THE
INSURRECTIONIST

THE
INSURRECTIONIST

A NOVEL

★HERB KARL★

ACADEMY

CHICAGO

Copyright © 2017 by Herb Karl
All rights reserved
Published by Academy Chicago Publishers
An imprint of Chicago Review Press Incorporated
814 North Franklin Street
Chicago, Illinois 60610

ISBN 978-1-61373-633-3

Library of Congress Cataloging-in-Publication Data
Names: Karl, Herb, author.
Title: The insurrectionist : a novel / Herb Karl.
Description: Chicago, Illinois : Academy Chicago Publishers, [2017]
Identifiers: LCCN 2016037879 (print) | LCCN 2016042115 (ebook) | ISBN
    9781613736333 (softcover) | ISBN 9781613736357 (PDF edition) | ISBN
    9781613736364 (EPUB edition) | ISBN 9781613736340 (Kindle edition)
Subjects: LCSH: Brown, John, 1800–1859—Fiction. | Abolitionists—United
    States—Fiction. | Kansas—History—1854–1861—Fiction. | Harpers Ferry
    (W. Va.)—History—John Brown's Raid, 1859—Fiction. | Antislavery
    movements—United States—History—19th century—Fiction. | BISAC:
    FICTION / Historical. | GSAFD: Biographical fiction. | Historical fiction.
Classification: LCC PS3611.A78355 I57 2017 (print) | LCC PS3611.A78355
    (ebook) | DDC 813/.6—dc23
LC record available at https://lccn.loc.gov/2016037879

Cover design: John Yates at Stealworks
Typesetting: Nord Compo

Printed in the United States of America
5 4 3 2 1

insurrection: A rising against civil or political authority . . .

—from Noah Webster's *Dictionary of the English Language* (1849)

A Note to the Reader

What follows—an account of the militant abolitionist John Brown's three-year war on slavery—is not entirely a work of fiction. Because I've drawn heavily from the historical record, most of the events depicted—as well as the characters—are real, and much of the dialogue has been taken, with some modifications, from reported speech and writings. When I've departed from the historical record, I've done so to preserve the drama of storytelling. My only other purpose has been to bring the characters to life by imagining what they may have thought and said.

The Backstory

The opening chapter of this narrative is about a real event that illustrates why the abolition of slavery was at the top of the political and social agendas of activists like John Brown. The event—which moved America closer than ever to civil war—was caused by circumstances that go back as far as 1619, when the first African slaves were brought to Jamestown in the English colony of Virginia. Over time that modest wave of slavery grew larger and rolled up the James River, spreading out to the low country from the Chesapeake to Georgia, finally settling in great tidal pools in the South's interior before drifting as far west as Texas.

In 1854—two and a half centuries after the introduction of slavery into colonial America—the US Congress passed the Kansas-Nebraska Act, a piece of legislation that created the territories of Kansas and Nebraska out of the vast chunk of land north of Texas, east of the Rockies, and westward along the Missouri River. Though it opened these territories to settlement and eventual statehood, the bill was bitterly contested. In it was a provision that violated the substance and spirit of the Missouri Compromise of 1820, an agreement prohibiting the extension of slavery within the boundaries of the two new territories. In essence, the disputed provision—known as *popular sovereignty*—effectively repealed the Missouri Compromise by allowing the settlers of each territory to decide at the ballot box whether they wanted to enter the Union as a free or slave state.

To the abolitionists—the vocal reformers in the North who were determined to root out slavery wherever it existed—and to the antislavery members of Congress, popular sovereignty represented one more concession to slaveholders, one more effort to appease Southerners fearful of losing congressional power and influence.

While it was politically beneficial to slaveholding interests that a balance of free and slave states emerge from the territories of Kansas and Nebraska, many questioned whether slavery would ever take permanent hold in a climate not suited to the South's labor-intensive cash crops of cotton, tobacco, sugar cane, and rice. Still, any act of Congress that appeared to validate slavery was an acknowledgment of what slaveholders claimed was among their constitutional rights. Popular sovereignty, in appearance if not reality, seemed to level the playing field for the slaveholding South.

If there were any doubts that the nation was divided into two sections—each with its own agenda, each following a path leading to permanent and irreconcilable differences—those doubts were erased on May 30, 1854, with the adoption of the Kansas-Nebraska Act. Its effects were immediate and demonstrable. Kansas Territory felt them first.

Northern industrialists, manufacturers, businessmen, railroad investors—and of course the abolitionists—all had a stake in Kansas. Their motives were economic, political, or purely moral. Through immigrant aid organizations, they offered incentives that created a steady stream of Northern settlers. It was hoped these settlers would one day gain the votes necessary to convert the territory into the free state of Kansas.

Since the Northern immigrants seemed to have an advantage, Southerners would have to respond quickly. On the eastern border of the territory lay Missouri—a slave state. Many Missourians simply crossed the border and laid claim to lands in Kansas before it was legally permissible to do so. Others—aptly called *border ruffians*—descended on towns and villages at election time, voted illegally for the proslavery agenda, chased Northern settlers from the polls, then headed back by nightfall to their homes in western Missouri. But by far the Southerners' biggest asset was President Franklin Pierce. Pierce was elected largely because he favored compromises with the slaveholding South. It was he who permitted the territorial government to have a proslavery identity. A proslavery Kansas seemed a real possibility.

Thus, in the summer of 1854 began the struggle over whether Kansas would be free or slave. It started relatively quietly. But eventually the stream of Northern immigrants turned into a river, swift and relentless, leaving behind not only settlements but thriving little towns—like Topeka and Lawrence—with hotels, stores, sawmills, brickyards, newspapers.

And when the proslavery territorial legislature ignored the Northern settlers, the Northerners called it "bogus" and formed their own government. Tempers grew short. Intimidation reigned. A shooting. Retribution. Skirmishes crackled along the Kansas-Missouri border like dry kindling. Two factions—one proslavery, the other pledged to a free state—were engaged in a little civil war of their own. It would come to be known as "Bleeding Kansas."

By the spring of 1856, violence and lawlessness in the territory had escalated. In Washington, DC, the Thirty-Fourth Congress was in session. Massachusetts Senator Charles Sumner sat at his desk in the Senate chamber writing notes on printed copies of a speech he'd delivered earlier on the Senate floor. He intended to mail copies to his friends and constituents and to newspapers across the nation. The speech was entitled "The Crime Against Kansas," and it was an indictment of everything being done to force Kansas Territory into the *embrace of slavery*. As he was writing, Sumner was unaware that a thousand miles to the west, men led by a notorious proslavery sheriff had ravaged the free town of Lawrence— looting its stores and homes, burning its most prominent hotel, and throwing the presses of the town's two newspapers into the Kansas River.

In this gathering excitement, Old John Brown was spoiling for a fight. He'd been in Kansas almost eight months and he was getting impatient. He had big ideas. He saw not only Kansas without slavery; he saw a nation without slavery.

And he claimed divine guidance. He said he was called by his God to make war on slavery.

1

May 22, 1856
Washington, DC

Shortly before one o'clock in the afternoon, Preston Smith Brooks—a slender, thirty-six-year-old congressman from South Carolina—entered the chamber of the United States Senate. Because of a hip injury suffered as a younger man, he walked with a slight limp and carried a cane. The cane—along with his superbly tailored three-piece suit, neatly trimmed goatee, and genteel manner—made Brooks one of the more recognizable members of Congress. Since the previous morning he'd been stalking Senator Charles Sumner, the antislavery crusader from Massachusetts. To Brooks's relief, their paths finally converged. His damaged hip throbbed, and he welcomed the opportunity to sit down. First, though, he took a moment to remind himself to control his emotions.

After all, he was about to commit an act of extraordinary violence.

The chamber was practically empty—the Senate having adjourned early—but some members still lingered, conversing in hushed voices in the lobby that hugged the semicircular walls. A few men were gathered in the columned loggia behind the Senate president's high-backed chair, above which hung a canopy of crimson drapery held in the talons of an ornately carved, gilded eagle. Brooks took a seat in the top tier of desks, across the aisle and three rows behind Sumner, who was absorbed in writing, the nib of his pen darting between an inkwell and the bundles of pages stacked before him.

In the lobby, not far from Sumner's desk, a young lady had snared a senator attempting to exit the chamber. Her voice, though barely audible, annoyed Brooks. He couldn't complete his mission in the presence of a lady. To do so would be inappropriate, a breach in the conduct of a gentleman. He felt his hand tighten around the cane he had selected for the occasion. It was one of many he'd collected since sustaining his hip injury, an injury that over the years had gradually worsened.

Now, poised to execute the plan he'd conceived only days earlier, he felt a rush of nervous energy work its way through his viscera. He was well aware that Sumner, even at forty-five, was an imposing adversary—six feet two, almost two hundred pounds, barrel-chested, his legs so thick they barely fit into the space under his desk. And while friends and family insisted that Brooks, a veteran of the Mexican War, hadn't lost his vigor and military bearing, the physically impaired congressman was no match for the robust Sumner.

The lady and the senator were still chatting in the lobby. So Brooks waited. His thoughts turned to the events that had brought him to this moment.

It was on Monday—three days earlier—that Brooks and a fellow South Carolina representative, the burly and mercurial Laurence Keitt, left their seats in the House and walked across the floor of the rotunda, avoiding the scaffolding of a hulking steam-driven crane. Renovations to the Capitol were in progress, and the crane was being used to remove the old copper-covered wooden dome, a legacy of Boston architect Charles Bulfinch. Viewed from Pennsylvania Avenue, the crane's mast and boom rose eighty feet above the rotunda and brought to mind the mast and boom of a great sailing ship—bereft of sails. The crane would remain in place until the eventual erection of a cast iron dome.

As the two men approached the main door to the Senate chamber, they were met by a throng of visitors searching for vacant seats in the already crowded galleries and lobbies. They had come to hear Sumner, an unflinching enemy of slaveholders and an eloquent speaker, a student of classical rhetoric fond of sprinkling his speeches with Latin phrases.

Sumner was slated to reenter the debate on slavery. It had been almost two years since he formally spoke on the issue in the Senate. That he waited so long was a disappointment to Massachusetts abolitionists. On this day, however, Sumner was ready to take the floor. Rumors had circulated for weeks. This was to be no ordinary tirade by a Northerner against the evils of chattel slavery. Brooks had a bad feeling about the speech and was eager to learn if his suspicions would be confirmed. He and Keitt found standing room in a lower doorway of the chamber.

It was an exceptionally warm day. The air was heavy with the odors of tobacco and perspiration; they commingled into a noxious mixture, prompting those in the Ladies' Gallery over-head to break out their fans. Brooks looked up at the ladies. He likened their fluttering fans to a covey of flushed quail.

On the floor, Senate president pro tem Jesse Bright of Indiana called on the senator from Massachusetts. Sumner strode to the speaker's rostrum and opened a leather binder

containing his speech—a speech that was to take two consecutive afternoons to deliver.

The territory of Kansas, he began, his words rippling
through the multileveled chamber with a steady and insistent
force, was being raped by factions from both the South and
the North, and if the present course of events was allowed
to continue, Kansas soon would become a new state locked
in the hateful embrace of slavery. Then, just minutes into his
speech, he lashed out at Brooks's fifty-nine-year-old cousin,
Andrew Pickens Butler, the South Carolina senator who was
one of the most vocal supporters of the Kansas-Nebraska Bill.
And Sumner's speech, if nothing else, was an unbridled attack
on the Kansas-Nebraska Bill—and its supporters.

"The senator from South Carolina," Sumner declared of
Butler, "has read many books of chivalry and believes himself
a chivalrous knight with sentiments of honor and courage. Of
course, he has chosen a mistress to whom he has made vows and
who, though ugly to others, is always lovely to him." A pause.
"Though polluted in the sight of the world, she is chaste in
his sight." Another pause. "That mistress is the harlot Slavery."

First a chorus of murmurs, then a palpable stillness fell on
the chamber. Even Sumner's critics, who earlier pretended to
be uninterested—shuffling papers and talking over his words—
came to attention.

It was worse than Brooks anticipated. Sumner had leveled a slanderous insult at an elderly relative in front of the
Senate and a sea of spectators. And he'd done so when his
cousin wasn't present to defend himself. The absent Butler
had chosen to spend a few extra days of rest—away from
the stress of Washington politics—at his beloved Stoneland,
a sprawling cotton plantation in Brooks's district of Edgefield
in the South Carolina upcountry.

Sumner wasn't finished. He soon expounded on the irony of Butler's use of the words *sectional* and *fanatical* to describe Northerners who favored a free Kansas. It wasn't the opponents of slavery who were sectional and fanatical, Sumner proclaimed; it was men like Butler, with their fanatical defense of slavery, who cleaved the nation in half, creating two sections—one North, the other South. After calling Butler one of sectionalism's maddest zealots, Sumner drew his attack to a close—for the moment, anyway. "If the senator wishes to see fanatics, let him look around among his own associates. Let him look in a mirror."

Keitt hissed through his beard. He was one of the fire-eaters, men prepared to lead the South out of the Union in order to preserve a unique way of life. "You abolitionist bastard," he muttered.

Brooks had heard enough. He turned, leaving Keitt behind, and snaked his way through the people gathered outside the chamber straining to hear Sumner's words. When Brooks reached the landing of the east portico he stopped and took a deep breath. It was good to be in the open air, away from the packed chamber. His anger subsided, but as he descended the steps he felt a sharp pain in his hip. The pain was familiar and made him wince, and he cursed aloud.

At the foot of the steps he paused. To his left and right the prodigious, newly constructed House and Senate wings, virtually completed, jutted into the plaza. The marble facades were burnished to a glaring white by the afternoon sun. Shading his eyes, he hailed one of the hackney coaches that lined the curb and directed the driver to his lodgings at a hotel on West Sixth.

Inside the cab Brooks rubbed his hip. The *clip-clop* of hooves and the clattering of steel-treaded wheels rolling over the broken cobbles of Pennsylvania Avenue gradually faded from his consciousness as he struggled to bring order to the jumble of thoughts swirling through his head. His cousin Andrew Butler had been publicly insulted, and for that there would have to be consequences. Because Butler was old—much older than Sumner—the task of righting the matter now fell to Brooks. The situation wasn't new to him. He understood the burden of being born a gentleman and a South Carolinian. His father, a slaveholding planter, had infused Brooks and his siblings with a sense of obligation to family, to South Carolina, and to those who were their equals: those who possessed slaves and large tracts of land—land that yielded rice and Sea Island cotton in the low country and short-staple cotton in the upcountry. For these landowners and their progeny there were duties, rules of conduct. It had to be so.

By the time he stepped out of the cab at his hotel, Brooks had gone lame. Though he tried to ignore it, the stinging in his hip came in bursts with each stride, and his body accommodated by turning his gait into that of an old man. He uncharacteristically waved off familiar faces in the lobby, told the desk clerk he'd take dinner in his room, and ordered two bottles of Madeira to be sent up immediately. And no visitors. He needed time to think, to gather himself.

That night he slept fitfully. The Madeira dulled the pain in his hip but not the memory that had haunted him for sixteen years. As he lay on his bed fully clothed, slipping in and out of consciousness, the images returned, as they had many times in the past—nagging him, goading him into reconstructing the events of a cold November day in 1840 on an island in the Savannah River just a few miles from his Edgefield home.

As dawn broke that day, a mist obscured a flurry of activity. A few men—three, maybe four—worked with axes to clear a field covered with cane and underbrush. At the river's edge, two skiffs were pulled ashore. In one of them sat two men. They passed a smoothbore flintlock pistol between them, testing the firing mechanism, cocking and releasing the hammer. Alongside the men lay an open leather case containing a matching pistol. These were not ordinary pistols. Brass engraved barrels, mahogany grips. They were designed for one purpose: to test the honor and personal courage of gentlemen who represented a privileged class, a class defined by bloodlines, professional status, and, to a lesser extent, wealth.

Observing the activity were the two principals. Brooks, then only twenty-one, his cloak drawn tightly against the morning chill, shifted his weight from one foot to the other. His opponent, arms folded, stood some distance away, teeth clamped onto the stump of a black cigar. By now the cause of their confrontation had lost its significance. All that mattered was the contest. Like knights of feudal Europe, the two men were to meet in a trial by arms that would not only test their courage—their manliness—but also affirm the beliefs of the class to which they both belonged. It was a ritual in which only true gentlemen were expected to participate.

By early afternoon the field had been cleared. The adversaries were called to their posts. They stood back to back, pistols in hand. The order came to march the customary ten paces. At sixty feet they turned, assumed the shooting stance, their bodies sidelong, and awaited the final command. At the call "Ready" they aimed—and fired.

In his hotel room Brooks tossed feverishly. His bed linens and shirt were soaked with sweat. The images that dominated his restless sleep lost their clarity, dissolved in shadows. Then, as had been the case in countless recurrences of the dream, he heard the booming reports of the pistols, felt the pain of the lead ball tearing through his flesh, narrowly missing his spine, shattering a portion of his pelvis, finally glancing off a bone in his arm. He howled.

Outside the room Keitt shouted, pounded on the door. "For God's sake, Brooks, are you hurt?"

Brooks lay on his bed barely aware of the commotion. Sunlight streamed through an unshaded window.

Again, Keitt's voice intruded into the room. "Open the door, Preston. It's Laurence. We need to talk."

Brooks struggled to compose himself. He stumbled to the washbasin, filled it with water from a pitcher, cupped his hands, doused his face. His attempt to bring some tidiness to his disheveled clothing was futile. He opened the door to a startled Keitt.

"Come in, Laurence. You must pardon my appearance. It's been a difficult evening."

"I should think it has," Keitt agreed. "And I'm afraid the worst lies ahead. The damned abolitionist is only half finished with his speech and already he's humiliated your cousin, called him a liar. He rails against the entire South, Preston, calls us *the slave power*—over and over: *the slave power*. There is no end to it. And the president—the scoundrel insults the president. He has no honor."

Keitt had come to escort Brooks to the Senate. It was almost noon, and Sumner was scheduled to resume his speech at one o'clock. But Brooks was hesitant, noncommittal. He needed time to devise a suitable response to Sumner's provocation.

Besides, he was in no condition to make an appearance at the Capitol. The Senate chamber already would be nearing capacity. He urged Keitt to go without him.

They could meet later, after the speech—maybe have dinner downstairs in the hotel dining room.

Brooks spent the remainder of the day in his room, leaving only briefly to pick up a copy of the *National Intelligencer* at the front desk. The parlor and lobby swarmed with guests, mostly Southerners. The chatter was about Sumner. It was impossible for Brooks to avoid being noticed. He politely excused himself from a phalanx of young men with notepads. Newspaper reporters. They knew he'd attended the first day of Sumner's speech. He had no comment.

At six o'clock Keitt was back at Brooks's door. He heaved his body into the room. The blood vessels in his eyes were red and swollen. He carried a stack of pages smelling of printer's ink and tossed them onto the bed.

"Sumner's speech," he said. "The bastard ordered copies to be printed, intends to mail them to every Northern newspaper."

Dinner could wait. The two men headed straight for the hotel bar.

As they walked through the parlor they were approached by several ladies, among them the wife of a South Carolinian prominent in President Pierce's administration. She was suppressing her anger as she stood before Brooks and expressed revulsion at what she called Sumner's "perfidious and vile treatment of Senator Butler and our glorious state." She said, "I am sure Sumner's treachery shall not go unchallenged by the good and righteous men of South Carolina."

The bar was overflowing—an amalgam of legislators and
Washington's distinctively Southern social elite, all just
returned from Sumner's speech. By the time they stepped
away from the bar, Brooks and Keitt were well fortified with
scotch whisky and advice on how to teach the damned Yankee
abolitionist a lesson in civility.

Keitt recited parts of the senator's speech. The worst of it
was the attack on the homeland, their hallowed South Carolina. Sumner had piled insult upon insult, condemning South
Carolina's long covenant with slavery and the slave trade. Keitt
was enraged, but Brooks expected as much. Sumner was, after
all, an abolitionist—the latest in a parade of abolitionists to
mock slavery as it existed in South Carolina and elsewhere.
Brooks and Keitt had been exposed to this sort of abuse for
most of their adult lives. To them, the struggle in Kansas
Territory simply gave the abolitionists an excuse to renew
their attack on the South's *peculiar institution.*

"They are different from us," Keitt said, referring to Northern abolitionists like Sumner. "They are not to be reasoned
with. And they have no understanding of good manners. Sumner is no gentleman and doesn't deserve to be treated as one."

Brooks respected Keitt even though he regarded his politics
as extreme. If Keitt had had his way, South Carolina would
have seceded from the Union years ago. He'd fallen under
the influence of men like Robert Barnwell Rhett and David
Jamison, and that meant Keitt regarded Northern abolitionism as an imminent threat to the South. He was immersed
in Southern chivalry with its code of honor; he longed for
the opportunity to defend Southern rights—on the battlefield
if necessary.

Keitt implored Brooks to act boldly. "The damned abolitionists want to take away our freedom," he said. "They

cannot be allowed to trample on our rights. They would have us change places with our servants." Like many slaveholders, Keitt chose to substitute the word *servant* for *slave*.

Brooks nodded politely. He knew what was expected of him and needed no encouragement. Insults had been delivered publicly. The reputation of an elder statesman, a blood relative—as well as the reputation of South Carolina—had been rudely besmirched. No apology was offered. Brooks knew he couldn't face his constituents, much less the entire state of South Carolina, without gaining satisfaction. The question that remained was how it would be obtained. And therein lay the problem.

"I'm sure you will do the right thing, Preston," Keitt said before retiring for the evening. "I only wish I were in your place. Nothing would give me greater pleasure than to put a ball through that cur's black heart."

———••••———

In the light of a whale oil lamp Brooks sat up in bed reading and rereading Sumner's speech. His hip ached and he couldn't sleep. He poured himself a glass of Madeira, but it only made him more agitated. He lay awake, pondering an honorable course of action. Sleep finally came.

He arose at dawn determined to act. Two days had passed since Sumner began his rant and there was still no hint of regret from the senator from Massachusetts. Brooks was groggy, hungover, but he wouldn't delay another minute. He felt drawn into a whirlpool of emotions—his own, those of his colleagues, and those shared by all Southerners. Charles Sumner had come to represent those abolitionists who were determined to make the South bend to their will. Brooks needed to do something and do it quickly. To hesitate any longer would be a sign of weakness.

Before leaving his room he paused at a brass umbrella stand beside the door. The stand was filled with canes he'd brought to Washington from his home in Edgefield. He removed one—a recent gift. It had a gold head, and its shaft was fashioned from a new material, gutta-percha—a latex compound that was rigid yet elastic enough to be used in the manufacture of golf balls. The cane had a hollow core.

Brooks arrived at the Capitol at eleven o'clock, hoping to confront Sumner before the Senate reconvened at noon for its Wednesday session. He knew Sumner typically walked to the Capitol from rooms he rented on New York Avenue. That meant he would approach the west portico from Pennsylvania Avenue. Brooks paced nervously, oblivious to the clutter, the construction shanties, the mounds of building materials.

He prowled the tree-lined path leading to the west front of the Capitol and eventually ran into his colleague and friend Henry Edmundson, a representative from Virginia. But no Sumner. Brooks was dejected. He had no interest in taking his seat in the House. He found a young page sitting on the Capitol steps and gave him a message intended for Keitt and James Orr, an upcountry congressman whose moderate political views Brooks respected. He wanted them to join him in his hotel room that evening, to get their advice on what he should do about Sumner.

The meeting with Keitt and Orr quickly turned ugly, the language rambling and heated. Brooks had been drinking. "The people want revenge," he said, "and I have failed to give it to them." He confessed he had no desire to challenge Sumner to a duel. To do so would be to regard him an equal. The code of honor governed only the conduct of gentlemen, and as Keitt had already made clear, Sumner was no gentleman.

"I intend to whip him," Brooks said, "as I would whip a servant who was disobedient or behaved badly. I have no whip, so I've chosen a cane instead."

While Orr urged restraint, Keitt spoke approvingly. "I envy you this opportunity, Preston," he said, "to strike a blow that might alter the destiny of our people. The abolitionists have degraded us, insulted us. They would take away our peace, our very existence." He paced about the room, his words taking on the passion that earned him his reputation as a radical secessionist. "We must defend our rights . . . our honor . . . and leave the consequences to God."

Between Keitt's exhortations and the wine Brooks had been consuming since early afternoon, Brooks began to find Orr's plea for calmness and reason less appealing. Orr must have sensed the futility of his arguments. He wished both men well and excused himself.

In a gesture Brooks would deny in the coming days and weeks, he reached into the umbrella stand filled with canes, removed one, handed it to Keitt. "I expect you to be ready should things not go well for me tomorrow," he said. "Use it, Laurence, if you must."

"Sir, I would be honored."

After Keitt's departure, Brooks collapsed in bed. Two nights of little sleep and heavy drinking left him sullen, edgy. He fretted over what lay ahead.

He didn't remember falling asleep.

A knock at Brooks's door at first light meant fresh water had been delivered. He brought the pitcher inside, washed, took a straight razor to the stubble on his face, then slipped into one of his finely tailored linen suits. He lifted the gutta-percha cane from the umbrella stand and gave it a quick snap against his thigh.

It was another warm spring day in Washington. Brooks's goal was the same as the day before. Only this time the deed would be done.

The plan to cut off Sumner outside the Capitol, however, proved fruitless. He again ran into Edmundson on the grounds near the west front. The two men spoke briefly, then together ascended the long flight of stairs to the rotunda. Each step sent a twinge through Brooks's hip, reminding him of the obligation he now carried like a millstone. While Edmundson went directly to the House, Brooks headed for the Senate in search of Sumner. He reached the door to the chamber breathing heavily.

The Senate was in session, but Brooks knew there would be an early adjournment in honor of the recent death of a congressman. He spotted Sumner at his desk, then returned to the vestibule. Though exhausted, Brooks was determined to stay until Sumner or the senators—whichever came first— vacated the chamber.

At twelve forty-five the senators began streaming through the doors. Brooks reentered the chamber and took a seat in the top tier of desks, across the aisle and three rows behind Sumner.

An hour had passed since the lady and the senator she held captive began their conversation in the lobby.

Brooks was glad to see that Keitt had joined the small group gathered in the loggia behind the Senate president's chair. Keitt glanced up, displaying the cane Brooks gave him the previous evening. He tapped his forehead with the tip. Brooks returned the gesture.

When Brooks turned his attention back to the lobby, he saw that the lady and the senator were gone.

A wave of uneasiness struck him. The punishment he was about to deliver had to be administered quickly, deliberately. He couldn't let his emotions get in the way. Nor could he wait any longer. It was apparent Sumner had no intention of completing his work anytime soon. Brooks stood up and stepped into the aisle, descended the three levels to Sumner's row, slid into position alongside the senator's desk. Sumner was still absorbed in his writing; he didn't seem aware of Brooks's presence.

"Sumner!" Brooks called out.

The senator looked up, squinted, a puzzled expression on his face.

Brooks continued, his words stiff and mechanical, evidence that he'd rehearsed them. "I have read your speech twice over carefully. It is my duty to tell you that you have libeled my state and slandered a relative, Mr. Butler, who is aged and absent, and I am come to punish you for it."

Brooks raised his cane and struck the side of Sumner's head sharply, near the temple, not a particularly forceful blow but one that surely stunned the senator. Sumner raised his hands in self-defense, attempted to rise from his chair. Then, as though a switch had been thrown, Brooks surrendered to an impulse—a primitive and dark impulse that loosed itself from a part of his brain over which he had no control. He found himself swinging his cane repeatedly, each blow crashing down on Sumner with greater fury, until the cane split into a clump of slender fibers. All that remained was the gold head and a section of the shaft that allowed Brooks to retain his grip on what no longer resembled a cane at all but looked more like a cowhide whip with its plaited thongs unraveled.

Brooks had intended to execute his mission without emotion. It was to be a simple act of punishment, a means of correcting behavior, as one would correct the behavior of a dog or a servant. But something went awry. The unspoken fears that slumbered in the deepest recesses of his being were awakened. And Sumner had come to embody all those fears: the loss of a way of life enjoyed on the piazzas of the great plantation houses . . . the loss of pleasures made possible by those who labored in the fields, served in the houses, who cooked, washed, cleaned, even took to their breasts their masters' babies as they would their own . . . the collapse of a social system that Brooks and others like him were required to preserve, a system that had already begun to suffer the stresses brought on by the constant pressure of the abolitionists, the growing acts of resistance in the settlements, the runaways. All of the demons were released upon the helpless Sumner, who was finally able to wrench himself from the confines of his desk. In a desperate, Samson-like effort, he rose, his powerful legs snapping the screws that fastened the desk in place. He tumbled into the chamber's center aisle, his face so lacerated and bloodied as to make it impossible to identify whose face it was.

All this in less than a minute, and Brooks was not done yet, though by now the spectacle claimed the attention of the stragglers who remained in the chamber. Several of them rushed to restrain Brooks, only to be challenged by Keitt, brandishing the cane he'd pledged to use should the need arise. He raised it over his head and shouted, "Let them alone. Let them alone, God damn you."

Keitt's efforts were unnecessary. Sumner lay on the floor unconscious, blood pulsing from deep wounds in his head.

A doctor was summoned.

As Keitt led Brooks out of the chamber, the pain in his hip returned, the chronic ache to which he'd grown accustomed. Brooks disliked admitting it, but the pain wouldn't go away. Nothing would ever change that.

———•••••———

One of the witnesses to the assault was a reporter from Horace Greeley's *New York Tribune*. After a doctor determined Sumner's wounds weren't life threatening, the reporter rushed out of the Capitol and headed for Samuel Morse's Northern and Eastern Telegraph office on the corner of Pennsylvania Avenue and Sixth Street. As he walked he took out his pencil and notepad and composed a message to the *Tribune*.

The reporter handed the message to J. R. Bailey, the agent in charge of the telegraph office. Bailey began tapping out the words in code:

Washington STOP *Thursday May 22* STOP *Vicious and cowardly attack in Senate chamber* STOP *Preston Brooks of South Carolina strikes down Sumner of Massachusetts* STOP *Defenseless Sumner beaten with cane while working at desk* STOP *Sumner collapses in pool of blood* STOP *Brooks flees as Sumner regains consciousness* STOP *More later* STOP

After the reporter left, Bailey gradually realized the seriousness of the message he'd sent. He took it upon himself to repeat the message, this time sending it along the western route, where it would be relayed through Pittsburgh, Indianapolis, and Saint Louis, reaching its terminus at a town along the Kansas-Missouri border.

2

Sixteen Hours Later
May 23, 1856
Kansas Territory

Word of the caning of Charles Sumner had yet to reach the company of Free State militiamen camped alongside Ottawa Creek south of the town of Lawrence. The sun had barely cleared the horizon and the men could feel the heat coming on. Spring thunderstorms had let up, and the temperature hovered in the nineties. The prairie grass was stunted and wispy. The men, however, went about their tasks with quiet resignation—cleaning weapons, stowing gear, rolling up blankets. Meanwhile, the one they called the old man grumbled and fumed, his discontent spreading through the camp like an outbreak of cholera.

John Brown—the man who came to Kansas Territory to fight slavery—was angry, and he wanted the people around him to know it. The town of Lawrence, a sanctuary for Northern immigrants, had fallen to an army of proslavery invaders, and he hadn't fired a shot in its defense.

He'd just turned fifty-six, and though his lean, once ramrod-straight frame had begun to buckle a little—giving the appearance his torso tilted forward slightly—he remained gritty and combative, more so than the other men in the company, all of whom were much younger. On this morning his chiseled, leathery face was exceptionally gaunt, the creases in his brow deeper. He'd stayed awake most of the night brooding over the debacle at Lawrence, struggling to devise a retaliatory response—a measure, in his words, so radical as to cause a restraining fear among the proslavery forces. By sunrise, what little moisture remaining in the grass had penetrated his blanket. The dampness added to his discomfort. But he'd come up with a plan.

It would involve some killing.

The old man had learned of the impending invasion two days earlier. He was with his sons at their homesteads, some thirty-five miles to the south of Lawrence, when a messenger on horseback reported that proslavery marauders were massing on a bluff above the town. The marauders, the messenger said, were Missouri border ruffians who were joined by Southern mercenaries. The whole whiskey-swilling mob was hell bent on ridding the town of Yankee abolitionists. The citizens of Lawrence needed help.

So Brown jammed a Colt revolver under his belt and gathered up a half dozen double-edged broadswords—sinister looking weapons that once served as sidearms for artillerymen during the Canadian Rebellion of 1837. Then he and his sons and the rest of the local militiamen set out for Lawrence—most of them on foot. They marched until late in the evening, camped briefly, then resumed early the next day. Within three miles of the town, another rider intercepted them, said they were too late. Lawrence had fallen. There was no resistance. The people fled or simply refused to fight.

"Cowards—all of them," Brown growled. His voice had a rasping metallic sound like someone who habitually drank whiskey and smoked tobacco. Neither was true. He never used tobacco of any kind and had only drunk whiskey once, after which he vowed to never again consume anything that caused him to lose control of his ability to reason.

"It's because of Robinson," one of the men offered. "He claims forbearance shows we're in the right and our enemies are the aggressors."

Brown had little use for Dr. Charles Robinson, the de facto leader of the Free State settlers who stood in opposition to the fraudulently elected proslavery legislature. Though Robinson had bestowed the rank of captain on Brown and given him command of a small group of militiamen, the old man viewed the doctor as a man to be pitied, a radical abolitionist who'd lost his nerve. As far as Brown could tell, Robinson had no fight left in him.

Brown asked, "And what does *forbearance* mean?"

No answer.

"I'll tell you what *forbearance* means," he bristled. "It means we are to act as slaves . . . and allow the enemy to have his way with us."

Brown urged the company to continue on to Lawrence, even though it was apparent the town had capitulated. But cooler heads prevailed, one of which belonged to his eldest son, thirty-four-year-old John Jr.

"Father," he cautioned, "there are hundreds of them and only forty of us."

So they turned around, Brown complaining about those who too easily surrendered to the minions of slavery. As they retraced their steps, the men marching at his side were forced to listen to him condemn the citizens of Lawrence for failing to defend themselves.

"We need more men like Thomas Barber," he fumed. Barber was shot dead because he refused to be cowed by border ruffians looking to torment antislavery settlers. Brown was at the Free State Hotel in Lawrence when Barber's body was brought in and laid out for public viewing. He witnessed the wailing of Barber's wife. It hardened his resolve.

During the intervals of silence that marked the long march back to their homesteads—when the constant placing of one foot in front of the other compelled the men to turn away from their comrades—Brown found himself gazing absently at the sparsely wooded prairie. It seemed to roll on forever, unlike the forested country of the Northeast he was accustomed to, where he found spiritual comfort in the chapels of sunlight hidden in dense stands of hardwood. He wouldn't admit it, but the open prairie made him feel uncomfortable, vulnerable at times.

* * *

The old man had moved to Kansas Territory almost eight months ago. He'd been reluctant to come. There were distractions, futile attempts to recover from business ventures gone sour. He failed as a wool merchant in Springfield, Massachusetts, and worked three farms in Ohio to pay off debts. If and when his financial problems were settled he hoped to join his wife, Mary, at their farm in North Elba, New York, in the wilderness of the Adirondack Mountains. The farm was a special place to Brown, a place where he was able to escape his financial difficulties—at least temporarily—and where he continued to help build an independent, self-sustaining community for runaway slaves. It was there he spoke to his wife about an idea that had been incubating in his mind for almost two decades. He wanted to muster an army of volunteers and strike a blow against slavery on Southern soil. For some time he leaked details of his intentions to a select few—abolitionists who promised to support him.

Meanwhile, five of his sons—two of whom were married with children—decided to leave farms in drought-stricken Ohio and make a fresh start in Kansas Territory. Brown's half sister Florilla and her missionary husband, the Reverend Samuel Adair, had already settled in the village of Osawatomie. The sons invited their father to come along. Even though he might not be interested in farming the land, he could at least help them defend their claims against proslavery marauders. He declined the invitation.

"I feel committed to operate in another part of the field," he said, intimating he was seriously considering an incursion into the South.

Then came a letter from John Jr. that changed everything. The letter stated that Kansas Territory was being invaded by mean and desperate men, armed with revolvers, bowie knives, rifles, and cannons. The targets of the invaders were Northern immigrants, who exhibited the "most abject and cowardly spirit." The immigrants needed to fight back, to organize into military companies. John Jr. and his brothers were ready to lead such an effort, but first they needed guns and ammunition.

"We want you to get us arms," the eldest son beseeched his father. "We need them more than we do bread."

Brown put his own plans on hold. He'd find a way to get the weapons to his sons—even if he had to deliver them himself.

He liquidated his business assets and arranged for the welfare of his wife and young daughters. Then, when he'd accumulated enough money and supplies, he and his son-in-law Henry Thompson picked up sixteen-year-old Oliver, the youngest of Brown's sons, and headed for Kansas Territory, walking alongside a horse-drawn wagon loaded with guns, ammunition, and other weaponry, all of it concealed under surveyor's instruments. Surveying was one of several trades Brown had plied over the years, so it seemed logical that it should serve as his cover if challenged during the journey through proslavery country.

On an unusually cold and windy day in October 1855, he arrived in eastern Kansas at the settlement his sons had staked out near Osawatomie. He found them and their families shivering and feverish. They had waited too long to build permanent shelters and were living in tents and log huts with canvas roofs and doors, unprotected from the winds and ice storms that swept through the prairie.

———————

Now, nearly eight months later, the old man had plenty to stew about as he plodded across the Kansas prairie, grumbling about the sacking of Lawrence.

With the sky darkening, the company, fatigued and hungry, had pitched camp at Ottawa Creek on land belonging to John Tecumseh Jones, better known as Ottawa Jones, a man Brown's age whose mother was a Chippewa from Indiana. Jones had come to the territory as a Christian missionary and ended up a prosperous farmer who served as spiritual advisor to the Ottawa tribe on its ten-square-mile reservation. In Jones and his wife, Brown found kindred spirits. They were intelligent, feared God, and prized action over inertia. They shared Brown's commitment to the abolition of slavery, and he shared their respect and affection for the native people. He was always welcomed at their spacious log home. This time, however, he chose to stay with his men. Within sight of Jones's house and barn, beside clear-running Ottawa Creek, Brown bedded down for the evening.

At dawn he was up and about, cooking breakfast for the handful of men he regarded as a little company of his own. The group included his unmarried sons—Owen, Frederick, Salmon, and Oliver—and son-in-law Henry Thompson. Though they marched with the rest of the men, their loyalty was clearly to Brown. They sat around a cooking fire as he served a meal of bacon and johnnycakes. Ottawa Jones had donated a pail of fresh milk.

Toward the end of the meal, Brown unburdened himself.

"Something must be done," he said. "Something *will* be done."

The men put aside their plates and looked to the old man.

His eyes glistened. "We cannot allow these acts of murder and destruction to go unpunished. I would rather be ground into the earth than passively submit to the barbarians."

Owen, the eldest of his unmarried sons at thirty-one, spoke up. "What do you suggest we do, Father?"

"Blood," he said, the metallic timbre of his voice infusing the word with such malevolence that men standing nearby abandoned their chores and moved closer. After a pause, he added, "I have said slavery is a sin before God. And there can be no remission of that sin without the shedding of blood." He turned, faced the fire, his hands clasped behind his back.

Most of the company, including Brown's married sons— John Jr. and Jason—were now gathered at the fire.

Brown surveyed the men crowding around him, many of whom he hardly knew. Except for his own boys, he doubted any of them could appreciate who he was and why he came to Kansas. He was an abolitionist—dyed in the wool, he liked to say. Blacks—free or slave—were his brothers, his equals. He took the words of the Declaration of Independence literally. And while he'd traveled to the South only once, he'd become a student of slavery. Like his father, he was a conductor on the Underground Railroad and escorted runaway slaves to freedom in Canada. He'd befriended former slaves, some of them leaders in the abolitionist movement. He had little formal education but was an avid reader of history and had a keen interest in slave revolts. He expressed admiration for the Haitian liberator Toussaint-Louverture and the rebel slave Nat Turner, whose 1831 rampage in Virginia resulted in the deaths of fifty-seven whites—men, women, and children.

The old man had come to view the South's slaveholding planters as members of a prideful aristocracy who persuaded themselves over the course of two hundred years that slavery was both natural and good. He believed the slaveholders ensured the preservation of slavery by creating a social order that placed the slave at the bottom of the heap, thus securing the supremacy and loyalty of all whites, regardless of wealth or position. And because slavery ultimately relied for its survival on violence and brutality—the lash, the irons, mutilation, the splitting apart of families—it had turned the South into a place where violence and brutality penetrated the very core of Southern life. "The South," Brown said, "allowed slavery to seep into its bones, and no amount of moral persuasion by antislavery Northerners would change that." He once told his friend and confidant Frederick Douglass—the former slave turned abolitionist—that slaveholders would never be induced to give up their slaves until they felt a big stick about their heads.

Brown had to remind himself that although the men waiting to hear him speak favored a free Kansas, they weren't
necessarily committed—as he was—to making war on the
very existence of slavery. Many of the Northern immigrants
saw nothing wrong with slavery—as long as it was kept out
of the territory. They came to Kansas because of incentives
provided by the immigrant aid organizations and because they
wanted to make a new life for themselves; they wanted to
plow the cheap, abundant, fertile soil of Kansas as free men,
and to most of them that meant free *white* men. They called
themselves Free State men, but often they were as racist as
the proslavery marauders who were trying to drive them out
of the territory. If they hated slavery it wasn't because they
felt it was a sin against God or a crime against humanity.
They hated slavery because it threatened their livelihoods.
How were they expected to compete and prosper in a country
that permitted slave labor?

Such was Brown's audience at Ottawa Creek. A gathering
of men who couldn't be expected to grasp the motives behind
the slaughter he would soon direct just a few miles from
where they stood. Rumors about Brown's intentions had been
circulating in camp since the previous evening. Some of the
men hoped he would dispel their anxiety. Others were just
curious. A few were prepared to join him, whatever his plan.

He began speaking in little more than a whisper. "You
men know the enemy has no fear. He commits his acts of
violence without a thought to the consequences. He thinks
we are cowards and this emboldens him to commit even
greater outrages."

A murmur of assenting voices.

"Remember these men," he said. "Charles Dow, shot in
the back by Frank Coleman. No punishment. Thomas Barber,

unarmed, shot by George Clarke. No punishment. Reese Brown, mutilated by a pack of hatchet-wielding scoundrels, flung onto his doorstep to bleed to death in the arms of his wife. No punishment—"

One of the men interrupted. "We all expect to be butchered, every damn Free State settler in the region."

"And you will," Brown responded, his voice growing louder, "unless the enemy learns there are two sides to this thing—that he cannot commit these crimes without fear of retaliation."

The sound of hooves hammering the dry ground shattered the moment. A lone rider came into view.

Brown stooped to pick up his revolver—then recognized the man as Gardner, one of Ottawa Jones's hired hands. Gardner reined in his horse at Brown's feet and slid from the saddle. He reached into his boot and withdrew a folded slip of paper moist with perspiration.

"They've murdered Senator Sumner," he said, thrusting the paper into Brown's hand.

The old man unfolded the message. Gardner apparently had misunderstood what it said. As Brown read the news of the caning, the image of a bloody, prostrate Charles Sumner flashed before his eyes.

He'd first met the senator in 1851 while dealing with the aftermath of an unsuccessful wool business in Massachusetts. It was a time of both disappointment and anticipation. The business had failed, but Brown had befriended leading abolitionists. He was pleased a senator from his adopted state was a champion of the antislavery movement.

The men were waiting for the old man to speak. Choked with rage, he said nothing, crumpled the paper, flung it into the fire.

Gardner continued his story. He'd been dispatched to Kansas City by Ottawa Jones to send a message to a Saint Louis grain merchant. The telegraph office was crowded with young men and women—refugees from the Lawrence invasion. They were fed up with the border ruffians and said they were returning to their homes in the Northeast. When Gardner turned to leave, the telegraph operator handed him a note, asking that it be delivered to Dr. Charles Robinson in Lawrence. Gardner tucked the message into his boot. He spurred his horse toward the postal road—a rugged but shorter route that ran close to the Kansas River. He ran into more refugees. They warned him to avoid Lawrence. It was late when he neared the town. He saw the flames of burning buildings and decided it would be too danger-ous to enter the town. He turned off the trail and headed for Jones's house. He'd ridden across the prairie most of the night, stopping only long enough to rest and water his horse.

Brown waited until Gardner finished. Then—in a voice cool and detached—he looked to his eldest son and said, "Jones keeps a grinding wheel in his barn. I have need of it."

Though Brown and his son had quarreled earlier over the decision to turn back from Lawrence, John Jr. didn't argue this time. He turned and headed for Jones's barn.

The men returned to their chores.

Brown walked to a large canvas rucksack that sat next to his blanket. He removed its contents: the short, double-edged broadswords sheathed in scabbards and attached to leather belts. He carefully laid them on the blanket.

For the remainder of the morning the men huddled in groups, spoke guardedly of their fears, questioned their willingness to do anything that might escalate the danger to themselves and their families.

Meanwhile, the grinding wheel turned, sending brilliant yellow sparks cascading from a broadsword's blade, reminding the men of Brown's intentions—the precise details still a mystery to most of them.

Later, as the old man moved about the camp, someone came forward to urge caution. He snapped back, "Caution? You want *caution*? I am eternally tired of the word *caution*. It is nothing but a word for cowardice."

As the noon hour approached, it was evident those willing to follow Brown were few in number. The five in his own little company could be counted on. The only other man to step forward was pugnacious Theodore Weiner, a powerfully built Austrian who backed down from no one. He came to Kansas by way of Texas and operated a dry goods store near the Browns' homesteads. Because he willingly catered to Free State settlers, he was the victim of constant threats from pro-slavery neighbors. Brown knew he could use Weiner when the Austrian declared, "I will cut the throat of anyone who wants to drive the Free State men from Kansas. It is the way we treat such pigs in Texas."

Brown still needed a wagon. Two days of marching had left the men fatigued. Another half day lay ahead. The men needed rest. The choices were limited. Only one wagon had been part of the expedition, a lumber wagon drawn by a pair of draft horses, and it belonged to James Townsley, who, reluctantly, was to become the eighth and final member of what Brown would later call his Northern Army.

At two o'clock the men loaded Townsley's wagon, the mess gear and rations first, then the bedrolls, then the rifles and pistols. Brown hoisted the rucksack containing the broadswords. He executed the task so deliberately it caused one of the spectators to comment, "Looks like he means business."

Brown's four unmarried sons and his son-in-law climbed aboard the wagon and seated themselves among the clutter, backs resting against the sideboards. Townsley took his place on the driver's bench. Weiner had come on horseback; he swung his imposing frame onto his mount.

The old man paused, looking north toward Lawrence. His eyes were fixed on a hazy column of smoke that curled upward, fading into the pale sky.

John Jr. stepped from the group of men assembled near the wagon. He approached Brown from behind, put his hand on the old man's shoulder. "Father," he said, "you must not do anything rash."

Brown stiffened. He moved to the wagon and pulled himself aboard, taking the seat next to Townsley.

As the wagon rolled past Ottawa Jones's farm, a cheer went up from those who stayed behind.

At the end of the lane was the Lawrence Road, the well-traveled thoroughfare connecting Lawrence with settlements to the south. Townsley halted his team at the intersection, then turned onto the road leading south. Weiner rode alongside.

The Jones farm had barely disappeared from view when Townsley began to voice his concerns. Earlier in the day, when Brown requested the use of the wagon, he'd been evasive. Now Townsley wanted specifics. What exactly did Brown intend to do?

The old man seemed not to hear. Perhaps it was the clattering of unsecured gear, the creaking of axles as they gave way to uneven terrain. The men in the wagon bed dozed.

At length Brown emerged from his cocoon of silence. What he said caused Townsley to shift his weight, slacken his hold on the reins. He turned to face the old man. "You cannot do this thing." Townsley was agitated by what he'd heard. "It will bring war to Kansas."

Brown nodded. "As God is my witness, it most surely will."

----------•◦◦•----------

The road was deeply rutted. Shallow outcroppings of limestone caused the wagon to pitch and yaw like a New England fishing dory on a roiling sea. From time to time the men in the wagon bed were jarred into consciousness. Brown, though, was hardly aware of the disturbances. He still agonized over the assault on Charles Sumner by Preston Brooks. The congressman from South Carolina had become a symbol of everything Brown deemed evil among the South's slaveholding elite. The slaveholders respected neither the laws of God nor the laws of man. And they hated abolitionists. In Brown's mind Brooks had raised the stakes in the battle for Kansas. Retaliation would take on new meaning.

It was dusk when Townsley guided his team onto the site Brown chose as a base of operations: a stand of cottonwoods on a bluff between two ravines, about a mile from Pottawatomie Creek. The land along the creek was home to proslavery settlers active in the territorial legislature.

Because he didn't want to draw attention to his encampment, Brown announced there would be no cooking fire that evening. The men washed down strips of dried beef with water from a nearby spring, then spread their blankets under the overhanging branches of the cottonwoods. Physically and emotionally spent, they were soon asleep.

Not the old man, though. He continued to wrestle with thoughts of the bloody work that lay ahead.

3

Seven Hours Later
May 24, 1856
Kansas Territory

A full moon illuminated the encampment between the two ravines. The men were asleep—except for Brown. It was his habit to rise before the others. Barefoot and carrying his stovepipe boots, he was on his way to a spring that percolated from the bank of one of the ravines. He paused to survey the campsite, taking in the rhythms of the slumbering men, gauging their resolve to do what he'd ask of them.

His eyes rested first on Oliver, just turned seventeen. The old man was barely able to detect his youngest son's measured breathing. Muscular, well proportioned, in splendid physical condition, Oliver's stature belied his passion for reading. Brown was unsure of Oliver's role in the work to be done. Maybe it would be better if he stayed behind.

Brown moved on, lingering beside twenty-five-year-old Frederick, whose thick frame was coiled into a tight knot—steeling himself, perhaps, against the severe headaches that had plagued him since his early teens. The old man was especially attentive to Frederick's condition, comforting him during the bouts of delirium and depression that accompanied the headaches.

His gaze shifted to Owen. Though he had philosophical differences with his elder son, Brown knew him to be loyal. Owen wouldn't wilt, regardless of the circumstances that might arise. A childhood accident had left him with a weakened arm, yet he'd overcome his handicap and had even taken a leadership role at the family's Adirondack homestead during Brown's frequent absences.

He scanned the rest. Nineteen-year-old Salmon occupied a spot near Henry Thompson, the husband of Brown's eldest daughter, Ruth. Though Salmon sometimes doubted his father's methods, he'd do what was required—as would Henry, who came from a family of Adirondack farmers that shared the old man's convictions. Henry was as committed to the abolition of slavery as the Browns.

There would be no problem with a snoring Theodore Weiner, even though the Austrian drank whiskey, a habit Brown grudgingly tolerated. Weiner was an angry grizzly ready to rip apart its prey, and right now the old man needed men like that. About James Townsley, though, he was uncertain. Townsley had spread his blanket at some distance from the others. If possible, he'd be held in reserve.

Brown reached the camp's perimeter and struck out for the spring. Water trickled down the limestone bank in silver ribbons, forming shallow pools that glittered in the moonlight. The old man sat down on a rock shelf, dipped his feet into one of the pools. His toes were encrusted with a muddy paste, a mixture of sweat and dirt that had worked its way through the cracks in his boots. He closed his eyes and felt the water's coolness creep up his legs, his spine, finally reaching a part of his brain long deprived of sensual pleasure. It startled him. He didn't come to this place to enjoy pleasant sensations. He came to collect himself, to bring order to his thoughts about the mission he'd carved out for the seven men waiting for his instructions. And he came for spiritual guidance; for this he prayed as the cool water washed over his feet, dispersing Kansas mud into the darkness.

It wasn't until the sun's fiery rim appeared on the horizon, signaling another day of searing heat, that Brown finished his meditation. He'd prayed hard, hoping for some kind of mystical confirmation of the events that were soon to unfold. Instead he was visited by the memory of an incident from his youth—an incident familiar to his family and to most who knew him personally.

It took place during the War of 1812 when, at the age of twelve, he was driving a small herd of cattle from his father's Ohio farm to General William Hull's army in Detroit, a journey of more than a hundred miles. On previous drives he'd accompanied his father, but this time he was alone. He stopped overnight at a boardinghouse where he and his father had stayed in the past. During the evening meal, in the presence of guests, the landlord praised him for being able to do a man's work at such an early age.

It was a moment of great pride for Brown. But then something happened that forever changed him. He watched helplessly as the landlord picked up an iron shovel and used it to beat a thin, shabbily dressed slave boy whose job was to serve the guests. Brown had befriended the boy on earlier visits but sat paralyzed, unable to raise a hand or speak a word in the boy's defense. He went to bed tortured by a feeling of self-loathing that went unrelieved, even after he vomited his supper. He stayed awake, reflecting on the hopeless condition of the boy and others like him who were taken from their families, sold by their masters, destined to a life with no father or mother to protect them.

The memory persisted—in his dreams or when he was alone or engaged in some mindless task. It was truly the catalyst, he'd later admit, that led him to declare eternal war on slavery.

He lifted his feet from the cool water and pulled on his boots. He reminded himself to write Mary, the wife who had shared his passionate antislavery feelings since they first married—she only sixteen at the time, he thirty-three and a widower of not quite a year. Mary had uncomplainingly assumed her role as head of household so her husband could pursue his cause. At their mountain farm in upstate New York she was attending to baby Ellen and two young daughters. The letters they exchanged continued to bind a relationship marked by Brown's lengthy absences.

Brown would write Mary, but first there was work to be done. He would wait until evening to announce his plan. In the meantime the men could stand easy and wait for the cover of darkness.

"Father?"

The voice was Oliver's. In each hand he held a tin pail, having been sent by his brothers to fetch water from the spring. "They are waiting for you, Father."

Brown returned to camp. Those not standing got up as he approached. He said, "Tonight we carry out the Lord's will."

The campsite, he said, needed to remain undetected, so again there would be no cooking fire. Whatever sustenance the men required would come from the dried rations. "This is a time to rest," the old man said, "to gather your strength and prepare for what lies ahead."

Throughout the daylight hours the men lounged, speaking in subdued voices—with the exception of Townsley. His agitated voice could be heard above the rest. Brown took him aside.

"Mr. Townsley, you have doubts about our mission."

"Sir, you are asking us to do what is unlawful."

"I serve a higher law, Mr. Townsley. The law I follow gives every man and woman the right to live free."

"If we commit this crime," Townsley said, "we will become fugitives in our own country."

Townsley was a housepainter and former cavalry soldier and had fought Indians in Florida. He came to Kansas Territory from Maryland—along with his wife and four children. As a Baltimore tradesman he felt the sting of slave labor, saw it drive away fellow tradesmen. Kansas offered him an opportunity to acquire land and compete fairly for work, and—though he suffered verbal abuse from his proslavery neighbors—he was willing to defend the Free State cause. He objected, however, to the extreme measures the old man had suggested during the ride from Ottawa Jones's farm.

"I hardly need remind you of the crimes committed by the enemy," Brown told him. "He has murdered. He has tortured. He has ordered us to submit to a legislature elected by Missourians who run off Free State settlers and stuff ballot boxes with illegal votes."

Townsley nodded.

"And the enemy doesn't cease his aggressive acts. Three days ago he looted and burned the free town of Lawrence."

Like a skilled debater, the old man was girding himself for the kill. "It is not only Kansas that is forced to bow to the slaver power, Mr. Townsley. In the United States Senate, a representative of the slaveholders struck down a senator from Massachusetts. The senator wanted nothing more than a free

Kansas, and because of this the slaveholders hated him. And so
he was attacked as he sat at his desk . . . defenseless. The cowardly perpetrator skulked away with neither fear nor remorse."

Townsley sagged under the weight of Brown's intractable
resolve.

"So you see, Mr. Townsley, it is no different in Washington
than in Kansas. The slave power wishes to own us all."

By now Brown's words had drawn the attention of the
others. They gathered around him.

Owen stepped forward. He described an incident that
occurred a few days earlier. More than two hundred Southern mercenaries—the main body of the army that went on to
sack Lawrence—had camped not far from the Brown settlement. The old man had responded by collecting his surveying
equipment and setting out to gather intelligence. He took
along Owen, Frederick, Salmon, and Oliver and proceeded to
establish a baseline through the middle of the camp. When
one of the mercenaries came forward to ask his intentions,
the old man said he was surveying land for the local Ottawa
tribe. Owen mimicked the trooper's response: "We don't aim
to trouble them as minds their business. But all them abolitionists, such as the damned Browns, we going to whip, drive
out, or kill—any way to get shut of them, by God."

Salmon spoke next. He told of the grand jury convened
by Judge Sterling Cato. Proslavery leaders sent the judge to
seek warrants for the arrest of the Browns in order to discourage antislavery resistance. "Cato was going to charge us
with violating laws made by the bogus legislature, said it was
treason to speak out against slavery."

"He's right," chimed in Henry Thompson. "Cato said anyone who refused to recognize the authority of the bogus legislature was a traitor."

Owen again: "Had Father not broken up the meeting, we all would have been arrested for treason. And that includes you, Mr. Townsley."

Weiner, too, had a story. He was harassed regularly by the Sherman brothers—three strapping Germans who bullied Northern immigrants, often stealing livestock from passing wagon trains. The tavern they operated served as a courtroom for the grand jury presided over by Judge Cato. Located at the junction of the Lawrence Road and Pottawatomie Creek, the tavern was a watering hole for proslavery locals and border ruffians. A drunken William Sherman showed up at Weiner's store on Christmas Day and unleashed a string of epithets, threatening to exterminate abolitionists and anyone else who catered to Free State settlers. Weiner put an end to the dispute by grabbing an ax handle and clubbing his opponent with a ferocity that wasn't expected from a Free State sympathizer.

While the men talked, Brown remained silent. The lines etched in his face seemed deeper than usual; his razor-thin mouth was turned down solemnly. He didn't want his words to be taken as justification for an act of revenge. The men meant well, but they were making his motives seem too personal, too limited. His real purpose was to change the enemy's perception of Northern immigrants, to turn around the image of Free State settlers as cowards easily intimidated, to show that Northern men were capable of acts of violence comparable to—maybe even worse than—anything meted out by the border ruffians.

"I have already told Mr. Townsley my aim," Brown said, his tone signaling that further discussion of the matter was concluded.

What Brown didn't say was that battling slavery in Kansas was only the beginning of a much larger mission. His sword would remain unsheathed until slavery and the wickedness it bred was completely eradicated—first from Kansas Territory, then from the rest of the nation. If the acts committed by his men in Kansas ignited a war to end slavery, so be it. The time and place didn't matter. It wasn't his choice anyway. His God, after all, had commanded this thing be done.

———•••—

By late afternoon dark clouds drifted in from the north. Brown marveled at the spectacle. It was as though he were looking at the underside of a tumultuous ocean.

With the coming of evening, the full moon bled through the clouds and mist enveloped the camp. Perhaps there would be relief from the heat. The scabbards containing the broadswords were wet with dew as Brown removed them from his rucksack.

The old man's eyes had taken on a luminous glow familiar to his sons. He called for the men, gathered them in a circle around the broadswords he'd laid on a blanket. He reached for the hand of the man on either side of him, invited the others to do the same.

Then he bowed his head and prayed: "Almighty God, sovereign judge of all humanity, we ask that you give these men the strength and the will to do your bidding. You have said those who rebel against your authority—those who love slavery and seek to profit from its wickedness—shall be devoured by the sword. And so we ask that you place in the hands of each of these men a sword of righteousness so that he may strike down those who have grown proud and haughty and do not fear your might. Let these men standing before you strike a blow of such terror and dread as will cause the slave power to know freedom is alive in Kansas Territory and that there are good men prepared to draw their swords in its defense. Bless these men that they may strike the first blow in a war that will bring an end to slavery. We ask this blessing in your name. Amen."

If any of those clasping hands on that warm, humid evening were capable of detaching from the old man's thrall, it was Owen. "Father sometimes bends the Lord's words to suit his purposes," he muttered under his breath. But even Owen succumbed to his father's incantation.

Though none of Brown's sons shared his rigid brand of Christianity, they'd absorbed his belief that it was the responsibility of each one of them to recognize evil and do everything possible to defeat it. They came to respect and admire their father's cause, the sacrifices he made as a conductor and stationmaster on the Underground Railroad, the constant stream of runaway slaves that passed through their home, his grand ambition to free the nation from the curse of human bondage. They were proud to be part of a family of abolitionists. Now, along with their sister's husband Henry Thompson, the storekeeper Theodore Weiner, and the reluctant housepainter James Townsley, they were on the verge of committing acts of horrific proportions.

Brown broke the circle first, stooping to pick up one of the broadswords. He approached Owen and seemed to embrace him as he reached around his son's waist and buckled on the leather belt from which hung the sheathed sword. Brown repeated the ritual with each man. They stood motionless in the quickening darkness, surrendering to his will.

The hour was late, almost ten o'clock, when Brown told the men to follow him to Townsley's wagon. He rolled back a canvas tarpaulin, under which lay a collection of firearms. He distributed the .36 caliber Colt revolvers, one for each man, the last for himself. He checked to make sure the cylinders were loaded and capped, then slid the pistol under his belt. The others did likewise.

"We are now soldiers in the Northern Army," he said. "As your captain I expect each of you to do his duty."

He turned to young Oliver and ordered him to stay in camp and stand watch over the horses and wagon. Then he lifted a tattered straw hat from the wagon's bed. Limp and misshapen, it clashed wildly with his black leather cravat, a staple of his attire, worn over the high collar of a white muslin shirt now fouled with sweat. He reached inside his coat and pulled out a slip of paper. In the mist-enshrouded darkness it was impossible to read, but he knew what it said. He waved it in the air and announced:

"The Doyles first. Then Wilkinson. Then the Shermans."

Before setting out for the timbered bank of Pottawatomie Creek, Brown cautioned his soldiers to remain silent. Townsley took the lead. He knew the dwellings of the men Brown named.

By eleven o'clock, they reached Mosquito Creek, a shallow stream that emptied into the Pottawatomie and ran through the claim of James Doyle.

Doyle was a hardscrabble Tennessee farmer who migrated to Kansas Territory to escape the disadvantages of subsistence farming in a slaveholding state. In Tennessee he supplemented his meager income by hunting fugitive slaves. When he settled in the territory he brought along two bloodhounds that had served him well tracking down runaways. With his wife Mahala and their four children—among them twenty-two-year-old William and twenty-year-old Drury—he staked out a claim on Mosquito Creek. However, he was unable to free himself from deeply held racial prejudices and soon aligned himself with his proslavery neighbors. He and sons William and Drury fell under the influence of the Sherman brothers. Together they drank whiskey at the Shermans' tavern, then amused themselves by intimidating Free State settlers. James Doyle sat on Judge Cato's grand jury—the one seeking to indict the Browns—while son William served as bailiff.

Brown and his men were nearing the Doyles' log cabin when the bloodhounds came bounding out of the mist. Townsley drew his sword and with a single stroke sent one of the dogs to the ground in a crumpled heap. The other fled yelping into the night.

Brown jabbed at the lifeless body with his boot. He heard muffled voices coming from the cabin. He chose Owen, Salmon, and Henry to accompany him to the cabin's front door. Townsley, Weiner, and Frederick would remain behind—unless called on for help. The old man made his way along a worn path to the crude, low-walled cabin. He pounded on the door and called out:

"We are lost and need directions to the Wilkinsons'."

A woman's voice responded, begging her husband to ignore the request. Brown heard the scraping of a wooden bar being lifted from metal brackets. He thrust his shoulder against the door and burst into the cabin. Owen, Salmon, and Henry were on his heels. A single candle flickered in the otherwise dark interior.

James Doyle, wearing only a pair of trousers he held up with one hand, stepped back, a puzzled look on his face. His wife and two youngest children—a teenage boy and a little girl—sat close together on one of the three beds in the dirt-floored room. The two older boys, clad in soiled nightshirts, stood nearby.

Brown pressed his pistol into Doyle's bare chest. "We are from the Northern Army," he said, "and we have come to take you prisoner."

The wife wept as she looked to her husband. "Haven't I told you what you were going to get for the course you've been taking?"

"Hush, Mother, hush," Doyle said. "I know this man."

Brown pointed to Doyle. "Take him." Then he waved his pistol at William and Drury. "And them as well."

Henry, Owen, and Salmon, their pistols drawn, shoved Doyle and his two sons outside the cabin.

"Not this one, sir," the wife sobbed, clinging to the boy sitting beside her. "Not this one, I beg you."

Brown paused, glanced briefly at the woman and her two young children, then turned and exited the cabin, shutting the door behind him.

Outside, in the hazy glow of the moon, Henry guarded a shivering James Doyle. Owen and Salmon, their swords unsheathed, prodded William and Drury along a wagon trail. They disappeared into the mist.

Brown followed at some distance, stopping as the sounds reached him.

What he heard reminded him of the ax strokes delivered to the skinned carcasses of deer he butchered occasionally for his family. The ax would slam into flesh, sometimes finding bone—the bone snapping sharply as it split into fragments. Except the slain deer wouldn't moan piteously, nor would there be the choking babble of curses drowning in blood-laced saliva.

When Brown next saw Owen and Salmon they were breathing heavily, their clothes sodden with blood and sweat. Blood dripped from their swords and hands. Blood merged with the sweat on their brows, producing pink rivulets—barely discernible in the soft glow of moonlight that clung to the mist.

"Finish it," the old man said, gesturing in the direction of the cabin, where Henry waited with James Doyle. They headed back.

Doyle, still gripping his trousers, seemed dazed. Owen and Salmon marched him down the same trail traversed earlier by William and Drury. This time Brown stayed close.

It was Salmon who wrenched Doyle from Owen's grasp, shoving the trembling man to the ground. With both hands clutching his sword as though it were an iron digging bar—one that might be used to break up hard clay in the farm country of Doyle's native Tennessee—Salmon raised it above his head, then plunged the blade into Doyle's abdomen, impaling him to the ground. Doyle's hands flew from his side, wrapping around the blade, the finely honed edges slicing into his fingers. His knees jerked upward. A piercing shrill welled up from deep within his chest.

Salmon released his grip and turned away. He found himself staring into the face of his father. "There," he rasped, his glazed eyes fixed on Brown. "You have your blood."

Brown looked down at the writhing body, listened to the shuddering death rattle until he could bear it no longer, drew his pistol, placed the barrel to Doyle's head and squeezed the trigger. The writhing ceased.

Owen withdrew the sword from the lifeless body.

The Sabbath had arrived, and the night of controlled frenzy hadn't yet come to an end.

Brown sent an exhausted Salmon and Owen to the rear, then collected Henry, Weiner, Frederick, and Townsley. They resumed their march along the Pottawatomie.

The killing of Wilkinson and the Shermans fell to Weiner and Henry. Brown, Townsley, and Frederick were witnesses.

Allen Wilkinson, a member of the proslavery legislature, was acting district attorney for Judge Cato's grand jury. One of the few literate settlers in the Pottawatomie region, Wilkinson was rabidly proslavery. Hours earlier on this, the evening he was to die, he'd boasted to his wife, "In a few days the last of the Free State settlers will either be dead or out of the territory."

The wife implored Brown to spare her husband's life. Brown shrugged. Wilkinson's death was no less violent than the Doyles'.

It was time to move on.

Tied to a hitching rail in back of the Shermans' tavern were three horses, one of which Townsley identified as belonging to William Sherman. All three of the brothers were on Brown's list, but on this night—as luck would have it—William was the only brother present, asleep in a back room. He was rousted from his bed, marched to the Pottawatomie, then ordered into the creek, where he found himself anchored in silt as though shackled in leg irons. He was an easy mark for the slashing blades of Weiner and Henry Thompson. Brown, Townsley, and Frederick stood on the high rim of the creek gazing through the mist at the dim spectacle below. The hulking William Sherman wouldn't yield without trying to defend himself. In the end he toppled into the water like a felled tree.

It was shortly after two o'clock on Sunday morning and the work was finally done. Five men lay dead—victims of an execution designed to create fear among those claiming allegiance to slavery. Five men who, besides being proslavery, had the misfortune of living in close proximity to one another alongside a creek in Kansas Territory.

The executioners stripped to the waist, waded into the Pottawatomie, rinsed their bloody swords in the slow-moving waters, wrung the blood from their shirts. When they emerged from the creek, they dropped to the ground like dead weight.

Townsley stood motionless alongside an agitated Frederick.

Brown distanced himself from everyone. In the darkness, he was invisible in a stand of timber that bordered the creek.

None of the executioners spoke except Owen. "There will be no more such work as this," he said.

———— •••• ————

Brown inspected the property he confiscated from the victims. Four horses pawed the dirt, uneasy among their captors. Stacked on the ground were six saddles, three rifles, a powder flask, and a bowie knife.

"We are at war," the old man said. "We take from the enemy what we need."

With the horses in tow, the soldiers of Brown's Northern Army trudged back to the encampment between the two ravines. For the first time since the ordeal began, they were able to reflect on what they had done.

Brown walked to one side, his head bowed and thrust forward, immersed in thought. He had accomplished his mission. Now let the word go out. Let the slave power know the war on slavery had begun in earnest.

The horses whinnied and shook their manes. Brown could feel the moisture in the warm air being lifted up. A gust of wind caused his straw hat to flap against his head. Jagged bands of lightning rippled across the night sky, illuminating the men in ghostly poses.

Brown was confident the rain would come; it would bring new life to the parched prairie—just as the blood spilled along the Pottawatomie would bring new life to the struggle against slavery in Kansas.

There would be guerrilla warfare, skirmishes with border ruffians and proslavery territorial militia. Maybe even action against federal troops acting under orders from President Pierce and Secretary of War Jefferson Davis.

Brown's army would be small. But a few men of principle who respected themselves and feared God could accomplish great things. Besides, the old man had connections—abolitionists in the Northeast who would supply him with money and guns once they learned he was determined to bring freedom to Kansas Territory.

4

Eight Days Later
June 2, 1856
Kansas Territory

At first light Brown was on his belly clutching a Colt revolver and crawling through grass he could have sworn had grown a foot since the rains returned to the prairie. The grass was lush and wet and dotted with purple wildflowers that seemed to have sprung up overnight. The old man couldn't avoid crushing them as he slithered upward toward the crest of a ridge, a vantage point from which he hoped to get a glimpse of the enemy.

The enemy was twenty-four-year-old Henry Clay Pate, a deputy US marshal and captain of a troop of Missouri militiamen hunting the Pottawatomie killers.

But now the hunters were the hunted.

———————————

News of the approaching Missourians had reached Brown at his encampment in the timber near the headwaters of Ottawa Creek, north of Ottawa Jones's farm. He and his men were in hiding—awaiting the repercussions of Pottawatomie—when Samuel Shore, a Free State settler from the nearby hamlet of

Palmyra, rode into camp and announced the Missourians had come and were seeking revenge. He told of cabins plundered and burned.

"The only thing that's protected us so far," Shore told Brown, "is the Missourians' fear that you and your men are lying in ambush somewhere close by."

Brown's eyes widened. Had Pottawatomie become the catalyst he hoped for? An event that would compel Free State settlers to abandon their fields and take up arms? Was it possible the war to end chattel slavery might begin in Kansas Territory?

Brown asked, "Mr. Shore, how many men can you furnish me?"

Shore hesitated. "My neighbors are afraid to leave their farms and families."

Brown said, "I am not willing to sacrifice my men without the hope of accomplishing something."

So Shore left, promising to return after he recruited enough volunteers to form—along with Brown's small company—a combined force capable of taking on the Missourians.

————

Soon after Shore's departure, a correspondent from Horace Greeley's *New York Tribune* stumbled onto the old man's camp. James Redpath was only twenty-two; he'd joined Greeley's newspaper intending to write about slavery. He spent a year traveling in three Southern states and witnessed enough depravity to convert him into an impassioned abolitionist. At the behest of Greeley, who openly opposed slavery, Redpath journeyed west to join the cadre of *Tribune* correspondents already reporting on the troubles in Kansas Territory.

Brown was pleasantly surprised when he learned the identity of his visitor. He knew of Redpath's work and had read some of his reports in the *Tribune*. He also knew that to achieve his goals he needed a favorable press, especially in the Northeast, where his benefactors resided. Anyone who wrote dispatches for a radical abolitionist like Horace Greeley was a valuable asset.

It was midday when Redpath was escorted to a clearing in the stand of trees surrounding the camp. The air was saturated with the aroma of simmering pork. Brown stood beside a cooking fire, a fork in his hand, leaning over an iron pot suspended from a tripod. He turned to greet Redpath.

"They tell me you work for Greeley."

"I do indeed, sir. And you, I trust, are Captain John Brown."

The old man nodded. "Please join us for dinner." He turned over the slab of meat; it sizzled and sent puffs of steam into the air. "This pig was liberated from its proslavery owner," Brown said dryly. "Gave its life for the cause of freedom."

Redpath hadn't expected droll humor from a man suspected of brutally murdering proslavery settlers.

Brown invited Redpath to sit with him in the shade of a hickory tree—but not before asking the Lord's blessing and seeing that his men were fed. With the addition of two new volunteers, the company had grown to ten.

As they ate, Brown and Redpath talked of the defeat of Lawrence, the timidity of the Free State settlers. Eventually the journalist broached the subject of Pottawatomie. He reached into his coat and pulled out a newspaper, unfolded it, handed it to the old man, and pointed to the banner headline:

WAR! WAR!

The story was printed on the front page of the *Border Times*, a proslavery weekly published in a town near Kansas City.

Brown read without commenting, showed no emotion even though the story incorrectly claimed eight men—rather than five—had been killed. It concluded with a plea for volunteers and money to fight a civil war that had broken out in Kansas. The old man refolded the paper and handed it back to Redpath.

The story was reprinted in other papers, Redpath said, but hadn't made its way out of Missouri. "I think Northern editors are too busy filling their pages with the destruction of Lawrence and the assault on Senator Sumner."

If Brown wanted recognition for Pottawatomie—recognition that would reach New York and the rest of the Northeast—Redpath was offering him an opportunity.

"I have nothing to say on the matter of the killings," Brown said, then added, "Nor do my men." He wiped his mouth with a soiled rag. "If you want my opinion on what appears to be the beginning of civil warfare in Kansas, I welcome it."

The old man's penetrating gaze unnerved the correspondent. Redpath must have felt the conversation had taken an unpleasant turn; he didn't want to alienate the one man he judged to be irrevocably committed to the abolition of slavery in Kansas. So he backed off. "I've seen what slavery has done to this country," Redpath said, "and I fear if you don't persevere all will be lost."

"Frankly," Brown said, slipping into a more genial mood, "my men and I feel as though we are the extreme outpost of the free North. We shall stay here and fight, young man. We shan't disappoint our friends."

Redpath then told of his frustration with the Free State politicians he'd met and interviewed in Lawrence and Topeka.

"There is much jealousy, selfishness, and unprincipled ambition," he said. He was beginning to doubt whether there were men in Kansas who were true champions of freedom.

The old man reached for Redpath's hand, a signal that it was time for him to be on his way. But first Brown summoned the men.

They gathered around him as he bowed his head and again gave thanks to the Lord for the meal they shared. He added a blessing for the young journalist in their midst, whom he hoped would be faithful to the truth when telling readers of the struggle for freedom in Kansas.

Before Redpath left the camp, he was moved to say a few words about Brown's soldiers. He admired their loyalty and obedience, how they earnestly went about their chores and seemed in good spirits despite their meager circumstances. They exhibited none of the swaggering, bullying traits of the whiskey-guzzling, tobacco-spitting border ruffians who roamed the countryside with no purpose other than to terrorize Northern immigrants and, more recently, to plunder and burn Free State settlements.

Brown's eyes gleamed. "Sir," he said, "I would rather have the smallpox, yellow fever, and cholera all together in my camp, than a man without principles. It is a mistake to assume bullies are the best fighters." He went on to explain that his men fought with a single purpose in mind: to oppose slavery. His underlying principles, he said, could be found in Holy Scripture and the Declaration of Independence. "We will succeed," he said, "if our purpose is such as to deserve the blessing of God."

Redpath was buoyed by Brown's words. As for the old man, he was confident he'd sown seeds that might one day yield a bountiful harvest.

The following evening Samuel Shore returned. He said the Missouri militiamen were bivouacked near Black Jack Springs, a three-hour ride from Brown's encampment. Some of the Missourians had ambushed a group of Free State settlers in the village of Palmyra. The settlers were afraid to fight back.

Shore said he was tired of being intimidated and that he was able to muster a group of volunteers. Were Brown and his men willing to fight the Missourians alongside his people?

Brown responded emphatically: "We are with you!"

Though Shore admitted his recruits were mostly boys in their late teens, he said they were eager to serve. With Shore's volunteers, the combined force now stood at eighteen. The enemy was presumed to be at least twice that number.

Shore departed, but not before making it clear that Brown was in charge. They agreed to rendezvous the following day at Palmyra.

During the ride to Palmyra, Brown learned of a prayer meeting in progress in a log cabin off the trail. When he was told the congregation was made up of Free State settlers, he expressed a desire to attend. His men waited outside the cabin while he dismounted and introduced himself to the preacher.

The old man was about to take a seat when Owen burst through the door and shouted a warning. Three horsemen were approaching the cabin, rifles braced against their saddles. The congregation spilled out the door—armed and ready to fight. Seeing they were outnumbered, the riders wheeled and fled. Brown's men pursued and eventually captured two, the third managing to escape.

Both captives confessed to being part of the Missouri militia camped at Black Jack Springs. When informed they were prisoners of the man accused of the Pottawatomie killings, they became exceedingly cooperative, disclosing the number of men in their company, the location of their encampment, and the name of their leader, and finally—though not asked— they recited a tale of interest to the old man. It seems the Missourians had raided the Free State village of Osawatomie. Their leader, Captain Henry Clay Pate, arrested two men outside the village who were believed to be members of the gang involved in the Pottawatomie affair.

With some trepidation, one of the captives said, "We was told they was the sons of Old John Brown."

As inscrutable as ever, Brown said nothing. He knew it was inevitable that his married sons, John Jr. and Jason, would be implicated in the killings. He'd even sent Owen to Osawatomie to warn them of possible recriminations.

Owen spoke up, his voice betraying some anxiety. "And what about the wives? My brothers had wives, and there were children."

"Hain't nobody seen no women, nor little ones neither. Reckon they hiding out somewheres."

The interrogation ended on a disturbing note. The captives told Brown that John Jr. and Jason were no longer prisoners of Pate. They had been turned over to the commander of a troop of federal cavalry bound for the proslavery capital of Lecompton.

Before leaving, Brown handed over the two captives to the preacher and his congregation.

The old man had wanted war. He'd gotten what he wanted—along with its unintended consequences. His married sons had nothing to do with Pottawatomie, yet they were now in the hands of the enemy. And Brown could do nothing about it.

Meanwhile, Shore and his volunteers were waiting to be led into battle. The attack on Pate's camp was supposed to begin the following day in the predawn hours.

Brown untied his horse, hoisted himself into the saddle. A sharp kick to the animal's flanks sent it galloping down the Santa Fe Trail toward Palmyra. The others followed, strung out in a line. The old man didn't see Weiner take a long pull on a jug of whiskey, then hand it to Townsley. He was absorbed in thoughts of fulfilling a destiny he believed was foreordained.

Brown finally reached the crest of the ridge. He'd crawled through the wet grass until his clothes were soaked. Below him lay the encampment of Pate's Missourians. In the gray dawn, the old man could see wagons. Horses were grazing. Otherwise, all was still. He was breathing hard as he laid his pistol aside, removed a brass spyglass from his coat pocket, and extended it to the maximum length. The first full rays of the sun were still minutes away.

He was eager to test his theories of guerrilla warfare. Only those closest to him knew of his ideas on wars of resistance, wars pitting small bands of revolutionary fighters against sovereign states. Not only did he admire Toussaint-Louverture, liberator of the slaves of Haiti, but he'd read about Javier Mina, leader of the Spanish resistance against Napoleon. He felt he had much in common with Schamyl, champion of the Muslim Caucasians who fought the Russians for thirty years, believing a small army of disciplined, God-fearing warriors could defeat a large army of well-armed combatants.

And Brown had his own ideas on how to wage a war requiring unconventional tactics. After visiting battlefields in Europe during an unsuccessful attempt to sell American wool abroad in 1849, he concluded that Napoleon and other commanders were wrong in believing high ground was necessarily a strong position in battle.

As he peered through his spyglass, he saw that Pate's encampment was situated at the base of a gentle slope that leveled off near the edge of a ravine. Pate had placed four supply wagons end to end in front of the ravine. A scattering of tents was visible behind the wagons. The horses and mules were tethered among the blackjack oaks, a stunted and spindly species that bordered the ravine.

Brown rolled onto his back, pressed steadily on the eyepiece of the spyglass until the brass tubes collapsed, then returned it to his coat pocket. He gazed at the brightening sky, pondering all the elements of Pate's position. Lying in a swale behind him, the men from his company—along with Shore's volunteers—awaited orders. They had come on foot, leaving their horses a few hundred yards to the rear in the care of one of Shore's boys and Brown's son Frederick, the latter suffering from another of his painful headaches.

The old man crawled to the swale and presented his plan. He'd already allowed for the element of surprise by beginning the attack when most of Pate's men would be asleep, some of them probably groggy from swilling whiskey the night before. He wanted Shore's company to proceed as speedily as possible to the left of Pate's wagons. At the same time

Brown's men would rush to the right. If fired upon, Shore's boys were to dive into the tall grass, wait for the shooting to ease, then continue forward, crawling on their bellies. There was to be no engagement with the enemy until the ravine was reached. In effect Brown and Shore would be executing a pincer movement, the object being to fire into Pate's men from opposite ends of the ravine.

As ordered, Shore's boys dashed down the slope toward Pate's left. Within a hundred yards of the ravine, however, the discharge of a sentry's musket sent a ball scudding over their heads. For the next two hours, Brown and his men—having reached the shelter of the ravine to Pate's right—listened to the exchange of gunfire between Shore's volunteers and the Missourians.

Shore's boys had failed to reach the ravine. In fact their only movement, Brown learned later, was to seek safety in the rear. Fortunately, a considerable number of Pate's men were also quitting the fight, leaping onto the backs of their unsaddled horses and spurring them toward Missouri.

While attempting to shoot one of Pate's fleeing Missourians, Henry Thompson took a ball in his side that lodged close to his spine. Still, he refused to leave his post, continuing to fire his revolver until his trembling hands were no longer able to cap and load cartridges. His eyes were fixed on a distant point in space when he told Brown, "I have taken a life, and if I'm obliged to surrender my own, I accept my fate." Henry hadn't been able to detach himself from the bloody work at Pottawatomie.

Brown now realized his ability to prolong the fight was in doubt. His company had dwindled to eight men. Those who remained included his sons Owen, Salmon, and Oliver, as well as the wounded Henry Thompson. Frederick was still

guarding the horses. James Townsley and Theodore Weiner
had determined the outcome of the battle was hopeless and
had chosen to walk away.

The old man was surprised when Shore showed up with
two of his volunteers. They had retreated to the ridge and
circled back during a lull in the shooting. Shore expressed
regret at his failure to occupy the ravine on Pate's left. "This
is all new to us," he said, adding that some of his boys had
been wounded.

"You needn't apologize, Mr. Shore. If there is a lesson here,
your boys will be better for having learned it."

Brown was glad to have the additional soldiers—although
he immediately sent Shore to seek reinforcements in Lawrence.

Meanwhile, the two boys from Shore's troop seemed to
have little enthusiasm for rejoining the fight. No matter.
Brown saw an opportunity to restore their will.

"If you won't kill the enemy," he told them, "you can kill
the enemy's ordnance." He ordered them to take a position
on a nearby hillock, where they were to fire on Pate's horses
and mules across the ravine. In a matter of minutes, they sent
a half dozen to the ground.

As if this development weren't enough to throw Pate's
remaining soldiers into a panic, a lone rider suddenly came
charging down the slope. He waved a short broadsword as
he rode back and forth in front of the wagons, somehow
managing to avoid the guns for which he was the sole target.

It was Frederick. He'd witnessed some of Shore's boys
retrieve their mounts and ride off and felt compelled to move
closer to the fighting. When he heard the screams of the
wounded and dying animals, he couldn't turn away. Whatever
his motivation, he held his life to be of little worth since the

Pottawatomie killings. He'd always been racked with guilt for one reason or another, even believing his excruciatingly painful headaches were a form of divine punishment. Apparently Pottawatomie had become for him an atrocity of such magnitude that he now felt permanently connected to Kansas and its fate. Brown and his soldiers were aware of this and consequently weren't nearly as shocked at Frederick's behavior as were Captain Henry Clay Pate and his Missourians.

"Come on, boys!" Frederick shouted. "We've got 'em surrounded! We've cut off their communications!"

Pate took the brash horseman at his word. He feared Free State reinforcements actually had arrived. So he sent forward two men carrying a white handkerchief attached to a ramrod.

Brown climbed out of the ravine to meet the men bearing the flag of truce. He asked, "Which of you is Captain Pate?"

"We are speaking for him," one of the men replied.

"I will talk with no one but Captain Pate," Brown said. "Go back and bring him out."

Brown knew he had the advantage and had no intention of relinquishing it.

Pate came forward and immediately began scolding Brown. "I should warn you," he said, "I am a deputy United States marshal under orders to search for persons for whom I have writs of arrest."

"Captain," the old man replied, "I understand exactly what you are and don't want to hear anything more about it." He paused to study his young adversary. "Now . . . have you a proposition to make?"

Pate ignored the question and continued to lecture Brown on the treasonous consequences of attacking a federal officer and a militia deputized by the government of the United States.

Brown interrupted. "Very well then. If you have no proposition to make to me, I have one to make to you—your unconditional surrender." He gestured toward the wagons, behind
which the Missourians waited, weapons still at the ready. Then
he turned to Pate and repeated the demand for unconditional
surrender. "Tell your men to lay down their arms."

Pate grimaced, but he gave the order and his men com-
plied, albeit reluctantly. Those who had remained at their
posts were loyal proslavery men. Even though three of them
were seriously wounded, they had little stomach for capitulat-
ing to a company of Yankees.

Brown's stern attitude belied the satisfaction he felt as he
paraded the prisoners of war in front of his soldiers; they had
lined up to meet him.

———•••———

It was shortly before noon, and the first regular battle of civil
warfare in Kansas Territory had come to an end. A small force
of Free State volunteers prevailed against a numerically superior militia from Missouri. In Kansas, in Missouri, and most
particularly in the Northeast—where abolitionist sympathizers
hungered for retribution for the caning of Charles Sumner
and the sacking of Lawrence—people would soon be learning
about what happened at Black Jack Springs.

Brown intended to exchange Pate and the captured Missourians for Free State men held by the territorial government. He
even drew up a surrender document in which he specifically
called for the release of his sons John Jr. and Jason.

It was late in the afternoon when the prisoners and their
equipment were secured in Brown's camp on Ottawa Creek.
A visitor was waiting for him. Twenty-six-year-old John Cook

was a handsome though somewhat diminutive young man with shoulder-length blond hair. He was part of a militia from Lawrence that Samuel Shore had rallied to Brown's aid—even though Pate had already surrendered by the time the militia arrived. Brown had been introduced to Cook some weeks earlier and remembered him as an enthusiastic advocate of the Free State cause.

Cook had studied law before coming to the territory. He was something of a lady's man, and though he was in Kansas to fight the enemies of freedom, he also was aware of the notoriety that might accrue to someone engaged in such an endeavor. He saw in Brown the selfless, idealistic hero he'd like to emulate—especially now, what with the old man's victory over the Missourians.

Brown was glad to see Cook. The old man was witnessing the disintegration of his company. Son-in-law Henry Thompson needed medical attention. Salmon, Frederick, and Oliver were weary of the fighting; too much blood had been shed over the past two weeks. Townsley had returned to his family. Weiner's store had been burned, and he'd soon leave Kansas permanently. Yet the old man knew the battle of Black Jack Springs had given him credibility as a guerrilla leader. And if he wanted to continue to fight he needed to rebuild his force. He needed someone who had access to young men imbued with the cause. He could use a man like John Cook.

"Black Jack is only the beginning," Brown told Cook. "There are more battles to be fought. The enemy is obstinate. He shan't give in easily."

Cook agreed. "How can I be of service, Captain?"

"I need men," Brown said. "Not just ordinary men. I need men who have a purpose in their lives and are willing to adhere to it in all trials, men who respect themselves, men who are temperate and fear God."

Brown went on to explain that his new company would be a model of efficiency and that he'd only accept volunteers who agreed to a set of written bylaws designed to ensure that the mistakes of Black Jack wouldn't be repeated. The enlistees would have to vow to uphold moral principles and follow a rigid code of conduct.

Cook left the camp impressed by the old man's intentions. He'd pass the word and do what he could to find the kind of men Brown was looking for.

——— •···· ———

Three days later, Colonel E. V. Sumner—a distant relative of the Massachusetts senator—converged on Brown's encampment with fifty US cavalrymen. Sumner had orders from President Pierce and the territorial governor to liberate Pate's militia. He was also authorized to disperse Brown's company and arrest the old man for treason and suspicion of murder, but he was content to recover the prisoners and leave Brown and his men alone when he determined—after a casual inspection—that none of them fit the descriptions in his arrest warrants. One of Sumner's officers, a young lieutenant named J. E. B. Stuart, found the colonel's decision grossly negligent, but he kept his mouth shut.

As Colonel Sumner led away Pate and his men, Brown grumbled that the action taken against him was another example of a corrupt federal government bent on supporting a corrupt and illegal territorial government.

It was a bittersweet conclusion to an otherwise successful action. Brown had enhanced his reputation as a dangerous man, someone to be reckoned with. A tacit warning had been issued to all Missouri marauders and their Southern allies: Northern men were no longer to be trifled with; they could fight and fight well. Still, the old man was unable to negotiate the release of any Free State prisoners, not even his sons. And he was forced to give up the weapons, ammunition, wagons, mules, and horses he took from Pate.

That evening Brown sat down in the light of a campfire and began to compose a letter to his wife, Mary. He drew partly on a biblical passage: "We have been, like David of old, *dwelling with the serpents of the rocks and wild beasts of the wilderness*, being obliged to hide away from our enemies. We are not disheartened though nearly destitute of food, clothing, and money."

The part about being nearly destitute was not completely true. Owen and Oliver had just come back from a raid on a dry goods store owned by a proslavery sympathizer. Since Brown now saw himself engaged in a full-scale civil war, he felt he was taking what he was entitled to—the spoils of war. The raiding party returned with a supply of pants, shirts, coats, hats, bandanna handkerchiefs, and other provisions, including a cow, all of it worth hundreds of dollars.

There were other peculiarities in the letter to Mary. Brown described the battle at Black Jack Springs in some detail but failed to mention Frederick's charge into Pate's guns. There was also a casual reference to Pottawatomie, Brown noting that "some murders had been committed at the time Lawrence was sacked."

Near the end of the letter he asked Mary to send a copy to Gerrit Smith, a wealthy New York abolitionist who had

5

A Month Later
July 2, 1856
Kansas Territory

It was a Wednesday morning when John Brown rode into Lawrence at the head of a column of fourteen mounted Free State fighters, most of them newly recruited. Piles of rubble were still visible along Massachusetts Street, a reminder of damage sustained when the town was sacked in May. Women eyed the riders warily, scurried across board sidewalks, ducked into stores.

Brown lifted his straw hat and wiped his brow on the sleeve of his black wool coat, a garment strikingly out of place in the oppressive heat. He came from the woods and thickets along Ottawa Creek, where he'd been *dwelling with the serpents of the rocks and wild beasts of the wilderness*, moving from one campsite to another, hiding from proslavery militias intent on killing him, avoiding contact with US troops not likely to be as lenient as Colonel E. V. Sumner.

The old man had been tending to a collection of invalids. His son-in-law Henry Thompson was still recovering from the wound suffered at Black Jack. Salmon had accidentally shot himself in the shoulder, and Owen, Oliver, and Frederick had come down with chills and fever. Brown felt poorly too. He was thinner, the flesh on his face drawn so close to the bone that his head looked like a skull.

Between the injured, the sick, and those who quit after Black Jack, Brown was left with only three able-bodied men—among them his son Jason, just released from the stockade in Lecompton. But the recruiting efforts of John Cook, together with the old man's growing reputation, had attracted eleven volunteers. The prospect of returning to action with a new company under his command had energized Brown, and the symptoms of whatever illness he was experiencing had practically disappeared as the column of horsemen made its way to Lawrence's Eastern House, a favorite lodging of Northern journalists.

Brown was in town to call on William A. Phillips, thirty-two, another of Horace Greeley's *New York Tribune* correspondents. Like James Redpath, Phillips was committed to the Free State cause. He was also a close friend of the Free State leader, Dr. Charles Robinson. Brown still had doubts about Robinson, saw him as a timid man who put too much faith in a peaceful solution to the troubles in Kansas. With regard to Phillips, though, the old man had heard good things. Redpath and other *Tribune* journalists saw Phillips as the most perceptive of Greeley's correspondents, someone dedicated to making sense out of the Kansas struggle and its implications for a nation steadily becoming more divided over the issue of slavery. Rumors had Phillips writing a book. He'd be someone worth meeting, someone who might be interested in Brown's purposes, what his beliefs were, and how they shaped his decisions.

The old man was usually skeptical of anyone with a preference for words over actions. He disliked many of the antislavery orators and editors, including the highly regarded William

Lloyd Garrison, publisher of the *Liberator*, considering them weak men who had no stomach for taking the fight directly to the enemy. Journalists who were at the front and witnessed firsthand the stubbornness of the slave power were the exception. Brown admired Elijah Lovejoy, the Illinois newspaper editor assassinated by proslavery thugs. When he was a young man mired in financial difficulties, Brown had attended a church service in honor of the slain editor. He'd listened to an account of Lovejoy's heroic stand against slavery and found himself slowly overcome by guilt. Lovejoy had sacrificed his life for a cause to which Brown was no less dedicated. But Brown had been consumed with fighting off creditors and responding to lawsuits. Near the end of the service he stood up, raised his right hand as though swearing an oath, and declared, "Here, before God, in the presence of these witnesses, I consecrate my life to the destruction of slavery."

Now, years later, Brown was intent on keeping his promise. Maybe Phillips was cut from the same cloth as Lovejoy.

The old man had his reasons for seeking out the *Tribune* correspondent. The first was to hand him a letter—Brown's personal account of the battle at Black Jack, written as a rebuttal to a *Tribune* story authored by Henry Clay Pate. Pate had written that deceitful tactics were used at Black Jack, that a pistol was held to his head when Brown ordered him to surrender.

Brown also wanted to escort Phillips to a convention of Free State legislators slated to meet two days hence, on Independence Day, in Topeka. He correctly assumed Phillips would be attending the convention, an assembly certain to be challenged as treasonous by federal and territorial authorities. If a crisis arose Brown wanted to be there, helping in any way he could, even if it meant fighting federal troops. He felt Phillips ought to take advantage of the protection he was being offered.

"I'm sure you are aware of the danger in traveling alone these days," Brown warned Phillips. "The border ruffians kill for the sake of killing."

Phillips didn't need to be reminded. He reported to the *Tribune* that murders along the border were frequent, many remaining undisclosed.

It also was obvious he wasn't awed by Brown's reputation. "The past thirty days have been described as a reign of terror, Captain," Phillips said caustically, "and the blame has been laid on the perpetrators of the Pottawatomie affair."

Brown had no desire to justify himself to Phillips. He hoped their meeting would be amicable and that the ride to Topeka would be an opportunity for a respected journalist to get to know the real John Brown. "Come with us," the old man urged. "You will be safe and we can talk about such matters as will make my purposes clear. I shall only say now that what I do, I do for the cause of liberty—and because I regard it necessary."

That afternoon Phillips joined Brown and his soldiers for the ride to Topeka. They took the California Road, headed west, skirting the proslavery capital of Lecompton, where John Jr. was still imprisoned. At dusk they reached Big Springs, turned off the trail, and moved onto the open prairie, a precautionary measure to avoid a confrontation with the enemy. They made camp on a hill near a creek. The horses were unsaddled, watered, and picketed in the tall grass. The men ate what they had—dried beef, cornmeal rolled into balls and cooked in the ashes of the campfire, all of it washed down with creek water.

Brown noticed that Phillips was reluctant to sample the charred bread balls. He chided the journalist. "I'm afraid, Phillips, you will hardly be able to eat a soldier's harsh fare."

Conversation around the campfire touched on a number of subjects, including Brown's theories of military tactics and strategy, the old man underscoring once again his belief in the superiority of the individual soldier over the most stalwart fortifications. "A few good men in the right, and knowing they are, can overturn a king," he said, noting that Nat Turner and his fifty rebel slaves held the entire state of Virginia at bay for five weeks. Brown reiterated his belief that a ravine could sometimes be a more defensible position than a hilltop.

During a lull in the conversation, Phillips turned to Jason and asked about the arrests that took place after Pottawatomie. One of Phillips's fellow correspondents, William Hutchinson of the *New York Times*, had written an account of the treatment John Jr. received while being conveyed to Lecompton by a troop of federal cavalry. Phillips found parts of the story hard to believe and was curious to hear what Jason had to say.

"What is it you would like to know, Mr. Phillips?" There was sadness in Jason's voice, and Phillips must have regretted broaching the subject.

Of all Brown's sons, thirty-three-year-old Jason came closest to being a pacifist. Though he shared the abolitionist sentiments of his father and brothers, he wanted nothing more than to lead the quiet life of a farmer. His trip west was marred by the death of his infant son Austin, struck down by cholera. He brought grape vines and fruit trees and dreamed of cultivating the rich soil of Kansas Territory and raising a family. While he was imprisoned at Lecompton the Missourians burned his house near Osawatomie, then trampled his plantings. His wife, Ellen, and their surviving child were able to find a safe haven in the village. After his release from prison, Jason believed he had no choice but to join his father's company. Though he was ready to leave the territory, he wasn't going anywhere until his brother was freed from the stockade at Lecompton.

Brown picked up a stick and poked at the embers in the smoldering campfire.

Jason gazed absently at the rekindled flames. He began to tell his story: "We all suffered, but none so much as my brother. They found him in the brush. He had been wandering for days, eluding the federals. He wasn't well. They tied his wrists behind him, then the upper part of his arms. The rope was hard and the commander of the troop set it with his teeth. Another length of rope was yoked to the bindings and tied to a wagon. They drove him afoot to Osawatomie—some eight or nine miles—while I rode in the wagon and witnessed his agony. They never loosened the rope around his arms. His flesh was so swollen it covered the rope. They drove him through the water of Bull Creek and the yellow flints at the bottom cut through his boots and lacerated his feet. When we arrived at Osawatomie and made camp, I found him chained to the center pole of the prisoners' tent. By this time he was quite insane, shrieking military orders, jumping up and down, casting himself about—"

Brown interrupted. "Enough, Jason. I'm sure by now Mr. Phillips has a good idea of the privations suffered by your brother."

Phillips turned to the old man. "I can understand why you would want to avenge such cruelty, Captain."

After a short pause, Brown said, "I do not act from revenge, Mr. Phillips. It is a feeling that does not enter my heart."

The sky was darkening as the men retired to their blankets—but not before listening to Brown recite the customary prayer. He gave thanks for the meager rations.

A cooling breeze provided some relief from the sweltering heat.

Having placed their blankets and saddles only a few feet apart, Brown and Phillips lay on the ground looking up at the night sky. The stars seemed exceedingly close, almost within their grasp. As the rest of the men slept, Brown talked and Phillips listened.

"How admirable is the symmetry of the heavens," the old man mused. "Everything moves in sublime harmony in the government of God." He paused. "Not so with us poor creatures. We put too much faith in the governments of men, I think, and not enough in the government of God."

Then Brown began to excoriate what he called the "professional" politicians. "You can never trust a professional politician," he said, "for even if he has convictions, he will sacrifice them for his own selfish advantage."

Phillips agreed. "I'm afraid we are all by nature a selfish lot."

"And therein lies our downfall," Brown acknowledged. "If our nation were organized on a less selfish basis, we would be better for it." He noted that selfishness cultivated material interests, a desire for personal pleasures, and that men and women had lost much by it. "When selfishness is deified, it can corrupt an entire society," he said, pointing to the elite Southern planters as an example. "They have grown accustomed to living a life unfettered by work and are unwilling to part with that life. To satisfy their selfish desires they have torn the humanity from the bosom of a people, adopting the belief that their slaves are less than human, mere property, no different from plows or livestock. Such a belief eases the slaveholders' guilt, but it brutalizes them, makes them capable of great cruelty."

Apparently Phillips was as willing to forgo sleep as Brown. The journalist redirected the conversation to a more personal subject. "They say you're a man of deep religious convictions, Captain. I should think your faith has influenced your actions in Kansas."

Brown took some time before responding: "My faith requires many things of me, among them a personal responsibility for those in need—and a responsibility to right the wrongs in society as I find them. It is my duty to act on these responsibilities—for duty is the voice of my God. A man is neither worthy of a good home here on earth, nor one in heaven, who is not willing to put himself in peril for a good cause."

Brown allowed his words to settle before adding, "There are many wrongs that need to be made right, Phillips. But slavery is clearly the sum of all villainies and its abolition the first essential work. I came to Kansas to do this work. If the American people do not end slavery speedily, human freedom and republican liberty will soon be empty phrases in these United States."

For a time neither man spoke as they both peered into the night sky. Brown, who relied on his own ability to tell time by observing the positions of the stars, suddenly stood. "It is nearly two o'clock, Phillips, and it is nine or ten miles to Topeka. We must be on our way."

The old man intended to reach Topeka before sunrise and wanted to conceal his movement as much as possible. Although Phillips tried to dissuade him from the route he chose—a rugged passage that required the fording of several creeks—Brown's mind was made up. He would take a straight course guided by the stars. When he awakened the men, they responded without saying a word, and in ten minutes all were in the saddle riding across the dark prairie.

The result was as Phillips predicted. After four hours of battling thickets and fording rivers, dawn arrived with the men wandering in the timber along a creek. Then, in the distance, came the faint strains of a bugle sounding reveille.

Brown guided his horse into the creek and up the opposite bank. The men followed. After he passed through the timber bordering the creek, he saw the movement of soldiers, the glint of the sun reflecting off the barrels of artillery. The old man had unknowingly come within a mile of the encampment of Colonel E.V. Sumner, the cavalry officer who had stripped him of his captives at Black Jack Springs.

Brown dismounted and removed the brass spyglass from his saddlebag. Beyond the encampment he could make out a cluster of buildings.

"It appears we have arrived at Topeka," he said, then turned to Phillips and suggested he ride into town with one of the men. Two riders were less likely to draw attention from the federals than a company of militiamen. Brown picked twenty-two-year-old August Bondi—an Austrian immigrant who was with him at Black Jack Springs. The rest of the company would camp in the timber and wait for Bondi to report back on conditions at the convention.

Brown said to Phillips, "You must urge the legislature to resist all who would interfere—even, if necessary, the federal troops. My men and I shall be ready when called."

Phillips reached for Brown's hand. "You have my gratitude," he said. "I hope we shall meet again—under happier
circumstances."

"Well, Phillips," Brown said, "tomorrow is the anniversary
of our nation's birth—a day when our ancestors declared their
independence from the shackles of an unjust government.
Perhaps history will be repeated in Topeka."

When Bondi returned the following afternoon, July 4, he
told of Free State supporters filling the streets of Topeka.
Colonel Sumner came into town and had his soldiers line
up in front of the building where the convention was being
held. His objective, Bondi learned, was to break up the Free
State convention; he had a cannon aimed at the door while
he read the order requiring the legislators to disperse. Then
Sumner told the people assembled in the street that carrying out his orders on this matter was "the most disagreeable
duty of his life."

The legislators agreed to leave, and the people made no
effort to protest. In fact, Bondi said, someone in the crowd
called for three cheers for the colonel. "Up went three loud
cheers and then three more for the Free State constitution
and three more for the legislators." As the troops rode off,
someone called for three groans for President Pierce. "The
colonel saluted us," Bondi said, "and we kept up the groaning
until the soldiers were out of sight."

Brown listened to Bondi's report but said nothing. Sumner's
response had been a sympathetic one, yet the old man was
bothered by it. As long as the Free State settlers believed that
important people—people like Colonel E. V. Sumner—were

supportive of their cause, they could be lulled into a false sense of security. Brown knew the enemy was intransigent and uncompromising and would take advantage of any sign of weakness.

Before breaking camp, the old man thought about snatching John Jr. from the military stockade at nearby Lecompton, where several other Free State men, including Dr. Charles Robinson, were being held as political prisoners. The plan was scrapped when Brown received word that his son was against any attempt to rescue him. Apparently John Jr. was being treated well; his wife Wealthy and their young son were permitted to live with him in the stockade, and—more important—John Jr. didn't want to complicate matters for the other prisoners. He and the others were likely to be set free anyway—possibly within two or three months.

Struggling to conceal his frustrations, Brown assembled the company. He needed time to sort things out, to make sure his next actions weren't done in haste. Though he wanted to lead his men into battle, he also wanted to return to his ailing boys—the wounded and sick who had been loyal to him at Pottawatomie and Black Jack. He refused to admit it, but his own health was failing again. He was experiencing the chills and fever that had tormented him sporadically in recent weeks. He needed to take care of his boys, but he also needed to recuperate from his own illness.

"I release you from duty," he announced to the men who had ridden with him to Topeka. "I expect to be active again and I hope you shall join me when I return. There is still much work to be done, but I must take leave of you at this time."

Brown shook the hand of each man, wished all of them well. Then he and Jason saddled up and headed for Ottawa Creek. The old man needed not only to tend to his invalids but also to prepare for his reentry into the war for a free Kansas. Federal forces were preoccupied with a surge in guerrilla activity; they wouldn't waste time focusing their attention exclusively on John Brown.

The violence in Kansas Territory was far from over. And Brown had no intention of retreating from it. He was merely biding his time, fulfilling obligations. His invalids either no longer wanted to fight or were too ill to think about anything but going home. Except for Frederick. He still felt bound to Kansas because of the guilt brought on by Pottawatomie.

Brown, however, was optimistic about the possibility of growing another following. Though he'd felt compelled to release the volunteers who were with him at Topeka, he was hopeful they would respond to his call when he returned to action.

Only one thing was certain. History wasn't repeated in Topeka—or anywhere else in Kansas Territory—on Independence Day, July 4, 1856. There was no battle against federal troops, no heroic defense of the Free State legislature. As far as Brown was concerned nothing had changed.

Shortly after he and Jason arrived at the encampment on Ottawa Creek, the old man was told that proslavery forces were massing along the border. Similar reports in the past had turned out to be greatly exaggerated.

6

Eight Weeks Later
August 28, 1856
Kansas Territory

Toward evening a herd of cattle churned the dry soil, sending a dust cloud rolling across the prairie south of Osawatomie. Outriders—their faces covered with bandannas—struggled to keep the cattle from straying. In front, clear of the suffocating dust, John Brown rode alone.

A young man repairing a rail fence strained to recognize the leader. When Brown came within hailing distance, the young man saw who it was and called his name. Brown broke off from the herd and turned his horse toward the fence.

"Fine looking steers, Captain," the young man shouted as Brown approached. "Where'd they come from?"

"It matters not," Brown replied. "They're Free State cattle now."

The young man smiled. Brown returned to the herd.

In the distance the old man spotted three horsemen riding hard in his direction. He rested a hand on his pistol, then saw that one of the men was his son Frederick.

"The Missourians, Father," Frederick shouted over the rumble of the cattle. "They're at the border. Lane and Walker need you in Lawrence."

Brown knew it was only a matter of time before Missouri militias would seek to avenge the growing number of raids on proslavery settlements. He had a decision to make—join up with Jim Lane and Sam Walker, both venerated leaders of Free State forces, or continue on his own. He'd been busy scouring the countryside around Osawatomie, seeking targets of opportunity for his newly formed Kansas Regulars—twenty-seven mounted men sworn to serve under his command.

Several weeks earlier, as the old man was nursing his ailing sons at the encampment on Ottawa Creek, he'd found time to spend with his host, Ottawa Jones. While Owen, Salmon, Frederick, and Oliver—and son-in-law Henry Thompson—convalesced, Brown dined with Jones and his wife in their double-walled log home. After supper he sat in Jones's parlor toiling over a document that would govern the conduct of men he planned to recruit when he returned to action. The *Articles of Enlistment and By-Laws of the Kansas Regulars* specified rules of engagement, court martial offenses, chain of command—but also reflected Brown's personal sensibilities:

All uncivil, ungentlemanly, profane, vulgar talk or conversation shall be discountenanced.

The ordinary use or introduction into the camp of any intoxicating liquor as a beverage is hereby declared disorderly.

While his thoughts were focused on returning to the fighting, the old man reconciled himself to the wishes of his boys. Owen, Salmon, Oliver, and Henry wanted to go home. When they were well enough to travel, Brown and Frederick loaded them onto a covered oxcart and headed north to Nebraska Territory.

When they reached Nebraska City, Frederick—who had been struggling with feelings of guilt since Pottawatomie—announced that he'd be staying with his father in Kansas. The rest of the boys boarded a ferry at the Missouri River.

Brown soon learned that Owen got only as far as the abolitionist community of Tabor, Iowa, where he was again stricken with illness and was taken in by a local minister. Salmon, Oliver, and Henry had continued their journey to North Elba, New York.

Even without his boys, the old man was confident he could start over. Somehow he'd find volunteers and build a new company, one that would bear his unique signature.

Brown and Frederick's presence in Nebraska City was timely. It coincided with the arrival of Jim Lane and Sam Walker. Lane had returned from a series of promotional speeches in the North, where he recruited four hundred emigrants, more than half of them young men starved for action, all of them waiting to be led into Kansas Territory. Walker had come up from Lawrence with his militia to escort Lane's caravan across the Nebraska-Kansas border. When Lane learned Brown was in town, he insisted the old man meet with him and Walker so they might talk about working together to advance the cause of freedom in Kansas.

A skeptical Brown showed up at the meeting. Unlike Lane and Walker, each of whom commanded armies numbering in the hundreds, the old man had no soldiers, having released them at Topeka. He sat tight-lipped as his hosts spoke of taking a more aggressive posture toward the proslavery militias. The meeting was interrupted by a bearded young man, an impressive physical specimen who looked like he'd been chiseled from a slab of Kansas limestone.

"I've asked Colonel Whipple to join us," Lane said. He introduced the young man as the leader of the Second Kansas Militia.

Colonel Whipple only knew Brown through stories he'd heard and read. He shook the old man's hand and said, "My compliments on your victory at Black Jack, Captain. You've enticed the wolves from their lairs so the rest of us can hunt."

Brown responded with an ambivalent nod. His instincts told him to make a mental note of this man. There was something about his manner, his piercing dark eyes. Later he learned that "Whipple" was a name Lane had given the colonel to conceal his identity from federal authorities. His real name was Aaron Dwight Stevens; before Lane recruited him, he'd escaped from the military prison at Leavenworth.

"Colonel Whipple will be taking a more active role in our operations," Lane said, then explained that his own involvement would be curtailed. He was told to remain in Nebraska, that he'd be arrested if he returned to Kansas. He said he'd shoot himself before abandoning the four hundred immigrants he brought to Nebraska City.

Brown grew weary of the talk. He appreciated Lane's situation but didn't see its relevance to his own aims. Lane was a Kansas man; he intended to do what he could to convert Kansas Territory into a free state. The same was true of Walker. Good men with good purposes. For Brown, however, a free Kansas was not his ultimate goal. In order to achieve what he wanted, the old man wouldn't hesitate to leave Kansas and "operate in another part of the field." He was glad, though, to have met Colonel Whipple.

Whatever lay ahead, Brown's actions would be exclusively his own. He wasn't interested in joining Jim Lane or Sam Walker or any other guerrilla leader. *New York Tribune* correspondent William A. Phillips—the man Brown conveyed to the Topeka convention—had it right when he said, "John Brown was not in the habit of subjecting himself to the orders of anybody. When there was work to be done, he would do it his way."

———————

After leaving Nebraska City, Brown and Frederick returned to Ottawa Creek, where the old man made an inventory of his needs.

For his army of Kansas Regulars, he wanted men who shared his purpose and moral values and were willing to submit to the code of conduct he'd drawn up at the home of Ottawa Jones. Son Jason was available—at least temporarily. His wife and child were safe at the Osawatomie home of Brown's half sister Florilla Adair. Jason again consented to join his father, even though by now it was well understood he deplored violence and had vowed to leave the territory as soon as John Jr. was released from prison—after which the two brothers, along with their wives and children, planned to return to Ohio.

Though Jason signed on, Frederick didn't. He chose to work independently as a messenger between Lawrence and Osawatomie, keeping the several guerrilla bands that operated in eastern Kansas aware of each other's actions.

Brown hadn't forgotten those who joined him on the ineffectual expedition to Topeka. These men and others, particularly the loquacious John Cook, had spread the word of

Brown's return. It wasn't long before volunteers—including some who served under him in the past—showed up at the camp on Ottawa Creek.

While Brown was quietly enlisting soldiers, the Free State guerrillas were engaging in a series of attacks on proslavery settlements near Lawrence. Ironically, the proslavery press claimed Brown was in command at virtually every one of the incursions. Those sympathetic to the Free State cause found the reports amusing. *New York Times* correspondent William Hutchinson, with tongue in cheek, dubbed Brown "the terror of all Missouri" and "the old terrifier." And in a letter from the stockade at Lecompton, John Jr. wrote Jason, "Father is an omnipresent dread to the ruffians. I see by the Missouri papers that they regard him the most terrible foe they have to encounter."

As the Free State offensive gained momentum, so did acts of retribution by the Missourians. David Hoyt—a well-regarded Massachusetts man—tried unsuccessfully to negotiate a truce prior to a Free State raid on a proslavery settlement. On his way home Hoyt was assailed by gunmen; they threw acid in his face before shooting him. His body was found on the prairie half eaten by vultures. The incident infuriated Free State settlers. Soon afterward, the murder of William Hoppe spawned even greater outrage. Hoppe was the innocent victim of a drunken proslavery man who made a six-dollar bet at a Leavenworth saloon that he could kill a Free State man and return with his scalp in no more than two hours. Within the prescribed time the man returned to the saloon and slapped Hoppe's bloody scalp on the bar.

By mid-August, looking prim and fit, Brown rode into the village of Osawatomie at the head of his company of newly enlisted Kansas Regulars. He'd traded in his black wool coat for a white linen duster; it flared out behind him, draping over his horse's haunches. He wore a new straw hat, the brim still rigid. He was clean-shaven and seemed fully recovered from the illness that had weakened him after Black Jack. Like other Free State guerrilla leaders, he was reaping the benefits of Northern immigrant aid societies that were pumping men, money, and weapons into the territory.

Osawatomie was a logical choice for Brown's headquarters. He knew the neighborhood. It was home to his relatives, the Adairs, and wasn't far from the homesteads his boys had staked out when they first arrived in Kansas. Also, he felt an obligation to defend the village that had been plundered by Henry Clay Pate as retribution for the Pottawatomie killings.

Immediately after setting up camp, the old man thrust his men into action, raiding settlements within a twenty-mile radius of Osawatomie.

It was during one of the raids that Brown encountered a twenty-two-year-old New Yorker and his band of Iowans. James Holmes came to Kansas hoping to serve as an agronomist for a colony of families from Pennsylvania, New York, and Ohio. When the colony failed to materialize, Holmes put together a group of Iowans looking for someone to lead them against the proslavery militias. Brown was impressed with the young man, thought he was wise beyond his years, and when he expressed an interest in joining his company, Brown apprised Holmes of the rules and regulations governing volunteers, then officially swore in him and his Iowans.

Though rumors of a large-scale invasion from Missouri persisted, Brown refused to be distracted. For seven consecutive

days he and his soldiers raided settlements south of Osawatomie. At dawn on Wednesday, August 27, they set out for
a ranch that belonged to the captain of a group of border
ruffians Brown suspected had taken part in a recent raid on
Osawatomie.

Brown said to Holmes, "We have a score to settle with
one of our enemies. He has failed to pay taxes on some cattle
he claims to own. We shall collect the taxes or repossess the
cattle."

Later that day Brown's men "repossessed" fifty head of
cattle from the ranch. The captain was not home. Brown told
the frightened wife she had nothing to fear, that he would
never hurt women or children.

And so, late in the following afternoon, while Brown and his
men were herding the cattle across the dusty prairie, they ran
into a hard-riding Frederick on the outskirts of Osawatomie.
Brown listened as his son told him of an army of Missourians massing on the border. Lane and Walker needed him in
Lawrence.

Brown made his decision. He shouted to Frederick, "Tell
them we have business here."

Frederick hesitated, wondered if there was anything else his
father wanted to add, but the old man seemed preoccupied
as he gazed in the direction of Osawatomie.

As Frederick sped away, the old man was already pondering
a line of defense. It would have to face northeast—the direction from which the Missouri invaders were likely to come.

The sky was darkening when his men turned the cattle
off the trail. Across the river on high ground lay his camp,

an abandoned ranch where there was plenty of grass for liberated cattle.

Brown and Holmes watched the cattle lurch and stumble down the river's steep bank. A sudden gust stirred the cottonwoods; the sound of rustling leaves was lost in the din of bawling cattle splashing through the water.

Holmes looked up at the sky. "Looks like we're in for some weather, Captain."

Brown shifted his weight in the saddle. He hadn't heard Holmes. He was deep in thought. He said, "If the enemy comes our way, we ought to have soldiers picketed in the village."

Holmes asked, "You want me to get my boys?"

Brown nodded. He gave Holmes the name of a family that would take in him and his Iowans. Dark clouds were forming as another gust rocked the branches overhead.

Meanwhile, Jason broke off from the herd, approached his father, spoke a few words, then rode off—to join his wife and child at the Adairs' cabin, Brown supposed.

The cattle had barely forded the river when the rain came—suddenly and torrentially. It chased the remaining men into a hay barn, where they spent the night supperless—some curled under canvas ponchos, the rest resigned to an evening of dampness, empty stomachs, and little sleep.

The inclement weather, however, didn't cancel a standing order: *When in camp a thorough watch shall be maintained both day and night.* Brown assigned two men to stand guard, one of whom was the young Austrian immigrant August Bondi.

———••••———

At dawn the old man was cooking breakfast. The rain had quit, leaving behind a dense fog. Corn coffee simmered over a fire. Smoke from damp wood billowed from under the pot, stinging Brown's eyes. In spite of the discomfort, he went about preparing a meal intended to satisfy the hunger of men who hadn't eaten for a day and a night. A slab of beef sizzled on an iron grate. The fog picked up the aroma, spreading it through the camp. The men congregated at the fire. Brown filled each man's cup, gave each one a thick slice of beef, then asked the Lord to bless the food and prayed that he and his soldiers might soon be granted the opportunity to battle the enemies of freedom.

He didn't have to wait very long.

The men were still eating when Bondi stepped out of the fog holding the arm of a young man, obviously distressed. The man had a message for Brown.

"Captain, it's the Missourians. They've killed Frederick."

The old man stiffened. Slowly he uncoiled. He reached for his rucksack, drew out a pair of revolvers, and tucked them under his belt.

The messenger said the Missourians were gathered below the ridge west of Osawatomie. An advance party had been scouting the village. There was a confrontation, and now Frederick, who spent the night at a cabin near the Adairs', was dead.

Brown pivoted and headed for the river, his long strides propelling him toward the crossing. He didn't look back to see if anyone was following.

His men scurried about, retrieving weapons. Strips of meat dangled from their mouths. They guzzled coffee and tossed empty cups to the ground.

The first soldier to catch up with Brown was twenty-three-year-old Luke Parsons. Parsons had joined the old man's company after Black Jack. Brown made a point of presenting

Parsons with a state-of-the-art, breech-loading Sharps carbine.

"Parsons, were you ever under fire?" Brown asked.

"No. But I will obey orders. Tell me what you want me to do."

Looking straight ahead, the old man said, "Take more care to end your life well than to live long."

The fog was dissipating, the sky brightening, as they entered the village. In the muddy road confusion reigned. Armed men raced for the blockhouse—a two-story log fortification equipped with gun ports. A few women—bags slung over their shoulders, children in tow—darted for shelter.

Word spread that Brown was in the village. His presence seemed to restore a measure of order. Men fell in behind him.

Jason came running. He was breathing hard. "Father, we must get Fred. They say he lies in the brush."

The old man, grim-faced, eyed Jason—but only briefly. A horse was bearing down, hooves tossing up clods of rain-soaked earth.

The rider was James Holmes. He reined in his mount. "Got a look at 'em, Captain. Just over the ridge. Waiting for I don't know what."

"Numbers," Brown said.

"Plenty," Holmes said. "And cannons, too. Six-pounders, I'd say."

"Numbers," Brown repeated.

"Hundreds, Captain. Two. Three. All mounted."

Brown was standing near the center of the village of Osawatomie. To the north was the river, to the south Pottawatomie Creek. He was on a flat plain that slowly rose to the crest of a ridge. He knew that beyond the ridge was the enemy—numbering in the hundreds and reinforced with artillery—no doubt forming into a line of battle at this very moment.

His mind raced as more horsemen bounded onto the scene. He recognized James Cline, another of the guerrilla captains who had been raiding proslavery settlements south of Osawatomie. The old man didn't care for Cline, even warned his soldiers to stay clear of Cline's men. They were too rowdy. But now Brown was forced to make a concession. He needed every available man.

A breathless James Cline: "It's hopeless, Captain."

Brown's response was unequivocal: "I shan't yield to the enemy."

"You don't understand," Cline persisted. "There's too many. They have artillery."

It was Cline who didn't understand. He didn't understand the depth of Brown's commitment. Brown's cause—the destruction of slavery—was God's work. The old man was utterly convinced of that. He'd told his soldiers, "One man in the right, ready to die, will chase a thousand." But he also understood that victory wasn't the only worthwhile outcome of battle. To fear no man and fight well—even in defeat—sent a powerful message to friend and foe alike. He once wrote, "Nothing so charms the American people as personal bravery." If Brown made a stand in Osawatomie—even though victory was unattainable—the enemy would know that in Kansas Territory there were men willing to sacrifice their lives for freedom. How could anyone—North or South—not honor such devotion to a cause?

Brown said to Cline, "If you fear the enemy, then go. If there are men in your company who wish to fight, they have my invitation."

Cline wouldn't be provoked into an argument. He knew firsthand of Brown's determination to crush the enemy. Just a few days earlier, while interrogating border ruffians, Cline's attention had been called to the brow of a nearby hill. Men on horseback led by Brown were charging Cline's encampment at full speed. The old man had mistaken Cline's company for the enemy. The two groups finally recognized each other, but the event was a sobering one for Cline and it caused him to doubt Brown's judgment. He wasn't eager to risk his life for a lost cause. He said to Brown, "My men may do as they choose." Then he dug in his spurs, sending his horse galloping toward the crossing on the river. Not all his men followed.

Brown turned to his soldiers: his regulars and those of Cline's troop who stayed, along with a few locals—altogether a force of fewer than forty men. Not very good odds, assuming the estimates of Holmes and Cline were correct.

The old man barked orders. To Luke Parsons: "Take ten men into the blockhouse. Hold your position as long as possible. Hurt the enemy all you can."

To Jason: "Stay close. I shan't lose another son this day."

To the rest: "Into the timber. We can at least annoy them from the flank."

Brown drew his revolvers and headed toward the trees bordering the river, the men hustling after him.

He placed them behind trees, concealed them in thick brush. He walked up and down the line, reminding each to hold his fire until the enemy was at close quarters.

"Keep cool," he said, "take good aim, aim low, and be sure to see your target in both sights."

They waited, all eyes on the crest of the ridge.

When the sun burned off the last remnants of fog, the Missourians rose up from behind the ridge in two ranks, a hundred or more horsemen in each rank. Their weapons—pistol, saber, musket—glittered like newly minted coins.

In front were two mule-drawn limbers, each towing a smoothbore cannon capable of firing a six-pound ball.

The men in the blockhouse were the first to lose their nerve. Believing they were easy targets for the cannons, they fled, most following Parsons into the timber to join Brown.

Seconds later the Missourians swept down the ridge in two thunderous waves. Brown's men—hidden in the brush and trees—let go with withering gunfire.

Some of the enemy dismounted and sought safety in shallow swales. They were unsure of where the bullets were coming from.

A veil of blue-gray smoke from the exploding black powder hovered over Brown's position. The artillerymen spotted it and turned their cannons. The first round of grapeshot tore into the treetops. Branches exploded. Chunks of wood rained down.

"Steady, boys," Brown called out. He said something else, but it was drowned in the noise. A second round of grape crashed into the timber, shearing the top of a hickory tree from its trunk.

The commander of the Missourians abandoned his horse, ordered the rest of his men to dismount. He attempted to rally them for a counterattack and pointed his saber toward the trees on the riverbank.

Brown walked down the line. "A while longer, boys," he shouted. "Keep it up a while longer."

As he spoke the artillerymen fired another volley. Two gusts of grapeshot ripped into the foliage. Brown felt a blow to his shoulder, called out to the nearest soldier, Luke Parsons.

"See anything on my back, Parsons? Any blood? Something hit me an awful rap."

Parsons looked. "Nothing, Captain."

"Well," Brown said, "I surely don't intend to be shot in the back if I can help it."

The Missourians concentrated their small arms fire on Brown's position. Musket balls hissed overhead. The loud crack of a nicked branch was followed by a humming sound as a bullet tumbled in the air. Buckshot raked the underbrush.

For nearly one hour, Brown's men held their ground against a superior force. The old man followed his instincts, taking advantage of the natural defenses provided by the wooded margin of the river. He'd confused an enemy of 250 men reinforced by two cannons.

Jason announced the inevitable. "Our men are leaving, Father. And we must, too."

In choosing to take a stand in the timber with his back to the river, Brown held the advantage over an enemy that fought in the open—uncovered, unconcealed. Now, in retreat, the reverse was true. It was he and his men who were vulnerable. There was no alternative but the river, a river that offered few places shallow enough to be forded easily.

Some of them swam—notably James Holmes. Others moved along the bank, looking for a manageable crossing. Those who made it across the river scrambled up the opposite side, all the while chased by gunfire.

Jason crossed ahead of his father, looked back at the old man wading in chest-deep water. "A strange sight was Father," Jason recalled later, "in his straw hat and white linen duster, the tails floating behind him like the wings of a swan, his revolvers held high in the air to keep them dry."

———— •••• ————

Brown learned that most of his soldiers escaped. Only one died as a direct result of the battle—shot as he jumped into the river. Two were wounded, four taken prisoner. He would never know, nor would anyone else, the exact number of enemy casualties. The old man claimed to have killed thirty-one or thirty-two and wounded forty or fifty.

The commander of the Missourians reported no troops killed, only five wounded—none dangerously. There was never an official record of Missouri casualties.

It was late in the day when Brown and Jason set out to retrieve Frederick's body. The Missourians were gone, and Jason had made sure his wife and child were safe. Before crossing the river, the old man reined in his horse on the edge of the high bank and gazed at the flames and smoke rising from the village.

He felt the sting of tears, calmed himself by repeating silently the mantra he professed to live by. *I do not act from revenge. It is a feeling that does not enter my heart.*

Sitting motionless in his saddle, he spoke to an audience much larger than just his son Jason.

"God sees it," he said. "I have only a short time to live—only one death to die—and I will die fighting for this cause. There will be no more peace in this land until slavery is done for. I will give the enemy something else to do than extend slave territory."

He wiped his eyes on the sleeve of his white linen duster, then uttered with the solemnity of a sacred oath, "I will carry this war into Africa."

Africa. Brown's code name for the South. The dwelling place of four million men, women, and children—held in bondage. When Brown arrived in Kansas Territory he hoped to challenge the slave power through violent action. Once there, he'd done what he thought necessary—at Pottawatomie Creek, at Black Jack Springs, and now at the Free State village of Osawatomie. As the summer of 1856—a summer that would be remembered as "Bleeding Kansas"—faded into autumn, it became clear to the old man he wouldn't be able to carry his war on slavery into Africa.

Not yet, anyway.

7

Five Months Later
January 19, 1857
Boston, Massachusetts

Agust of cold air hit John Brown in the face as he stepped out of a hack onto the ice-covered cobbles in front of No. 4 Court Street—the law office of Charles Sumner, newly reelected senator from Massachusetts. It was early in the afternoon, and the normally busy street was deserted. With his hands buried in the pockets of his wool overcoat, Brown aimed himself at the front door. He was pleased to have been granted a visit with Senator Sumner—the victim of the assault that provided the final nudge, launching Brown and his boys into a night of bloody assassination.

———————

After the battle at Osawatomie, Brown saw that a change was coming to Kansas Territory. President Pierce had appointed a new territorial governor—John W. Geary. An imposing figure at six feet six inches tall and 260 pounds, he quickly brought the warring factions under control. With the aid of a beefed-up US cavalry, Geary orchestrated an informal truce between Free State guerrillas and proslavery militias, then

96

defused a planned raid on Lawrence by twenty-seven hundred Missourians.

Brown brooded over the cessation of hostilities. He was convinced the Missourians would strike again, and he was suspicious of Geary's motives. The governor had rounded up border ruffians but also targeted Free State fighters—including Jim Lane, Sam Walker, and Brown himself.

Another disappointment for Brown was the attitude of his married sons, John Jr. and Jason. Like their younger brothers who had already left the territory, they were weary of the violence and wanted to escape the desolation of eastern Kansas.

The old man was reminded of the ruinous condition of the settlements when he and Jason left their hiding place after the fighting at Osawatomie and were riding to Lecompton to meet John Jr. who—with several Free State leaders charged with treason—was to be released from the stockade by order of Governor Geary. Brown took a circuitous route to avoid federal scouts. It allowed him to inspect John Jr.'s abandoned homestead and keep a promise to assess the damage and determine if anything was worth salvaging.

Brown and Jason rode past deserted farms and scorched fields, saw cabins ravaged by fire with hardly a sign of life anywhere except for an occasional cow—ribs bulging, belly swollen—foraging between rows of charred corn stubble.

As they approached familiar territory, the old man drew in his reins.

Before him lay an expanse of bottomland. He guided his horse to the blackened shell of a small log cabin. A path led to what once was the cabin's front door. He dismounted and walked to a wall of half-burned logs, a place where once a threshold might have been.

He stepped inside the cabin's collapsed interior. Fragments of charred timbers were indistinguishable from stone and iron.

Jason scanned the rubble from his saddle. "Nothing, Father," he said.

Brown probed with his boot. He bent over and reached into one of the ash-covered mounds. He pulled out a book, its cover and spine seared black. He fanned the pages. They crumbled to the touch. He tossed the volume aside, pushed away more debris, found more books, all partially burned, all giving off the odor of stale smoke.

Brown knew his eldest son prized his books. He'd brought four hundred volumes to Kansas from his Ohio farm. They represented a lifetime of reading and collecting.

Jason said, "You've done what was asked of you, Father. My brother needs to know there is nothing left."

The old man continued to shuffle through the charred remains. He marveled that not a single book was totally destroyed.

"Strange, is it not?" he mused. "Books do not burn so easily."

Jason nodded.

"I recall Mr. Douglass saying a book inspired his escape from slavery," Brown said. "I'm sure he would be comforted to know these books were able to resist the fires of the slave power." Brown was referring to his friend Frederick Douglass, the former slave who now edited and published a widely circulated abolitionist newspaper.

The ride to Lecompton was interrupted again when Brown and Jason came to the smoldering ruins of Ottawa Jones's double-walled log home—once a safe haven for the Brown family. A band of Missourians—part of the militia that Brown fought at Osawatomie—had been instructed to kill Jones and destroy his house and cattle. The Missourians wanted to send a message: collaborating with Free State settlers wouldn't be tolerated. Jones and his wife escaped. Not so a hired hand. His throat was slit.

Jason stared at the remains of the Joneses' cabin. He was overcome with a sudden and deep sorrow brought on by the events of the summer: the Pottawatomie killings, the torturous ordeal of his brother John Jr., the constant worry over the well-being of his wife and child, the burning of his crops by Pate's men, his reluctant involvement in the fighting at Osawatomie, and, finally, the murder of his brother Frederick.

Brown sensed Jason's anguish, saw he was on the verge of tears. "You must not let such as this get in the way of your duty," the old man said. "Take care to let nothing get in the way of your duty—neither wife, nor child, nor a good man like Jones."

"I do not weep for Jones, Father. I weep for all of us—whether against slavery or for it. Such a terrible waste. The killing, the burning—"

"I feel no more love for this business than you. I merely dread the consequences we shall face if we do nothing."

Jason then began to relate the story of an event he hadn't disclosed to his father, an event that took place on the evening before the battle at Osawatomie. He confessed he hadn't joined his wife and child at the home of Brown's half-sister Florilla. Instead he went to the aid of a family that was nursing a severely wounded boy who served in the proslavery militia Brown was to face at Osawatomie.

"I cleansed his wound of maggots, Father," Jason said. "I dressed the wound, bathed him, and changed his clothes. He told me he thought abolitionists were savages until he was brought to us. As he lay there, pale and exhausted from loss of blood, he spoke of his home and friends in Mississippi and how he wished he had never come to Kansas. He asked if I would take care of him for the few hours he had left. As I sat by his bed and saw tears flowing from a heart full of sorrow and trouble, a boy alone among strangers and far from home, I said to myself . . ." He paused to breathe deeply. "I said to myself: if these are some of the things that make war glorious and honorable, deliver me from the honor of war."

Jason's confession confirmed what Brown already suspected. His son would be of little use to him in the future. The old man dug his spurs into his horse's flanks. Lecompton was still hours away.

At the stockade in Lecompton, the reuniting of Jason and John Jr., the exchange of embraces, left little doubt in Brown's mind that his married sons and their families were determined to leave Kansas—as soon as possible.

With the restoration of peace and the coming of winter, the old man questioned his own need to remain. Maybe it was a good time to take advantage of his growing reputation. Abolitionists in the Northeast would be eager to hear him tell of his battles in Kansas. Perhaps they would see fit to provide him with the money he needed to build a truly potent force—say, a hundred men who could patrol the border between Kansas and Missouri. With $30,000 and a wagonload of Sharps carbines he could return to the territory in the spring and become a formidable opponent to the enemies of freedom.

Brown arranged passage to Ohio for his sons' wives and children. They would take the shorter route through Missouri by boat and rail—an option made possible by the cease-fire imposed by Governor Geary.

Meanwhile—to avoid federal troops—Brown, Jason, and John Jr. would take the overland route through Nebraska. They would leave Kansas in two wagons, one crammed with weapons, cookware, and other personal belongings, the other filled mostly with hay—under which lay a fugitive slave from Missouri whom Brown had agreed to transport to freedom.

Barely averting capture in Nebraska, the old man's party arrived safely in Tabor, Iowa—the abolitionist community where Owen had found a temporary home while recovering from the ailment he suffered after the fighting at Black Jack. Owen welcomed his father and brothers. The fugitive slave was turned over to a local conductor on the Underground Railroad. The weapons and supplies were put in storage.

Brown intended to return to Tabor.

Jason and John Jr. took passage on a stagecoach bound for eastern Iowa. From there they would complete the journey to Ohio by rail. Brown, meanwhile, had again been stricken with chills and fever, and he and Owen were forced to remain in Tabor. After a week in bed under his son's care, Brown felt well enough to continue. He and Owen climbed aboard the wagon that had brought him from Kansas. They headed east.

Brown needed money and guns. He needed Massachusetts.

Now, almost three months later—having traversed half the continent in a horse-drawn wagon—Brown found himself standing in the cobbled street outside the Boston law office of Senator Charles Sumner. He leaned into the icy wind as he crossed the street and headed for the front door.

The old man felt a rush of warm air as Sumner invited him inside. A fire blazed on the hearth, providing much of the illumination in the small room, its windows stained with soot. Shelves of books lined the walls, and well-worn leather armchairs surrounded a library table that took up most of the floor. The table was festooned with stacks of papers.

Brown removed his overcoat and handed it to Sumner, who struggled to hang it in a narrow closet.

In appearance the two men were a study in contrasts. Sumner, the Harvard-educated lawyer who socialized with Boston's intellectual elite, was bedecked in a tweed coat, vest, wool trousers, and a pair of gaiters that covered his finely crafted shoes. Brown wore a black frock coat buttoned almost to the neck, a leather cravat, and rough-textured trousers tucked into his stovepipe boots. He looked like a farmer in Sunday attire.

The senator may have dressed like a gentleman, but his clothing couldn't disguise his frail condition. Brown was saddened to learn that Sumner still suffered from the wounds inflicted in the Senate chamber by the South Carolina congressman Preston Brooks. Even in the dim light the old man saw the senator's pallid complexion, the blackened hollows under his eyes.

After obligatory comments on Boston's harsh winter weather, the two men settled into chairs at the library table.

The meeting had been arranged by Franklin Sanborn, the twenty-five-year-old secretary of the Massachusetts State Kansas Committee, one of the private organizations that provided money and supplies to Kansas migrants. Sanborn enjoyed an almost sycophantic attachment to a circle of influential Massachusetts abolitionists, several of whom he'd already introduced to Brown. He was delighted to bring together one of the Senate's champions of abolitionism and an acclaimed chieftain of the Kansas wars. At first, Sumner was reluctant to agree to the meeting; his precarious health had left him a virtual recluse.

"Sanborn has spoken highly of you, Captain Brown, but that was hardly necessary," Sumner said. "We've read of your exploits. Your efforts to discourage those who would bring Kansas into the fold of the slave power are well known."

"I have merely answered the call of the Lord," Brown said. "It is my duty."

Sumner, too, knew something about duty. His life was wrought in the selfsame crucible. He was a disciple of the Unitarian minister William Ellery Channing, and as such he had dedicated himself to the improvement of society. Sumner had an agenda: prison reform, public education, the international peace movement, temperance, and of course the abolition of slavery. He spoke in a thin, halting voice. "As you can see from my present condition, one must accept the fact that there is sometimes a price to pay for doing one's duty."

"I don't wish to cause you further discomfort," Brown said, "but I must tell you that the bravery you exhibited has been a source of inspiration to me and my soldiers. And I would like to thank you on behalf of Northern men who continue to fight for freedom in Kansas."

Sumner was growing weaker. Yet he couldn't pass up an opportunity to educate Brown on the political realties both men faced.

"Don't expect the slave power to change because of what happens in Kansas," Sumner said. "We have just elected a new president—a man from Pennsylvania—who will no doubt continue the policy of appeasement followed by his predecessor. I'm afraid there is too often little difference between Northern men and Southern men, and this is especially true when greed holds dominion over what is right." Sumner was determined to finish what he had to say, even though his voice had begun to crack. "I have long questioned the unholy alliance between the cotton-planters and flesh-mongers of Louisiana and Mississippi and the cotton-spinners and human traffickers of New England—between the lords of the lash and the lords of the loom."

So saying, the once sturdy and vigorous senator from Massachusetts gave out a long sigh and let his body collapse limply into the leather armchair.

It was an awkward moment for Brown. While he felt privileged to have been taken into the confidence of a man he held in high esteem, he'd not yet divulged the special reason for his visit. Given the senator's obvious misery, he wondered if perhaps the timing wasn't right. Then again, there might not be another opportunity. Brown pushed back his chair and stood.

"Senator Sumner, before I leave, I would be most grateful to see the coat you wore when assaulted by that coward from South Carolina. I understand you keep it here."

His voice almost a whisper, Sumner replied, "You understand correctly, Captain Brown. I keep it as a reminder of the barbarism that has taken hold of the slave power. I'm afraid the ladies in my family have banished it from our home." He struggled to rise.

"Please," Brown implored, motioning for the senator to remain seated.

Sumner pointed to the closet where earlier he'd hung Brown's overcoat.

Brown squeezed into the tiny space. The glow from the hearth cast a muted light on the frock coat hanging next to his overcoat. He let his fingertips glide over the dark folds of dried blood that saturated the coat from shoulder to shoulder, covering the lapels, leaving them stiff as untanned cowhide. He reached inside and felt the hardness where blood had penetrated the lining and gathered in clumps. He drew the coat to his face and inhaled deeply as though the pungent odor might merge into his being.

Later, as he prepared to leave, Brown was tempted to embrace his host, but he instead contented himself with a handshake, executed gingerly because of the senator's frail condition.

The old man departed with a sense of renewal. He'd completed a pilgrimage, received an audience from a guardian of the faith, and looked upon a sacred relic. The experience left him euphoric.

Outside, the sun hadn't broken through the thick cloud cover. It was getting colder and the wind came in blasts that numbed the flesh. Still, Brown eschewed an approaching hackney coach, choosing instead to walk to his hotel. He'd endured worse conditions on the Kansas prairie. As he walked he reflected on what had happened since his arrival in Boston. In two short weeks Franklin Sanborn had introduced him to arguably the most important New England advocates of the antislavery movement. He was offered generous sums of money. He was held up as a hero. The Massachusetts State Kansas Committee had given him custody of two hundred Sharps breech-loading rifled carbines—presently in storage in the basement of a house in Tabor. And no mention was made of Pottawatomie. The meeting with Sumner was a fitting climax to what he considered a good start toward acquiring the money and weapons he needed for his return to Kansas.

In his hotel room Brown sat on his bed and pulled off his boots. He was feeling some discomfort from the bowie knife that was tied to his leg with strips of leather. It was the same knife that had been part of the cache of weapons he acquired at Pottawatomie, and he carried it for self-defense. The walk to the hotel caused the knife's double-edged tip to rub flesh from bone, and he hadn't been aware he was bleeding. He held the knife with the tip pointing at the ceiling and watched the blood slide down the blade like dark syrup.

Before turning down the bedcovers he knelt and prayed that he would soon be able to renew his war on slavery, acknowledging that his destiny was not in his hands but in God's.

A little over a week after Brown's meeting with Sumner—on Tuesday, January 27, 1857—Preston Smith Brooks, the South Carolina congressman who had caused the Massachusetts senator so much pain, died in a Washington, DC, boardinghouse. He was thirty-seven.

Sumner was visiting a friend, the poet Henry Wadsworth Longfellow, when he learned of Brooks's death. Longfellow wrote in his journal that Sumner did not express any personal feelings about Brooks but spoke of him as "a mere tool of the slaveholders, or, at all events, of the South Carolinians."

When Brown received the news, he was on his way to visit two men who were to continue to play a significant role in his life: Frederick Douglass and Gerrit Smith. The old man stepped off a train in Rochester, New York—Douglass's hometown—and read the report of Brooks's death in the *New York Tribune*. Had he read the paper thoroughly he would also have noticed an article predicting that the nation was headed toward a serious economic crisis.

Brown was looking forward to his meetings with Douglass and Smith, but he had unfinished business in Boston and planned to return there as soon as possible. He also had a strong desire to see his family. He'd been away from the North Elba homestead for almost a year and a half.

8

Three Months Later
April 30, 1857
North Elba, New York

At dusk Brown stood outside the unpainted frame house gazing at iconic Whiteface Mountain. He watched as a low cloud rolled in and slowly engulfed the pale granite slopes. Like the mountainside covered in mist, everything he'd been promised—the money, the weapons, the supplies to equip a hundred soldiers, the freedom to use these assets as he saw fit—was now shrouded in uncertainty. The fundraising tour that began by exceeding his expectations had ended in a sudden reversal.

Forces were at play he didn't understand and couldn't control. The nation was sliding into a recession, and the consequences were particularly harsh in the Northeast: business failures, growing fears among land speculators and railroad investors, cutbacks in employment as factory owners laid off workers. The money Brown had been offered was no longer available, and he wasn't able to accept the realities causing his financial backers to tighten their belts.

Even the Supreme Court's decision on Dred Scott, the slave who waged a ten-year legal battle for his freedom, failed to pry open the purses of the abolitionists. Brown was in

Boston when the slaveholding chief justice from Maryland, Roger Taney, delivered the court's judgment on March 6. Taney said slaves were never intended to be citizens of the United States, that they were personal property entitled to no rights of any kind. The ruling infuriated the abolitionists, but the surge in contributions Brown expected never materialized.

The news from Kansas was equally dismal. Though Governor Geary resigned under pressure from the new president— James Buchanan—the warring factions remained subdued. Not at all what Brown hoped for. And though another wave of Northern immigrants had flooded the territory, the new settlers were more interested in acquiring land than fighting for a free Kansas. Still, Brown knew it was only a matter of time before the settlers would have the political clout their numbers alone would produce. He fretted that the war on slavery in Kansas was coming to an end and that his sources of funding had all but dried up.

In the tiny settlement of North Elba, guarded by mountains and thick forests, the old man sought consolation among those with whom he felt most comfortable—his family and the colony of fugitive slaves attempting to create farms in the wilderness. In such a remote place, no US marshal was likely to pursue him. Despite a hurried stopover in mid-February—at a time when he was still optimistic about the future—Brown had been unable to enjoy an extended visit to his Adirondack home in two years.

He loved the mountains and rugged meadows, and he missed mingling with the black families that were given acreage by his friend and advocate Gerrit Smith. The wealthy abolitionist owned vast tracts of land in western and northern New York. Brown had promised to avail the colony of his knowledge of subsistence farming in the severe climate;

he would do so, he told Smith, in exchange for some land for himself. The deal, executed a decade earlier, marked the beginning of the relationship that eventually yielded financial support for the old man's war on slavery.

As the skies darkened over the North Elba homestead, Brown considered his options and prayed for guidance. In the morning he'd be leaving for the West. He wouldn't see his wife and young daughters again for many months.

When first he arrived at the farm eleven days earlier, he yet again was ailing with chills and fever. Awaiting his return were his wife, Mary, and three young daughters: thirteen-year-old Annie, ten-year-old Sarah, and two-year-old Ellen. Also present were Owen, Salmon, and Oliver—all having returned safely from Kansas—and Brown's twenty-one-year-old son Watson, who had recently married Isabella, the sister of Henry Thompson. While his father and brothers and Henry were in Kansas, Watson had stayed behind to help his mother.

In the evenings Brown and Mary lay on the small bed on the ground floor of their sparsely furnished home, little Ellen asleep on a pallet beside them, Annie and Sarah in an adjacent bedroom, the three unmarried sons in the loft above.

Brown spoke to his wife of men of wealth and position, men who looked upon him as someone capable of cleansing the nation of its vilest sin. He also disclosed the doubts that had caused him so much anguish in recent weeks. He described the reception he got from the abolitionists who were introduced to him by Franklin Sanborn of the Massachusetts State Kansas Committee.

"When I first went to them," Brown said, "they wanted to hear my stories." So he told them about Black Jack and Osawatomie and how the border ruffians murdered Frederick. He showed them the chains worn by John Jr. after he was driven barefoot across the prairie until he'd almost gone mad. He told them how the rest of the boys fought courageously, how they suffered terrible wounds and sickness.

"I thought they trusted me," Brown said of his abolitionist allies. "I told them I had no other object but to serve the cause of liberty."

As he spoke, the wife who had borne him thirteen children, who had stoically accepted her husband's longstanding promise to defeat slavery, who had endured the personal hardships his mission had caused their family, who had come to believe in his divine inspiration, now listened to him, his words weighed down with disappointment.

"They insisted on harnessing me to Kansas," he said. "They wanted me to expose my plans. I told them no one knows my plans—except perhaps one."

He told Mary of his relationship with the prosperous businessman George Luther Stearns, the most generous of his Massachusetts supporters. Stearns was a self-made man who acquired his wealth through his own talents, an achievement the old man admired. He visited the Stearns mansion in suburban Medford several times and captivated the family with stories of his Kansas exploits. It was Stearns, as chairman of the Massachusetts State Kansas Committee, who transferred to him those two hundred Sharps carbines. The guns, however, were only to be used in defense of a free Kansas. And while Stearns also saw to it Brown was supplied with the sidearms he wanted—two hundred .31 caliber six-shot Maynard revolvers—they, too, were restricted to the fighting in Kansas, fighting that had become almost nonexistent.

Stearns's wife had even persuaded her husband to open his personal bank account to Brown. But again there was a stipulation that money drawn from the account was only to be used for actions taken against proslavery forces in Kansas, a circumstance that seemed less likely with each passing day.

Other commitments went unfulfilled. In New York, the National Kansas Committee—which promised him $5,000—claimed to be experiencing the effects of the recession. The committee was on the verge of bankruptcy; no longer was there money to spare for an army of one hundred soldiers.

A speech the old man gave on the floor of the Massachusetts legislature resulted in praise for his efforts but no offer of funds for weapons, ammunition, or supplies.

Then there was Boston's Amos Adams Lawrence, heir to mercantile businesses and textile mills. He'd already invested heavily in the Kansas migration; the most important immigrant settlement in the territory had been given his name. Lawrence agreed to help support Brown's family, but he was reluctant to contribute to an army of one hundred men without first assessing the present situation in Kansas. He had no desire to see the renewal or expansion of hostilities unless absolutely necessary. It wouldn't be good for business.

Brown couldn't understand why the elites of New England— some of them descended from ancestors who gave birth to a nation professing liberty as its core value—wouldn't gladly part with their abundant wealth so he might carry out his mission. He claimed that he, too, was a descendant of one of the *Mayflower* pilgrims, and though his Puritan lineage hadn't provided him the financial advantages of those from whom he was seeking help, he was willing to sacrifice his life for the cause of freedom.

"It wasn't as though I were asking for an extravagant sum," he grumbled to Mary. At a time when the average annual wage was between $700 and $900, the cost of supplying a hundred soldiers with horses, feeding the men and their mounts for a year, purchasing saddles, harnesses, tents, wagons, cooking and eating utensils, blankets, knapsacks, entrenching tools, holsters, spurs, and a minimal supply of ammunition—all of it seemed a bargain in light of the $30,000 he was seeking.

At Sanborn's urging, Brown had hit the lecture circuit, telling his stories in the cities, towns, and villages of Massachusetts and Connecticut. But seeking money in this fashion didn't sit well with him. He felt he was begging. He especially didn't like the questions about how he planned to use the money. He couldn't disguise his frustration when he repeated to Mary the words he uttered many times over the years: "I told them I obey the laws of God and adhere to the promises of the Declaration of Independence. To act on these principles is my sacred duty."

Still, Brown's willingness to act—in direct, often violent ways—captured the imaginations of the New England men and women who saw him as the embodiment of ideals they claimed to live by. Never was this more apparent than during the old man's visit to Concord and its distinguished residents Ralph Waldo Emerson and Henry David Thoreau. They met at the Thoreau home, a boardinghouse run by his mother, and listened to Brown's Kansas stories. They shared their mutual disdain for Judge Taney and the Dred Scott ruling, then attended a speech the old man was slated to give at the Concord town hall.

"It is better," Brown told his audience, "that a whole generation of men, women, and children should pass away by violent death rather than that a violation of the Holy Gospel or the Declaration of Independence be further tolerated."

Emerson and Thoreau bonded with the old man. His words echoed their doctrine of independent action engendered by obedience to a higher law, a doctrine they had been writing and lecturing about for years.

But there was a trace of contempt in Brown's voice when he told Mary, "I have done—and will continue to do—what they only *talk* about." It was the same attitude he held toward highly regarded abolitionists like William Lloyd Garrison and Wendell Phillips. "All talk and no cider," the old man groused.

However, he didn't question the authenticity of Thomas Wentworth Higginson—the thirty-three-year-old irascible minister from Worcester who used the pulpit to advance his political agenda. Higginson was a man of action. He wore a scar on his chin, the result of a saber slash received during an attempt to rescue the runaway slave Anthony Burns. Burns had been a victim of the Fugitive Slave Act, one of a series of federal laws—the so-called Compromise of 1850—that required local authorities in the North to assist Southern slave catchers. The Fugitive Slave Act radicalized many Northerners who previously favored more moderate approaches to the abolition of slavery. Higginson had led the charge up the steps of Boston's city courthouse, where Burns was held prisoner. The rescue attempt failed, but that didn't diminish Brown's respect for Higginson and his courageous act.

The old man had been introduced to two of Higginson's coconspirators in the Burns affair: the radical cleric Theodore Parker and the social reformer Dr. Samuel Gridley Howe, both active in the Massachusetts State Kansas Committee. Like the men of letters from Concord, Parker and Howe were much impressed with Brown. They compared him to Oliver Cromwell, the Puritan warrior who overthrew the British monarchy in 1649. The old man smiled at the comparison. He admired Cromwell, even owned a copy of Joel Headley's biography, which portrayed the Puritan as a patriot directed by God to rid his nation of sin and corruption. That both Cromwell and Brown were accused of committing bloody atrocities wasn't a problem for the abolitionists from Massachusetts.

Mary listened to her husband relate the story of the event that caused his hasty return home. In early April he'd received a letter from his son Jason, then farming in Ohio. Jason wrote that a deputy US marshal was on Brown's trail and was coming to arrest him. The old man took refuge in the home of Judge Thomas Russell, one of the more moderate of the Massachusetts abolitionists. Russell lived in a secluded Boston suburb, and he and his wife offered their home as a temporary hideout. Brown barricaded himself in an upstairs bedroom for ten days and came to the dinner table each evening with two revolvers tucked under his belt. He rolled up a trouser leg to reveal the long bowie knife strapped to his leg.

"I told Mrs. Russell I hoped I wouldn't soil her expensive furniture or stain her plush carpets with my blood. I warned her—if the US hounds showed up, I'd not be taken alive."

It was at the Russells' that Brown's malarial sickness returned. In between episodes of violent tremors he wrote "Old Brown's Farewell," a document seething with sarcasm, intended for the New England benefactors he believed had deserted him. In the final lines he lamented that he was unable to secure "amidst all the wealth, luxury, and extravagance of this heaven exalted people, even the necessary supplies for a common soldier."

When Stearns's wife visited Brown at the Russells', he handed her a copy of his "Farewell." After reading it, she felt embarrassed by the comfort her husband's wealth afforded her family; she knew Brown's family suffered constant deprivation as he struggled to raise money, and she later claimed she considered liquidating her husband's estate and giving the proceeds to Brown so that he might accomplish his mission.

Brown confessed to his wife that even though he appreciated the tangible and moral support given him by the Massachusetts abolitionists, something about them gnawed at his conscience. Yes, they hated slavery. But did they truly believe men and women of color were their equals? Brown's black sympathizers, especially Frederick Douglass, warned him to be wary of the subtle racism that lingered among well-meaning white people.

Only a few times did Brown's nocturnal soliloquies at the North Elba farmhouse reveal genuine optimism. He told Mary of a fundraising visit to Canton, Connecticut—the town in which his mother and father had lived for many years. While there he visited his family's former homestead and noticed a granite tombstone leaning against a wall. The stone once marked the grave of his grandfather, a captain in the Revolutionary War. The old man spoke proudly of his grandfather, a man he said died fighting for liberty. "The stone shall be delivered here to North Elba," he told Mary, "and I will add to it the name of Frederick, who perished in Kansas for the same cause."

He also told Mary about Charles Blair, a forge-master who worked for the Collins Company—a Connecticut foundry with an excellent reputation for manufacturing fine-edged tools. Blair attended one of Brown's speaking engagements and responded to it favorably. The two men chanced to meet the following day at a drugstore. After learning of Blair's occupation, Brown reached into his carpetbag and pulled out a two-edged dirk, a knife with an eight-inch blade carried by soldiers in the Scottish Highland regiments during the eighteenth century. He'd taken it from one of Pate's men at Black Jack.

Brown handed the knife to Blair and asked, "If I had a use for one of these attached to a six-foot pole, could you fashion such a formidable weapon?"

Blair nodded.

"What if I needed a thousand?"

Brown told Mary he signed a contract with Blair for the manufacture of one thousand pikes. He didn't tell her for what purpose the pikes were intended, but he did say that rifles and pistols had no place in the hands of inexperienced men. And he didn't mention the cost of the pikes. At a dollar each, the deposit on the $1,000 investment depleted a fair amount of his cash.

The last piece of favorable news was about a forty-five-year-old Scotsman named Hugh Forbes whom Brown met during a fundraising trip to New York City. Forbes had fought with Garibaldi in the failed Italian Revolution of 1848–49. He'd written a book based on his experiences and said he came to New York to be part of a second American revolution, a conflict he hoped would result in the abolition of slavery. When Brown met him, Forbes was barely scraping by as a part-time journalist and fencing instructor.

Brown explained to Mary that Forbes might be the missing piece to a puzzle—someone who could drill recruits and prepare them for any eventuality, including an invasion of the South. Forbes had signed on as Brown's drill officer and agreed to write a handbook, an introduction to the strategies and tactics of modern warfare and the duties of a soldier. His services didn't come cheap. Forbes wanted a monthly salary of one hundred dollars and additional money to cover expenses. And he expected to be paid in advance.

Between the cost of Blair's pikes and the demands of Forbes, Brown had practically exhausted his remaining funds. He'd return to Kansas, he told Mary, believing that God would somehow see fit to help him.

———•••——

For ten consecutive evenings, lying beside his wife in the darkness, Brown talked as his dutiful and compassionate wife listened, both of them waiting for the symptoms of his illness—which had become chronic—to subside.

Now, on the eve of his departure, Brown stood outside the North Elba farmhouse and watched an immense cloud continue its descent onto Whiteface Mountain. It was growing late and he felt a chill in the air, yet he didn't turn away until the mountain disappeared.

His family was waiting for him, crowded around the iron stove, its warmth radiating into the candlelit parlor that served as Brown's writing room. They knew he'd be leaving in the morning, and he still hadn't disclosed his plans. Mary had heated a large pot of cider. And of course there would be singing, one of the few indulgences the old man allowed himself.

The room was filled with his sons, young daughters, and eldest daughter Ruth and her husband Henry Thompson, the wounds he sustained at Black Jack now healed. Of those gathered in the parlor only little Ellen was oblivious to the moment. She still was not totally at ease with the father she viewed as a stranger. Brown went to her, hands extended, but she retreated into Mary's arms.

The old man's taut lips gave way to a rare smile as he drew himself into the most erect posture his ailing body would allow. His eyes burned with the familiar glow.

"I have promised others I would return to Kansas," he said, "and I shall keep that promise." He turned to Mary. "Our family has sacrificed much, but the Lord has chosen us to make sacrifices. He has given our family a purpose that requires sacrifices."

Ruth, sitting on the floor beside Henry, reached for her husband's arm. Intelligent, perceptive, pregnant Ruth—the daughter with flaming red hair who respected and loved her father but feared his power to hold sway over an audience. "Father," she said, "even those not of our blood have sacrificed much." She wasn't seeking validation for Henry's service; rather, she was worried her father would ask her husband to follow him into yet another violent skirmish.

Almost whispering, Brown responded, "My dear Ruth, many shall be called upon to *remember those that are in bonds as bound with them.* But only a few shall have the courage to answer."

Ruth squeezed Henry's hand. Little Ellen hugged her mother. Annie and Sarah, on the cusp of adolescence, sat motionless. The sons nodded compliantly.

Brown's dominating will was at work again, his rasping metallic voice slowly rising in volume: "For twenty years—since the time I took an oath consecrating my life to the destruction of slavery—it has been my aim to fight slavery on the enemy's soil. I fought in Kansas and I shall return to

Kansas. But I sense the hour is near when I shall take this war into Africa." He let the words settle, studying the faces of Oliver, Salmon, Watson, Owen, and Henry, then added, "Those who are willing to act should be prepared."

Young Oliver wasn't going to let the old man spoil the evening. "Enough, Father," he said, "lest we are dispatched to the infernal regions before tasting Mother's cider."

Watson went outside for wood, and he and Oliver stoked the iron stove. Mary and Ruth ladled the hot liquid into cups. When everyone was seated, Brown asked the Almighty to bless the occasion, reminding everyone present not to forget those millions still held in bondage. Then he called for Annie to bring Ellen to him. With Annie perched on one knee and Ellen on the other, the doting father sang his favorite hymn, "Blow Ye Trumpet, Blow," while the rest joined in the refrain:

> *The year of jubilee is come!*
> *Return, ye ransomed sinners, home!*

The next morning Brown embraced the members of his North Elba family, including little Ellen, who finally had come to accept as her father the strange man with the glittering eyes. The old man kissed Mary and told her he'd write often and that the girls should continue to study their Bibles. Annie and Sarah wept.

Of his three unmarried sons, only Owen agreed to accompany the old man on his journey back to Kansas Territory. The two men tossed their carpetbags onto the bed of a wagon owned by Lyman Epps, a neighbor and former slave.

Epps would take them the thirty miles to Westport on Lake Champlain. From there they would travel by steamboat to the southernmost tip of the lake, then to Albany by canal boat on the Champlain Canal, then to points west aboard the cars of the recently completed New York Central Railroad.

9

One Year and Eight Months Later
December 20, 1858
Vernon County, Missouri

Snow swirled in the hazy glow of a moon veiled by clouds as twenty-four horsemen—rifles slung across their backs, pistols holstered under wool coats—traversed the undulating farmland of southwestern Missouri. They slouched in their saddles and retreated deeper into their coats as the temperature dropped steadily.

Their leader struggled to follow a trail slowly disappearing beneath the falling snow. He'd adopted the alias Shubel Morgan and wore a full beard. To those strung out in a column behind him and to the runaway slave Jim Daniels who rode at his side, the new name and beard were irrelevant. He was still John Brown.

"No need to worry, Captain," Daniels called out. "Been down this road before."

Daniels had fled across the Missouri border in search of Brown, rumored at the time to be in southeastern Kansas Territory near Fort Scott. If Daniels could find the old man and get his help, he hoped to rescue his pregnant wife and two children from being put up for auction at a nearby plantation whose owner had recently died. The members of Daniels's family were to be sold separately, and at least one of them was bound for Texas.

The old man had intended by now to be in the southern Appalachians raiding plantations from Virginia to Alabama, but because of threats made by someone he once trusted, he had to change his plans. He was looking for an excuse to draw attention to himself, something worthy of inclusion in Northern newspapers, something that would placate his principal benefactors: New York's Gerrit Smith and the five men from Massachusetts—George Luther Stearns, Franklin Sanborn, Thomas Wentworth Higginson, Samuel Gridley Howe, and Theodore Parker—all of whom anguished over the possibility they would be linked to him as coconspirators in a slave uprising intended to terrorize the South. Brown was convinced that his God had sent Jim Daniels to him in a time of need. And so—instead of taking his war on slavery into Africa—he was back in Kansas attempting to snatch a handful of slaves from a plantation in Missouri.

He and his men had left at dusk from the tiny settlement of Trading Post, north of Fort Scott, with Daniels as their guide. Brown recruited half the company himself; the rest were volunteers from James Montgomery's Free State militia, the Jayhawkers.

At midnight the column reached the Little Osage River in Missouri's Vernon County. The plantation where Daniels's family was quartered was less than a mile away. During the ride Daniels spoke of slaves kept at a neighboring farm; they would be grateful, he said, to be freed from bondage. Brown responded by dividing his men into two groups. Fifteen would stay with him; the remaining eight would go with Aaron Stevens, once introduced to Brown as Colonel Whipple, the powerfully built, dark-eyed young man who escaped from the military stockade at Leavenworth and was the leader of Jim Lane's Second Kansas Militia. Stevens was now one of the old man's trusted soldiers.

"Take whatever you need from the enemy," Brown told Stevens. "We shall have many miles to travel, many mouths to feed, before we deliver the children of Israel out of Egypt."

Stevens nodded. He was accustomed to the biblical allusions. The two men parted, agreeing to rendezvous at the Little Osage when the work was done.

The wind had freshened, battering Brown with squalls of wet snow, but the weather was of little concern to him. He was leading an armed incursion into a slave state and soon would be liberating human beings from the shackles of slavery. At last he'd been given an opportunity to carry out his mission. It wasn't what he expected, but he was grateful, and he closed his eyes and offered a silent prayer of thanks.

At length his party came to a split-rail fence, then an iron-picketed gate hinged between stone pillars. On either side of the pillars the rail fence faded into darkness.

Daniels said his wife and children waited somewhere beyond the padlocked gate.

Brown pointed to a section of the fence. "Take it down!"

The men poured through the breach, turning their horses onto a tree-lined lane. In the moon's dim light the old man was able to make out a two-story house. It loomed like a fortress.

More than a year and a half had elapsed since Brown departed North Elba with his son Owen, climbing aboard the cars of the New York Central Railroad at Albany. His destination was Kansas with an intermediate stop in Ohio. During the journey he spoke to Owen of his disillusionment with what was happening in the territory. The letters he'd received, the newspaper accounts—all confirmed his worst fears. If politicians like Dr. Charles Robinson had their way, Northern settlers would yield to policies of appeasement and compromise. There would be no more fighting. The slave power was entrenched in Washington and would find a way to perpetuate itself—if not in Kansas, then elsewhere.

"I may be an old man," Brown told Owen, "but I don't intend to die before I fulfill my destiny. God has charged me with a mission. It matters not where I fight. I can die on a plantation in Virginia just as easily as on the prairies of Kansas."

Brown came close to dying before he reached Kansas. He spent two months with friends and relatives in Ohio—most of the time recuperating from his chronic illness.

During his convalescence he wrote letters to Kansas friends inquiring about the likelihood of renewed border conflicts and the availability of recruits for an army of one hundred soldiers. And he continued to ask for money from his principal benefactors.

Responses were disappointing. His friends urged him to stay put; the border was quiet. Several of his former soldiers had returned to farming. James Holmes, one of the old man's stalwarts, had staked out a claim in Emporia. In the Northeast, the recession was becoming more severe, money was getting tighter, and Brown's financial backers were feeling the effects.

Finally, in August 1857—aboard a horse-drawn wagon—Brown and Owen rolled into Tabor, the abolitionist community in the southwestern corner of Iowa where the old man and his boys had sought refuge in the past. There were citizens in Tabor willing to aid Free State fighters. It was a good place for him to set up his base of operations before reentering the territory.

His first task upon arriving was to take an inventory of weapons. Aside from his own personal cache of arms, the two hundred Sharps carbines from the Massachusetts State Kansas Committee remained in storage in the home of a local minister. The two hundred .31 caliber Maynard revolvers purchased by George Stearns were still in eastern Iowa, where they would remain until Brown claimed them. And the pikes ordered from Connecticut forge-master Charles Blair were put on hold; the old man had no way of paying the balance he owed on them.

Though Brown found the carbines fouled with grease, they weren't his main concern. A rift had developed between him and Hugh Forbes, the one-hundred-dollar-a-month drill officer, who showed up in Tabor just two days after the old man's arrival. There was no one—other than Owen—for Forbes to train. Brown had failed to recruit a single soldier.

Forbes said he'd been misled, but Brown blamed the situation on the two-month delay caused by his illness, something Forbes would have known about if he'd answered the old man's letters. The failure of Forbes to reply had vexed Brown, especially since he'd sent his drill officer six months' salary in advance.

While Forbes waited for recruits to materialize, the old man cleaned weapons. He now believed the possibility of renewed hostilities in Kansas was slipping away, and his thoughts had shifted to a plan for invading the South.

When he tried to discuss his plan with Forbes—who insisted on being addressed as "Colonel"—he was met with resistance. The two argued incessantly, first about how to wage war against slaveholders, then about how Forbes might benefit from the generosity of Brown's benefactors, men the colonel referred to sarcastically as "the humanitarians."

"Forbes has become a burden to me," Brown complained to Owen. "I grow weary of the bickering."

An issue dividing the two men was the role to be played by slaves in the invasion Brown was planning, an invasion that would require liberated slaves to join the old man's army.

"Whether he is free or slave," Brown asserted, "the black man must fight for his freedom. He must join in the war on slavery—or the nation will never respect him."

Forbes argued, "It's foolish to think that men ignorant of the use of arms or the conditions of battle could contribute effectively to a war against their oppressors."

Brown countered, "Nat Turner and fifty men held Virginia for five weeks."

Forbes again: "A slave who is not given advance warning of an uprising or who isn't already in state of agitation will answer your call reluctantly or not at all."

Forbes continued to find fault with Brown's ideas. And he was obsessed with money. He had needs Brown hadn't been aware of, claiming to have a wife and children living abroad in poverty. If he didn't send them a decent allotment very soon their survival was in doubt. "I must take care of my family, Captain. Surely the humanitarians will understand."

Even though Brown's personal bank account had dwindled, he might have been more sympathetic to Forbes had their relationship not begun to unravel. The old man even had come to believe the colonel wanted to assume a more prominent role in the plan for invading the South. Could it be, Brown grumbled to Owen, that Forbes saw himself as the leader of such an invasion?

For the moment Brown was confined to Tabor, unsure of his next move, annoyed by his carping drill officer, depressed by the state of affairs in Kansas, and anxious about the depletion of his money.

Then came the news that the Kansas territorial election had resulted in a Free State victory. Thirty-three of the fifty-two seats in the legislature were won by Free State candidates, and a Free State man was elected to represent the territory in the US Congress. There was no doubt peace was coming—sooner rather than later. Brown resigned himself to the fact he was no longer needed in Kansas. He could set his sights exclusively on taking his war on slavery elsewhere. He'd been thinking about the Allegheny Mountains of northern Virginia.

First, though, he was obligated to keep his promise to return to Kansas—maybe not to fight but rather to find men who were willing to join him in striking a blow on Southern soil. He sent a note to John Cook, the young man with long blond locks who already had demonstrated his ability to rally volunteers to Brown's cause. Brown wrote that he was in Iowa but hoped to get to Lawrence very soon and wanted Cook to arrange a meeting. "Be sure to invite all who wish to continue the fight against slavery," the old man wrote. "Tell them to bring their arms and ammunition."

Before leaving for Kansas, Brown penned a letter to his Massachusetts supporters indicating he was "in immediate need of from five hundred to one thousand dollars for secret service and no questions asked."

Somehow he'd find the soldiers and money to begin a campaign in the Southern states. "God will not let me fail," he told Owen.

Shortly thereafter, Brown's faith was rewarded. He received $250—part of it from George Stearns, the rest from Kansas militants who coveted the old man's Sharps carbines. He wasted no time purchasing a fresh team of horses for the wagon trip to Lawrence.

While Owen guided the team along the road from Tabor to Nebraska City—the first leg of the journey—Forbes, who insisted on coming along, voiced his grievances. Brown had deceived him, he said. He'd been promised employment for a full year. Nonsense, Brown replied; Forbes had been hired on a monthly basis with only the first six months guaranteed.

The colonel continued his rant. What about the humanitarians—the Massachusetts men who cherished freedom and were committed to the abolition of slavery? Why hadn't they delivered on their promises? How was it possible, Forbes groaned, that he—who fought alongside and gained the respect of the great Italian revolutionary Giuseppe Garibaldi—was reduced to begging? How was he to care for his wife and children?

Brown endured Forbes's harangues during the twenty-mile trip to Nebraska City. He decided the colonel had become a liability. Perhaps Forbes should return to New York City, where the prospects for earning money were better. Brown opened his carpetbag, took out some cash, and handed it to the colonel. Then he reached into his coat pocket and withdrew an envelope.

"I have written a letter of introduction to my good friend Frederick Douglass. You may wish to avail yourself of his hospitality." Brown paused before adding, "I expect to be mustering my new recruits in Ohio. Perhaps you will be able to join us there."

Forbes took the money and envelope without uttering a word. Maybe he was thinking about the long stagecoach ride to Iowa City, the nearest railhead for trains bound for the

East. Or maybe he viewed Brown's talk of mustering new
recruits as wishful thinking.

Owen gave the reins a shake, and he and the old man
continued on to Kansas. They hadn't traveled far when Owen
said, "I fear we've not heard the last of Colonel Forbes."

———

When he arrived in Lawrence, Brown received another wind-
fall. Stearns had once more honored his request. An agent of
the Massachusetts State Kansas Committee presented the old
man with a bank draft in the amount of $500.

Now Brown had the means to vigorously pursue recruits.
With Cook's help, he started enlisting volunteers, among them
two men who would become part of his inner circle: Aaron
"Colonel Whipple" Stevens and John Henry Kagi, a bright,
self-educated journalist and lawyer who once taught school
in Virginia and served in Stevens's Second Kansas Militia.

Brown told his new volunteers to meet him in Tabor,
where he'd reveal his plans and unveil a store of weapons
and supplies.

Nine men were waiting when he and Owen returned to
the Iowa village. Those present soon learned the old man
had no intention of resuming activities in Kansas, a disappointment to Cook, who was anticipating more raiding of
proslavery settlements.

But Brown had a different agenda. He said he planned
to launch an invasion into the South by the coming spring
and that he wanted to set up a "military school" to sharpen
fighting skills and instill discipline in the soldiers he hoped to
recruit. Though he hadn't decided on an exact location for the
school, he was certain the Lord would provide the necessary

guidance. The confidence the old man exuded—coupled with the cessation of hostilities in Kansas and the two hundred Sharps carbines he laid out for inspection—erased any doubts the men may have had.

———•••———

It was a cold and blustery morning in early December 1857 when Brown and his company of nine volunteers left Tabor. They marched behind two covered wagons, each drawn by a two-horse team. The wagons were filled with crates of Sharps carbines, cooking gear, blankets, tents, and provisions. An icy wind gnawed at toes and fingers, and in the evenings the men huddled around a cooking fire while Stevens—in his baritone voice—led them in the singing of Brown's favorite hymns. The misery induced by the harsh weather drew the men closer together.

As they approached the eastern border of Iowa on the last day of December—having marched almost three hundred miles—Brown decided they had gone far enough. In the village of Springdale, populated largely by Quakers, he found someone willing to house and feed the men through the winter—in exchange for his two teams of horses and the wagons. After the supplies and weapons were unloaded and stored, the old man put Stevens in charge of drills and marksmanship.

Then he continued on—alone. There was much to be done in preparation for the invasion.

———•••———

For some time Brown had been deliberating about a scheme for recruiting more men. It involved organizing a convention of free blacks and former slaves residing in Canada West, a territory nestled among three of the Great Lakes—Huron, Erie, and Ontario. Almost forty thousand people of color lived in Canada West, most of them former slaves, some freeborn and well educated; they had established communities with schools that provided instruction in literacy, mathematics, and the applied subjects of agronomy and the mechanical arts. Such communities would be ideal destinations for the slaves—especially women and children—the old man intended to liberate.

To bring his convention to fruition Brown needed the support of the core financial backers he'd come to rely on, and he also hoped to draw on the resources of prosperous persons of color scattered throughout the Northeast.

But before taking the first step toward realizing his grand ambition, the old man wanted to make sure future generations would know that whatever the outcome of his attempt to free slaves on Southern soil, his cause would be viewed as a righteous one and his aims were in keeping with the ideals of the Founding Fathers. To this end, he intended to put his beliefs and purposes into writing—a document that would serve as a manifesto justifying what he regarded as the most important action in America since the Revolutionary War. Before creating such a document, he needed someone who would listen to his ideas, someone with a sympathetic ear. So he headed for Rochester, New York, the home of his longtime friend and ally Frederick Douglass.

En route to New York, Brown stopped briefly at the Ohio farm of his eldest son, John Jr., who was still haunted by his experiences in Kansas. He said he'd received a letter from Franklin Sanborn of the Massachusetts State Kansas Committee.

THE INSURRECTIONIST   133

"Sanborn says that someone he knows nothing about has been up to mischief," John Jr. told his father. "Apparently your Colonel Forbes wrote Senator Sumner and Dr. Howe. He denounced you and threatened to do great harm to your plans if he isn't paid what he's owed."

Brown didn't seem overly concerned. The new year—1858—had just arrived, and he was excited about the prospects of realizing his life's goal. He was poised to strike a blow against slavery on Southern soil—something he'd been contemplating for more than two decades. Before continuing his journey to New York, he told his son, "We shall wait and see how far Forbes is willing to go."

———————

Frederick Douglass's home was situated on a hill not far from Lake Ontario on the outskirts of Rochester. As a stationmaster on the Underground Railroad, Douglass chose the location for its remoteness; it wasn't unusual for runaways to hide in his barn before escaping to Canada. The seclusion was ideal for Brown. He could work without having to worry about federal marshals or inquisitive neighbors.

The youthful appearance of the thirty-nine-year-old Douglass belied the fact he was among the most highly regarded and eloquent spokesmen of the abolitionist movement. His broad, angular face with its prominent jaw was framed by a mass of thick, black hair. In contrast, Brown—now nearly fifty-eight—was still whip-thin and slightly stooped, his face etched by long exposure to the elements. Though the two men differed markedly in age and appearance, they shared a bond of mutual respect. Since their first meeting nearly ten years earlier, Douglass had gradually come to accept the old man's belief that slavery could be eradicated from the South only through violent action.

During Brown's three-week stay in Rochester, Douglass became a captive audience as the old man hammered out the details of his multifaceted plan. It began with a constitution.

"A constitution for what?" Douglass asked.

"A constitution that will serve two purposes, my friend—the first being to create a provisional government with all the powers necessary to ensure order and security for men and women who will be experiencing freedom for the first time." He studied the reaction of his host, then added, "My aim, as you know, is to gather up many hundreds from the plantations, and I do not intend to allow my efforts to turn into anarchy."

Douglass said, "And this constitution will eliminate such a possibility?"

"Indeed—but it also shall have a larger purpose."

Since they first met in 1848—when the old man was in the wool business in Massachusetts—Douglass had known about Brown's dream of liberating slaves. However, talk of a constitution and a provisional government was new to him.

Brown continued: "The constitution will express everything that lies at the heart of this nation's calamitous illness—an illness brought on by a slaveholding elite that has usurped the powers of the government." His voice grew louder. "Our spineless president bows to the slave conspiracy, and the slaveholding chief justice declares the black man to be less than human, mere chattel, having no more rights than a mule."

Brown reached into his pocket, pulled out a handkerchief, and mopped his brow. "The people of this nation must understand that it is not I who will have incited an uprising among the slaves. It is the slaveholder who has declared a most barbarous and unprovoked war on those he holds in bondage. He has violated the truths set forth in the Declaration of Independence. He has corrupted the purpose of the federal constitution in order to satisfy his wicked desires." Brown paused, waited for his passion to cool, then added, "The time has come to make slavery totter from its foundation."

The old man had spent himself—emotionally if not physically. Douglass urged him to rest. There would be other opportunities to talk.

Before retiring for the evening, Douglass mentioned that he had received a visit from Hugh Forbes. The meeting turned out to be a disappointment, he said. "All the man could talk about was his destitute circumstances and that he was in dire need of money." Douglass admitted he expected more of Forbes, especially since the colonel came with a letter of introduction from Brown.

From early morning until late in the evening, Brown worked on his constitution, as well as his own version of the Declaration of Independence. His constitution was simplistic, seeming at times to be a parody of the US Constitution; it affirmed the rights of a diverse society, promising freedom and equality not only to slaves but also to others who were oppressed, including women and native peoples. Both documents addressed the injustices of a government held hostage by slaveholders.

As he wrote, Brown worried his words would be interpreted as a pretext for an armed rebellion against the federal government—which was never his intention. He saw his constitution as an instrument advocating reform, providing a model for a more perfect Union. To guard against misinterpretation, he concluded with a caveat:

The foregoing Articles shall not be construed so as in any way to encourage the overthrow of any State Government of the United States, and look to no dissolution of the Union, but simply to Amendment and Repeal.

On the eve of his departure from Rochester, Brown was riding a wave of optimism that receded only slightly when Shields Green—a fugitive slave employed by Douglass—handed him another angry letter from Hugh Forbes. Green, who was privy to some of the conversations between Douglass and Brown, had come to admire the old man and felt he had much in common with the ideas he heard expressed.

The letter from Forbes contained the usual threats but had little effect on Brown; his enthusiasm was still intact as he took time to write Franklin Sanborn, inviting him and the other Massachusetts men—his core benefactors—to attend a meeting at Gerrit Smith's Peterboro estate near Syracuse. Smith's home was to be the old man's next stop. The letter began:

God has honored but comparatively a very small part of mankind with such mighty and soul-satisfying rewards. . . . I expect to effect a mighty conquest even though it be like the last victory of Samson.

The meeting at Gerrit Smith's was important to Brown. He couldn't take his war on slavery into the South without the support of his backers. So he was disappointed that none of the Massachusetts men showed up except Sanborn. But he was glad to hear Sanborn say he would write a report of the meeting and pass it on to the others when he returned to Boston.

The gathering took place in an upper room of the Peterboro mansion on February 22—George Washington's birthday. Only Brown, Smith, and Sanborn were present as the old man laid out the constitution he'd drawn up at Douglass's home and told of his desire to launch an invasion into slave territory somewhere east of the Alleghenies.

"Gentlemen," he said, "I aim to restore our slave-cursed republic to the principles of the Declaration of Independence and am prepared to die in the attempt."

Both men were puzzled by Brown's plan. A constitution? A provisional government? And what about numbers? It seemed like the old man was willing to undertake an enormous task with a relatively small number of soldiers.

Nothing either of them said could dissuade Brown. He countered every objection, cutting off debate with the words "If God be for us, who can be against us?"

Smith looked to Sanborn and said, "You see how it is. Our dear friend has made up his mind to his course and cannot be turned from it. We cannot give him up to die alone. We must support him."

When Brown left Smith and Sanborn, he began a two-month journey that took him to New York, Massachusetts, Connecticut, and Pennsylvania. He met with other well-heeled abolitionists—black and white—and told them of his plans for a convention and subsequent invasion. Of course he would gladly accept donations to support his venture.

By the end of his journey, he was ready to head to Canada West and the place he chose for the convention: the town of Chatham, located some fifty miles east of Detroit. But first he would return to Iowa to pick up the men he'd left in the capable hands of his drill officer, Aaron Stevens. The volunteers who'd endured the hardships of marching across Iowa in the dead of winter had earned the right to be introduced to the men he hoped to recruit in Canada West.

When the company finally got to Chatham, Brown was told that the invitations he extended to his six principal benefactors were declined. Not even the consistently loyal Sanborn chose to come. Apparently Hugh Forbes's campaign of misinformation was working.

Of the forty-five men who attended the Chatham convention, one-quarter were from Brown's military school in Springdale. His promotional efforts netted only thirty-four former slaves and free blacks. He expected hundreds. No matter. He announced he was ready to begin his invasion; those wishing to join him should be ready to assemble at a location near the border of Virginia.

As the convention drew to a close, Brown received an urgent message summoning him to Boston. His benefactors—who now identified themselves as "the secret committee"—had made a decision that would require him to revise his plans. They needed to talk to him—immediately.

Before leaving, Brown told the men he brought from Springdale to find whatever work they could during his absence—but they should be ready to report to him at a moment's notice. For the impatient John Cook, who expressed an interest in scouting possible sites for the invasion, Brown had a special assignment: Find a job in a town in northern Virginia. Reconnoiter the surrounding countryside and gather intelligence. The town the old man had in mind was located some fifty miles northwest of Washington, DC, at the confluence of the Shenandoah and Potomac Rivers. It was situated in a region of gentlemen farmers who possessed few slaves. It was a mill town and the site of a federal armory: Harpers Ferry.

When Brown's cab pulled up to his Boston hotel, he was exhausted. He'd been continuously on the move for almost five months, traveling throughout the Northeast, soliciting money and attempting to recruit soldiers, his odyssey finally coming to an end at the convention in Canada West. And while he always took pride in being well groomed and neatly attired when in the company of his benefactors, on the day he was to meet them his clothing was soiled and he hadn't shaved.

Higginson met him at the hotel and gave an account of what had transpired in recent weeks. Other members of the secret committee, Higginson said, met earlier and reached an agreement. "They want you to suspend plans for operations in the South. It appears Colonel Forbes has made them nervous."

Higginson said Forbes had accelerated his vendetta of character assassination and that he traveled to Washington, where he spoke to antislavery senators, including New York's William Seward, New Hampshire's John Hale, and the junior senator from Massachusetts, Henry Wilson. Forbes had slandered Brown and named the members of the secret committee as coconspirators in a plan to invade the South in order to incite a slave uprising. According to Higginson, things spun out of control when Forbes declared that textile manufacturer Amos Adams Lawrence stood to make a fortune with the increase in the price of cotton goods that was sure to follow an invasion of a Southern state. Forbes had tried to create the impression that the whole venture was nothing more than a scheme to make money.

Higginson said the secret committee dreaded seeing its work shattered by the allegations of a lunatic. "I'm afraid the charge of sedition would be too much to bear for most of them." Not so for Higginson. The man who had tried to free the fugitive slave Anthony Burns urged Brown to go ahead with his plans regardless of the consequences.

"But they hold the purse," Brown said. "I am powerless without them." The old man finally realized he'd underestimated the dissatisfaction of Forbes and overestimated the number of men who would join his crusade. And now he was broke.

Later, when Stearns, Howe, and Sanborn arrived at the hotel, Brown was prepared for the worst. Stearns said, "We don't want you to abandon your plan, merely to postpone it."

Sanborn added, "Forbes has become a pariah. We have no choice."

A visibly distressed Howe: "Captain, you must return to Kansas. It's the only way to cast doubt on Forbes and his accusations."

Then Stearns made an offer. He wouldn't recall the fire-arms Brown had been provided. They could be used at his discretion. "But you must agree to tell us nothing of your future plans," Stearns said. "Your actions will speak for themselves." He reached into his pocket and withdrew a cloth bag secured by a leather drawstring. "There are five hundred dollars in gold in this bag. The committee is willing to raise more—when you return from Kansas."

Brown was puzzled by Stearns's stipulation but asked no questions. He'd take the money and do as his benefactors wished. He'd go to Kansas—again—and find a way to minimize the damage inflicted by Forbes. He'd do something that would call into question Forbes's claim that an invasion of the South was imminent. And after things quieted down he'd accept Stearns's offer of additional funds.

The old man's return to Kansas couldn't have been timed any better. Details of an atrocity in the Fort Scott area had reached Boston newspapers. There had been a massacre of Free State settlers by proslavery marauders. Brown thought an opportunity might lie hidden within this tragedy.

Wearing a full beard, he quietly slipped into Lawrence in late June 1858. Though most of the soldiers who went with him to Canada were left to fend for themselves, the old man asked Aaron Stevens, John Kagi, and twenty-four-year-old Charles Plummer Tidd—another man enlisted by John Cook—to meet him in Kansas. Their experience in the skirmishes of 1856 would be useful, and maybe they could help recruit a few veteran fighters.

Brown drew up a document, the title of which included his new alias: "Articles of Agreement for Shubel Morgan's Company." As word spread that Shubel Morgan and John Brown were one and the same, volunteers stepped forward. Soon Brown had enlisted enough men to make himself visible in southeastern Kansas, the only part of the territory where clashes between Free State and proslavery factions still persisted.

When not bedridden with severe and prolonged attacks of
his chronic malarial fever, Brown led his new company as it
patrolled the area around Fort Scott, scene of the recent massacre. Though he despised those who participated in the massacre, Brown wasn't interested in revenge. He'd only engage
the enemy if challenged. However, if he were presented with
an opportunity to fulfill his mission—the divinely inspired
mission that took precedence over all else—he wouldn't hesitate to act.

And so, almost twenty months after boarding a train in Albany
with Owen, Brown had traveled to Kansas, back to the East
for the Chatham convention, and back to Kansas again.
Though he'd experienced his share of disappointments, he
felt closer than ever to realizing his goal of taking his war on
slavery into Africa. All he had to do to get the funding he
needed was discredit the rumor that he was conspiring with
abolitionists in the North to start a slave uprising.

His unexpected encounter with the fugitive slave Jim Daniels had come to him as divine intervention. When Daniels
asked for help in rescuing his pregnant wife and children from
the auction block, the old man was happy to oblige. Such a
rescue was sure to the draw the attention of the newspapers.
His benefactors in the Northeast would have evidence that
Hugh Forbes's insinuations were false and that John Brown
was still roaming the Kansas-Missouri border.

It was after midnight when the men Brown led into Missouri drew in their reins and came to a halt in front of the two-story house at the end of a snow-covered lane. The moon was still veiled by clouds, but the snowfall had eased. The house was cloaked in dark shadows as the old man sat motionless in the saddle, gazing at the elevated veranda. For many years he'd dreamed of freeing hundreds of slaves—maybe thousands. He was now about to rescue far fewer from a plantation in Missouri.

One of the men shouted, "There's smoke coming from a chimney, Captain."

The men were cold. They were getting impatient.

Then the flickering light of a candle appeared in an upstairs window.

Daniels had told Brown the deceased owner's relative—a man named Hicklin—had taken up temporary residency in the house. He had a wife and children.

Brown called to John Kagi. "Looks like the tenant is awake." He pointed to the candlelight in the upstairs window. "You know what to do."

Kagi dismounted and headed for the front door.

Brown gave his reins a shake and motioned for Daniels to follow. As they reached the back of the house, the slave quarters came into view—two windowless log cabins. Daniels leaped from the saddle and ran toward the larger of the two cabins. The moon had slipped from behind the clouds, bringing the scene into sharper focus. It didn't require much illumination for Brown to see that the woman Daniels was embracing was indeed great with child.

The old man dismounted and walked his horse back to the veranda. Daniels and his wife and children and an older black man followed. There were others, Daniels said, but they'd been sent to plantations at distant locations out of fear that they—as Daniels had—might run away.

Kagi had stoked the fire in the parlor; the newly liberated slaves warmed themselves at the hearth. Parked outside was an old Conestoga wagon harnessed to a yoke of oxen. The wagon had been appropriated from the barn and was being loaded with bedding, clothing, and provisions. Hicklin and his family watched from the vestibule.

"Well, you seem to be in a pretty tight place," Brown told Hicklin. "But you shan't be hurt if you behave yourself."

One of the men stuck his head inside the door. "Captain, the wagon is loaded and all is ready."

The emancipated slaves boarded the Conestoga.

Brown turned to Hicklin. "I hope you understand we are but doing our duty. To do otherwise in the presence of the barbarities of slavery would be an eternal disgrace." He mounted his horse and added, "You have been visited by Old John Brown of Osawatomie, Kansas. Be advised to remain here with your wife and children until the sun rises."

It was well past midnight and more work remained. Daniels suggested that slaves at a plantation three-quarters of a mile away would welcome a visit.

In half an hour the company arrived at the plantation of John Larue. Larue anticipated an encounter with Free State guerrillas and was prepared to resist.

"Alright then," Brown shouted. "We'll burn you out."

Larue surrendered, and five more liberated slaves climbed aboard the Conestoga wagon. The old man also confiscated several horses and a quantity of provisions, and he brought along Larue and his houseguest as hostages.

The only troubling event of an otherwise successful mission was revealed hours later when Brown met up with the rest of his soldiers at the Little Osage River. A somber Stevens stood amid the property he'd seized: eleven mules, two horses, and a covered farm wagon loaded with salted meat and barrels of flour. He'd liberated only one slave, a young woman who knew Daniels and his wife.

Stevens's demeanor had nothing to do with his failure to liberate more slaves. He'd shot dead the owner of the farm he invaded. And he'd done so in the presence of the man's thirteen-year-old son.

Stevens struggled to control his emotions. "It grieves me deeply, Captain. He fired first and I had to defend myself."

Brown stepped forward, placed his hands on Stevens's shoulders, and—speaking as earnestly as a minister to a member of his congregation—said, "An all-knowing God decides all things."

Apparently Brown's God decided the old man's deeds should be made known quickly—and the news created anger and terror along the border. Missouri planters, fearing more raids, sold their slaves south or sent them east to plantations in the interior of the state. At the same time, Free State settlers in southeastern Kansas braced for retaliation from Missourians.

Meanwhile, newspaper stories leapfrogged eastward: from Lawrence to Saint Louis to Chicago to Cleveland to New York to Boston. Horace Greeley's *New York Tribune* correspondents and William Hutchinson of the *New York Times* rushed to inform their readers of Brown's raid and his liberation of the slaves. The magnitude of the event grew when the governor of Missouri offered a $3,000 reward for Brown's capture.

President Buchanan was obliged to make a token gesture; he offered a bounty of $250.

As for the local newspapers, not all were favorable to the old man. Yet he'd accomplished what his benefactors hoped for. Hugh Forbes would vex him no more. As far as the people in the Northeast were concerned, Brown had never left Kansas.

The old man may have missed his first opportunity to take his war on slavery into the South. But he wouldn't miss the next. For the moment, however, he was committed to shepherding a wagon filled with fugitive slaves to Canada—eleven hundred miles from the Kansas-Missouri border.

10

Four Months Later
April 29, 1859
North Elba, New York

Brown had written Mary that he'd be home by early spring. By then she'd have heard or read about his emancipation of the eleven slaves from the Missouri plantation. After the slaves were aboard a ferry bound for Canada, he intended to return to North Elba, confident he'd be able to carry out a plan for invading the South.

But first he wanted to see his wife and young daughters— perhaps for the last time.

When he arrived with a stranger at the Adirondack homestead, Mary was startled by the change in her husband's physical appearance. She'd last seen him on the eve of his final expedition to Kansas—the expedition whose purpose was to divert attention from threats made by Hugh Forbes. Prior to his departure he was clean-shaven, but he now wore a full beard that cascaded down his face in bone-white waves.

The stranger was a former member of James Montgomery's Kansas Jayhawkers—twenty-six-year-old Jeremiah Goldsmith Anderson. Anderson had joined Brown for the Missouri raid, then accompanied him on the trip east at the insistence of John Kagi, who was worried about the old man's deteriorating health. The bouts of chills and fever had become more debilitating, and Kagi felt Brown ought not travel alone.

Mary ushered her husband and Anderson into the warmth of the parlor. They were cold and wet, having trudged along a muddy road in drizzling rain for the better part of the day. In the glow of a cast iron stove stood the three daughters, freshly scrubbed and neatly attired, each nearly a year older than when Brown last saw them. Like their mother, the girls were struck by the change in their father's appearance. Little Ellen, now almost five, had been reluctant to approach him on previous occasions, but she seemed quite happy to see him and was the first to step forward. A bedraggled Brown dropped to one knee and lifted her into the air.

"My dear daughter," he said, kissing her on the cheek, "you shall soon be old enough to understand why your father has spent so little time in your company."

He stood up and held out his hands to fifteen-year-old Annie and twelve-year-old Sarah. Both were waiting patiently for their father's attention, exhibiting the self-restraint emblematic of the Brown household.

The old man looked to his companion. "Children," he said, "this is Lieutenant Jerry Anderson—a soldier from Kansas."

Brown had barely finished his sentence when he began to cough violently. Mary told the girls to bring water, but it took minutes for the coughing to subside. When the old man finally was able to talk, he blamed the cold and rain.

It wasn't long, however, before his chronic illness returned. He took to his bed the following afternoon, and for the next ten days he was nursed by Mary and the girls while Anderson tended to the livestock and performed other chores around the farm.

A procession of visitors converged on the house almost daily. It included Brown's sons Salmon, Oliver, and Watson—by now all married—and their wives; daughter Ruth and her husband, Henry Thompson; Henry's brothers, twenty-five-year-old William and twenty-one-year-old Dauphin; and members of the North Elba community of former slaves.

The visitors came to stand at the foot of the bed and pay their respects, but Brown had little to say. Once again his body had betrayed him, and he found it difficult to accept another setback at a time when he was so close to fulfilling his mission. Tormented by a fever that left him lying in pools of sweat, he spent the intervals, when the symptoms abated, reflecting on his final days in Kansas.

———————

Brown had left Kansas under a cloud of controversy. Dr. Charles Robinson condemned him, fearing his liberation of the Missouri slaves would disrupt the delicate transition of power resulting from Congress's rejection of a proslavery territorial constitution. Brown was vilified in Missouri and Kansas newspapers for jeopardizing the lull in hostilities. The *Leavenworth Herald* carried an editorial stating there was "no earthly excuse" for the old man's Missouri raid. Even the Lawrence papers chided him; they worried the progress made by the Free State cause would be dashed by another episode of "Bleeding Kansas."

The criticism festered in Brown; he'd wanted to respond to it publicly, but he was busy transporting the liberated slaves out of Kansas, contending with roving bands of Missourians intent on repossessing their stolen chattel.

The caravan was made up of the Conestoga wagon with
its human cargo and a horse-drawn farm wagon filled with
provisions. Tethered behind were the horses and mules confiscated during the raid. Because the Conestoga's ploddingly
slow team of oxen took almost two weeks to cover a distance
of fewer than a hundred miles, Brown sought to replace it.
He sent Aaron Stevens and Charlie Tidd to requisition a pair
of draft horses. Also, there had been a delay caused by the
birth of a boy to the wife of Jim Daniels.

While Kagi scouted for safe houses along the trail to
Nebraska, Brown and his refugees found shelter from a mid-
winter snowstorm. They were welcomed by a family that
knew the old man and regarded the Missouri raid a worthy
undertaking. When everyone was settled in, Brown took time
to answer his critics. He wanted to defend his liberation of
the slaves but also to expose the collusion and collaboration
operating at the highest levels of government. So he sat down
and composed an open letter to Greeley's *New York Tribune*.

He began the letter with a description of the seemingly
pointless massacre that took place near Fort Scott prior to
his return to the territory. "Eleven quiet Free State citizens,"
he wrote, "were taken from their work and homes, lined
up and shot, resulting in five killed, five wounded, one having escaped unhurt." However, he noted, when he and his
men raided Missouri in order to restore eleven slaves to their
"natural and inalienable rights, with but one man killed, all
hell was stirred from beneath." Furthermore, Brown claimed
the governor of Missouri requested the aid of the federally
appointed governor of Kansas in order to capture the perpetrators of the "dreadful outrage" while a federal marshal was
"collecting a posse of Missouri (not Kansas) men" in order to
track down the fugitive slaves.

The old man wanted his readers to know that the federal government again had surrendered its authority to the slave power, allowing crimes committed by proslavery men to go unpunished while bringing the full force of the law to bear on Free State men who were acting on principles contained in the Declaration of Independence. The letter eventually found its way onto the pages of the *Tribune* and other Northern newspapers.

Brown had another matter to attend to before leaving Kansas. He wouldn't depart without saying good-bye to the person he took into his confidence at the encampment outside Topeka on the eve of Independence Day in July 1856. To Brown, William A. Phillips was a journalist who, despite his close connection to Dr. Charles Robinson, hadn't been tainted by a lust for power. Brown was convinced Phillips had a better grasp of the Kansas situation than other journalists; he'd written a book that Brown felt proved his judgment correct. The old man had acquired a copy—published in Boston in the fall of 1856—after his first meeting with the men who were to become his principal Massachusetts benefactors. In *The Conquest of Kansas by Missouri and her Allies*, Phillips included a description of Brown:

Tall and stern-looking, hard-featured and resolute, there is something in Captain Brown's air that speaks the soldier, every inch of him. He is not a man to be trifled with; and there is no one for whom the border ruffians entertain a more wholesome dread than Captain Brown. They hate him as they would a snake, but their hatred is composed of nine-tenths fear. Although the captain is a practical man, he is one of those abstruse thinkers who have read much and thought more. In his opinions he is inexorably inflexible, and the world would pronounce him a "fanatic."

He is one of those Christians who have not quite vanished from the face of the earth—that is, he asks the blessing of God when he breaks his bread, and does not, even in camp, forget his devotions in his zeal against the border ruffians. There is not a more stern disciplinarian in Kansas.

However, when Brown invited Phillips to meet him at the Whitney House in Lawrence, the antislavery journalist's attitude had changed. Like Dr. Robinson, Phillips was disturbed by Brown's foray into Missouri, believing it imperiled a peaceful resolution to the troubles in the territory and harmed the chances of Kansas being admitted into the Union as a free state. Phillips came to the Whitney House reluctantly, approached Brown in the hotel's lobby with skepticism.

"You wished to see me, Captain?"

Brown reached for Phillips's hand. "I couldn't leave Kansas without bidding farewell to one who has so unselfishly devoted himself to the cause of liberty. Come, my friend, we must talk. Perhaps we shall not meet again—at least in this world."

The old man led Phillips to his room—a small, unheated space containing a bed, a small table, and two chairs. Neither man removed his coat as they took a seat at the table. The only warmth came from a shaft of sunlight streaming through a window.

Brown immediately launched into a monologue on the rise of slavery in America. "The Founding Fathers were opposed to slavery," he intoned. "The whole spirit and genius of the American Constitution antagonized it and contemplated its early overthrow. But then, as the demand for their crops increased and machines made the harvesting of cotton more profitable, the planters commenced to extend slavery throughout the South and into the West." Brown's eyes flashed as he shifted to the political changes orchestrated by the slaveholding elite. He told how they gradually were able to seize control of the federal government. "Then began an era of political compromises, and men full of professions of love of country were willing—for peace—to sacrifice everything on which the republic was founded."

Brown abruptly pushed away from the table, stood, and began pacing. "And now," he said, hands clasped behind his back, shoulders thrust forward, "we have reached a point where nothing but war can settle the question."

Phillips's furrowed brow indicated he had doubts about what the old man was telling him.

"It's true," Brown insisted. "If the Republican Party candidate is elected to the presidency next year, there will be civil war."

The old man continued, arguing that the successes achieved in Kansas by the Free State forces had merely checked, not defeated, the slave power. "We are now in a treacherous lull before the storm," he said, his words resonating with absolute conviction. "We are on the eve of one of the greatest wars in history, and I fear slavery will triumph, and there will be an end to all aspirations for human freedom."

Brown returned to his chair. His voice softened. "For my part, I drew my sword in Kansas and I will never sheathe it until this war is over."

Phillips finally spoke. He knew it was Brown's goal to conduct incursions into southern states. He said he feared such guerrilla activities would ultimately lead to the war Brown described, and that he and others like him would be responsible for it. "It is better to trust events," Phillips admonished the old man. "If there is virtue enough in our people to deserve a free government, they will have it."

Brown grew sullen. "You forget the fearful wrongs that are carried on in the name of government and law."

"I do not forget them," Phillips replied. "I regret them." He went on to question Brown's intention to recruit young black men from the slave population for his army of liberation. "The blacks are a peaceful, domestic, inoffensive race," the journalist said. "In all their sufferings they seem incapable of resentment and reprisal."

"You haven't studied them right," Brown protested, "and you haven't studied them long enough. Human nature is the same everywhere."

Phillips countered: "I fear for *all* your men—both black and white. It alarms me that you would lead them into some desperate enterprise where they would be imprisoned and disgraced."

The journalist's refusal to endorse Brown's mission was a disappointment. "Well," the old man said, rising again from his chair, "I thought I could get you to understand this. The world is very pleasant to you. But when your household gods have been broken as mine have been, you will see all this more clearly."

Phillips should have expected his criticisms would be taken as a sign of disloyalty. "Captain," he said, turning to leave, "if you thought this, why did you send for me?"

Brown put his hand on Phillips's shoulder. "No—we must not part thus. I wanted to see you and tell you how it appeared to me. With the help of God, I will do what I believe is best."

The old man's eyes were rimmed with tears as he reached for Phillips's hand. He squeezed it firmly.

It was indeed the last time the two men would see each other—at least in this world.

Brown's frustration was eased when Charlie Tidd rode into Lawrence leading a pair of husky grays. He and Stevens had acquired the horses from a proslavery man who was alleged to have stolen them from a Free State settler. Now the pace of the journey could be accelerated. A pair of workhorses would be pulling each wagon, and Brown could sell the oxen, putting additional money into his pocket for expenses.

The caravan departed Lawrence bound for Holton, a village north of Topeka, where the wagons were to be met by Stevens and Kagi.

But another blustery snowstorm moved onto the prairie, and Brown and his people were forced to seek refuge in some small cabins near Straight Creek, a stream that cut across the trail and was swollen by a premature thaw. While they waited for a lull in the storm, a local farmer informed Brown that a posse led by a US marshal was scouring the neighborhood and would probably arrest him as soon as the weather cleared.

Brown immediately sent Tidd to find Stevens and Kagi and anyone else willing to help. "Tell them Pharaoh seeks to block our exodus from Egypt."

A day and a half later the storm passed and the skies cleared.

One of Brown's scouts reported that the posse he'd been warned about was lying in ambush, waiting for the caravan to ford Straight Creek. Meanwhile, Stevens and Kagi arrived with reinforcements. Twenty-two men—including those from Brown's company—were now standing by, ready to do the old man's bidding.

One of the volunteers spoke up: "What do you propose to do, Captain?"

"Cross the creek and move north."

"But Captain, the water is high and I doubt we can get through."

Brown's response was as icy as the frozen puddles that dotted the ground. "I have set out on this road, and I intend to travel it straight through. The Lord has marked out a path and I shall follow it."

And follow it he did. When his men reached the creek, Brown told them to dismount and march directly into the bone-chilling water.

On the opposite bank the Missouri lawmen looked on in disbelief as Brown's men, carbines at the ready, advanced. When it was obvious they had no intention of turning back, the marshal leaped onto his horse and made a speedy departure.

Chaos reigned as his deputies followed, stumbling over each other in a race for the horses secured among the leafless trees bordering the creek. Panic-stricken, they dug their spurs into the animals with a fury that forever preserved the event in the memories of those who witnessed it.

The final action of the old man's storied career in Kansas would be known thereafter as the Battle of the Spurs. "Old Captain Brown is not to be taken by boys," noted a report of the incident in a Leavenworth newspaper, "and he cordially invites all proslavery *men* to try their hands at arresting him."

The caravan crossed the border into Nebraska and headed for Iowa. Kansas Territory had seen the last of John Brown.

————— •••• —————

The wagons made it to Tabor without further incident. But the Iowa town that had welcomed Brown in the past now harbored doubts about his recent actions. Residents of the abolitionist community, like settlers and politicians in Kansas, were critical of his Missouri raid and feared retribution if they appeared too friendly.

The old man asked the town's mayor for permission to explain his actions at a public meeting. He assumed he'd be praised for rescuing the slaves; perhaps some of the people even might be willing to help defray the cost of conveying the slaves to freedom in Canada. His request received a less than enthusiastic response, though the mayor agreed to let him speak to a small group of concerned citizens gathered in a church.

As Brown stood in the pulpit and began to tell his story, a prominent physician and slaveholder from nearby Saint Joseph, Missouri, entered the church. With his gaze fixed on the visitor, the old man said, "One has just come to this meeting whom I would prefer not to hear what I have to say and therefore I respectfully request him to withdraw."

The visitor took a seat and folded his arms defiantly. The grim-faced audience sat in stony silence. Stevens rose and declared in a voice seething with contempt, "So help me God, I never will sit in council with one who buys and sells human flesh."

Together, Stevens and Brown headed for the door. The rest of Brown's men followed. As he walked out of the church, the old man said in a voice loud enough to be heard by all present, "We had best look to our arms. We are not yet among friends."

The caravan left the following day.

His rejection by the citizens of Tabor didn't deter Brown. If anything, it emboldened him. Knowing that bounty hunters would be looking to collect the rewards posted for his capture, he told Kagi he'd no longer engage in evasive maneuvers by choosing remote roads and avoiding towns. Henceforth, the caravan would take only the main roads across Iowa. "Any who try to take me and my company are cowards," he said. "We are in the right and ought not fear any man."

Traveling in the severe winter weather had taken a toll on the old man. He was suffering from a "terrible gathering" in his head, and breathing was becoming difficult for him. He told Kagi his failing health was becoming as much his enemy as slavery.

The farther the wagons moved east, the more cordially he was received by the citizens in the villages and towns of Iowa. He found many Iowans openly hostile to the Fugitive Slave Act. Since slave catchers were combing the area for runaways and didn't hesitate to kidnap persons of color, whether slave or not, the Iowans figured that if the rights of free blacks could be violated, everyone's rights were in jeopardy. They viewed Brown's taking of the Missouri slaves as a much-needed expression of outrage against a law that denied the principles on which the nation was created.

No Iowan was more receptive to Brown than Josiah Grinnell, the founder of the town bearing his name and the most notable abolitionist in the state. Grinnell showered Brown with praise, resupplied the caravan with provisions, and arranged for the liberated slaves to be taken to Chicago by rail.

When the caravan reached the railhead near Iowa City, the freight car commissioned by Grinnell hadn't yet arrived. For their safety and comfort, Brown took the refugees to a family in the nearby Quaker village of Springdale, once the location of his military school. The old man had time to retrieve the weapons that had been in storage there since the previous winter. Fifteen cases of Sharps carbines and five boxes containing two hundred pistols were loaded onto the Conestoga.

Brown also had an opportunity to meet two Quakers who expressed an interest in joining him. Young Barclay Coppoc had been to Kansas and knew the old man by reputation. Older brother Edwin listened to the stories Barclay told of Brown's deeds. Signing up for duty meant both men would have to renounce their religious commitment to nonviolence. They did so gladly.

The freight car finally arrived, coupled between a locomotive and a passenger car. The refugees got on board. Brown had already purchased seats in the passenger car for himself, Kagi, and Stevens. The old man needed to get to Chicago in order to arrange for the transportation of the liberated slaves to Detroit.

Meanwhile, the wagons—filled with crates of carbines and revolvers hidden under mattresses—were left in the hands of the remaining soldiers: Jerry Anderson, Charlie Tidd, the Coppoc brothers, and two others. They were to continue overland to Ohio, where Brown intended to store the weapons and sell the wagons and horses and the rest of the confiscated livestock. As usual, he was in desperate need of cash.

Chicago—a city of almost a hundred thousand—turned out to be as responsive to Brown's needs as the tiny Iowa village of Grinnell. He'd been told about an ambitious thirty-nine-year-old Scottish immigrant who had opened a private detective

agency in the city and put an end to a series of train robber-
ies. His name was Allan Pinkerton. Brown learned Pinkerton
was also a social activist who fought for universal suffrage in
Scotland and had taken up the cause of abolitionism since
coming to America. The Scotsman knew about Brown and
was happy to assist. Pinkerton not only found another railroad
car for the refugees, he also collected $500 from friends and
business associates.

As soon as Pinkerton put the money in Brown's hands,
the old man experienced a remarkable recovery from the
"terrible gathering" in his head. He told Kagi and Stevens
he was more certain than ever he was destined to fulfill his
mission. He put Kagi in charge of the railroad car with its
cargo of emancipated slaves while he and Stevens took the
first available train to Detroit.

On the morning of March 12, 1859, Brown, Kagi, and Stevens
stood on a wharf on the Detroit River. Alongside were the
women and men rescued from slavery. Together they had
completed a journey across two territories and four states in
the dead of winter and, along the way, celebrated the birth
of a twelfth freedman to the wife of Jim Daniels. The couple
named their new son John Brown Daniels.

The liberated slaves were subdued yet profoundly moved,
some weeping quietly, others seeking out Brown's hand as
they filed past him and stepped onto the ferry bound for
Canada and a new life of freedom.

Coincidentally, Frederick Douglass happened to be in
Detroit for a speaking engagement. Word of Brown's deed had
spread through the city. When the old man was discovered at

the railroad station, he was invited to a reception for Douglass at the home of a local black leader. Brown accepted the invitation and shortly thereafter found himself in the company of a dozen men, some of whom he knew from the Chatham convention. Brown thought it appropriate to disclose the new timetable for his invasion and to make a plea for recruits and money. However, he soon found himself embroiled in an argument with Douglass that raised the eyebrows of those present—all of whom held both men in high esteem. The argument stemmed from Brown's announcement that he was considering arming liberated slaves with weapons he intended to take from the US armory at Harpers Ferry, Virginia.

Later, when he returned to the railroad station, the old man told Stevens and Kagi, "I'm not sure our friend is as committed to the war on slavery as I once thought. Mr. Douglass discourages our efforts to move boldly against the slave power."

At dusk, Brown, Kagi, and Stevens boarded a train bound for Cleveland, where they would wait for the wagons and livestock to catch up. Once he reached Ohio, the old man wanted to take advantage of every opportunity to raise money and enlist soldiers.

Cleveland was rife with posters offering hefty rewards for Brown's capture. Yet, flanked by Kagi and Stevens, the old man walked the streets with renewed confidence, often passing by the office of the federal marshal who put up the posters. Like other staunchly antislavery towns and villages in northern Ohio, Cleveland was in no mood to see a man with Brown's reputation thrown in jail. In fact there was a demand

for him to speak at a public venue—which he was happy to
do for a modest admission charge.

A Cleveland newspaper advertised Brown as the "terror of
all Border Ruffiandom" and announced he'd be giving "a true
account of the recent troubles in Kansas and of the late invasion of Missouri and what it was done for, together with other
highly interesting matters that have never yet appeared in the
papers." The turnout at a downtown lecture hall was modest—
a result, perhaps, of a combination of inclement weather and
a competing event: a rally protesting the arrest and trial of
persons who participated in the rescue of a runaway slave captured in the village of Oberlin, twenty miles west of Cleveland.

After his speech the old man was approached by the
Cleveland Plain Dealer's city editor, whose pseudonym was
Artemus Ward. Brown was familiar with the journalist, knew
him to be cynical toward those who professed high-minded
ideals. But, as had been the case since he began his crusade,
Brown viewed the press as his ally. It was important his name
and cause be placed before the public as often as possible—
even if the result wasn't always to his liking.

"Well, Captain," Ward queried, "do you intend to continue
to drive proslavery settlers out of Kansas?"

"I have never driven men out of Kansas," Brown replied.
"I believe in settling matters on the spot, using the enemy as
I would fence stakes—driving them into the ground where
they can become permanent settlers."

The journalist fought to suppress a smile. He said, "You
know, of course, President Buchanan has put a price on your
head."

"Two hundred fifty dollars," Brown responded with feigned
pride. "And I have put a price on *his* head." He paused, then
quipped, "Two dollars and fifty cents."

As they left the lecture hall and leaned into the gusts of a rainstorm, the old man turned to Kagi and Stevens and said, "I think Mr. Ward got what he came for."

The story appeared in the *Plain Dealer* the following day. "A man of pluck is Brown," Ward wrote. "He shows it in his walk, talk, and actions. . . . A resolution approving his course in Kansas was introduced and adopted by the audience. He thanked the audience very sincerely, although he was perfectly sure his course was right all along."

The wagons and livestock had not yet arrived from Iowa when Brown left Cleveland and set out for the Ohio homesteads of sons John Jr. and Jason. Stevens went along, but Kagi—now a part-time correspondent for Greeley's *Tribune*—stayed behind. He figured the Oberlin affair would be of interest to his abolitionist boss.

Brown's visit to Jason in Akron confirmed the old man's expectations. Jason would have nothing to do with a plan to invade the South. He'd fought in Kansas but had no desire to continue to participate in his father's war on slavery. Jason was a farmer, not a warrior. But steady, reliable Owen—who was helping Jason with the spring planting—said he would be ready when called.

Brown and Stevens traveled next to Ashtabula County, east of Cleveland, to the home of John Jr. and his family. His eldest son told Brown that he—like his brother Jason—was no longer able to serve as a soldier in the old man's anti-slavery campaign. He said he still hadn't recovered from the physical and emotional wounds of Kansas, but he agreed to a noncombatant role. He'd oversee the storage and delivery of weapons and ammunition, assist in recruiting, and act as a liaison between Brown and his men—many of whom would be separated from their leader while final preparations for the invasion were completed.

John Jr. then introduced his father to forty-four-year-old Dangerfield Newby, a recently manumitted slave whose wife and children were held in bondage in Warrenton, Virginia, forty miles south of Harpers Ferry. Newby was active in Underground Railroad activities but was hoping to find a way to free his family; he wanted Brown to know he was available for service. The old man told him that it would soon be possible to satisfy his wishes and that John Jr. would let him know when and where he was needed.

When Brown and Stevens returned to Cleveland, Kagi had good news. The wagons had arrived. As soon as the guns could be delivered to John Jr., the wagons and livestock would be ready for auction. Kagi also had much to say about the trial of the thirty-seven professors and students from Oberlin College who had been charged under the Fugitive Slave Act with rescuing the runaway slave. The trial had attracted a crowd of almost twelve thousand antislavery protestors.

Kagi said, "If the people of Ohio bespeak the attitude of the rest of the North, the time to strike a blow against slavery couldn't be better than at this very moment."

Brown liked what Kagi had to say and gave him a vigorous nod of approval.

"That's not all, Captain. I've signed up two more men."

Kagi was referring to twenty-four-year-old Lewis Leary and Leary's twenty-five-year-old cousin, John Copeland. Their parents were from North Carolina and had moved to Ohio in order to escape the racism they were subjected to as free blacks. Copeland attended Oberlin College, and Leary worked as a harness maker. When Kagi met them they were among the protestors supporting the rescuers of the runaway slave. They had read about Brown's Kansas activities and were eager to join his company.

"Tell them the call to action is close at hand," Brown told Kagi. "They should take care to alert their families."

———————

The sale of the wagons and livestock took place in front of a Cleveland hotel where Brown and his men had taken rooms. The old man was enjoying a rare period of extended good health and was decidedly optimistic about the future. His men sat on the steps of the hotel, ready to assist in the auction. Brown had shed his mantle of solemnity and seemed amused by the gaggle of prospective buyers assembled in the street.

"Where's the title to these horses?" someone shouted.

"No title necessary," Brown shouted back. "These animals are to me like slaves are to the Vermont judge who said he wouldn't consider a slave as property until the owner produced a bill of sale from the Almighty."

Laughter.

"You mean the horses come from slave country?"

"They are good abolitionist horses now," Brown declared. "I converted them." When the auction concluded, Brown did well enough to send Mary a bank draft for $150.

The respite from his illness, however, was short lived. The chills returned, along with the gathering in his head. When he resumed his journey, Brown wasn't traveling alone. At Kagi's insistence, Jerry Anderson accompanied him to attend to his needs.

While Brown and Anderson traveled to New York by rail, the men who remained behind—including Kagi and Stevens—found temporary jobs, as they had after the Chatham convention. They wouldn't stray far from northeastern Ohio. The old man wanted to be able to muster them quickly.

Before reaching the North Elba farm, Brown made two stops in western New York, the first at the Rochester printing shop of Frederick Douglass. Brown was still disturbed by the confrontation that took place in Detroit and didn't want to jeopardize his relationship with the man he wanted with him when the invasion commenced. Douglass agreed to meet with him before the blow was struck.

Brown next visited the Peterboro estate of his patron Gerrit Smith. At a gathering of abolitionists hosted by Smith, Brown told the story of the Missouri raid. It moved some to tears. Smith reiterated his faith in Brown and handed him $400, adding that he planned to raise several hundred more.

Prospects for the future looked bright as Brown and Anderson left Smith's mansion and boarded a train bound for Albany; from there they would travel north by boat before completing the final miles to North Elba on foot. Brown told Anderson that he longed for his family and the comfort of his remote community. He missed the mountains and forests of the Adirondacks.

———— ••••• ————

Now, lying on his back in the bedroom of the North Elba farmhouse, still in despair at having to be treated like the invalid he'd become, an anxious Brown stared at the ceiling. He could smell the aromas coming from the kitchen. Mary, with the help of the girls, was preparing the evening meal.

Brown could hear the distant, rhythmic cracking of logs being split; Jerry Anderson was performing yet another task that allowed Mary to devote more time to her husband's care. Brown appreciated Anderson's help but didn't like what it implied—that he was dependent on others. He hated being bedridden, rendered helpless by an affliction that struck with little warning. Especially since he was so close to carrying out the plan he'd been contemplating for twenty years. He now had the weapons he needed. George Stearns soon would supply him with the money he needed. And though he hoped to raise an army of one hundred soldiers, he wouldn't be deterred if he had to carry on with a smaller force. After all, he'd declared publicly that a few good men in the right—and knowing they are—could overturn a king.

He was glad he'd gotten commitments from Oliver and Watson, as well as son-in-law Henry Thompson's brothers, Will and Dauphin. Neither his son Salmon nor Henry—both of whom fought in Kansas—could be persuaded to join him. Though Salmon still possessed the family's antislavery fervor, he was skeptical about the old man's ability as a tactician and even told Oliver to be aware of "Father's insistence that everything should be arranged perfectly before making a move." Salmon warned his brother, "Beware that his dalliances don't get you trapped."

Confinement to his bed caused the old man much grief. He feared the delay his present infirmity produced might prompt his benefactors to abandon him. Already there had been too many delays. Sanborn wrote him that a member of the secret committee Brown deeply admired—Thomas Wentworth Higginson—was expressing doubts as to whether the old man would ever live up to his promises. Brown's desire to strike a blow on Southern soil, in Higginson's words, "had begun to seem rather chimerical."

"I am not dead yet," the old man muttered as he pushed away the covers and forced his legs over the edge of the bed. The thump of his feet hitting the floor brought daughter Annie to the door.

"Father," she said, "you must not get up. You're not well—"

"Tell your mother I shall be eating her soup. I have been lying in this bed too long. Lazarus already had risen by now."

So saying, the old man willed his body to respond, refusing to allow Mary to assist as he struggled to dress himself.

Later, at the kitchen table, they all joined hands—Mary, the three daughters, and Jerry Anderson. Brown asked his God to bless the food that had been set before them. He asked a special blessing for those held in bondage.

Hardly a word was spoken during the meal. The old man swallowed only a few spoonfuls of Mary's soup. He was still sick, but he wouldn't allow himself the luxury of a lengthy recovery. Stearns was waiting for him in Boston. Cook was gathering intelligence in Virginia. John Jr. was guarding an arsenal of weapons and telling prospective recruits that an attack on Southern slaveholders was near. Kagi was in Cleveland, waiting to head south with the rest of the company as soon as the old man gave the order. And one thousand unfinished pikes were in the hands of toolmaker Charles Blair in Connecticut; Brown had no intention of leaving the pikes behind.

It was early in the evening when the old man stood with Anderson in front of the North Elba farmhouse and gazed at Whiteface Mountain. The fading twilight had transformed remnants of ice and snow at the summit into patches of gold. It was a fleeting moment, and Brown had seen the spectacle before and wanted Anderson to witness it with him.

"In four days, I shall reach my fifty-ninth year," Brown said, his eyes still fixed on the mountain. "I am not afraid of dying. A man dies when his time comes. But I hold a commission from God Almighty to act against slavery, and much remains to be done."

11

Four Months Later
Late August 1859
Southern Pennsylvania

Brown sat on a stone slab on the floor of a limestone quarry that had been carved out of the wooded uplands on the outskirts of the town of Chambersburg. Steep walls rose from a basin strewn with rubble. At one end of the basin a pool of tepid water bloomed with green algae. Leaning against the slab were a Sharps carbine and a fishing pole. A blanket and a rucksack lay at the old man's feet. Since the quarry hadn't been worked for years, he felt it was remote and secluded enough for a meeting with Frederick Douglass. This was the meeting Douglass had agreed to attend when Brown was ready to launch his invasion.

Douglass had arrived in Chambersburg by rail the previous morning. Traveling with him was Shields Green, the fugitive slave whose friendship Brown cultivated during the weeks he spent at Douglass's Rochester home drafting a constitution for a provisional government. Douglass and Green were staying with Henry Watson, a local barber who let slip the fact that the acclaimed orator would be stopping in Chambersburg before returning to New York. A representative of the mayor had met Douglass's train to welcome the distinguished

visitor and invite him to speak at the town hall the following evening. Douglass accepted the invitation, hoping that in
doing so there would be no questions asked about the reasons
for his layover and the identity of his traveling companion.

In the morning, before opening his shop, the barber led
Douglass and Green to a gravel ramp, the quarry's only
entrance and exit. Douglass and Green descended to the
quarry floor.

Brown stepped forward to greet his visitors. His skin was
pasty and deep lines were visible under a beard trimmed back
from its former length. Beads of sweat clung to the ridges of
his brow. Douglass presented the old man with an envelope
containing some cash, a token of appreciation from a mutual
friend in New York.

In the sweltering August heat, surrounded by precipitous
walls that shut off any hope of a cooling breeze, Douglass and
Green sat down on a block of limestone and listened while
Brown paced, detailing his plan for invading Virginia. High
above, John Kagi patrolled the rim of the quarry, a carbine
slung over his shoulder.

As Brown spoke, Douglass seemed distracted, the expression
on his face alternating between perplexity and exasperation.

The old man stopped pacing. "It's settled, Fred," he
declared. "I mean to take the armory at Harpers Ferry—the
musket factory, the arsenal, the rifle works . . ." His voice
trailed off.

Douglass took out a handkerchief and blotted the moisture
from his face. "Forgive me, John, but you're still talking about
attacking a federal installation." A pause. "That's insurrection."
Another pause. "That's treason."

"Call it what you will," Brown said. "I shall take Harpers
Ferry. It was my hope that you would stand with me."

Douglass already had expressed doubts about Brown's plan. And just days before his arrival in Chambersburg he'd made his feelings known again during a meeting he and Brown attended in Philadelphia, where Douglass had stopped to take part in an antislavery rally. Brown had gotten word of the rally and was concerned that such an event—so close in time and place to Harpers Ferry—would create a climate of suspicion that could jeopardize the invasion. His apprehension was confirmed when he got to Philadelphia in time to hear one of the rally's leaders make a speech in which he claimed there was "a grand project afoot" involving an army of Northern blacks that soon would be marching south. When the rally was over, Brown and Douglass—along with several of Philadelphia's most influential black citizens—sat down to talk. Brown expressed his concerns, then announced he was on the verge of executing a plan that would send fear into the hearts of slaveholders. To Brown's chagrin, Douglass seemed indifferent and made no effort to endorse the plan. The old man returned to Chambersburg worried that the confidence of his Philadelphia allies had been shaken and their support compromised.

Now, at the quarry, Douglass continued to question Brown's judgment. "The measure you propose will be construed as an attack on the federal government," Douglass insisted. "It will array the whole country against us—the North as well as the South."

Brown didn't like defending the mission that represented his life's calling, especially when the person challenging him was someone he thought shared his beliefs and trusted him. He said, "Maybe an attack on the government is just what this nation needs."

Douglass persisted. "I know nothing of the tactics of an armed incursion, but from what you've told me you will be entering a perfect steel trap. Once in, you'll never get out alive." He lifted his arm, made a sweeping motion, his fingers tracing the rim of the quarry. "This place is no different from where you are going. Here there are high walls; there you will be surrounded by mountains and hemmed in by water."

Douglass obviously was unfamiliar with Brown's theories of guerrilla warfare, particularly his belief that high ground wasn't always a strong position. "If necessary, I can cut my way out," the old man said. "Besides, I shall have hostages."

A look of astonishment spread across Douglass's face.

"I shall take a number of the best citizens in the neighborhood as prisoners," Brown asserted. "If worse comes to worst, I shall use them to dictate terms of egress."

Though he must have sensed the futility of arguing with the old man, Douglass refused to give up. He cited plans Brown had spoken of during their ten-year friendship. "I recall you telling me that if you could drive slavery out of one county in a Southern state, it would be a great gain; it would weaken the slave system throughout the entire region. By making the slaveholder's investment insecure, you would be destroying its value." Brown's new plan, Douglass lamented, bore little resemblance to the one described by the Kansas warrior who came to Rochester to draw up documents for a provisional government to be established in the Appalachian Mountains.

They wrangled until the sun dipped below the rim of the quarry, the high walls casting the basin in shadows.

Douglass stood. "I've agreed to speak to the citizens of Chambersburg this evening," he said. "My train doesn't leave until noon tomorrow. We'll meet again in the morning. Perhaps, after a night's rest, we'll both see things differently."

Brown's lips were pressed tightly together. He nodded, avoided Douglass's eyes, grasped the outstretched hand, then Green's—the latter having remained silent throughout the lengthy debate.

Kagi escorted Douglass and Green back to town and the home of the barber, Henry Watson. Kagi would stay at the boardinghouse Brown was using as his mailing address. He'd return in the morning with Douglass and Green.

Having chosen to remain at the quarry, Brown opened his rucksack and pulled out a chunk of dried beef, muttered a few words of gratitude to his God, then ate, waiting for the darkness.

Lying on his blanket under the stars, the rucksack as his pillow, the old man thought about Mary and the evening they had spent together before he and Jerry Anderson departed for Massachusetts. He'd been suffering from his chronic illness and couldn't sleep. Yet he felt a need to talk, and Mary was his sounding board as he spoke of his purposes and his plan for invading the South.

Long before he'd sent John Cook to reconnoiter Harpers Ferry, Brown had expressed a desire to secure a cache of arms for what he hoped would be an ever-expanding army of freedom fighters. From his time in the wool business, he'd observed firsthand the lax security at the federal armory in Springfield, Massachusetts. He expected the armory at Harpers Ferry to be no different. But now that he possessed two hundred Sharps carbines and an equal number of revolvers, and intended to acquire a thousand pikes very soon, his need for weapons wasn't as crucial as it had been.

Still, he believed the mountains of northern Virginia were ideally suited for an initial thrust into the South. He was aware that a principal route of the Underground Railroad had its origin near Harpers Ferry, which meant shuttling liberated women and children to the North wouldn't be a formidable task. And he also felt he knew the character of the inhabitants of the region, both in southern Pennsylvania and northern Virginia; among them there had to be willing accomplices.

Mary listened as her husband railed against a nation asleep, a nation that had gone numb to the principles embodied in the Declaration of Independence. The armory at Harpers Ferry, he told her, operated under the authority of a federal government that sanctioned slavery. And since the government had become an accessory to a crime that violated the principles on which the nation was founded, he felt perfectly justified in attacking it. It was his duty to do what was necessary to awaken a nation that had lost its moral compass.

Brown spoke of his most powerful collaborators—the journalists. He saw what they had done for him in Kansas, whether favorable to his actions or opposed. If he could capture a federal armory—a victory greater than anything he'd accomplished in Kansas—the newspapers would do the rest. The nation will have been awakened, and the trumpet will have sounded for the slaves; they would know their friends had come and were ready to lead them to freedom.

When he and Anderson departed the Adirondack homestead, Brown hadn't fully recovered from his illness. But he could stay no longer. There were matters demanding his attention—the most important being the money promised by George Stearns, chief spokesman for the secret committee.

The old man told Mary he'd return to say good-bye after he'd taken care of his obligations.

En route to Boston, Brown and Anderson stopped in Concord, where they met Franklin Sanborn. Sanborn had arranged a celebration for Brown's fifty-ninth birthday—a dinner hosted by Henry David Thoreau. Later in the evening Brown spoke at the Concord town hall to an audience that included Ralph Waldo Emerson.

Accompanied by Sanborn, the old man conducted another fundraising campaign in and around Boston. He met with his abolitionist supporters, among them secret committee member Dr. Samuel Gridley Howe. Brown was introduced to Howe's wife, Julia, and made a favorable impression. But the old man was never at ease with the formality and polite conversation expected in the parlors of his prospective donors. When told by one of his hosts that "firmness at the ballot box by the North and West" would solve the slavery issue, Brown retorted, "Nothing but bayonets and bullets can settle it now."

At the Boston hotel where he and Jerry Anderson were staying, Brown met Stearns, who told him that he and Gerrit Smith had raised $2,000. That evening Brown and Stearns enjoyed a relaxed dinner in the hotel dining room. They talked freely about a variety of subjects—from the unrealized potential of Samuel Morse's telegraph to the steam locomotive and its role in the nation's westward expansion, to their support for the advancement of women's rights. Out of respect for the wishes of Stearns and the other secret benefactors, Brown was careful to avoid naming the exact target of his invasion.

The next morning he and Anderson headed for Collinsville, Connecticut, home of Charles Blair, the toolmaker Brown had contracted to fabricate the pikes. Two years had passed since the old man placed the order and handed over a deposit. Blair admitted he had quit working on the pikes some time ago. They were to be used, after all, in Kansas, and the troubles in Kansas had all but disappeared.

"You finish them," Brown snapped. "I'll put them to good use." Blair said he'd do his best but couldn't promise a completion date.

As the fundraising campaign came to a close, Brown added the money from Stearns to what he and Sanborn collected. The old man figured he had enough to go forward with his plan. If he were to strike the blow on the Fourth of July—a date suggested by Sanborn as symbolically appropriate—he'd have to move quickly.

By the end of the first week in June, he'd completed his business in New England and—as he promised Mary—he and Anderson paid a final visit to North Elba. It was a time for farewells—perhaps the last days he'd spend with family and neighbors at the Adirondack homestead. As soon as he arrived, however, he was stricken with yet another attack of his malarial illness. But he wouldn't allow it to interfere with his work. He needed to assess the recruiting efforts of John Jr. and to make preparations for the shipment south of guns and supplies. Though he was barely able to travel, he headed for Ohio in the company of Jerry Anderson and youngest son Oliver. Brown's son Watson would have gone along had his wife, Isabella, not given birth a few weeks earlier. Watson promised that he and Isabella's brothers—Will and Dauphin Thompson—would join the company as soon as Brown announced he was prepared to launch the invasion.

When Brown arrived at the Ohio farm of John Jr., he found his eldest son still plagued by the physical and emotional stress suffered in Kansas. He'd become paranoid about the weapons stored in his barn and was convinced that federal marshals were on the verge of discovering them. Though Brown was saddened by his son's condition, he promised that the guns would be transferred to another hiding place. Then he gave him money to make a trip to Canada—to inform those who attended the Chatham convention that the invasion date was drawing near.

Brown's next stop was Cleveland, where John Kagi still worked as a part-time journalist for Horace Greeley. Kagi had kept in touch with the steadfast few who remained committed to the mission; they were ready to muster, he told Brown, just as soon as he gave the order. After asking Kagi to see to the transfer of the guns from John Jr.'s barn to a secure location, Brown announced he'd be calling for them, along with the men, as soon as he found a temporary receiving depot somewhere in southern Pennsylvania.

By the time Brown picked up Owen at Jason's farm in Akron, the end of June was near, and it would be impossible to strike a blow by the Fourth of July. But at least Brown was ready to head south. With Owen as the new addition to his party, Brown set out for Chambersburg, a town close to the borders of Maryland and Virginia. The four men— Brown, Owen, Oliver, and Jerry Anderson—henceforth would be known to strangers as Isaac Smith and sons.

The choice of Chambersburg—fifty miles north of Harpers Ferry—was no accident. It was once the home of Martin Delaney, a free black who had migrated to Canada and was instrumental in organizing the Chatham convention. Delaney assured Brown there were people in Chambersburg who would assist him—among them Mary Ritner, the widow of the son of a former Pennsylvania governor who also happened to be an abolitionist. Mrs. Ritner had converted her home into a boardinghouse. Delaney also mentioned a conductor on the Underground Railroad, the barber Henry Watson. When Brown and his three "sons" reached Chambersburg, Mrs. Ritner offered her house as a destination for freight and volunteers. The barber said he, too, was willing to help.

The old man's next task was to find a location that could be used as a staging area capable of housing men and arms until he was ready to launch the invasion. On July 5, he found such a place, a small farm in the Maryland hills five miles northeast of Harpers Ferry. The farm belonged to the heirs of a local physician, Dr. Booth Kennedy. Brown was able to rent the property until March of the following year. Included in the price of thirty-five dollars were a two-story split-log farmhouse and a log outbuilding across the road. As soon as he signed the lease for the Kennedy farm, Brown sent Oliver back to North Elba with a letter asking Mary and daughter Annie to join him. He needed to create an illusion of normalcy at the farm, and he believed the presence of women would divert attention from the men and arms arriving from Chambersburg. Mary wasn't willing to leave her young daughters, but fifteen-year-old Annie was eager to go. And it didn't take much persuasion from Oliver to get his new wife, Martha, just turned seventeen, to take Mary's place. The couple had been married a little over a year, and Martha welcomed the opportunity to be with her twenty-year-old husband right up to the time of the invasion.

The two young women arrived at the farm in mid-July. Shortly thereafter the men and freight began trickling in from Brown's Chambersburg headquarters. Meanwhile, he busied himself creating alliances in the neighboring rural communities. He met with black ministers, conductors on the Underground Railroad, and members of secret antislavery societies. He also walked the streets of Harpers Ferry with John Cook, who had been gathering intelligence for more than a year. Brown wanted to personally observe the armory's security measures and view the locations of the various government facilities.

By mid-August, however, the process of gearing up for the invasion had slowed to a crawl. Brown was disappointed he didn't get the response he expected from those who attended the Chatham convention. He was particularly disheartened when Richard Realf, a young Englishman, failed to come. Realf had been with him during the trek across Iowa in the winter of 1857. A journalist and poet with a deep commitment to the abolition of slavery, Realf was inspired by Brown's idea of forming a provisional government for the slaves he intended to liberate. Brown had told Realf, "If a third party doesn't step between the slaveholder and the slaves, the slaves will one day rise up against their masters, and the result will be a bloody war of extermination," then added that he—John Brown—would act as the third party. And the provisional government with its constitution, Brown said, would bring order to the influx of slaves and keep bloody excesses to a minimum.

Aside from the lack of volunteers, the old man had other concerns. The men at the farm were getting restless; they'd made unauthorized jaunts into town when he was away. They wrote letters disclosing information that should have remained confidential. And Cook, who was obliged to marry a young girl he'd gotten pregnant, was spending too much time talking to strangers. Brown worried the whole operation would be betrayed by an indiscreet comment.

To compound difficulties, he was running short of cash. It embarrassed him that he had to beg for more money. So he wrote John Jr., who had just completed a recruiting trip to Canada, to do it for him. "It will cost no more for you to solicit for me a little more assistance while attending to your business," he wrote his son.

John Jr. immediately went to Boston, where George Stearns presented him with a draft for $200 along with a message: "Tell your father we have the fullest confidence in his endeavor, whatever may be the result." Brown was relieved to receive the money. It arrived just as he was preparing to meet with Frederick Douglass at the quarry outside Chambersburg.

Now, as he lay in the stillness of the dark quarry with his head resting on his rucksack, Brown fretted over his meeting with Douglass. Maybe Douglass was right. They both might think differently in the morning. He looked up and saw the stars shimmering in the night sky. At times like this he felt closest to his God. Slowly he drifted into sleep.

Brown had been awake for some time when the doleful cry of a mourning dove prompted him to sit up and pull on his boots. In the gray dawn he picked up his canteen and walked up the gravel ramp. He stopped at a stream that flowed through a wooded area. He washed himself, filled his canteen, and returned to the quarry floor.

It was a little after eight o'clock when Kagi arrived with Douglass and Green. Kagi went back to patrolling the rim of the quarry. Douglass and Green made their way down the ramp.

Brown opened the conversation by asking Douglass about his speaking engagement at the Chambersburg town hall. "I was received very well," Douglass said, adding that he was forced to pause several times because of outbursts of applause.

As their conversation turned to the invasion, it became clear that Brown hadn't altered his position. His mind was made up. "My men are ready," he said. "And I am ready to lead them." He was as immovable as the block of stone on which Douglass and Green were sitting.

"If you fail," Douglass said, "it will be fatal to all engaged. But it will be worse for those you liberate. For them, death will be a welcome deliverance from the wrath of their masters."

Though he was resigned to the inevitable, Brown made another plea. As if he were a father about to leave home on a perilous journey, Brown took hold of Douglass's arm. "Come with me, my friend. I shall defend you with my life. I want you for a special purpose. When I strike, the bees will begin to swarm, and I shall want you to help me hive them."

As expected, Douglass declined. He'd continue to fight slavery—but not alongside John Brown. The old man would have to hive the bees without him.

Meanwhile, the fugitive Shields Green—who had listened patiently for several hours while uttering hardly a word— declared that he wanted to go with Brown. An illiterate slave who had tasted freedom, Green had come to respect and admire the old man and his cause. Later, as Douglass boarded a train in Chambersburg, Green was already at Henry Watson's waiting to be shuttled to the Maryland farm.

Three days after Douglass's departure, Brown was sitting at a table in Kagi's room in Mary Ritner's boardinghouse. He was writing a letter when Kagi walked in and laid a newspaper on the table. It was the most recent edition of a Chambersburg weekly, the *Valley Spirit*.

"You'll be interested in this, Captain," Kagi said. He tapped his finger on a headline that bore Douglass's name. Brown put his pencil aside and began reading:

> Frederick Douglass, a gentleman of color, paid our town a visit on Saturday last to brighten the prospects of his Republican friends who are now so hopelessly in the "dark." There is no calling into question the extraordinary ability of Mr. Douglass as an orator. He is an elegant and powerful speaker, and he possesses a clear well modulated voice and a style of elocution unaffected and impressive. His discourse was well received by a large and attentive audience and was interrupted by occasional demonstrations of applause from those who seemed disposed to favor his peculiar doctrine. His aim is to place the negro on an equality with the white man—to have him eat at the same table, sit in the same pew, and vote at the same ballot box. He would appear to forget altogether that the Creator Himself has made a distinction when He established the great and immovable barrier of color between the races . . .

Brown finished reading, laid the newspaper on the table, folded his arms across his chest, and lowered his head. Kagi remained standing, waiting for Brown to say something.

When the old man finally spoke, the rasping metallic voice seemed to be weighed down by a great sadness. "I am afraid, Kagi, we hardly grasp the magnitude of this nation's illness. If we succeed in our efforts to help the slaves achieve freedom, it shall be only a first step. Those who come after us will have more miseries to face. I have no doubt the time of healing will be long and painful."

The newspaper story left Brown dejected, but he couldn't dwell on it. There were more immediate and practical matters on his mind. He'd hoped to have at least fifty soldiers, all trained and under arms, before launching the invasion. It was now apparent he'd have to make do with fewer than half that number. And though he was encouraged by the responses he'd gotten from slaves and free blacks from neighboring plantations and settlements, he wasn't sure how many would show up. Perhaps they would come in greater numbers after he'd taken the armory. But if something went wrong, it would be like Douglass said—the runaways would suffer greater consequences than his regular soldiers.

The old man had planned to strike within a few days, but it was beginning to look more like weeks. He picked up his pencil, forced himself to complete the letter he'd been working on, though his thoughts were elsewhere. He looked up as Kagi turned to leave. Kagi was a loyal and able follower—the person he designated second in command of his army of liberation. The old man felt he needed to say something reassuring. He was aware of Kagi's skepticism when it came to matters of religion, that he claimed it was impossible to know of the existence of a deity. Still, Brown chose words that mirrored his own faith.

"We must remember," he said, "God reigns in the best possible manner. Our destiny is in his hands."

Kagi gave a nod, and Brown resumed writing.

12

Two Months Later
October 15, 1859
Kennedy Farm, Western Maryland

The air was heavy with the threat of rain as Brown guided a one-horse covered wagon onto the lane leading to the farmhouse in the hills of western Maryland. Since mid-July the wagon had been transporting men and freight from Chambersburg. This time the only passenger was twenty-two-year-old Francis Jackson Merriam, frail and blind in one eye. The wagon's arrival at dusk brought to a close the endless waiting for volunteers to show up at the Kennedy farm.

Merriam was the grandson of the president of the American Anti-Slavery Society and had traveled with James Redpath on a fact-finding tour of Haiti and the slaveholding states. What Merriam witnessed appalled him, and he was eager to convert his abolitionist zeal into action. Redpath, the journalist who accidentally stumbled onto Brown's camp in Kansas, was by now an unapologetic promoter of the old man. Merriam had listened as Redpath spoke enthusiastically of Brown and his cause, disclosing what he knew of the plan to invade Virginia. When Merriam learned he might be able to join Brown's company, he collected some money—$600 in gold—and boarded a train in Boston bound for Chambersburg.

"The good Lord in heaven who furnishes our daily bread sent him to Father with his money just at the moment it was needed," said Brown's daughter Annie when she heard about Merriam's decision.

As Merriam handed Brown a fistful of double eagles, the old man breathed easier. He would soon dispatch his new recruit to Baltimore to make some emergency purchases. Even though there was a tidy sum left over, Brown intended to live off the spoils of war for the foreseeable future.

The wagon carrying Brown and Merriam to the small split-log farmhouse was transporting more than the two men. Concealed under a canvas tarpaulin were much-needed tools and munitions: a sledgehammer, a crowbar, a pair of wire-cutting pliers, a large quantity of percussion caps, and a case of .52 caliber paper cartridges.

The farmhouse rested on an elevated stone basement. A flight of stairs led to a porch that opened into a living room and a kitchen. A narrow staircase in the living room provided access to an attic that served as sleeping space for some of the volunteers, the log outbuilding across the road accommodating the rest.

Brown and Merriam climbed the porch stairs and entered a room filled to capacity. Among crates of weapons and ammunition stood twenty men, many of them bearded, some wearing clothes that hadn't been washed since Annie and Martha returned to North Elba. The reception was restrained, the men having been told by Brown to avoid any commotion that might draw the attention of suspicious neighbors. The warning became so ingrained in the men that Annie, during her stay at the farm, had taken to calling them her "invisibles."

Brown interrupted the amenities with a speech, brief and to the point: "Men . . . tomorrow we begin our war against chattel slavery. It shall take place five miles distant from where we are presently gathered. Look to the man next to you and know that he, like you, has come here for one reason: to free the slave—the slave who has been denied what is promised in the Declaration of Independence. You shall be armed with the weapons of war, but you also shall be armed with the knowledge that what you are doing is right."

For the newcomers, the words triggered a rush of blood that warmed them on the damp and chilly October evening. For the rest of them it brought to mind an earlier meeting at the farmhouse, prior to the old man's rendezvous with Frederick Douglass at the quarry near Chambersburg.

The company then was composed of sixteen men, and Brown had decided to gather them together and announce his decision to invade Harpers Ferry. It had been his habit to remain circumspect about such matters, disclosing information only when he felt it necessary. When the men heard that the invasion would begin with a raid on the armory, those who had no knowledge of the plan were shocked. An argument erupted that threatened to disrupt the whole operation.

"We came to free slaves from the plantations," complained a disgruntled Charlie Tidd. He spoke for all who had doubts about the wisdom of striking a federal installation. Tidd had participated in the liberation of the eleven slaves from Missouri, and though he was a trusted and reliable soldier, he wasn't easily intimidated—by Brown or anyone else.

"And we shall do that," the old man retorted. "But only after we have taken the armory." He paused to read the faces of the men before adding, "When the citizens of Harpers

Ferry find their town has been invaded by armed men—men of color as well as white men—the news will spread quickly. And when we break down the armory doors, the worst fears of the slaveholder will have been realized: his slaves in rebellion and fully armed."

The words didn't satisfy Tidd. His grumbling stirred others—including two of the old man's sons, Oliver and Watson.

Brown responded by offering to resign his post. Someone else could assume the role of commander in chief. He was willing to follow whoever wanted to lead.

His strongest supporters were John Kagi, Aaron Stevens, and John Cook, each having been privy to a more complete picture of the old man's plan, each willing to commit fully to a raid on the armory. The men deliberated briefly, then all of them reaffirmed their faith in Brown. Oliver, remembering Salmon's words of warning, turned to brothers Owen and Watson and whispered, "We must not let our father die alone."

Tidd, however, still sulked. He stormed out of the farmhouse and stayed three days at Cook's rented rooms in Harpers Ferry "to let his wrath cool off."

Brown blamed the blowup on the fact that his volunteers were impatient young men. All but two were in their twenties. Some had been living at the farm for three months and were tired of being cooped up. They were bored with breaking down and cleaning their weapons, honing their aiming skills, making leather slings, holsters, and ammunition pouches—all done within the cramped quarters of a small living room and an even smaller attic. When the boxes containing the thousand pikes reached the farm—unassembled—the men were grateful to be doing something different. But it didn't take long for the boredom to return. Using an auger and hammer to rivet metal blades to six-foot ash poles became another tedious, repetitive task.

They relieved the tedium by playing cards and checkers, and they amused themselves bantering with Annie and Martha. But by far the most pleasurable diversion was the debating—contrived by Brown as a means to challenge the men's thinking. On days when he wasn't scouring the countryside for recruits, the old man showed up at the farm—usually with Kagi and a wagonload of supplies. The men would gather in the living room and the contest would begin, often with a topic taken from Thomas Paine's *Age of Reason*. Stevens owned a dog-eared copy of the pamphlet, and at Brown's request he'd read a passage aloud. At the end of the reading, the men responded, arguing for or against the meaning of the passage as they understood it.

It didn't seem to bother Brown that Paine repudiated organized religion and sought to debunk the Bible. While the men argued whether the Bible could ever be viewed as the literal word of God or if an organized religion was necessary to a moral and happy life, Brown listened, occasionally raising a question that would prompt closer examination of the text.

Annie was amazed at the depth of insight displayed during the debates. "Father," she said as she and Brown sat on the porch keeping an eye out for strangers, "it would be most unfortunate if your soldiers were one day made out to be a wild, ignorant, fanatical, and adventurous lot of rough men. This is not so."

Brown responded with a rare smile, imperceptible beneath the beard that had begun to grow back to its former length. He couldn't hide his eyes though; they took on the familiar glow as he let his mind drift, contemplating those who chose to share his destiny.

He was especially pleased with the two men who formed
his inner circle—Kagi, the journalist who practiced law, and
Stevens, the former cavalry soldier who escaped from the
military prison at Leavenworth. They understood his mission
and were ready to follow him anywhere—to their deaths if
necessary. They had been with him during the marches across
Iowa and had participated in the Chatham convention; they
were key figures in the Missouri raid and the transporting of
the freed slaves to Canada.

Twenty-four-year-old Kagi, of course, was Brown's choice
to take his place should he fall in battle. The old man found
him to be intelligent, knowledgeable, and serious about his
duties. Kagi had no use for trivial matters, especially his
appearance. His hair was in permanent disarray, and he often
could be seen with one pant leg tucked in his boot, the other
bunched around his ankle. When he wasn't making a modest
living as an antislavery journalist, he rode the Kansas prairies
with Stevens and the Second Kansas Militia.

During the first winter journey across Iowa from Tabor
to Springdale, as the men talked of their Kansas experiences
around a campfire, Brown heard Stevens tell of Kagi's encounter with Rush Elmore, a proslavery territorial judge from Alabama who possessed a strong sense of personal honor. Kagi
had retired to his blanket early, so Stevens was able to recite
the story without causing his friend any embarrassment. It
seems Elmore was offended by a newspaper article written by
Kagi that accused the judge of a fraudulent ruling in a case
involving a Free State settler. With a revolver in one hand and
a club in the other, Elmore ambushed Kagi, first hitting him
on the head with the club, then firing at him from behind a
stone pillar. One of Elmore's shots struck Kagi in the chest,
but a thick notepad absorbed the bullet. With blood streaming

down his face, Kagi drew his own pistol. Elmore continued to shoot while circling the pillar. The confrontation came to an end when Kagi's only shot penetrated the judge's groin.

Stevens concluded the story with "The judge lived, but the House of Elmore was no more."

Though it brought a smile to faces numb from the Iowa cold, Stevens's story was a testament to Kagi's physical courage. There were other qualities that drew him to Brown. The son of an Ohio blacksmith, Kagi appreciated the dignity of those who labored in the trades—something that Brown, who spent his early life as a tanner, was pleased to learn. As a boy Kagi excelled in school and was sent to a Virginia academy to continue his education. While immersed in his studies he observed the institution of slavery up close—and came to detest it. Still, his proficiency in mathematics, English, Latin, and French, afforded him an opportunity, at seventeen, to take a teaching position at one of the local schools. But because he allowed his antislavery feelings to creep into his lessons, he was branded a subversive and forced to leave—first his teaching job, then Virginia.

The old man saw in Kagi a reflection of himself, someone who loved freedom so much he couldn't abide slavery from the very first time he witnessed it. What Kagi felt as a young student in Virginia, Brown had experienced as a twelve-year-old watching that slave boy being beaten with an iron shovel. Brown and Kagi had seen slavery drain the humanity from its victims—both the slave and the slaveholder.

In twenty-eight-year-old Aaron Stevens, Brown found something different but equally worthy. Stevens had the physical stature that commanded attention. At six-feet-two, weighing over two hundred pounds, he was the tallest and sturdiest of Brown's volunteers. His piercing dark eyes had

the power to induce palpitations in the heart of an ordinary
private or a superior officer. Stevens's experience as a sixteen-
year-old enlistee in the Mexican War, as a cavalry officer in
the Far West, and as a commander of a Free State regiment in
Kansas, had made him well qualified to run Brown's military
school in Springdale.

In Nebraska City, where he was first introduced to Stevens
by Jim Lane, the old man had sensed an aura of confidence and
tenacity. And when he learned the details of the young officer's
court martial offense and subsequent imprisonment, he knew
Stevens was someone he wanted with him. The incident that
resulted in Stevens's arrest occurred while his regiment was
fighting Apaches in New Mexico. His regimental commander,
coincidentally, was Colonel E. V. Sumner—the same Colonel
Sumner whom Brown faced outside Topeka after the battle
at Black Jack Springs. Stevens was accused of assaulting the
regimental major, who had ordered a soldier to be severely
punished for a minor infraction. Stevens felt the punishment
was barbaric, so he attacked the major, chastising him verbally
as he beat him with a bugle. At his trial, Stevens was convicted
and sentenced to death by hanging. However, a number of his
fellow soldiers made a plea to President Pierce for clemency—
resulting in a commutation of the sentence to three years' hard
labor in the army's prison at Leavenworth. He escaped, joined
Jim Lane's Free State militia, and adopted the alias "Whipple."

Brown viewed Stevens as a soldier who witnessed absolute power exercised unjustly on a helpless victim. The regimental major's action was immoral and unfair, and Stevens
could neither accept nor ignore it. His act of insubordina-
tion—though extreme—risked everything: his rank, his good
name, his career, his life. Yet it was an act that was to gain
him Brown's respect and admiration.

In the old man's eyes, Stevens stood among those who subscribed to a higher law—a law that transcended the laws of man and, in Stevens's case, the laws of the US Army. He'd entered the pantheon that included Emerson, Thoreau, Higginson, and Brown himself. Stevens fought for a cause he believed was morally defensible, and he felt it was his duty to willingly sacrifice his life for that cause. Brown knew he would lead by example.

Curiously, the religious beliefs of Kagi and Stevens differed radically from Brown's own. Kagi would have been labeled an agnostic in a later century; Stevens claimed to be a Spiritualist, someone who found God in nature rather than in the Bible and believed one's spirit survived the death of the body. Brown made no attempt to convert either man to his Christian faith. He appreciated the religious freedom guaranteed every American in the US Constitution.

Annie, in her innocence, told her father, "If the term Christian means a follower of Christ's example, Kagi and Stevens are uncommonly good and sincere Christians."

In fact, during her stay in Maryland, Annie made other observations concerning matters of religion. She heard her father's response to a question about his financial backers: Did the money for expenses come from conservative or liberal Christians? Brown confessed it came from the liberal ones—to which Charlie Tidd responded, "I thought so. The conservative ones do not often do such things."

When volunteers stopped arriving at the farmhouse, Annie and Martha returned to North Elba. They had done what Brown asked—having stayed at the Maryland farm for nearly three months, attending to the housekeeping, the cooking, washing the men's clothes. Their principal task had been to create the illusion the Kennedy farm was inhabited by a family, albeit a large family, ruled by the patriarch Isaac Smith, a.k.a. John Brown.

———————

With the arrival of Francis Jackson Merriam and the supplies purchased with his $600 in gold, Brown's confidence was renewed as he delivered his brief speech on the eve of the invasion. After finishing, he stood back, observing the men he'd soon be leading into Virginia. They chatted amiably amid the crates of carbines and pistols, the kegs of black powder, the boxes of cartridges and percussion caps, the piles of leather slings and ammunition pouches.

He was especially gratified that the five men of color— whom he regarded as indispensable to the mission—had quickly blended into the group. John Copeland and Lewis Leary, enlisted by Kagi during the protest against the capture of the fugitive slave in Ohio, reached the farm only hours before Brown drove up with Merriam. Yet they moved with ease among their new comrades. The same was true of both Shields Green—the runaway who had worked for Frederick Douglass—and Osborne P. Anderson, the sole black delegate from the Chatham convention to reach Maryland. They had been at the farm just three weeks and were welcomed into what Anderson, a printer from Canada, described to Brown as "a true brotherhood of freedom fighters." Anderson beamed as he told the old man he was thankful to be part of an anti-slavery family that had an "inflexibility of purpose without a hint of milk and water sentimentality." "Your house," he told Brown, "is a place where no hateful prejudice dare intrude its ugly self, no ghost of intolerance dare seek a space to enter." The men called him "Chatham," partly because of his involvement in the convention, but also because it enabled them to make a distinction when speaking about the other Anderson—Jerry.

The last of the five blacks was Dangerfield Newby. At forty-four, he was the eldest of the volunteers—tall and sinewy, a physical specimen who despite his age was the envy of the younger men. He had a personal stake in Brown's war on slavery; his wife and children were still held in bondage in a Virginia community located at the foot of the Blue Ridge Mountains south of Harpers Ferry. Though he was committed to Brown's mission, Newby harbored some hope of rescuing his family. Brown told him that the provisional army would be moving south along the Blue Ridge, launching raids on plantations from mountain strongholds, and that a rescue attempt was a real possibility. Newby showed the old man a letter he carried in his shirt pocket. It was the last letter he received from his wife before he left Ohio for the Maryland farm:

My dear husband,
You cannot imagine how much I want to see you. I want you to buy me as soon as possible, for if you do not get me, somebody else will. It is said Master is in want of money. If so, I know not what time he may sell me and then all my bright hopes of the future are blasted, for there has been one bright hope to cheer me in all my troubles, and that is to be with you. If I thought I would never see you, this earth would have no charms for me.

Oh dear Dangerfield, come this fall without fail, money or no money. I want to see you so much. The baby has just commenced to crawl.

Your affectionate wife, Harriet

Brown watched as Newby introduced Copeland and Leary to a Sharps carbine. The new recruits were getting a crash course in the use of a potent weapon.

There was other work to be done. The outbuilding across the road from the farmhouse contained the pikes, and Brown wanted them moved to a hiding place in back of the house. The sun had set and it was safe for the men to go outside. They were forbidden to leave their quarters during the daytime, so a temporary escape from confinement was a welcome relief. Brown gave the order to transfer the pikes, and the men filed out of the living room onto the porch and down the flight of stairs. A cold, drizzling rain started to fall as they headed toward the outbuilding.

Brown, meanwhile, pulled Kagi and Stevens aside, motioning for them to follow him into the kitchen. The few embers that still burned in the stove warmed the room. The old man took a candle from a shelf, opened the door to the stove's firebox, held the wick against the coals until it ignited, then placed the candle on a tin plate in the middle of the kitchen table. Kagi and Stevens took a seat as Brown reached under the table and dragged out the carpetbag that served as his portable file drawer. He reached into it and removed a sheet of stationery, placing it on the table.

He'd drawn a map of the part of Harpers Ferry known as the lower village, a strip of level ground that came to a point at the juncture of the two rivers—the Potomac and the Shenandoah. The lower village was where the main buildings of the armory were located, and he'd made crude images depicting each facility: the musket factory with its mills and machine shops, the arsenal across the street from the factory's main gate, where the finished muskets were stored, and the rifle works, which stood several hundred yards west of the arsenal on an island in the Shenandoah.

He tapped his finger successively on each of the facilities, marked I, II and III. "These are the places I wish to occupy." He raised his head and declared emphatically, "When we establish a presence in each location, we will have seized the armory at Harpers Ferry."

Brown again looked to the map, dragged a finger between images of the two bridges—the covered railroad bridge that linked Harpers Ferry to Maryland and points east, and the wagon bridge that crossed the Shenandoah and led to a road running south along the Blue Ridge.

He said, "We shall station sentries at the bridges to make sure our paths of egress remain open."

Then he said to Stevens, "Aaron, you shall be collecting the hostages. The great-grandnephew of General Washington may prove a boon to our cause."

The old man was referring to Colonel Lewis Washington, a slaveholding gentleman farmer whose home was located five miles west of Harpers Ferry, just off the newly resurfaced macadam turnpike that ran to the county seat in Charles Town. As a descendant of the leader of the American Revolution, Colonel Washington would be an ideal hostage.

Brown had learned about the colonel—as well as other slaveholders who lived close to Harpers Ferry—through the undercover work of the effusive twenty-nine-year-old John Cook. He'd managed to ingratiate himself with the locals— one of whom was Colonel Washington. It was during a visit to the colonel's plantation that Cook was invited to view some gifts presented to the nation's first president: a pair of flintlock pistols from France's Marquis de Lafayette and a sword alleged to have belonged to Frederick the Great of

Prussia. Cook also made note of the fact the colonel owned a large, four-horse farm wagon.

Even though Cook was a capable soldier—the most proficient marksman in the company—he was a source of consternation to Brown. In some ways Cook was the opposite of Kagi. Personal appearance meant nothing to Kagi, whereas it mattered much to Cook. His long blond hair seemed to get an excessive amount of care; his face with its intense blue eyes was almost always clean-shaven, and his attire was too flamboyant for Brown's simple tastes. As to his motives, the old man always worried that they were misplaced. Was he truly committed to the cause? Or was he seduced by the lure of adventure and personal notoriety? And he talked too much. It was Cook whom Brown was complaining about when he wrote to Kagi in Chambersburg, "If someone must write some girl or some friend, telling (as some have done) all about our matters, then we might as well get the whole published at once in *The New York Herald*. Anyone is a stupid fool who expects his friends to keep for him that which he cannot keep to himself." That Cook had been compelled to marry a local girl he impregnated further justified Brown's concerns about motives and commitment. Still, the work Cook had done over the past year should have entitled him to a seat alongside Kagi and Stevens. But because of Brown's doubts about Cook's character, he was excluded. His intelligence-gathering, however, wasn't unappreciated, especially the news about Colonel Washington's farm wagon. Brown had plans for its use.

Now, at the kitchen table, Brown leaned forward, his gaze moving from Kagi to Stevens. "Cook has spoken of relics the colonel has in his possession. Some pistols, I believe, and a sword presented to General Washington by the King of

Prussia." He paused. "I think it would be useful for us to acquire these relics."

Stevens's response was immediate, almost reflexive: "And you shall have them, Captain."

Kagi, however, tilted back in his chair. He'd been with the old man for two years, had studied him, observed his talent for the dramatic and how he sometimes resorted to actions that were as symbolic as they were practical. He knew that Brown had something in mind for the relics; they weren't going to become plundered souvenirs. At the Chatham convention, Kagi had watched as the old man presented his constitution, a document that was more than an instrument intended to create order and discipline among newly freed slaves; it was also something tangible that would justify Brown's war on slavery to future generations. Perhaps if Kagi had been at Pottawatomie, he would have felt that he'd once more witnessed the old man's inclination toward the dramatic and the symbolic.

Brown said, "I want Colonel Washington to present these relics to our man Osborne Anderson. Anderson being a person of color, and persons of color being only *things* in the South, it is proper the South be taught a lesson on this point."

Kagi raised an eyebrow.

Brown didn't notice. His eyes were focused on the map. He pointed to where he'd drawn an *X* representing the log schoolhouse that stood on the Maryland hillside above the Potomac a little more than a mile from the covered railroad bridge. After the hostages were taken, Brown explained, the colonel's wagon would be used to transfer arms from the Kennedy farm to the schoolhouse, a location more accessible to the Blue Ridge. From there—after the armory had fallen—the weapons would be taken across the Shenandoah River as the company moved south along the Blue Ridge. In the meantime the schoolhouse was to serve as a rallying point for the others.

The *others*.

Brown had been in contact with slaves in neighboring settlements—both in Maryland and Virginia—since he first arrived at the Kennedy farm. If and when they came to him, the arms would be waiting at the schoolhouse—a place out of harm's way, yet close enough to the armory to allow the runaways to judge whether the invasion was successful. Brown worried that his decision to begin the operation so precipitously might not allow enough time for them to respond. But he couldn't delay any longer. Rumors were circulating that he'd been betrayed, that lawmen were about to descend on the farm. To spread the word that the invasion was in progress, Brown had to trust the "underground wires"—the system of word-of-mouth communication that worked so efficiently for the slaves.

In the dim candlelight, Kagi and Stevens waited for the old man to continue. He hadn't spoken about a strategy for exiting the Ferry. Maybe he wasn't sure it was the right time to do so. Maybe he felt his exit plan was contingent on the response of the slaves. If so, a decision would have to wait until he and his men were occupying the village. Or maybe the old man had no plan for evacuating Harpers Ferry—he'd let his God make the decision for him.

Kagi and Stevens were reluctant to raise the question themselves. They had given Brown their trust and, like the rest of the men, they were imbued with a higher purpose, aptly expressed by one of his soldiers in a letter home: "Yes, Mother, I am warring with slavery—the greatest curse that ever infested America." The problem with having a sense of higher purpose was that it had a way of obscuring matters that otherwise would be essential to an undertaking as ambitious as the capture of a federal armory.

So it was with some hesitation that Kagi finally offered, "We must not be tardy in our retreat from the Ferry, Captain."

Brown moved to the stove. He opened the door to the firebox, tossed in the map. As he watched the flames rise from the smoldering coals, he said, "I shall convene a general council tomorrow morning for the purpose of giving the men their assignments. Since we'll not depart until nightfall, they will have only the daylight hours to prepare themselves."

The old man's failure to acknowledge Kagi's word of caution was forgotten when Stevens laughed. "Don't worry, Captain," he said. "There'll be enough time for me to make sure the new ones don't shoot themselves in the foot."

The briefing was over.

It was time for the two men Brown considered his consummate freedom fighters to rejoin their comrades. Kagi and Stevens would make sure the men got a good night's rest. Once the invasion began, they would be expected to remain awake and vigilant into the early morning hours.

Brown would remain in the kitchen overnight. He would sleep in a chair—as he had many times in the past. The warmth of the stove would be a comfort should his chronic illness make an untimely visit.

He returned to the table, sat down, reached into the carpetbag for a clean sheet of paper. He wanted to share his thoughts with Mary and his daughters on this, the eve of an event that would forever define his life and the lives of those in the adjacent room. Before he began to write, he peered into the carpetbag. It was filled with papers—printed copies of his constitution, some certificates he'd made for the men he intended to commission as officers, other documents he'd been working on since Kansas. The bulk of the bag's contents, however, consisted of letters, many from family and friends and a fair number from his financial backers, including the members of the secret committee.

For a moment he thought about tossing the letters from his most prominent benefactors into the stove's firebox; thus the letters would yield to the same fate as the map he'd drawn of Harpers Ferry. But he didn't. Instead, he shoved the carpetbag under the kitchen table, picked up a pencil, and began to write.

13

Eight Hours Later
October 16, 1859
Kennedy Farm, Western Maryland

It was well before daybreak when Brown started preparing breakfast for his twenty-one soldiers. He'd emptied the basement larder of eggs, cornmeal, and a slab of salted pork. The aroma of bacon frying in an iron skillet drifted through the house, and a pot of corn coffee simmered on the stove.

The men straggled into the kitchen and filled tin plates. It would be their last hot meal before setting out for Harpers Ferry.

Brown gave them time to finish eating before he entered the cramped living room with Kagi and Stevens. The room was gray and damp, and sunlight bled feebly through two small windows. Plates were pushed aside as Brown called the meeting to order.

The men had seated themselves among the clutter of gun crates, powder kegs, and blankets scattered on the floor. Kagi and Stevens remained standing, the old man inserting himself between them.

To give the proceedings a tone of formality, Kagi called the roll. Then Brown held up his tattered Bible and read a chapter on the obligations of free men toward those held in

bondage. After reciting a brief prayer, he turned to Osborne
Anderson and asked him to come forward and take charge
of the meeting. It was important to Brown that a black man
assume a leadership role in a council whose purpose was to
wage war on slavery.

The first order of business was Brown's presentation of the
provisional army's table of organization. In addition to nam-
ing a commander in chief (himself), an adjutant (Kagi), and
a battalion commander (Stevens), he announced that their
force would be divided into companies, each commanded by
a captain, with lieutenants underneath them to lead smaller
groups of men. Each of the four companies in the First Battalion would consist of 72 officers and men, a total of 228
soldiers.

"Of course," Brown noted, "we are now only a small part
of what we shall become." He said he eventually expected
to be joined by slaves and free blacks from the settlements
in Virginia and Maryland that he'd been visiting since early
August. "In the meantime we shall be a company with a
disproportionate number of officers to privates."

Next came the marching orders—the tactical scheme Brown
devised and the duties of each soldier. "We shall depart for
the Ferry tonight at eight o'clock," he said, adding that Francis
Merriam and twenty-year-old Barclay Coppoc, the younger
of the two Quaker brothers, would remain at the farm under
the supervision of Owen. They were to guard the munitions
and supplies that would be moved later to the schoolhouse,
a destination for runaway slaves and a location closer to the
path Brown intended to take when he headed south to occupy
mountain refuges in the Blue Ridge.

The purpose of launching the invasion at night, he
said, was to take advantage of the element of surprise and

reduce the possibility of encountering anyone during the march. "We must make as little noise as possible so as not to attract attention," he cautioned. "And we must keep our arms secreted."

He'd already spoken with Stevens about concealing the Sharps carbines. Each man was to take one of the gray wool blankets and make a slit large enough for his head to pass through—thus creating an improvised poncho. Draped over them, the garments would hide the carbines, as well as the pistols and ammunition pouches, and would insulate the men from the weather.

The five-mile march to the Ferry was to be made in a column of twos, each pair of men maintaining a suitable distance from those in front and behind.

John Cook and Charlie Tidd were to cut the telegraph lines attached to the covered bridge that crossed the Potomac. The bridge not only accommodated the railroad but also had a plank roadway for vehicular and foot traffic. Cook and Tidd would lead the column, Brown to follow in the covered wagon, its bed filled with a stack of pikes, two dozen carbines, some pine-knot torches, tools, a box containing bandages and medicine, and a basket of oats for the horse.

It was the task of Stevens and Kagi to seize the night watchmen—the first of whom was stationed at the railroad bridge, the second inside the main gate of the musket factory.

After the railroad bridge watchman was taken, Brown's son Watson—along with twenty-two-year-old Stewart Taylor—would be posted as sentries. Taylor was a late addition to Brown's army, a short and stocky Canadian who saw no action in Kansas but was at Springdale for military training under Stevens. Taylor attended the Chatham convention, afterward taking a temporary job in Illinois, where he lost track of Brown and worried he'd be left out of the invasion. When he finally received a letter from Kagi, he immediately reported to the Maryland farm. He was passionate about the abolition of slavery and claimed "fate had decreed him for this undertaking." He told Annie he felt he'd be killed in action, but according to her, "It didn't cause him to behave the least bit cowardly." Like Stevens, he was a Spiritualist who believed in the immortality of the soul.

While Watson and Taylor guarded the covered railroad bridge, Oliver and twenty-six-year-old Will Thompson, the brother of Watson's wife, Isabella, would occupy the bridge over the Shenandoah.

Taking possession of the arsenal—the walled compound across from the musket factory's main gate—fell to Edwin Coppoc, Barclay's older brother, and twenty-two-year-old Albert Hazlett. Hazlett, who served with James Montgomery's Jayhawkers in Kansas before joining Brown for the Missouri raid, was one of the men who helped shepherd the liberated slaves to Canada.

Brown himself would take charge of breaching the gate to the musket factory. He wanted to set up headquarters in the firehouse, a sturdy brick building with a large cupola that housed a brass bell used to summon villagers in the event of fire. The firehouse was located just inside the gate and featured three sets of double doors. Behind two adjacent double doors stood the fire wagons—one a bucket carrier, the other a suction engine. The third double door opened to a watch room separated from the fire wagons by an interior brick wall. The watch room with its iron stove would be reserved for Brown and the people he intended to take as hostages. Jerry Anderson and Will Thompson's younger brother Dauphin were to be stationed at the firehouse to guard the hostages and the captive watchmen and anybody else rounded up during the operation.

Brown said he'd wait until the musket factory and arsenal were secured before taking the rifle works and capturing hostages from plantations near the Charles Town Turnpike. Soldiers not given specific duties were to wait for further orders.

The assignments having been given, Brown allowed his eyes to settle for a moment on each man. They all leaned forward in anticipation of his closing words.

"Gentlemen," he said, "this is the Sabbath—the sixteenth day of the month of October in the year of our Lord one thousand eight hundred and fifty-nine. Be assured the nation will remember that on this day the war against chattel slavery was begun, a day when the promise of the Declaration of Independence was fulfilled and the Lord's instructions heeded. *Do unto others as ye would that others should do unto you.*"

All eyes were on Brown as he tucked his Bible under his arm and headed for the kitchen, and nobody moved until Osborne Anderson announced the meeting was adjourned.

Kagi and Stevens stayed with the men. There was unfinished business that required their attention. Kagi filled out certificates for those who were to serve as officers. Although Brown had offered commissions to Osborne Anderson and the other men of color, they all declined. Stevens, meanwhile, took the latest arrivals aside and read them the constitution of the provisional government, afterward administering the oath of allegiance as specified in Article 48.

Together, Stevens and Cook held a training session on the use of the carbines and pistols. For some of the volunteers it was their first exposure to guns. Later, the men were told to rest, that they would be doing their work when the residents of Harpers Ferry were asleep.

Alone in the kitchen, Brown leafed through his Bible. From time to time he could hear the voice of Stevens asserting itself over the din of activity in the adjacent room.

"With this carbine you are worth ten men with muzzle loaders."

Stevens was right. Skilled shooters equipped with Sharps breech-loaders could produce several times the firepower of men armed with muskets requiring powder and ball to be rammed down a barrel after every shot.

"And don't forget to blow the excess powder off the breech before you pull the trigger. Your darlings back home shan't like it if you show up with powder burns all over your pretty cheeks."

Laughter.

The old man had put his Bible aside and was removing papers from his carpetbag when he felt the blood draining from his extremities. He touched his brow; it was wet and cold. He prayed he wasn't experiencing another attack of his malarial illness—not now, not within hours of launching an invasion he'd been anticipating for decades. He closed his eyes and willed the symptoms to subside.

He was bent forward at the table, his head resting in his cupped hands, when Owen appeared at the kitchen door. "Father?"

Brown raised his head. "Sit down, Owen." The voice sounded weak.

"You don't look well, Father."

"It shall pass."

Owen was familiar with the signs of his father's illness: the pasty complexion, the sweating. He'd nursed him in the past and now watched as the old man struggled to compose himself. When Owen tried to persuade him to delay the invasion, the response was unequivocal: "I'll not postpone this action another day, another hour, another minute."

Owen knew it was useless to argue. He said, "I came to tell you what we've learned from Newby." Because Dangerfield Newby knew the Harpers Ferry area well enough to avoid the slave patrols, he'd been given permission by Brown to gather intelligence from neighboring farms.

"And what does Newby have to say?"

"Another slave, Father. A suicide. The day after his wife was sold south. He was found hanging in an orchard nearby. That's six altogether since we've been here—five murdered, one suicide. All within a few miles."

Brown let his head slump to his chest. Owen got up to leave.

"Wait."

The old man gestured for his son to remain seated. Owen had come at a time when the old man needed to talk. And Owen was available, perhaps by chance, though Brown placed little stock in chance. The Lord had brought his son to him in his time of need.

"What is it, Father?"

"I have been troubled by the opposition of some of the men, Owen. I almost considered abandoning the undertaking."

"We've gone too far for that," Owen said.

Brown straightened himself, drawing on strength he held in reserve. He took a rag from his coat pocket, wiped the sweat from his forehead and beard. Owen would understand what he had to say. Of all his sons, Owen was the steadiest. He'd been at Pottawatomie and Black Jack and would have fought at Osawatomie had he not come down with his own debilitating illness. He was the only son willing to accompany him on his return to Kansas in the spring of 1857. And when it was time to commit to the Virginia invasion, Owen did so without hesitation.

The words Brown confided in Owen were spoken solemnly: "We have only one life to live and once to die. And if we lose our lives in this endeavor it will perhaps do more for our cause than our lives could be worth in any other way."

Owen pushed back his chair. He'd served his purpose, having listened to his father purge himself of doubts. Anyway, it was apparent from the languid gaze—focused on nothing Owen could discern—that Brown's mind was drifting. So Owen stood and quietly slipped out of the kitchen.

Brown's thoughts wandered to his other sons, sons with whom his relationship was enigmatic at best. It confounded him that he was thinking about anything but the mission on which he was about to embark.

———————

Seven of Brown's boys had reached adulthood in an era when infant mortality was commonplace. The four sons from his first marriage—his wife having died in childbirth—included Owen, John Jr., Jason, and Frederick. Mary gave birth to Watson, Salmon, and Oliver. When they were babies stricken with illness or disease, Brown treated all of them with tenderness and affection. It wasn't unusual for him to respond to their cries in the middle of the night, holding them close and crooning a favorite hymn. But this changed as they grew older. Displays of affection were replaced by a demand for obedience erected on a foundation of spiritual duty. He continually reminded them to fear God and follow the Commandments.

No memory of his sons was more vivid to him then when, as a young father, he administered a most extraordinary form of punishment to ten-year-old John Jr., the one to whom he gave his own name with the expectation that the hopes and dreams of the father would be taken on by the son. Young John had been guilty of a number of minor transgressions, and Brown devised a system for holding him accountable, entering the offenses in a logbook along with the number of lashes to be meted out as punishment for each offense. When Brown deemed it was time to settle the account, he found a beech switch and the whipping commenced. However, after only a few lashes he stopped, removed his shirt, then ordered his astonished son to take the switch and lay it on him until drops of blood showed on his back. Brown wanted to demonstrate an act of atonement, that the sins of the guilty could be absolved when the innocent submitted to punishment intended for the sinner.

Years later Brown came to believe that this lesson—like others he tried to teach—produced the opposite effect, turning his sons away from a Christian faith rather than leading them to it. The boys grew to manhood questioning their father's rigid brand of Calvinism. But it didn't affect their belief in his cause. They didn't need the justification of Holy Scripture to know slavery was wrong and worthy of eradication.

Brown's religious indoctrination and harsh disciplinary practices—coupled with his desire that the boys become independent thinkers—yielded other unintended consequences. After the battle at Black Jack Springs, Oliver, then seventeen, got into a physical confrontation with his father. Oliver had taken a pistol from one of Henry Clay Pate's men, intending to give it to a relative. But Brown objected, insisting the relative would never use the weapon, and tried to take it away from Oliver. With Salmon encouraging his younger brother, a scuffle ensued. Oliver grabbed his father's arms and pinned him against a wagon. When Brown demanded to be let go, Oliver—in a reversal of roles—told him, "Not till you agree to behave yourself." It took a while for the old man to discover that his child-rearing methods had prompted his sons to challenge his authority, and that this was especially true of Oliver and Salmon.

As the boys matured, Brown continued to ask much of them, though he rarely acknowledged their sacrifices—or did so only when they weren't around to hear his words of praise. When John Jr. was falsely implicated in the Pottawatomie killings and driven to the brink of insanity during his forced march across the Kansas prairie, Brown seemed to repress the incident, interrupting Jason as he told the story of John Jr.'s ordeal to William A. Phillips, the *New York Tribune* correspondent. However, during a fundraising tour in New England, Brown proudly revealed the grisly details of his eldest son's suffering—even held up the chains used to restrain him.

It was the same with Frederick, murdered at Osawatomie. Though Frederick's charge into Pate's men at Black Jack marked the turning point of the battle, Brown made no mention of it in his letters. But later, when he promised Mary that he would inscribe Frederick's name on the tombstone of his grandfather, he elevated Frederick to the status of the man he regarded a hero of the Revolutionary War.

Then there was Jason, self-described as the greatest coward in the family. Brown had come to accept his son's compassionate nature—revealed so vividly after the battle at Osawatomie when he told of nursing the wounded Southern boy, the story that concluded with a fierce denunciation of the "honor of war." Brown knew then what he suspected all along—that

Jason was a kind, loving human being incapable of the warrior mentality necessary for fighting the slave power. It hadn't come as a surprise when Jason declined to follow him to Virginia.

Not so with Salmon. His failure to join Brown for the invasion was difficult to accept. Salmon had been faithful to the cause since Kansas, but attempts to persuade him to come to Virginia were fruitless. Was it the controlling influence of his wife, who wouldn't allow him to say good-bye to his brothers Watson and Oliver because she feared he'd join them? Or did he truly doubt the wisdom of his father's plan to attack a federal armory? Brown didn't know of the warning Salmon had offered Oliver regarding their father: *Beware that his dalliances don't get you trapped.*

Though he couldn't get Salmon to commit, Brown had managed to entice Watson and Oliver in spite of resistance from their wives, both of whom had good reason to want their husbands to remain at home. Watson's wife, Isabella, had a new baby, and Oliver's Martha was pregnant, something she discovered shortly after leaving the Kennedy farm.

It was especially difficult for Watson to leave his young wife and child. In his letters from Maryland, he wrote Isabella, "I think of you all day and dream of you at night. I would gladly come home and stay with you always but for the cause that brought me here—a desire to do something for others and not live wholly for my own happiness." Then later, "Oh, Bell, I do want to see you and the little fellow very much, but I must wait . . . I sometimes think perhaps we shall not meet again. If we should not, you have an object to live for—to be a mother to our little boy."

Like his brothers, Watson grew up admiring his father's dedication to a cause that promised to change the course of the nation. But Watson hadn't gone to Kansas, so he only knew of his father's actions from what he read and what his brothers told him. Now it was his turn to serve. Brown reminded him, as he had Jason after the battle at Osawatomie, "to take care to let nothing get in the way of your duty—neither wife nor child." Watson would go to Virginia, even though he harbored doubts about his father's plan.

As Brown sat at the kitchen table in the Maryland farmhouse musing about what might have been, it didn't cross his mind that his sons had a genuine affection for him, in spite of the relentless demands he placed on them and despite the fact that when they were armed and under his command, he regarded them as soldiers—no different from the rest of the men in his company.

To his sons, however, Brown would always be their father, and for their service to him they wanted nothing in return—other than his approval.

It was late in the afternoon when the old man discovered he'd fallen asleep in his chair at the kitchen table. There was a chill in the air, the last embers in the stove having turned to ash. He was acutely aware that no sound was coming from the adjacent room, and for an instant he was struck by a feeling of dread; he'd lost track of time and felt disconnected from the men. In his haste to get up from the table, he stumbled, then righted himself and headed for the porch. He found Kagi and Stevens sitting in the chairs normally occupied by whoever was assigned the watch.

Stevens stood up. "Anything wrong, Captain?"

Brown shrugged. He thought it better not to express his irritation at having slept away hours that could have been put to better use.

"Didn't want to wake you, Captain," Kagi offered. "Owen said you needed rest."

"What about the men?"

Stevens: "Resting if not sleeping. They've done about all they can do."

"Have they eaten?"

Kagi: "Some dried beef and biscuits—and the apples. They filled their pockets with the apples." Cook had brought a bushel of apples donated by a local farmer.

Stevens scanned the gray sky. "More rain seems likely, Captain."

Brown nodded, though he felt disoriented. The sense of losing control he experienced when he awoke in the kitchen had unnerved him. "The men should be readying themselves," he said brusquely. "And they need to load the wagon. I shall have words for them." Repeating a series of orders made him feel better. He needed all his wits about him in order to lead his men on a mission, the outcome of which—as he intimated to Owen earlier—was not as certain as he once believed.

"Everything will be ready, Captain," Kagi assured him. "The men will do their duty."

The old man trusted Kagi and Stevens implicitly. He turned and walked back to the kitchen, where he'd left a pile of papers lying on the table. He may have been bothered by a feeling of uncertainty, but at least he could put the contents of his carpetbag in order.

Darkness came early to the Maryland farm. Low clouds pressed down on the tiny house, blocking out the moon and stars. A light rain fell.

Brown walked out of the kitchen onto the porch and peered through the open doorway of the dimly lit living room. The room was alive with the chaotic activity that precedes the order and discipline at the start of a military operation. The old man watched as his soldiers buckled on the leather belts from which hung the pouches filled with cartridges and percussion caps.

Stevens was making sure the pouches were situated properly. "Cartridges on the left, boys. Caps on the right."

Brown had instructed Stevens to give each man forty of the .52 caliber paper cartridges for their Sharps carbines, along with a generous supply of percussion caps. However, the old man hadn't acquired a sufficient quantity of tape primers for the Maynard revolvers. His soldiers would have to get by with what was available, enough primers for a six-shot load for each revolver.

In a room that barely accommodated the men—providing they stayed in one spot—the tangle of activity Brown witnessed was almost comical. His soldiers were in good spirits, testing the fit of their homemade ponchos, avoiding collisions as they donned the cumbersome garments.

No one seemed aware that Brown was watching—except Kagi. When he saw the old man standing in the shadows outside the door, he turned around and retreated through the crush of bodies to the back of the room, then ascended the flight of stairs leading to the attic. He returned carrying a large burlap sack.

The men quieted and gave their attention to Kagi.

Holding the sack aloft, he said, "Captain Brown has pre-pared us for an evening such as this." He reached into the sack and pulled out a glossy, broad-brimmed slouch hat. He gave it a toss, then reached into the bag and pulled out another. The hats were waterproof—made of canvas and treated with pine tar and shellac. They'd been purchased in Philadelphia after Brown attended the meeting with his abolitionist allies. Kagi made sure every man had a hat.

As Brown stood on the porch observing the almost jubilant activity, he felt some relief from the despair that had been gnawing at him most of the day. He was pleased to see his volunteers uniformly attired in identical gray pon-chos and black slouch hats; they truly looked like a military unit.

The mood of the men changed when Brown entered the room. Elation was transformed into earnest anticipation.

More than anything else, the old man wanted the inva-sion to serve as a signal to anyone—whether enslaved or free, whether black or white—who wished to join him in a war of liberation. The invasion would be a successful first step if he awakened the nation to his cause and struck fear in the hearts of the slaveholding elite. When the slaveholders learned of the invasion, he wanted them to "imagine the whole North was upon them pell-mell." But at the same time he had no desire to engage in a violent confrontation with the residents of Harpers Ferry. He'd taken this into account as he thought about the final remarks he wanted to make to his soldiers before the march to the village.

"And now, gentlemen," he said, "let me press this one thing on your minds. You all know how dear life is to you and how dear your lives are to your friends. And, in remembering that, consider that the lives of others are as dear to them as yours are to you. Do not, therefore, take the life of anyone if you can possibly avoid it. But if it is necessary to take a life in order to save your own, then make sure work of it."

───────

Promptly at eight o'clock Stevens formed the men into two ranks in front of the farmhouse. Since early afternoon there had been rain, but it finally stopped and the night air turned colder. The wool blankets would make the march to the Ferry more bearable. Low clouds continued to obscure the moon and stars.

Brown was walking down the porch steps as Owen brought up the one-horse covered wagon. A few words passed between them as the old man hoisted himself onto the seat. He surveyed his soldiers, saw the wisps of vapor from their breathing. He took up the reins and gave the order to move out.

Cook and Tidd went first, Brown next in the wagon, the rest following in pairs in accordance with the sequence pre-scribed earlier.

The five-mile march to Harpers Ferry was a slow, muddy, mostly downhill slog from the Maryland Heights—a plateau some thirteen hundred feet above a macadam road that ran alongside the Potomac. As the procession neared the entrance to the covered railroad bridge, the moon broke through the clouds, disappearing just as quickly, but not before the men got a glimpse of the village. It rose up a steep hill in terraces.

The moon also revealed a thin layer of mist suspended over the river like a shroud.

───────

Occupy the musket factory, the arsenal, and the rifle works. Capture high-profile hostages. Wait to be joined by the runaways and others who learn of the invasion. Seize whatever arms can be carried off easily. Retreat to the mountains before having to deal with organized resistance.

That was the plan.

14

Minutes Later
October 16, 1859
Harpers Ferry, Virginia

Even though the march down the steep, rain-sodden road from the Kennedy farm had taken longer than expected, Brown and his eighteen soldiers saw no one. They arrived at the covered railroad bridge a little after ten o'clock. John Cook and Charlie Tidd moved ahead of the company in accordance with Brown's instructions. By the time the rest of the men caught up, Cook had snuffed out the lamp mounted over the bridge's entrance. Tidd, meanwhile, had removed his poncho and cartridge belt and was clambering up the side of the bridge with a pair of wire-cutting pliers.

While Tidd severed the telegraph line connecting Harpers Ferry to Baltimore and Washington, DC, the men formed a semicircle around the wagon. Brown told them to transfer their carbines and belts to the outside of their ponchos. He wanted his men to enter the village like legitimate soldiers—their weapons in plain sight.

They resumed the march across the bridge—a span of about three hundred yards. Aaron Stevens and John Kagi had taken the lead. Their task to intercept the watchman on duty was accomplished successfully a few minutes later. Bill

Williams surrendered without resistance, thinking at first he was the victim of a hoax.

When the men neared the junction—where the tracks split to accommodate the two railroad lines that used the bridge—Stewart Taylor and Brown's son Watson assumed their posts as sentries. Brown and the remaining soldiers, with the watchman under guard, exited the bridge and waited as Tidd cut the wire running to the telegraph key inside the office of the village's stationmaster.

Moments later they reached Potomac Street—a strip of cobbled pavement lined with shops and lodging establishments and bracketed by the Galt saloon and the US armory's musket factory. At the factory's main gate, the road veered to the left and merged into Shenandoah Street. Parallel to Potomac Street were the tracks of the Baltimore and Ohio Railroad line; they ran behind the Wager House, a hotel whose parlor also served as a waiting room for passengers traveling to Baltimore and Washington, DC. Though the street was deserted, Brown made note of the light coming from the windows of the Galt saloon. He surmised that some late-night patrons were fortifying themselves for another week of work in the armory's machine shops. The clatter of his wagon as it moved over the rough cobbles went unnoticed. Brown and his men arrived at the musket factory's front gate without incident.

Constructed of eight-foot-tall wrought iron pickets, the factory's double-swinging gate was hinged between stone columns. The columns and pickets were repeated at intervals on either side of the gate and formed part of the fence that protected the facility from undesirables—undesirables such as Brown's armed men, which must have been how they were perceived by the night watchman Daniel Whelan, who heard the wagon approaching. He stood inside the gate with his lantern, peering through the iron pickets.

When Brown demanded that he unlock the gate, Whelan refused. Stevens viewed the watchman's loyalty to the government as a temporary nuisance. He reached between the pickets and grabbed Whelan's coat while Tidd boosted Cook to the top of the nearest stone column. From his perch Cook kept his pistol trained on Whelan as more than a dozen carbines were aimed at the watchman's head.

Stevens's words sent a chilling message to Whelan: "Be very still and make no noise, else you will be put to eternity."

Kagi, meanwhile, removed the crowbar from the wagon and inserted it between one of the links in the chain securing the padlocked gate. The link snapped and Brown and his men passed through the gate, having accomplished their initial objective: the occupation of the musket factory.

The old man guided the wagon to the brick firehouse. The building's three double doors faced a spacious yard, from which Brown would be able to observe activity within the compound of workshops and mills. From the gate he would have a straight-line view of the short strip of Potomac Street—including the Wager House and Galt saloon. Diagonally across the street from the gate stood the arsenal, the second of his objectives.

Though the rifle works—the last facility Brown intended to occupy—was several hundred yards away, the firehouse's proximity to both the covered railroad bridge and the bridge across the Shenandoah made it a logical choice for his headquarters. And as he'd mentioned when outlining his plan, the firehouse's watch room, warmed by an iron stove, would be an agreeable place in which to confine the prominent citizens he intended to use as hostages. What he hadn't told his men was

that capturing someone like the great-grandnephew of George
Washington was likely to elevate the curiosity of newspaper
editors. After Brown freed the hostages and headed for the
mountains, he wanted reporters who descended on Harpers
Ferry to have at their disposal some newsworthy sources.

Before he left the Kennedy farm, Brown had made it clear
that he didn't want to subject the residents of the Ferry to any
unnecessary danger. Yet he understood, as the commander of
an invading force, that his actions had to be taken seriously—
which meant instilling a measure of fear in the villagers. And
so, as the two captive watchmen stood outside the firehouse
beset by uncertainty, Brown told them, "I came here from
Kansas, and this is a slave state. I want to free all the slaves
in this state. I shall soon have total possession of the armory,
and if the citizens interfere with me I must burn the town
and have blood."

Stevens then directed the prisoners to the watch room,
leaving them in the custody of Jerry Anderson and Dauphin
Thompson. Brown climbed down from the wagon. He was
ready to cross the street and take the arsenal.

Since no watchman was on duty inside the arsenal, Albert
Hazlett and Edwin Coppoc merely had to enter the grounds
from an alley in the rear. They took possession of the larger
of two storage buildings. Using the crowbar, Coppoc forced
open a door, and he and Hazlett went inside.

The arsenal and the musket factory were now in Brown's
hands. The rifle works was the next objective.

Fog had begun to settle on the lower village. Brown welcomed it, knowing it would give him and his soldiers added
concealment. As they neared the wagon bridge over the
Shenandoah River, Will Thompson and Oliver left the formation to take their posts. Brown and the remaining soldiers

continued their march to a causeway arching over a narrow channel between the mainland and the island on which the rifle works was located.

The cluster of workshops that made up the works was constructed decades after the musket factory and arsenal—hence its relative remoteness. The original purpose of the gunsmiths employed at the rifle works was to create cutting-edge weapons and innovative manufacturing processes. A former gunsmith at the facility was Christian Sharps, the inventor of the breech-loading rifle that eventually morphed into the carbine Brown had supplied to his soldiers. The old man had a genuine appreciation for what was being accomplished at the rifle works, but he didn't target it for that reason. It was the last facility of the armory, an armory that wouldn't be completely under his control until the rifle works was occupied. From Cook's surveillance report, Brown learned it was patrolled by a lone watchman—an elderly gentleman who, coincidentally, was the father of Bill Williams, one of the watchmen already imprisoned at the firehouse. An unarmed Sam Williams surrendered when he saw the display of force that greeted him at the gate. He stood shivering amid his captors, unsure of his fate, as Brown gathered his soldiers together to disclose the details of the final phase of the operation.

First, though, he made an announcement: "Gentlemen, we have taken the US armory at Harpers Ferry, Virginia. And we have done so without the snap of a gun or any violence whatsoever."

On an evening when the point of land flanked by the Potomac and Shenandoah Rivers was obscured by darkness and fog, the muted glow of the watchman's lantern made it impossible for Brown to read the expressions on the faces of his men at that special moment. No matter. The Lord had seen fit to honor his efforts, and for that he was thankful.

He assigned the task of garrisoning the rifle works to Kagi and John Copeland. Both men could be relied on, even though Brown was putting them at great risk; they would be isolated on an island at the farthest point from the old man's headquarters. He promised to reinforce their position as soon as possible.

It was time for Stevens to take charge of a detachment whose main purpose was to capture slaveholders to be used as hostages. Colonel Lewis Washington and John Allstadt owned farms just off the Charles Town Turnpike four miles west of Harpers Ferry. As Brown had explained earlier, Stevens was to appropriate the colonel's four-horse wagon and use it to transport Washington and Allstadt—along with their male slaves—to the firehouse. Stevens also was to do what he could to spread word of the invasion to other slaves in the area, many of whom already knew it was coming.

The detachment included veteran soldiers John Cook and Charlie Tidd and three of the recent arrivals: Osborne Anderson, Shields Green, and Lewis Leary. As Stevens led them away, Brown was left with two soldiers—Dangerfield Newby, the manumitted slave and eldest member of the company, and twenty-year-old William "Billy" Leeman, the youngest though not the least experienced of Brown's men. Leeman was only seventeen when he joined Brown's Kansas Regulars in September 1856. Annie noticed at the Maryland farm that Leeman exhibited an adventurous spirit, occasionally escaping to the village even though her father had forbidden such conduct. She said he "smoked a good deal and drank sometimes" and was one of the hardest of her "invisibles" to keep caged. Brown never doubted Leeman's commitment to the cause and rewarded him with the rank of captain. Still, he felt compelled to assign Leeman duties that ensured his adventurous spirit would be kept under control.

It was not yet midnight when Brown, Newby, and Leeman—along with their prisoner Sam Williams—arrived back at the musket factory. Jerry Anderson met them at the gate and reported that Will Thompson and Oliver had arrested a father and son at the Shenandoah wagon bridge. They were on their way home from a late-night revival meeting. After dropping the two captives at the firehouse, Oliver and Will were getting ready to return to their posts when Bill Williams—the watchman seized on the railroad bridge—announced that the person scheduled to relieve him was a young Irishman with a no-nonsense reputation who wasn't likely to be taken without a fight. Worried about the safety of his brother, Oliver had grabbed a handful of pikes, and he and Will had hustled to the bridge to alert Watson and his fellow sentry Stewart Taylor.

Brown didn't like the fact that the Shenandoah Bridge had been left unguarded. It rankled him that Oliver had acted without consulting him. Before deciding what to do about the situation, the old man wanted to reassure his prisoners he meant them no harm. So he entered the firehouse's watch room and stood with his back to the five captives huddled in a corner. He warmed his hands over the iron stove.

"I have not come to rob you," he said, turning to the prisoners. "My only aim is to free the slaves. There will be others joining you. If you do not attempt to escape you shall be allowed to return to your loved ones."

A voice from the shadows: "How long will you keep us?"

A long pause, then in Brown's rasping voice: "It is in God's hands."

The cold, damp night air jolted the old man as he left the watch room. He shivered, worried that he might suffer another attack of his chronic illness. As he stood outside the firehouse, he told himself to put such thoughts out of his mind. There were decisions that needed to be made. Oliver and Will had abandoned their posts. He would have Newby and Leeman take their place.

Before he was able to give the order, the early morning stillness was shattered by a gunshot, a dull report unlike the loud crack of a Sharps carbine. The shot came from the railroad bridge, and Brown assumed it was from a Maynard revolver, the sidearm carried by his soldiers. He moved tentatively toward the fence separating the musket factory from the railroad platform. He heard rapid footfalls and the panting of someone running across the platform. A door slammed shut.

"What shall we do, Captain?"

Brown was unaware that Newby had followed him and was standing in the dark only a few feet away.

"We shall do nothing until we know more than we do now," the old man said. Then, guided by the odor of smoke coming from the chimney of the watch room's stove, he and Newby made their way back to the firehouse.

What if the shot had aroused others? Brown didn't want word of the invasion to reach the locals prematurely—not before Stevens returned with the hostages and certainly not before runaway slaves had a chance to join him. In the meantime he wanted Newby and Leeman on the street. They could detain anyone who might be a threat and keep an eye out for runaways.

Brown picked up a lantern, told Dauphin Thompson to continue guarding the prisoners, then sent Newby and Leeman to patrol Shenandoah Street. He posted Jerry Anderson at the gate, gave him some instructions, and was on his way to the covered bridge when someone called out from the darkness.

"Father, is that you?"

"Watson?"

"Yes, Father. Oliver has a gash in his leg and I need to stop the bleeding."

As Brown searched the covered wagon for the box containing bandages and medicine, Watson told of Oliver and Will showing up at the railroad bridge, that they arrived just moments before the relief watchman.

"We told him to halt, Father," Watson said. "But he wouldn't listen."

"And you shot him?"

"We had him in our grip but he gave Oliver an awful blow."

"You shot the watchman?"

"I don't think we hit him, Father."

Brown found the medicine box and removed some gauze and sticking plaster. He considered expressing his disappointment at the actions taken but thought better of it. The damage already was done. Since the relief watchman was allowed to escape, he must surely have alerted others. Now there was a need to have extra men close by. Maybe Oliver and Will ought to remain with Watson and Taylor on the railroad bridge. But that meant Newby and Leeman would be on their own, monitoring all activity between the musket factory and the Shenandoah Bridge. The old man was uncomfortable with the situation but felt he had no choice.

After Watson returned to the railroad bridge to care for Oliver, Brown resumed his pacing outside the firehouse. He pondered the new developments.

15

One Hour Later
October 17, 1859
Harpers Ferry, Virginia

The eastbound Baltimore and Ohio express train hadn't figured into the old man's plan. It was scheduled to stop briefly at Harpers Ferry—to pick up or drop off mail—before continuing on to Baltimore. At 1:25 AM, the train rolled past the musket factory and approached the railroad bridge. A dense, wet fog had settled on the tracks.

The train's locomotive—with its fuel tender, mail car, and passenger coaches trailing behind—coughed smoke and cinders into the early morning darkness. Most of the villagers were asleep; they were accustomed to the screeching of metal on metal as the engineer alternately applied and released his brakes in order to bring the cars to a stop at the platform behind the Wager House.

Conductor A. J. Phelps, lantern in hand, stepped off the mail car followed by his baggage master. The two men walked ahead of the locomotive to a section of curved track the B&O shared with the Winchester and Potomac Railroad. Tracks for both lines converged at the railroad bridge with its two separate points of entry—one for the B&O trains heading east along the Potomac, the other for the Winchester and Potomac line paralleling the Shenandoah River. It was Phelps's duty to make sure a mechanical switch was properly positioned to allow the train to follow the correct tracks onto the bridge.

As he bent over to inspect the tracks, Phelps remarked to his baggage master that he thought it odd the bridge watchman hadn't met the train as he normally did. The conductor was about to signal the engineer to proceed when someone burst through the back door of the Wager House. Whoever the person was seemed in a frightful hurry, scuttling across the tracks toward Phelps and the baggage master. Phelps held up his lantern to see who it might be, but the fog had further reduced visibility in the darkness.

"'Tis me, Captain. Patrick Higgins. The watchman."

The stress in the young Irishman's voice was apparent to Phelps. He and Higgins traded pleasantries regularly whenever the B&O express stopped at the Ferry. As Higgins stood in the yellow halo of Phelps's lantern, the conductor noticed the cloth bandage wrapped around the watchman's head. Blood had seeped through.

"Good Lord," Phelps exclaimed, "what's happened to you?"

"They shot me, Captain. The bridge is crawlin' with gunmen—and the town, too, it pains me to say."

Phelps listened as Higgins gave an account of the events that had transpired since he arrived at the bridge to begin his midnight shift. He lived in Sandy Hook, Maryland—a little over a mile from the Ferry—and he was supposed to relieve fellow watchman Bill Williams. When Higgins reached the watch shack on the Maryland side of the Potomac, he saw that the bridge light had been extinguished and Williams was nowhere to be seen. After pulling a lever that recorded the beginning of his shift, Higgins started out across the bridge.

He hadn't quite gotten to the fork where the tracks diverged when four armed men confronted him.

"They hollered at me to halt, Captain. Didn't know what *halt* meant anymore than a hog knows about holiday. Then one of 'em grabbed me arm, said I was his prisoner. Well, I give the lad me Sunday punch and took off. That's when they shot me in the head." Higgins pointed to his bandage. "Nothin' serious, Jesus be praised." He gestured toward the village's terraced hillside. "Just now come from Bill's house, and his old lady says he ain't showed up. Come close to runnin' into another of them desperados on me way back to the hotel. Armed to the teeth he was." The watchman let out a sigh. "Somethin' needs to be done, Captain."

"You are quite right, Patrick," Phelps replied. "We need to find out what's amiss before the situation gets out of hand." He told Higgins to go back to the Wager House and tend to his injury. Phelps, meanwhile, would have a look for himself. With his baggage master following, he disappeared into the covered railroad bridge's cavernous interior. As he neared the spot where the B&O and Winchester and Potomac tracks merged, his lantern picked up the glint of gun barrels. From the shadows came a shout, but the conductor chose not to respond. He beat a hasty retreat, nearly colliding with the baggage master. Phelps went straight to the engineer and ordered the train to be backed up to a point near the water tower on the grounds of the musket factory. The conductor barely finished giving his instructions when he heard the loud explosion of a gunshot. It came from the railroad bridge.

Nervous chatter arose in the coaches.

Then came a cry of pain from the Winchester and Potomac tracks, a good fifty paces from where Phelps stood with the baggage master and engineer.

Passengers were beginning to evacuate the train as Phelps scrambled onto the railway platform. He cautiously made his way to the Winchester and Potomac trestle, where he found a man staggering in the roadway beside the tracks. Heyward Shepherd—the night porter for the B&O—was bleeding from a wound in his chest.

In the light of Phelps's lantern, Shepherd recognized the conductor. "Captain," he groaned, "I been shot."

Conductor A. J. Phelps and bridge watchman Patrick Higgins were not alone in their concern about what was transpiring in the lower village of Harpers Ferry. From the veranda of his bachelor's quarters—a second-floor dwelling above a tobacco shop on Potomac Street—thirty-four-year-old John Starry, a local physician, had an unobstructed view during daylight hours of both entrances to the covered bridge, as well as the short span of Potomac Street that made an abrupt turn in front of the main gate to the musket factory. However, at 1:25 AM—because of the darkness and fog—he could see virtually nothing.

Starry was a light sleeper and had been awakened earlier by a noise he wasn't able to identify. After more than an hour tossing in bed, unable to sleep, he got up and put on his robe. He stepped onto his veranda as the B&O express squealed to a stop. Minutes later he was startled by the same gunshot and cry that had captured the attention of Conductor Phelps. It didn't require the light of day for Starry to realize that extraordinary events were taking place a few hundred feet from where he stood. He gazed down on a murky scene, the only illumination coming from the Wager House, the nearby

Galt saloon, and a solitary lantern that bobbed in the dark like an enormous lightning bug.

He was about to go back inside and get dressed when he heard voices below. He bent over the veranda and saw three men, one holding a torch aloft. He noticed the broad-brimmed hats worn by two of the men. The hats were made of a glossy material that reflected the torch's flames. The doctor listened as harsh words were spoken.

As the men walked off in the direction of the musket factory, Starry quickly dressed. He picked up his medical bag and raced down the flight of stairs to the flagstone walkway on Potomac Street. When he reached the Winchester and Potomac trestle, he saw Conductor Phelps and the baggage master. He identified himself and said he heard a gunshot followed by someone crying out in pain.

"Over there," Phelps said, pointing to a squat building—the office of Fontaine Beckham, the stationmaster who also served as the village's mayor.

More shots rang out.

"I must return to my passengers," said the agitated conductor. As he and the baggage master hurried away, Phelps shouted over his shoulder, "Be forewarned, Doctor, enemies are in our midst."

Starry found Heyward Shepherd inside the stationmaster's office lying on a bench. Blood was leaking from his chest and spilling onto the floor. While Starry examined the wound, the porter remained conscious and spoke haltingly. It was his job to be on hand for the arrival of evening trains, and he was on his way to work when he met an injured Patrick Higgins returning from Bill Williams's house. When he learned Williams was missing, he was determined to look for the watchman—despite Higgins's warning that armed men were roaming the streets. He heard the screeching brakes, knew the express train had arrived, and decided to temporarily abandon his duties. He walked to the covered bridge, noticed that the telegraph wire that ran from the bridge to the B&O office had been cut. He entered the bridge but couldn't see anything in the pitch blackness and had to feel his way along the railing separating the tracks from the plank roadway. There was a hostile shout and he started to turn back, then suddenly felt like he'd been stabbed with a red-hot poker.

Shepherd struggled to take a breath. He asked the doctor for water.

Starry, meanwhile, had assessed the seriousness of the wound. The bullet entered Shepherd's lower back and passed through soft tissue, exiting on the right side of his chest. The doctor judged there was little he could do. "I'll have someone bring you a blanket and water," he said. "Try to lie as still as you can."

John Starry would spend the next twenty-four hours trying to find out why a band of strangers had disturbed the peace of his village.

Brown was pacing outside the firehouse when he heard the rumbling of the B&O express approaching the Ferry. He listened to the piercing shrill of the locomotive's brakes as the train rolled to a stop opposite the Wager House.

From where Brown stood he could make out the fuzzy glow of a lantern. He heard voices and moved to the fence, his eyes straining to penetrate the darkness and fog. Why wasn't the train moving on? It was supposed to stop only briefly.

Then came a gunshot, a loud crack—not at all like the muffled explosion Brown had heard earlier, the explosion he now knew was from a pistol that had been fired at the fleeing relief watchman. No—this was the distinctive crack of a Sharps carbine, and it was followed by a cry of pain.

Though Brown had experienced the uncertainty of warfare at Black Jack, this was different. He was literally blind to what was going on around him. He went to the wagon, reached into the bed, and lifted out one of the pine-knot torches and struck a match. The torch flared.

The voices coming from the railway platform grew louder. He was unaware passengers were disembarking from the train and seeking refuge in the Wager House. He moved to the gate, nodded to Jerry Anderson, then marched down Potomac Street, heedless of the commotion.

Two men were walking toward him, their glossy broad-brimmed hats reflecting the torch's flames. His sons—Watson and a hobbling Oliver—met him at the tobacco shop, beneath the veranda of Dr. John Starry. Watson spoke excitedly of someone who had entered the covered bridge from the Winchester and Potomac trestle.

Oliver: "We shouted a warning, Father."

Watson: "There was confusion."

Oliver: "We couldn't see."

Brown: "You were not to shoot unless your lives were threatened. Those were my orders."

Watson wanted to tell his father that he and Oliver did what they thought was right, but Brown had already turned around and was headed back to the musket factory. Watson and Oliver fell in behind, the latter struggling to keep up.

As they passed the Wager House, the light from the torch exposed a man brandishing a pistol.

"You had better go back where you came from," Brown snapped. The man glanced at Watson and Oliver, saw the carbines, and disappeared into the darkness.

The old man wasn't ready to make any radical changes to his plan just yet. If the underground wires were carrying news of the invasion to northern Virginia and western Maryland, as he hoped, there was still time for runaway slaves to come to the Ferry. In the meantime, he was impatient for the return of Stevens and the hostages.

⁕

Brown, of course, didn't know that Dr. John Starry had been observing perplexing activities from a veranda overlooking Potomac Street and that he'd soon head into the night to prowl the railroad platform behind the Wager House. The doctor was trying to gather information that would help him understand why his village was under siege and who would mortally wound the porter Heyward Shepherd for no apparent reason. Inexplicably, Starry managed to evade capture.

It would not be until later, however, with the first hazy sign of daylight, that the doctor would decide to act. He began by sending a messenger to nearby Charles Town. The messenger was to tell the authorities to muster the Jefferson County militia and come quickly. Starry then sent a man to arouse citizens in neighboring communities, and yet another to stop all eastbound trains from coming to the Ferry. Then he saddled his horse and rode up the hillside to warn the armory's acting superintendent, stopping first to alert the watchman at the rifle works. When he discovered the watchman wasn't on duty, he assumed the deeds he witnessed earlier had spread beyond the railroad platform and the covered bridge. After warning the acting superintendent, Starry decided to set out for Charles Town himself—just in case the messenger he sent hadn't been able to convince the town's leaders of the gravity of the situation. Before leaving the Ferry, he made a final stop at the home of the Lutheran minister, where he asked that the bell in the church's steeple be rung as a signal the village was in peril.

———————•••••———————

Meanwhile, with dawn still hours away, Brown continued to pace outside the firehouse, unaware he was a victim of the fog of war.

16

One Hour Later
October 17, 1859
Harpers Ferry, Virginia

By 3 AM the railroad platform behind the Wager House was a netherworld of darkness and fog. Passengers from the B&O express milled about, occasionally running into one of Brown's soldiers, exchanging a few words before moving on.

On the grounds of the musket factory there was a sense of relief as Aaron Stevens pulled up to the main gate in Colonel Lewis Washington's four-horse farm wagon. The wagon was packed with male slaves, four owned by Washington, six by his neighbor John Allstadt. Close behind was the colonel's carriage with John Cook driving; seated in the carriage were Washington, Allstadt, and Allstadt's teenage son. The rest of Stevens's detachment—Lewis Leary, Osborne Anderson, Charlie Tidd, and Shields Green—trailed on foot, as did a knot of six young black men who had joined the procession from farms south of the Charles Town Turnpike. They knew the invasion was coming but hadn't expected it so soon.

Brown met Stevens at the firehouse. In the amber glow of a coal oil lantern, Brown saw that Osborne Anderson already had begun distributing arms to the amalgam of runaways and liberated slaves. A few stood to one side, seemed tentative handling the pikes. Others were eager for an assignment.

Stevens reached under the wagon's seat and removed the "relics" he'd taken from Colonel Washington—the sword and flintlock horse pistols presented to the colonel's famous ancestor. Before handing the sword to Brown, Stevens announced with mock formality, "As you ordered, Captain, this sword— once the property of the leader of the American Revolution— was surrendered to our man from Canada." An embarrassed Osborne Anderson glanced at Brown and forced a grin.

The old man acted like he hadn't heard. He took the sword, removed it from its scabbard, and studied it for a moment, trying to imagine it in the hands of General Washington. Just as Washington had fought for the freedom of his countrymen, so too was Brown willing to fight for the freedom of the slaves, shedding his blood if necessary. With the sword at his side he'd be connected to a revolution begun decades ago—a revolution he felt wouldn't be completed until the nation purged itself of chattel slavery. He gave the pistols a cursory inspection, then returned the sword to Stevens and headed for the firehouse.

While Stevens and his detachment had been gathering hostages, several more villagers were captured and confined to the watch room, including the bartender of the Wager House, who had walked up to the front gate waving a pistol.

When Brown entered the watch room, it contained more than a dozen prisoners. He took Colonel Washington aside and introduced himself, then repeated what he'd told the others earlier, that his intention was to do him and the Allstadts no harm, that he came to Virginia to free the slaves and that he selected the colonel for the "effect it would give our cause having one of your name as a prisoner." He assured Washington that the sword and pistols would be returned in due course. Before leaving, he apologized for any inconvenience the colonel might suffer during his confinement.

Though the comfort of his prisoners was a concern, Brown was facing more pressing issues. He needed to dispatch the colonel's wagon to the Kennedy farm to pick up the arms and supplies and transport them to the schoolhouse—the staging area for his escape to the Blue Ridge and a destination for slaves seeking to join him.

While the farm wagon's horses were being watered and fed, Brown shifted his attention to the stalled B&O express. He sent one of the prisoners with a message for the conductor: the train would be allowed to continue to Baltimore unmolested.

Conductor Phelps, however, was worried the invaders had sabotaged the railroad bridge. The messenger returned with Phelps's response: "I'll not cross the bridge until daylight that I might see whether it is safe."

Brown shrugged. He'd get back to the conductor later.

He summoned Cook and Tidd, assigned them the task of driving the wagon to the Kennedy farm. He wanted some of the newly arrived blacks to go along, to help with moving the crates of guns and to provide security. Choosing who was fit for such duty was more difficult than he anticipated. Several of the slaves taken from Colonel Washington and John Allstadt appeared hesitant, so Brown left it to Osborne Anderson to determine those likely to be reliable soldiers.

Aside from overseeing the transfer of arms from the farm to the schoolhouse, Cook and Tidd were to seize another prominent hostage: a slaveholder named Terence Byrne whose estate was located near the Kennedy farm.

Before sending the wagon on its way, Brown told Dauphin Thompson to fetch Billy Leeman and bring him back to the firehouse. Even though it meant Dangerfield Newby would now be patrolling Shenandoah Street alone, the old man was worried about Leeman and thought it better that he accompany Tidd and Cook, both of whom knew about the young man's sometimes erratic behavior.

———————

The farm wagon—with a contingent of the new arrivals on board—departed at 4 AM, after which an uneasy quiet set in, though muffled voices could still be heard coming from the railroad platform.

It was during this period of relative calm that an excited Jerry Anderson brought news. "Captain," he said, "*they* are coming."

In groups of two or three, noiseless on bare feet, black men were approaching the musket factory's main gate. Brown never was able to determine the exact number; the most accurate count would have to come from Osborne Anderson, who continued arming them with pikes. He even gave Sharps carbines to the few he judged capable of using them.

The old man had wanted to express his gratitude to each new volunteer, but dawn was approaching and his duties as commander in chief were mounting. He hadn't forgotten his promise to reinforce John Kagi's position. He called up Lewis Leary, told him to take five of the runaways and join Kagi and John Copeland at the rifle works. The rest of the new arrivals were sent either to assist Newby on Shenandoah Street or to serve as rotating replacements for the sentries on the covered railroad bridge.

Brown thought about having runaways relieve Albert Hazlett and Edwin Coppoc, both of whom had been standing

guard inside the arsenal since before midnight. But he settled
on two of his regulars, Osborne Anderson and Shields Green.

The first rays of sunlight were piercing the clouds that
sagged over the lower village when Jerry Anderson came
forward holding a Sharps carbine in one hand and the arm
of Conductor Phelps in the other. Brown and Stevens were
engaged in a heated exchange outside the watch room, and
Anderson was reluctant to interrupt. He looked to Brown
and said tentatively, "Sir, there is someone who wishes to
speak with you."

Anderson released Phelps's arm.

"Oh, yes," Brown said, "you are the one I told some time
ago to leave the Ferry."

An irritated Phelps replied, "I was stopped by armed men
on the bridge and wouldn't allow the train to pass under such
conditions. The safety of the passengers is my responsibility."

"You needn't worry about the safety of your passengers,"
Brown said. "It is not my intention to harm anyone. I have
not come to spill blood."

Phelps, however, had firsthand knowledge that proved otherwise. He said, "I don't know who you are and why you are
here, but if I can inspect the bridge to make sure it is safe
for the train to cross, I'll gladly depart at once."

"I am Osawatomie Brown of Kansas," the old man said
matter-of-factly, "and I have come to free the slaves of Virginia." He turned to Stevens. "Come, Aaron—we shall escort
the conductor and his train across the bridge."

With the sword of George Washington strapped to his
waist, Brown led the conductor and Stevens—who carried

a Sharps carbine over his shoulder—to the railroad platform and the waiting train.

The locomotive's boiler was fired and the train was ready to move. The engineer released a cloud of pent-up steam from the funnel-shaped stack. Seconds later all passengers were aboard. Flanked by Brown and Stevens, Phelps stepped in front of the locomotive and began the tedious work of examining the ties and rails, a task made more difficult in a gray dawn whose pale light filtered through the openings at the top of the covered bridge's walls and barely illuminated the interior.

The engineer eased the locomotive's throttle forward, making sure to keep a safe distance behind the men who walked in front of the train. The B&O express—idle for nearly five hours—moved slowly ahead.

It soon became clear to Phelps, as he reached the midpoint of the bridge, that sabotage was unlikely. Brown sensed the conductor's relief and hoped to remove any tension that existed between them. He said, "You doubtless wonder that a man of my age should be here with a band of armed men. But if you knew my history you would not wonder at it so much."

Phelps still regarded Brown as a dangerous adversary and couldn't put his distrust aside so easily. The welfare of his passengers was more important to him than Brown's history. The conductor's eyes stayed focused on the rails as he spoke: "You say it is not your intention to spill blood." A pause. "But blood has been spilled. I tended to a man who was mortally wounded."

Phelps turned to face Brown directly. "What is puzzling to me," he said, "is your claim that you have come here to liberate the blacks. Yet the person I saw dying was a black man, albeit a free black man, but a man respected by all who knew him."

The words startled Brown. It was his first knowledge that the cry of distress he'd heard had come from a black man. His mind flashed to Potomac Street and the confrontation with Watson and Oliver, the harsh words spoken in the light of a pine-knot torch. He felt a pang of nausea, not unlike the sensation he'd experienced long ago when he witnessed a defenseless slave boy being beaten with an iron shovel.

"If someone dies," Brown said, "I am very sorry. It was not by my orders."

Stevens heard the despair in the old man's voice and felt compelled to speak out in his defense. "No fault of yours, Captain. Just a bad decision on the part of those stationed on the bridge."

Nothing Stevens could have said would dispel Brown's regret that soldiers under his command were responsible for the unnecessary shooting of a black man. He was struck by the irony of it. And there was another possible consequence. If word of the shooting spread to the neighboring countryside through the underground wires, the slaves he expected to join him might feel betrayed. They might look at the invasion as a plot conceived by white men to entrap slaves who were contemplating rebellion against their masters.

As the end of the bridge came into view, Phelps acknowledged the train was no longer in danger. Brown told him he was free to go, adding that he realized the conductor—at his first opportunity—would be informing his superiors about what was taking place at Harpers Ferry. "You may also tell them that this is the last train that shall be allowed to pass either east or west. Any attempts to do so will be at the peril of those in charge."

Then Brown did something that surprised Phelps. He reached for the conductor's hand and said, "I hope those waiting for your passengers are not too troubled by their tardiness."

Phelps stepped aboard the moving mail car. He stood for a moment and watched Brown and Stevens disappear in the shadows. The conductor found himself somewhat mystified by the man he believed threatened the safety of his passengers. Despite the revelations of Patrick Higgins, the shooting of Heyward Shepherd, and the delaying of his train, Phelps's attitude toward Brown was evolving. If the old man's goal was truly what he said it was—to free the slaves of Virginia—he might be misguided or foolish, but he certainly was no thief, and he seemed genuinely concerned about the train's passengers.

The conductor couldn't help being impressed by the sheer magnitude of the task Brown had set out to accomplish. Phelps had seen evidence of the old man's success when he observed at daybreak a number of men—most of them black—congregating in the yard of the musket factory. The lingering fog prohibited an accurate estimate of how many men he saw, but at 7:05 AM, when the train made its first emergency stop at Monocacy, Maryland, Phelps telegraphed the B&O's master of transportation in Baltimore that an insurrection was in progress at Harpers Ferry. Then—to ensure that his message would be given immediate attention—he added that the insurrectionists were 150 strong.

Brown walked with a heavy heart as he and Stevens followed the tracks back to the village. The old man was still anguishing

over the shooting of Heyward Shepherd and wondered if
the slaves in Maryland and northern Virginia were coming
to the schoolhouse and the Kennedy farm as they had the Ferry.

The two men stopped at the junction inside the bridge,
where Will Thompson, Oliver, and several runaways had taken
over sentry duties for Watson and Stewart Taylor. Brown had
made a decision. He dispatched Will to the farmhouse with
a message for Owen: "Tell him our friends are finding their
way to the musket factory. If all continues to go well, we
shall be leaving the Ferry very soon."

When Brown emerged from the bridge, Potomac Street
was eerily quiet. The buildings fronting the street, including
the Wager House and Galt saloon, were devoid of activity.
Inside the musket factory's gate, however, there was movement—though not the kind Brown expected. He hoped to
find the yard teeming with runaways. Instead he saw white
men lined up next to the firehouse; Watson, along with Jerry
Anderson and Stewart Taylor, was herding them into the
watch room.

Watson spotted Stevens and the old man and stepped forward to meet them. He said he'd been detaining villagers
since the train departed. He said most of the detainees were
workers reporting for their morning shifts but some were
armory officials—including the armory's acting superintendent, A. M. Kitzmiller, captured on Shenandoah Street by
Dangerfield Newby.

Brown asked Watson if any new volunteers had come.

"None, Father."

"They will come," the old man said. "There is still time."

In truth, though, there was no time—or precious little of
it—remaining. The golden hour was at hand, and the opportunity for Brown to collect his people and arms and escape

from the Ferry was diminishing with each passing minute. Earlier, when Jerry Anderson brought Conductor Phelps to the firehouse, Stevens was trying to persuade Brown that they should leave immediately, that the men and arms at the Kennedy farm should be brought directly to the musket factory and from there, via the Shenandoah Bridge, the entire company ought to flee to the natural strongholds that lay within the Blue Ridge. "We can be hiding safely in the mountains before noon," Stevens had argued.

But Brown wouldn't hear it. He still expected a surge of new volunteers. "We must be patient, Aaron," he said. "The Lord will not let our work go unrewarded."

Now, as he stood with Watson in the yard of the musket factory, the burden of leadership was weighing on the old man. Decisions had to be made that would affect the outcome of the invasion, and Brown never liked making a decision unless he was comfortable with its probable consequences. Yet he had found himself constantly making decisions, none of which he was able to give more than a moment's thought. His actions were no longer of his choosing; they were being dictated by circumstances over which he had no control. That the runaways had stopped coming added to his frustration.

His burden seemed to grow even larger when he was told by Watson that the prisoners in the watch room had expressed fears; they were concerned about their families. "They want their wives and children to know they'll not be harmed, Father."

"I don't want to create fear among the villagers when it is not warranted," Brown said. Then, after a pause, he added, "Nor is it my intention to harm innocent civilians."

If Brown's response contained a veiled reference to the shooting of Heyward Shepherd, Watson chose to ignore it—though he sometimes wondered if his father realized how his words, so often a source of inspiration, were capable of inflicting deep wounds.

Brown lowered his head, tugged at his beard, thought about what his son had said. Maybe the prisoners who were especially fearful could be allowed to return to their homes—with an armed escort, of course. After alleviating the worries of their families, they would be brought back to the watch room.

Watson was on his way back to the railroad bridge when Brown looked up to see Jerry Anderson running toward him, arms waving. "Captain," he shouted. "A message from Kagi . . . He says a man on horseback came to the rifle works . . . Rode off in an awful hurry when he didn't see the watchman . . . Kagi says we must leave the Ferry, sir."

Brown grimaced. "Tell him he must hold on." The old man wanted to add a few more words of encouragement but was distracted.

The village suddenly was besieged by the sound of church bells.

At the same moment, aboard the B&O express bound for Baltimore, Conductor Phelps had managed to convince his superiors—during the train's second emergency stop at Ellicott's Mills—that what he described in his first telegraph message was genuine. The new message was forwarded to the White House and President James Buchanan, who in turn relayed it to Virginia governor Henry Wise and Major General George Stewart, commander of the First Light Division, Maryland Volunteers.

At Harpers Ferry the church bells finally fell silent.

From where he stood on the grounds of the musket factory, Brown had a good view of the village, with its tiny houses clinging to the steep hillside. He felt something of a kinship with the men who lived in the houses. They weren't slave-holders. They worked in the armory's mills. Some probably possessed attitudes toward slavery similar to his. And they certainly wouldn't be willing to sacrifice their lives to preserve a plantation system that was as remote from their experience as someone living in New York or Massachusetts.

Then, as his eyes continued tracing the hillside, the old man noticed the smoke that had been curling upward from chimneys was beginning to disappear. Fires on hearths and in stoves were being extinguished. The streets slowly were coming alive. Men, women, and children were abandoning their homes, scurrying toward higher ground as though escaping a rising flood.

Brown turned around and faced the mountains that rose vertically above the converging rivers. To the east, across the Potomac, the fog that earlier covered the lower village floated in wispy bands along the rocky face of the Maryland Heights. To the south, across the Shenandoah, the brilliant fall colors had faded from the Blue Ridge.

The old man recalled his last meeting with Frederick Douglass at the quarry on the outskirts of Chambersburg.

This place, Douglass had said, *is no different from where you are going. Here there are high walls; there you will be surrounded by mountains and hemmed in by water. . . . You will be entering a perfect steel trap.*

17

Four Hours Later
October 17, 1859
Harpers Ferry, Virginia

All morning there had been intermittent rain.

Shortly before noon Watson came running from the railroad bridge. He was heading for the firehouse to let Brown know that a large body of armed men was poised to enter the bridge from the Maryland side of the Potomac. "You must hurry, Father!"

Brown had just selected ten prisoners from the thirty crammed into the watch room and was moving them into the adjacent engine room. These were the ten he planned to use as bargaining chips in the event he needed them to negotiate a retreat. The surge of runaway slaves he anticipated hadn't materialized, so he was forced to consider all his options.

Earlier, as Brown watched the villagers abandon their hillside homes, Aaron Stevens brought him the news that one of the men had killed another resident of the Ferry. Stevens said it was an act of self-defense. Though the shooting may have been justified, Brown loathed drawing civilians into his war on slavery. If they continued to become casualties, his purpose would be misunderstood. He needed to do something to reassure the people of Harpers Ferry that they were not the enemy.

He decided to take Watson's earlier suggestion. "The prisoners with families will be taken to their homes, Aaron, and they will be brought back when it is made clear we intend them no harm. I don't wish to cause wives and children undue suffering."

Stevens nodded.

"And Aaron . . ."

"Captain?"

"We don't want the prisoners to go hungry." A pause. "Perhaps we can release the man employed at the Wager House . . ."

"The bartender?"

"Yes, the bartender. We shall negotiate an exchange: the bartender for breakfasts for the prisoners."

As Stevens turned to leave, the old man was feeling light-headed, as though he were on the verge of another episode of his chronic illness. But he wasn't going to let the symptoms interfere with his duties. The invasion may have been foundering, but he'd right the ship. Allowing the prisoners to meet with their families, feeding them—these were decisions that would demonstrate his humanity, show that his captives weren't his enemies and that he was holding them only so he could make a successful retreat from the Ferry.

By ten o'clock, the prisoners—including those who had enjoyed a brief reprieve with their families—were back in the watch room eating the breakfasts supplied by the Wager House.

Brown, meanwhile, had received another plea from John Kagi. Gunsmiths were showing up for their shifts at the rifle works, and though they were being turned away, Kagi feared they'd return, armed and ready to take back their workplace. Brown could only respond with the words he'd already uttered: "You must hold on."

The old man hadn't given up hope that a favorable outcome to the invasion was still possible, that an army of runaways still might come to the musket factory, that Owen—having transported the weapons and supplies to the schoolhouse— would be marching across the railroad bridge with a small army of his own, and that using hostages to negotiate a retreat would prove unnecessary.

When Will Thompson and Billy Leeman trudged back from the Maryland Heights with the captured slaveholder Terence Byrne, Brown was counting on an encouraging report. Had Owen and the others finished moving the arms to the school- house? Had any new volunteers showed up?

"The work is still going on, Captain," Thompson said, add- ing that the rain had turned the road into a quagmire and that a large wagon like Colonel Washington's—even though drawn by four strong horses—was having difficulties with the heavy load. He said he'd overtaken Tidd and his helpers as they were making their first run to the schoolhouse. Another remained before the transfer of weapons and supplies was completed.

Then Thompson disclosed information he knew would please the old man: "We have new recruits, Captain. Owen said they came last night."

Brown asked for numbers, but Thompson wasn't sure. All he could say was that the black men he saw unloading the wagon at the schoolhouse were jubilant at having rid them- selves of the shackles of slavery.

While Thompson and Brown talked, Leeman was silent; his glossy slouch hat was pulled low and shaded his eyes.

He'd done what the old man ordered—the slaveholder Terence Byrne had been removed from his estate and was now in the watch room with the other prisoners.

Brown acknowledged Thompson's report, told him to return to his post on the railroad bridge. And though there was something about Leeman's behavior that bothered the old man, he ordered him to rejoin Newby's patrol on Shenandoah Street.

As the noon hour approached, Brown was jarred by a wave of self-doubt. His belief that he'd be joined by hundreds of runaway slaves hadn't happened. Not a single volunteer had appeared since the predawn hours when an excited Jerry Anderson announced that small groups of black men were converging on the musket factory. And at the Maryland farmhouse the number of new arrivals sounded modest at best. Brown wondered: Had he waited too long? Had he wasted time attempting to allay the fears of the prisoners? Was his release of the train premature? These questions, coupled with the return of symptoms of his illness, left him struggling to control an invasion that was rapidly deteriorating. Perhaps the Lord had a different plan for him, a plan he wasn't yet privileged to know.

He'd deliberately not spoken to the prisoners about terms of retreat, knowing that to do so would have been an admission the invasion wasn't going well and that he needed to prepare for the worst. As the morning wore on, however, he decided to meet with those he intended to use as hostages.

He summoned Stevens, told him to bring out the ten prisoners deemed most influential, a group that included slaveholders Lewis Washington, Terence Byrne, and the Allstadts, and A. M. Kitzmiller, the armory's acting superintendent. As they were being moved from the watch room to the engine room, a breathless Watson—having sprinted from his post on the covered bridge—reached the firehouse. Armed men, he shouted, were entering the bridge from the Maryland side of the Potomac.

"You must hurry, Father!"

The old man stood rigidly in place and said nothing as Stevens ordered the hostages to return to the watch room.

It was now clear to Brown that he'd delayed too long and, as a consequence, was in a position he'd hoped to avoid. His aim was to accomplish his goals without the shedding of blood: *Occupy the musket factory, the arsenal, and the rifle works. Capture high-profile hostages. Wait to be joined by the runaways and others who learn of the invasion. Seize whatever arms can be carried off easily. Retreat to the mountains before having to deal with organized resistance.* But blood had been shed, and now he'd have to fight. To do otherwise—to surrender—would mean the invasion was an aberration, something that ought not to be taken seriously. He'd come too far to see his efforts vanish in the shadows of irrelevance.

He said to Watson, "We will give the troops on the bridge a warm reception." Then to Stevens, "We will hold on to our positions. If we cannot bring our adversaries to terms, we will die like men."

Any symptoms of illness or anxiety had disappeared. Brown's raspy voice spit out orders. The men posted outside the musket factory's gate were to be brought in immediately. Stevens was to fetch the men patrolling Shenandoah Street while Jerry Anderson and Watson rounded up those stationed at the arsenal and the covered railroad bridge. It was too late to warn Kagi at the rifle works.

They came on the run, black men and white, clutching Sharps carbines. Some found it difficult to keep up with the old man as he led them down Potomac Street toward the Galt saloon. He positioned them at the corners of shops, had them kneel behind the steps of elevated porches. Instead of hiding them behind trees bordering a river—as he had at Osawatomie— he made use of any kind of cover and concealment available along the cobbled street.

The drumming of boots on the bridge's plank roadway grew louder.

There was scarcely enough time for him to call out his final instructions. "Wait for my command before you shoot," he shouted.

As the old man spoke, a company of fifty men emerged from the railroad bridge and turned onto Potomac Street. They marched in unison, five ranks deep, ten men abreast, muskets shouldered. The first two ranks completed the turn and came on line.

Brown stepped into the street from behind the tobacco shop—the same tobacco shop over which resided Dr. John Starry, the person responsible for mustering the company of Charles Town militiamen that now marched on Potomac Street.

The appearance of the bearded old man—unarmed except for the sword he held at his side—brought the company to a halt. The first rank dropped to a kneeling position, muskets ready. The men behind moved their muskets to the shooting position and remained standing.

Whether the first shots fired by the militiamen were intended as a warning, or whether the shooters were simply unnerved by the old man's disregard for his own safety, is unclear. When the smoke from their muskets thinned, Brown was still standing.

He raised the sword that once belonged to George Washington and gave the order to commence firing. From their scattered positions his soldiers responded with a volley that drove the militiamen back to the covered bridge.

The superior firepower of the breech-loading Sharps carbines blunted several more assaults, but it was evident that numbers alone would eventually favor the militia. The skirmish came to an abrupt conclusion with the arrival of rain. Not the cold drizzling rain that had fallen at intervals throughout the morning, but a sudden downpour that threatened to dampen the ammunition of combatants on both sides.

For the exhausted militiamen it was an excuse to remain inside the covered railroad bridge or move their wounded to the less toxic environment of the Wager House.

Brown had no choice but to order his men to fall back to the firehouse. The rain-soaked wool ponchos had become a burden and were shed by those who still wore them.

18

Minutes Later
October 17, 1859
Harpers Ferry, Virginia

In the semi-darkness of the firehouse's engine room, Brown's soldiers—drenched and cold—leaned their carbines against the fire wagons. They checked their ammunition pouches for wet cartridges. The old man was relieved that no one complained of wounds, but he was puzzled that the only black men present were Osborne Anderson, Dangerfield Newby, and Shields Green. Where were the runaways? Brown recalled placing at least a half dozen on Potomac Street. He would have known if any were killed or wounded. Had they judged the invasion doomed? The words of Frederick Douglass echoed in his ears: *If you fail it will be fatal to all engaged. But it will be worse for those you liberate. For them, death will be a welcome deliverance from the wrath of their masters.*

Brown was again faced with conditions he hadn't foreseen. Even with Sharps carbines, he couldn't expect the soldiers gathered in the engine room to chase the militiamen from the railroad bridge. They could simply pull back to the other side of the Potomac, take cover, and pick off his men as they attempted to leave the bridge. Besides, he wouldn't consider making a break without John Kagi, John Copeland, and Lewis

Leary—still at the rifle works awaiting his orders. And he was unwilling to abandon Owen and the men moving arms and equipment to the schoolhouse. As he pondered the situation, Dauphin Thompson came from the watch room and told him the prisoners offered no resistance during the fighting even though they were forced to share close quarters with the slaves guarding them.

The old man had another decision to make. If he was going to use the prisoners to negotiate a retreat, he had to do it now. But before beginning the negotiations, he wanted to bargain from what he considered a position of strength. He wanted to be able to tell those with whom he'd be negotiating that he still occupied the armory.

The rain had stopped and there was no indication the company holding the covered railroad bridge was preparing for another attack. So Brown told Osborne Anderson and Albert Hazlett to go back to the storage building at the arsenal and wait for further orders. Then he turned to Newby and Leeman and told them to take a position outside the fence that surrounded the arsenal grounds—a position where they could observe activity on Shenandoah Street between the wagon bridge and the musket factory. Shields Green stepped forward and volunteered to go along, and Brown approved. He'd grown to appreciate the zeal of Green, whose hatred of slavery was as profound as his own. And to make sure the soldiers at the rifle works were aware of what was happening, Brown sent Jerry Anderson with yet another message for Kagi: he was to remain at the works until arrangements for the retreat were completed. The rest of the soldiers—including those formerly posted on the covered bridge—were to take defensive positions along the musket factory's iron-picketed fence.

Brown took Aaron Stevens aside, told him he needed a few minutes alone. Stevens could see the signs of fatigue on the old man's face but reminded him, "We need to move quickly, Captain."

With his head down and his torso bent forward in the familiar pose, the old man headed for the covered wagon he'd driven from the Maryland farmhouse. He pulled back a canvas flap and peered into the wagon's bed. The extra carbines and pikes had already been moved to the engine room. The torches and tools remained, but they were of no use to him now.

He lifted the lid from a wicker basket filled with oats, scooped up a handful, and walked to where the horse he called Dolly was harnessed to the wagon. He'd given her the same name as the horse that took him to Kansas, and he'd grown as fond of the new Dolly as he had the old. They had made many journeys together since his arrival in Maryland. She was a small but strong horse and as tenacious as Brown. He saw that her coat was wet and matted. For more than fourteen hours she'd withstood the rain, the cold, and the occasional bursts of small arms fire. The old man extended his hand with the oats. She ate. He took her halter and gave a gentle tug, then led her across the musket factory's yard until they reached a vacant area between a warehouse and a forging shop where there was a tub used by blacksmiths to quench hot metal. The tub was filled with water, and Brown felt it would be a good place to leave Dolly and the wagon—until he was ready and able to retreat from the village.

By the time Brown returned to the firehouse, the ten hostages he'd selected earlier had been transferred to the engine room—a dark place where the only natural light came from high, arched transoms. Still, the old man felt it wasn't as vulnerable to an attack as the watch room with its large, mullioned windows.

Even with the removal of the hostages from the watch room, twenty prisoners remained penned inside. Dauphin Thompson secured the door before he and the slaves guarding the prisoners joined the others in the engine room.

As the hostages huddled together, Brown said, "Gentlemen, perhaps you wonder why I've selected you from the rest. It is because I believe you to be the most influential. And I have only to say now that you will have to share precisely the same fate that your friends extend to me and my men."

Brown intended to tell the hostages what was in store for the prisoners still confined in the watch room—that he planned to release them as soon as he felt it feasible to do so—but he was distracted by a volley of gunshots, apparently fired at some distance from the firehouse. Brown and Stevens stepped outside to assess the situation. The shooting had stopped and was replaced by the clatter of boots striking the cobbled pavement outside the gate to the musket factory.

Jerry Anderson, Shields Green, and Billy Leeman were running toward the gate. They were breathing with difficulty when Brown and Stevens met them.

Anderson spoke first: "They're everywhere, Captain . . . Couldn't get near the works." He paused to take a deep breath. "I fear it is all over for Kagi and his men."

Stevens was concerned about the missing soldier: "What about Newby?"

"Dead, sir," Anderson replied grimly, then looked to Green before adding, "But his murderer is no more. Green here made sure work of it."

Brown pressed his lips together. It crossed his mind that Newby may have been the first of his soldiers to be killed in the line of duty. Whatever the case, the old man was now resigned to the fact that his invasion was no longer the one he'd planned at the Maryland farmhouse.

Stevens, realizing the urgency of the situation, looked to Brown. "Captain," he said, "we'll need the men stationed at the arsenal."

Before Brown could reply, more gunfire crackled in the distance. Then, as though the shots were a signal, the hillside above the musket factory erupted in muzzle flashes. Brown and his soldiers found themselves caught in a hailstorm of lead balls.

The old man made no attempt to take cover, nor did he tell anyone else to do so. He stood erect and quite still—as though he were in no danger—while bullets burrowed into the firehouse's brick walls and shattered the transoms.

"Run, boys!" Stevens shouted. He grabbed Brown by the arm, dragging him along. As the last man heaved himself inside the engine room, Stevens pulled the heavy doors shut.

In the dimly lit space, amid the glut of wagons and fire-fighting equipment—with musket balls pecking at the walls and shards of glass cascading from the transoms—stood a knot of humanity: ten hostages, four liberated slaves, nine of Brown's soldiers. With the exception of Stevens, who still held his captain by the arm, the eyes of everyone—soldiers, hostages, liberated slaves—were fixed on the old man, expecting him to announce their collective fate . . . or at least bring order to a situation that seemed to be devolving into chaos.

Though he couldn't help sensing the tension that filled the room, Brown felt strangely removed from it, almost as if he were outside looking in, a spectator rather than a participant. Yes, he was trapped. Yes, he was unable to cut his way out against a superior force. Yes, he'd lost men—Newby and possibly others at the rifle works and the arsenal. But he refused to believe his God had abandoned him.

He pulled his arm from Stevens's grip. "We must not despair," he said, the words intended only for Stevens. "We shall continue to do our duty. We can only trust the Lord to reveal the true purpose of this time of tribulation."

When Brown spoke next, his voice was strong and steady and aimed at the hostages: "We shall soon discover if those shooting at us have any regard for the lives of their fellow citizens."

The old man surveyed the room, aware for the first time of Billy Leeman's absence. No matter. He'd inquire about him later. First, though, he had a request for the hostages. He asked for a volunteer to carry a message into the street.

An elderly gentleman—Reason Cross—stepped forward, claimed he was sure to be recognized as a longtime resident of the village. Brown nodded, then asked for a volunteer among his own men to accompany Cross. All were willing, but Brown picked Will Thompson.

The old man's message to his adversaries was simple: His soldiers—wherever they happened to be located—were to be allowed to return safely to the musket factory, after which he'd load his wagon with the hostages. Soldiers and hostages would then proceed across the railroad bridge until they reached the Maryland side of the Potomac, where the hostages would be released; he'd take his chances against anyone pursuing him.

With Will holding a pike flagged with a white handkerchief, he and Cross left the engine room. The gunfire subsided. Brown peered out the partially opened door as the two men passed through the gate and moved onto Potomac Street.

Seconds later the shooting resumed.

Brown turned around and saw that the hostages had separated themselves and were clustered against the back wall. He said to them, "It seems your friends do not hold your lives so dearly." He would have said more had Stevens not interrupted, insisting he be sent out immediately—this time in the company of a hostage who was sure to be treated in a civilized manner. Stevens pointed to the acting superintendent of the armory. Stevens was angry, said he'd take Kitzmiller and wouldn't hesitate to use his Sharps carbine on anyone, including the acting superintendent.

Watson, disturbed by what might have happened to Will, told Brown he intended to go along. He reminded his father that Will was the brother of his new wife and was therefore part of his family.

Stevens was barely able to hold his anger in check. He shoved Kitzmiller out the door. The acting superintendent dug into his pocket for a handkerchief—waved it frantically as Stevens prodded him with the barrel of his carbine. Watson—also armed with a carbine—walked close behind. The three men disappeared beyond the gate.

As Brown paced nervously inside the engine room, gunfire once again broke out, this time in concert with angry shouts.

Then, as though on cue, the sky darkened and once more a hard rain fell. The gunfire ceased.

Though Brown had kept his emotions under control throughout the morning and early afternoon, his patience finally reached the breaking point. He startled everyone in the engine room as he raised his voice and declared: "I had it in my power to destroy this place in half an hour—but I would not do it. It was not my aim. Now my attempts to leave peaceably are ignored." He eyed the eight remaining hostages and said, "It distresses me that I can no longer assure your safety. You must protect yourself as best you can."

Oliver approached his father, pleading that he be allowed to look for Watson. The old man refused, afraid his youngest son would become yet another casualty.

With the prospect of a negotiated retreat unlikely, Brown prepared for the fight he knew was coming. He told the men to take the axes and picks from the fire wagons and dig gun ports into the brick walls. The extra carbines were to be loaded and placed alongside the gun ports. When the attackers came, the old man wanted to be able to maintain continuous fire while the carbines were being reloaded. He cautioned his soldiers not to shoot anyone unarmed.

As the men began the work, a groan came from the yard. It was barely audible above the steady tapping of rain on the firehouse's slate roof. Oliver didn't bother to ask his father's permission; he rushed outside and returned seconds later with his brother draped over his shoulders. Oliver gently laid a bleeding Watson on the floor.

Brown hovered over his wounded son, found the hole where a ball had penetrated his abdomen. The old man knew that even with medical attention the wound would cause much pain and suffering. Death would come slowly.

In a weak voice, Watson said, "They gave no quarter, Father."

"And Captain Stevens?"

Watson had to muster the strength to respond. "In the street, Father."

They lifted Watson and placed him under the larger of the two fire wagons. The old man removed his son's coat and spread it over him, told him to rest.

One of the hostages—a young shopkeeper named Joseph Brua—offered to make another attempt to deliver Brown's message. The old man declined, said there was no guarantee Brua wouldn't be shot by his own people. But the shopkeeper persisted, even swore to return to the engine room after he told Brown's adversaries they were endangering the lives of the hostages. Brown reluctantly nodded his approval.

The rain had slackened by the time Brua returned. While he hadn't been able to persuade the leaders of the militia to accept Brown's demands, he was able to get help transporting a severely injured Aaron Stevens from the street to the parlor of the Wager House.

"He is a very fortunate to be alive," Brua said. "His wounds would have snuffed out the life of someone of a lesser constitution."

The attack the old man anticipated finally came, though not from the direction he expected. Dauphin Thompson was standing watch at the door when he saw men approaching from the opposite end of the yard. Carrying shotguns and pistols, they were marching down the alley between the workshops and mills.

Brown would learn later they were railroad men—conductors and freight handlers from Martinsburg, one of the towns alerted by John Starry.

The old man was now down to only six able-bodied soldiers. He told each man to take two carbines and form an irregular line outside the firehouse. They were joined by one of the liberated slaves—Allstadt's coachman, Jim.

The railroad men charged the firehouse but weren't prepared for the firepower of the Sharps carbines. The clash was intense but brief. A third of the railroad men suffered wounds and were forced to withdraw—but not before they broke the watch room's mullioned windows, freeing the prisoners Brown planned to eventually release.

When the Martinsburg troop retreated, Brown discovered his only casualty was Stewart Taylor—the Spiritualist from Canada who believed it was his destiny to be killed in action. He was shot in the throat and died almost instantly. The freed slave Jim had carried his body into the engine room.

Before going inside, the old man saw that the terraced hillside was alive with armed men. He knew the lower village soon would be overflowing with companies of militia.

There was nothing for him to do but wait.

Inside the engine room the hostages shivered. The liberated slaves continued gouging gun ports into the walls. The remaining able-bodied soldiers tended to their carbines, cleaning them as best they could and taking turns standing watch at the doors.

The old man tried to comfort Watson. The ball that entered his abdomen had pierced his bowel and infection had set in.

As Brown predicted, the militias poured into the village. The firehouse gradually was surrounded, though no attempt was made to launch an assault. The leaders apparently were content to seal off any possibility of escape.

Small arms fire continued to pepper the firehouse incessantly. An exasperated Edwin Coppoc was determined to retaliate. As he stood watch at one of the double doors, he spotted someone near the B&O water tower. "If that fellow keeps on peeking," he said, "I'm going to shoot."

Moments later the man stuck his head out and Coppoc fired. He didn't know that he'd killed an unarmed Fontaine Beckham, the B&O stationmaster and mayor of the village.

Oliver, like Coppoc, had grown increasingly weary of the constant exploding of bricks and glass and the thumps of musket balls slamming into the engine room's thick oak doors. The situation was made unbearable by the pleas of his dying brother. He was unable to help Watson and felt a nagging guilt whenever he heard his brother's groans. When it was Oliver's turn to stand watch at the door, he didn't hesitate to react to a shooter taking aim at the firehouse from the railroad overpass. He stepped outside to get a clear view of his target but never had a chance to squeeze the trigger. A ball shattered his sternum, sending splinters of bone into vital organs. He was brought inside and placed alongside Watson. Oliver died a short while later.

Though the old man had accepted what was fast becoming a tragic outcome to his plan to free the slaves of Virginia, he was comforted by the belief that suffering was an integral part of his faith. He knelt beside Watson—who begged to be put out of his misery—and whispered, "You must have patience, my son. You will get well. But if you die, you will die for a glorious cause." He brushed his lips against Watson's forehead.

Meanwhile, the gunfire was increasing in intensity and volume. The hostages were braced against the back wall as the last fragments of glass from the transoms were blown away. Brown's soldiers crouched low, as did the liberated slaves. The old man's posture, however, was unchanged. He stood as erect as his body would allow.

When the barrage was all-consuming, when everyone inside the engine room was rendered immobile and talk was impossible, Brown made a mental inventory of the status of his twenty-one soldiers:

Dangerfield Newby—killed.

Oliver Brown—killed.

Stewart Taylor—killed.

Watson Brown—engine room, mortally wounded.

Aaron Stevens—Wager House, wounded.

And while he presumed Will Thompson was still alive, he wasn't sure about Billy Leeman. Earlier, Jerry Anderson had told him Leeman was sickened by the killing of Newby and that, when the rest of the men retreated to the engine room, Leeman ran for the Potomac. As for the men stationed at the rifle works—Kagi, Leary, and Copeland—Brown could only guess their fate. The same was true of the men at the arsenal—Albert Hazlett and Osborne Anderson. And he knew nothing about the soldiers who were assigned the task of moving arms and equipment from the Kennedy farm to the schoolhouse. The rest—Shields Green, Jerry Anderson, Edwin Coppoc, and Dauphin Thompson—were the men with him who were still able to fight. Though there was much he didn't know, the old man found satisfaction in having done his duty as commander in chief. He'd attempted to account for the whereabouts and condition of each of his soldiers.

The shooting never stopped, though it diminished as dusk approached, replaced in part by the wrath of angry villagers, their cursing inflamed by the free whiskey dispensed at the Galt saloon.

Darkness had come when Brown noticed the light from a lantern across the yard. A shadowy figure was moving near the warehouse where the old man had left his horse and wagon. Shields Green also saw the lantern; he stood at one of the gun ports and was taking aim when Brown called out, "Don't shoot. That man is unarmed."

Brown nudged the door open and gave a shout: "*Halloo. You shan't be harmed if you come forward.*"

The man with the lantern took Brown at his word. He approached the door and said, "I am Captain Sinn, Sixteenth Regiment, Maryland Volunteers."

The old man replied, "I am Osawatomie Brown of Kansas."

19

Eight Hours Later
October 18, 1859
Harpers Ferry, Virginia

During the night a cold front pushed the rain south, leaving behind an icy fog that settled over the lower village. By 7 AM the fog began to lift.

In the firehouse's engine room, the sunlight filtering through the shattered transoms did little to warm the occupants. For them, sleep had come in brief snatches. It wasn't the cold that kept them awake but rather the knowledge that dawn promised a reckoning, a settling of accounts, a summation of costs incurred over the past thirty-three hours.

The previous evening Brown had been told by Captain J. T. Sinn—Sixteenth Regiment, Maryland Volunteers—that federal troops were on their way from Washington, DC, to quell the disturbance at Harpers Ferry. Sinn claimed there were enough volunteers already on hand to take care of the situation but officers in charge of the several militias deemed it prudent to wait for the professionals.

Brown had invited Sinn into the engine room, hoping an outsider would respond favorably to a proposal that had been rejected by the local citizens. "I've tried to negotiate a retreat from the village," Brown told Sinn, "but the men I sent bearing a flag of truce were shot down like dogs."

"You and your men must expect to be treated like dogs when you take up arms and violate the peace of those who mean you no harm."

"I bear no malice toward the citizens of Harpers Ferry," Brown protested. "My aim is—and always has been—to help the slaves of Virginia seek freedom."

"Whatever your intention, you have killed people in this village, and the citizens are angry and would have revenge." Sinn cocked his head, pointed a finger at one of the shattered transoms. "Listen," he said.

Through the dark, glassless openings came the howling of the drunken mob, background noise to the occasional discharge of a firearm.

Brown said, "When I took possession of the village, I could have massacred the inhabitants—but I did not. I fought only those who fought me."

"Not so," Sinn replied. "A shot fired from this building killed an unarmed citizen, the mayor of the village . . . a man I am told was much loved."

"If this is true," Brown said, "it was a mistake and I regret it."

Sinn said the shooting of Mayor Beckham had incited the most shocking acts of revenge. He told of a young man Brown deduced was Will Thompson, how he'd been cursed and dragged from the Wager House, executed, and tossed into the Potomac. He described another victim—in all likelihood Billy Leeman—who was shot in the face while attempting to swim across the river, then propped against the rocks and used for target practice by the militiamen on the covered bridge. Sinn recoiled as he told of the desecration of Dangerfield Newby's dead body. "Disgraceful," he said. "Some of the villagers cut off his ears as souvenirs."

Brown listened, his eyes taking on a watery glaze.

Sinn said he'd been to the Wager House and seen Aaron Stevens lying on a bench, his head covered with blood. "They would have killed *him* too—had I not intervened. Some local boys were taunting him, threatening to shoot him, but he never flinched."

And what about the rifle works? Did Sinn know anything about the men stationed at the rifle works?

"All dead. Except for a light-skinned Negro. They wanted to hang him on the spot, but a doctor came to his rescue. He's in the custody of the sheriff."

The occupants of the engine room were able to hear only fragments of the conversation.

"Before I came here," Brown said, "I knew what I and my men might have to endure. I weighed the responsibility and did not shrink from it. I said if we must die, we die knowing our purpose is right."

Sinn was mystified; he shook his head. "I confess I have no sympathy for the actions you've taken. Yet I regard you a brave man."

Brown responded with the words he'd uttered many times: "I only claim to be doing my duty. To sit still and do nothing in the presence of the barbarities of American slavery is an eternal disgrace."

Sinn didn't argue the point. He operated a livery stable in Maryland and owned no slaves.

Brown moved to where Watson lay on the floor clenching his teeth, trying not to surrender to the pain. The old man knelt and took Watson's hand, looked up at Sinn and said, "This is the third of my sons to have sacrificed for the cause of freedom. The first died in Kansas." He eyed Oliver's body. "Another lies here beside his brother."

Sinn was moved by Brown's words, saw the agony on Watson's face. "Allow me to summon a doctor," he said.

"I thank you for that," Brown said. "My only request is that I be allowed to leave the village with all my men—living or dead. We shall take the hostages across the bridge, after which they will be set free."

"I can guarantee nothing," Sinn replied, "but I'll make your wishes known."

Sinn picked up his lantern, thought about reaching for Brown's hand, decided against it, headed out the door into the cacophony of shouts and curses.

The old man knew another violent confrontation lay ahead. He unbuckled his belt and removed the scabbard holding the sword that once belonged to George Washington. He didn't want harm to come to a relic that in his mind was a symbol of his nation's struggle for freedom. He placed the sheathed sword on the sideboard of the bucket wagon. Before returning the belt to his waist, he shifted the ammunition pouch to its original position.

Shortly before midnight Captain Sinn reappeared. With him were a doctor and Sinn's superior, Colonel Edward Shriver, the commander of the regiment of Maryland volunteers. While Sinn stood holding a lantern, the doctor opened his medical bag and examined Watson's wound.

Colonel Shriver, meanwhile, introduced himself to Brown and told him straightaway that the militia leaders had denied his request for a negotiated retreat. Shriver said the lives of Brown and his men already were forfeited. He looked to the prisoners in the back of the room. "In light of present circumstances," he told Brown, "I urge you to release these unoffending gentlemen you hold as hostages."

"I have secured the hostages for the safety of my men and intend to use them accordingly," Brown replied.

"I must warn you," Shriver said, "this building will be taken at dawn. In order to ensure the safety of the hostages, we shall refrain from firing our muskets. We shall use only the bayonet."

Brown showed no emotion. "I am prepared to die," he said.

The doctor finished applying a gauze bandage to Watson's wound. He stood and whispered something to Sinn, then walked to the door where Colonel Shriver waited. Before departing, Sinn paused to speak to Brown: "The doctor tells me your son's condition is grave. He tried to staunch the bleeding and hopes to do more in the morning."

Brown nodded. He knew what awaited him and his men. He also knew surrender wasn't an option. The Lord had led him on a path of righteousness and he wouldn't turn back. He thought of the words he'd spoken at the farmhouse in the presence of Owen: *We have only one life to live and once to die. And if we lose our lives in this endeavor it will perhaps do more for our cause than our lives could be worth in any other way.*

The old man wasted no time preparing a defense against a possible assault. He took a coil of rope from a fire wagon and handed it to Edwin Coppoc, told him to lash both sets of doors together. The two fire wagons were rolled to the front as obstacles to anyone attempting to breach the doors.

The four soldiers still fit for action—Coppoc, Shields Green, Dauphin Thompson, and Jerry Anderson—now bore the burden of defending a cause that seemed certain to deprive them of their young lives. It wasn't surprising that at least one of them entertained thoughts of surrender. Such was the case with Dauphin Thompson, the younger brother of the man whose death was described by Captain Sinn. Dauphin had overheard a conversation between Brown and one of the hostages, the armory paymaster. The paymaster said Brown and his men were committing treason against Virginia and the United States.

Dauphin spoke up. "Is it true, Captain? Are we committing treason against our country by being here?"

There was a lull in activity as the occupants of the engine room—an audience composed of those who hated slavery as well as those who felt entitled to its beneficence—turned their attention to the challenge levied against the old man by one of his own.

After a long pause Brown said, "You must remember that it is the slaveholder who is committing treason." Another pause. "Our nation was founded on the promise of freedom. By holding men and women in bondage, the slaveholder has declared war on the nation. If it be treason to take up arms to free the prisoners of that war, then our cause—no matter what others choose to call it—is right."

Once again Brown had drawn on his powers of persuasion—with apparent success. His men, including young Dauphin, went back to work.

There was little talk during the few remaining hours before dawn. When preparations were completed, the only sounds heard inside the engine room were the groans of a dying Watson.

By seven o'clock what little sunlight that was able to penetrate the fog had filtered through the shattered transoms and partially illuminated the engine room's dank interior. The hostages, numb from the cold, stood shivering against the back wall. The liberated slaves squatted behind the fire wagons. One of them—Jim—made it clear that if an attack came he would fight alongside Brown's soldiers.

Even though the fog was lifting, the old man had decided that poor visibility made the gun ports unusable. He didn't want harm to come to an unarmed person or someone not directly engaged in an attack. He told the men to train their weapons on the doors. The firepower of the Sharps carbines, he said, would discourage any attempt to gain entry.

Meanwhile, new sounds were coming from outside the fire-house. The bellowing of the drunken mob had been replaced by the assertive tones of voices issuing commands . . . the clamor of boots scuttling across the yard . . . the clash of metal on metal as bayonets were fixed to muskets.

Then silence.

With his carbine at the ready, Brown stood at one of the double doors. He nudged it until the ropes gave way and allowed him to peer through a narrow slit. He saw two figures emerge from the fog. They were walking toward him. One was clad in the uniform of a US cavalry officer, the other held a flag of truce.

The officer was J. E. B. Stuart, the young lieutenant who'd been present after the fighting at Black Jack Springs when Brown was forced to give up the supplies he'd confiscated from the militia leader Henry Clay Pate. Stuart had questioned the failure of his commander, Colonel E. V. Sumner, to arrest Brown and charge him with treason.

"Aren't you old Osawatomie Brown of Kansas whom I once had there as my prisoner?" Stuart asked as he stood gazing at the bearded face.

"Yes," Brown replied, "but you did not keep me."

"This is a bad business you are engaged in," Stuart said. Before the old man could respond, the lieutenant announced: "The United States troops have arrived, and I am sent to demand your surrender."

"Upon what terms?"

Stuart explained that his commander had been assigned a company of ninety marines and was preparing to storm the engine room. "If you lay down your arms," he said, "my colonel will protect you and your men from the local citizens and guarantee you a fair trial by the civil authorities."

"I cannot agree to such terms," Brown replied. "You must tell your colonel that I should be allowed to leave this place with my men and the hostages. After we cross the river, I shall release the hostages. The colonel and his troops would then be free to pursue me."

"I have no authority to agree to such an arrangement," Stuart said. "My orders are to demand your surrender on the terms I've stated."

"Well," Brown said, "rather than hanging by a rope elsewhere, I prefer to die just here."

"Is that your final answer?"

"As I said, I prefer to die just here."

Stuart bowed and turned to leave.

From the back of the room Lewis Washington called out to the lieutenant. "Sir, you must arrange a meeting between Captain Brown and your colonel. Surely they will be able to settle this affair peaceably."

"My colonel will never accede to any terms but those he has offered," Stuart replied, then added, "You needn't worry about your safety and that of the other hostages. I assure you it shan't be compromised."

Brown pulled the door shut. He wasn't aware Stuart had given his colonel a prearranged signal, letting him know the terms of surrender had been rejected. The colonel—a fifty-two-year-old career army officer from Virginia, Robert Edward Lee—directed the leader of the marines to begin the assault.

20

One Minute Later
October 18, 1859
Harpers Ferry, Virginia

Brown had positioned himself between the two fire wagons. To his left—under the suction engine—lay the bodies of Stewart Taylor and Oliver. To his right—under the bucket wagon—lay Watson, quietly praying for his death. Brown shouted some words, but they were drowned in the pounding of sledgehammers. Meanwhile, the door at which the old man had met Lieutenant Stuart shivered with each blow, the strands of rope absorbing most of the force.

The pounding stopped.

Moments later it resumed, but the noise of the collisions was louder. The sledgehammers had been replaced with a ladder used as a battering ram. The batten near the bottom of the door cracked, causing two of the oak staves to cave inward. Then came another strike. It split the batten in half, further shoving the staves into the room, leaving enough space at the base of the door for a man to wriggle inside.

Brown and his soldiers fired a volley into the splintered door.

The smoke from detonating black powder filled the room, made it hard to see the marine crawling through the opening.

He rose to his feet, armed only with a sword, and moved past the fire wagons to the middle of the room. He was followed in quick succession by four more marines, each dragging a musket, each musket equipped with a bayonet.

Voices cried out, but another volley from the Sharps carbines rendered the words unintelligible.

The smoke thickened. Brown's eyes were focused on reloading his carbine when he glimpsed a sword's descending blade; it grazed his head and struck his shoulder near the neck. The blow drove him to his knees.

The marine wielding the sword redirected his attack, thrusting the tip of the blade into the blue-gray haze at what he must have judged was Brown's chest. It was a mighty thrust, but it missed the target, crushing the old man's leather ammunition pouch, half filled with paper cartridges. When the marine withdrew his sword, it was bent practically in half. He grabbed the collapsed blade and began swinging the weapon like a battle-ax, striking Brown—once, twice, thrice—until there was neither movement nor sound coming from the body that lay at his feet, a body barely visible in the smoke-filled room.

Brown heard nothing. Not the calls of surrender from his soldiers. Not the voice of a hostage pointing and shouting, "There is Osawatomie." Not the cries of Dauphin Thompson or Jerry Anderson—both mortally wounded from bayonet stabs.

According to a report issued later by Lieutenant Israel Green, the leader of the storming party, the assault lasted fewer than three minutes. Green noted that one of his men was killed, another slightly wounded.

Brown—his body gashed and bruised—was alive.

Lieutenant Green later blamed himself for Brown's good fortune. In his haste to respond to the order to muster his marines and rush to Harpers Ferry, Green inadvertently had strapped on his ceremonial sword—a finely crafted weapon whose dull blade and blunt tip made it ill suited for hand-to-hand combat.

As for the other occupants of the engine room, all the hostages survived. Of the four liberated slaves, Jim—who was as committed to the fighting as Brown's soldiers—fled and was later discovered floating facedown in the Shenandoah River. Another of the slaves was killed during the assault. A third was arrested, dying shortly thereafter of pneumonia while in captivity; the remaining slave somehow managed to dissolve into the crush of villagers demanding swift justice for the invaders.

"Kill them! Kill them!" the villagers shouted as they poured into the musket factory's yard.

Colonel Lee ordered the marines to restrain the mob while Brown was carried to the office of the armory paymaster. Edwin Coppoc and Shields Green—both unhurt—were moved to the firehouse's watch room, along with Watson, who was judged to be beyond medical help. The lone survivor of the fight at the rifle works, John Copeland, was brought in by the sheriff and locked up with his comrades in the watch room.

Meanwhile, in the paymaster's office, Brown—the left side of his face swollen and bleeding—lay on the floor on a straw-filled mattress. Though his injuries were painful, he willed them to a remote region of his consciousness. He was far more afflicted with a sense of personal failure, the belief that he made miscalculations and that the collapse of the invasion could have been avoided. But his commitment to his purpose was undiminished. His faith required him to right the wrongs in society as he found them, and because slavery was the worst of all wrongs, its abolition was his sacred duty.

Next to Brown lay Aaron Stevens, who had been transferred from the Wager House. Stevens's wounds—shotgun
pellets lodged in his head and shoulders—were more serious
than the old man's, but Colonel Lee judged that with medical attention he'd survive. While the two men waited for a
doctor, they could hear the angry cries of the citizens outside the paymaster's office. As difficult as their situation was,
it didn't deter Brown from cautioning Stevens to take care
not to betray his fellow brothers in arms—those transporting
weapons and ammunition from the Maryland farmhouse, as
well as Osborne Anderson and Albert Hazlett, who—as far as
the old man knew—were still at the arsenal. He wondered if
any managed to escape. Captain Sinn had said nothing about
activity on the Maryland side of the Potomac or the taking
of prisoners inside the arsenal gates.

As the old man weighed these and other questions, the door
to the paymaster's office opened and Colonel Lee appeared.
He was with the doctor who had attended Watson.

Brown said to the doctor, "You saw my son."

"I examined him this morning." The doctor's tone changed
as he added, "It saddens me to say there is little we can do."
A pause. "But his spirit is good. I heard him tell a reporter
he had done his duty as he saw it."

He had done his duty. The words brought a small measure
of satisfaction to Brown as he continued to show no outward
signs of the grief he felt for those who perished during the
invasion.

The doctor inspected Stevens's wounds and explained to
Colonel Lee that removing the pellets from Stevens's head
and shoulders would require a surgeon. He moved to Brown,
pushed aside the blood-encrusted beard. "This wound is not
severe," he said. He lifted Brown's shirt and noted the bruises

on the shoulder and the gashes on the neck and back. "These will heal," he said.

Knowing there were other men requiring medical attention, the colonel dismissed the doctor, then said to Brown, "The telegraph wires your men destroyed have been restored. As a consequence, news of what happened here has spread quickly. I'm afraid a number of influential men—and some newspaper reporters—will be coming, and they will want to interview you." Lee waited for a response, but when none came he declared in a gesture of magnanimity, "If you see this as an annoyance or painful in any way, I shall be happy to exclude all visitors from the room."

Though his jaw ached and speech was difficult for him, Brown said, "I am grateful for your concern, Colonel. But I am glad to make my motives clearly understood."

Lee walked to the door. He had other matters on his mind, among them information he received from the hostage Terence Byrne. Byrne had told him about the weapons that were being transported from the Kennedy farm to the schoolhouse, and Lee had responded by sending Lieutenant Stuart and a detachment of marines to look into the situation. The colonel was eager to learn what Stuart had discovered.

From the floor of the paymaster's office, Brown could hear marines dispersing the villagers. He also could hear the labored breathing of Stevens, who lay beside him. He knew his comrade would suffer his wounds bravely.

Brown found himself thinking about something Lee had said. The colonel had claimed the telegraph was responsible for the swift response to the invasion and that because of the telegraph "influential men" accompanied by newspaper reporters were aboard trains speeding toward Harpers Ferry. For quite some time—several years, in fact—Brown had regarded the telegraph and the steam locomotive as the great inventions of his era, had even spoken to his benefactor George Stearns about their unrealized potential as he and Stearns dined together in a Boston hotel just a few months earlier. Brown was especially intrigued by the telegraph; he thought it was much more than a means for the railroad lines to manage their schedules, even though it was used for such. Brown had told Stearns that the telegraph and the steam locomotive had shrunk the nation, brought people closer together than was ever before possible.

Now, because of the telegraph, journalists on their way to Harpers Ferry would be able to send their reports to newspapers near and far—reports that in some cases would appear in print within hours of their transmission.

Brown soon would have a chance to tell his own story, to explain what his motives were and, in so doing, reach the hearts and minds of a vast audience in both the North and the South. Was this God's plan for him? To sheathe his sword and do nothing more than speak his true purpose? If he could do this, would his invasion still be a failure? Once more, he reasoned, the newspapers would be his allies—as they had been in Kansas. When the visitors came to ask him questions, he'd choose his words wisely.

By midafternoon a dozen men were crowded around Brown and Stevens, both still lying on their straw-filled mattresses. Among those present was Virginia's Governor Henry Wise, who came by express train from the capital in Richmond. Representative Clement Vallandigham of Ohio, an outspoken advocate of proslavery interests, had boarded a train in

Washington, DC, as soon as he learned the perpetrators of a servile insurrection had been arrested. Virginia's Senator James Mason came from his nearby home. Others in the room included Colonel Lee, Lieutenant Stuart, and three journalists, one of whom—a correspondent for the *New York Herald*—recorded practically everything that was said during an interview lasting almost three hours.

It became clear that many of the questions Brown was asked were intended to induce him to incriminate others. Mason did his best to get the old man to admit he was part of a conspiracy financed by abolitionists. Vallandigham followed Mason's lead, hoping to implicate a political rival—the former antislavery congressman Joshua Giddings, reputed to be Brown's friend. The old man deflected such questions, but when the opportunity arose to defend his cause, his responses were elegant and to the point.

Reporter: "Upon what principal do you justify your acts?"

Brown: "Upon the Golden Rule. I pity the poor in bondage that have none to help them. That is why I am here. Not to gratify any personal animosity, not for revenge, not because I have a vindictive spirit. It is my sympathy with the oppressed and wronged—who are as good as you and as precious in the sight of God—that has brought me here."

And later, speaking directly to the correspondent from the *Herald*: "I want you to understand that I respect the rights of the poorest and weakest of colored people oppressed by the slave system just as much as I respect the rights of the people of our nation who are the most wealthy and powerful. That is the idea that has moved me—and that alone. We expect no reward except the satisfaction of endeavoring to do for those in distress and greatly oppressed as we would be done by."

Hoping to wrap up the interview so he could wire his story back to New York, the *Herald* reporter asked Brown if there was anything else he wanted to say. The old man responded, "I have only to say that I claim to be here to carry out a measure I believe perfectly justifiable. Not to act the part of an incendiary or ruffian but to aid those suffering great wrong." Brown scanned the room before adding, "I wish to say, furthermore, that you had better—all you people of the South—prepare yourselves for a settlement of that question that must come up for settlement sooner than you are prepared for. The sooner you are prepared the better. You may dispose of me very easily; I am nearly disposed of now. But this question is still to be settled—this Negro question, I mean. The end of that question is not yet."

As the reporters raced for the B&O Railroad office to telegraph stories to their newspapers and to alert their editors that more details were coming, the "influential" visitors stepped outside the paymaster's office to discuss a document Senator Mason held up during the interview. Mason had spoken of it as a "constitution" and asked Brown for an explanation, admitting he hadn't yet had a chance to read it. Brown replied, "I wish you would give that paper close attention."

The document was one of many Lieutenant Stuart came across during a search of the Kennedy farmhouse earlier in the day. Stuart had found Brown's carpetbag. It was filled with documents—copies of the constitution for the provisional government and a substantial amount of personal correspondence. The letters, many of them from Brown's most active supporters, were of particular interest to Governor Wise—a gaunt, quick-tempered slaveholder who already had announced publicly that he favored Virginia's secession from the Union.

Wise spent most of the afternoon at a table in the Wager House parlor surrounded by his staff, reading the letters aloud, looking for proof the invasion was instigated by wealthy abolitionists. Before he retired to his room, he was convinced he had enough information to bring charges of conspiracy against the members of Brown's secret committee and several other individuals, among them Frederick Douglass.

———

Brown was standing beside his mattress in the paymaster's office inspecting a large bruise on his side when Colonel Lee came at dusk to tell him Watson was near death. Lee said, "Your son is totally at peace despite the suffering he has had to endure."

Brown thanked the colonel, tucked his shirt into his trousers as he gazed down at a sleeping Stevens. The old man was gratified to learn Watson soon would be escaping his pain. He couldn't have accepted Watson's fate so easily—as well as all the other lives that had been sacrificed because of his decisions—were it not for his abiding belief that his actions were predestined by his God.

Lee, meanwhile, out of respect for the grief he presumed the old man was feeling, stood quietly for a few minutes. Then he informed Brown that he and Stevens, along with the men currently held under guard in the firehouse, were to be taken by train in the morning to nearby Charles Town. Once they arrived at the county seat, Brown and his surviving soldiers were to be confined in the Charles Town jail while a grand jury investigation was in progress. A squad of marines currently posted outside the paymaster's office would remain in place until Brown and his men were safely aboard the train to Charles Town.

The colonel excused himself. Brown returned to his mattress.

The old man hadn't slept since the invasion began. He'd been under constant stress during the past forty-eight hours and had suffered symptoms of his malarial illness. Now he found himself overwhelmed by fatigue. In spite of his wounds and the myriad concerns that swirled in his head, he slipped into a deep sleep.

He even dreamed. The dream had come to him many times over the years—a dream in which a young John Brown witnessed a thin, poorly clad slave boy being beaten with an iron shovel.

21

Nine Days Later
October 27, 1859
Charles Town, Virginia

On the morning Brown's trial was to begin, his physical appearance had improved. Though the gash on his neck wasn't healed completely, the swelling under his eye had subsided and he no longer wore a bandage around his head. In his cell in the Charles Town jail he sat on his cot, a collection of newspapers spread out before him. Sunlight filtered through a barred window that overlooked a yard surrounded by a high brick wall. On the stone floor beneath the window was a table covered with more newspapers.

Aaron Stevens lay nearby, still suffering the effects of shotgun pellets embedded in his skull and shoulders. Brown read aloud from the newspapers while Stevens listened dutifully, even though his head ached and he found it difficult to concentrate. Still, the news reports made it obvious to the ailing Stevens that the invasion of Harpers Ferry had instilled fear and outrage among slaveholders throughout the South.

Along one wall of the cell a fire burned in an inordinately large fireplace. The jailer had started the fire the previous evening in anticipation of an early morning frost. The warmth it gave was a comfort to both men but especially Stevens.

With his blanket pulled up to his chin, he was resigned to the fact that he'd probably receive little additional medical attention, but he was grateful his wounds had been cleaned and bandaged.

Brown had been awake since before dawn. He'd dressed and stoked the fire and at first light was looking through the newspapers provided by his jailer—stout, round-faced John Avis. Avis lived with his wife and child in quarters across the corridor from the cells occupied by Brown and the others taken at Harpers Ferry. It was his wife's job to cook for the prisoners and tend to their laundry and other needs, all of which she undertook without a trace of contempt, having found the new arrivals courteous and respectful.

A bond of sorts had begun to develop between Brown and Avis. As a captain in the Charles Town militia, the jailer had been in charge of a company summoned to the Ferry by the physician John Starry. Avis and his men were partly responsible for bringing about Brown's final retreat to the firehouse's engine room; it wasn't unusual for the old man to acknowledge his opponents' mettle, and he felt Avis and his company deserving. Though the jailer expressed no sympathy for Brown's actions, the two men had opportunities to talk. Brown was able to explain his purpose and that he drew inspiration from Holy Scripture and the Declaration of Independence.

The jailer soon became the old man's only source of reliable information—information that included what had become of the rest of Brown's soldiers. The old man learned of the men who had escaped—Charles Plummer Tidd, Barclay Coppoc, Francis Jackson Merriam, Osborne Anderson, and his son Owen. John Cook and Albert Hazlett had also managed to escape, but in the past few days they'd been hunted down and would soon join the prisoners in Charles Town.

With genuine remorse Avis also told him of the men who didn't survive—how the dead were tossed into shallow riverbank graves and that medical students were allowed to dig up some of the corpses and carry them off for laboratory dissection. Through the sharing of this and other personal information, Brown's relationship with the jailer became close, so much so that Avis extended the old man favors, among them paper and pencil so he could write letters. The jailer also turned a blind eye as newspapers from distant cities in both the North and South found their way into Brown's cell, smuggled in by reporters and visitors.

Brown, along with his fellow prisoners—Stevens, Edwin Coppoc, Shields Green, and John Copeland—already had appeared at a series of preliminary hearings. In front of a packed courtroom they listened to testimony from a list of witnesses that included the hostages held in the engine room. When the examination was over the prisoners were asked to choose whom they wished to represent them.

With one eye peering out of a slit in his swollen face, Brown rose from his seat. An injury to his jaw caused him pain as he spoke, but he felt obligated to make sure his adversaries understood that he had no doubts about the legitimacy of his purpose and that he was quite willing to face the consequences of his actions.

"I did not ask for any quarter at the time I was taken," he said. "The governor of the state of Virginia tendered me assurances that I should have a fair trial, but under no circumstances whatever will I be able to have a fair trial. If you seek my blood, you can have it at any moment without this mockery of a trial . . . I have now little further to ask, other than I may not be foolishly insulted only as cowardly barbarians insult those who fall under their power."

Governor Henry Wise may have tendered Brown assurances, but as long as Wise had a say in the matter, the man who violated the sovereignty of Virginia was going to be subjected to the full extent of the state's judicial powers. When the train from the Ferry carrying the governor and his prisoners pulled into Charles Town, Wise summoned Richard Parker, the judge who presided over the circuit court.

"We must bring Brown to trial without a moment's delay," the governor told Judge Parker, "before the black Republicans get their hands on him."

Wise was referring to certain members of a national political party that had been in existence only five years: the Republicans. The radical wing of the party—the so-called black Republicans—hated the existence of slavery in a nation that claimed individual liberty as a core value. Wise suspected the black Republicans might attempt to bring Brown to trial in federal court—a logical choice, given that Brown's headquarters was located in a federal armory and that much of the fighting took place on armory grounds. If the black Republicans succeeded, Wise thought they might use the trial to advance their antislavery agenda. And even if the black Republicans didn't meddle, Wise wanted to make a statement: Virginia had the right to act unilaterally when it was threatened with insurrection. As a politician who had called for his state's secession from the Union and as a Southerner who clung tenaciously to a code of honor—having survived no fewer than eight duels—Wise was embarrassed that Virginia militias didn't defeat the handful of insurgents at the armory, choosing instead to rely on federal troops. He felt

Virginians ought to be able to take care of themselves, and he didn't want the federal government nosing around where it didn't belong. However, the more he thought about the situation, the more he saw Brown's actions furthering the case for disunion—for the South breaking away from the North and forming its own confederation of states, a possibility he was inclined to favor.

Whatever its eventual impact, the invasion of Harpers Ferry—at least the exaggerated reports circulated at the outset—created an enormous stir, rekindling nightmares of another Nat Turner revolt, something that had haunted Virginia slaveholders for nearly three decades. In order to calm fears and send a message to abolitionists with thoughts of imitating Brown, Governor Wise wanted justice administered swiftly. And he had a valid excuse for doing so. The semi-annual term of the circuit court was nearing its conclusion, and if Brown wasn't brought to trial immediately he couldn't be tried for another six months. Too much time for Virginians consumed by fear and anger to have to wait.

Wise may have despised Brown's aims, but he admired the old man's courage, his willingness to die for what he believed in. After listening to him speak his mind from a mat on the floor of the armory paymaster's office and chatting with him as he was being taken to the train for the trip to Charles Town, Wise said of Brown, "He is a bundle of the best nerves I ever saw—cut and thrust and bleeding and in bonds. He is a man of clear head, of courage, fortitude, and simple ingenuousness. He is cool, collected, and indomitable, and he inspired me with great trust in his integrity as a man of truth." Wise no doubt had experienced the old man's ability to captivate an audience, a skill that knew no boundaries—affecting friends and enemies in equal measure.

Brown's parting words to the governor were uttered on the railroad platform in Charles Town. The old man waited with his hands cuffed behind his back as militiamen stood ready to take him and his comrades to their jail cells. Jeering citizens milled about; one came forward and called Brown a robber.

Brown looked the man in the eye and declared, "It is you who are robbers—you slaveholders." He paused, surveying the rest of the people on the platform and added, "And you who choose to do nothing about it."

An annoyed Wise chose to respond: "Mr. Brown, the silver of your beard is reddened by the blood of crime, and it is meet that you should eschew those hard words and think upon eternity."

"Governor," Brown said calmly, "I have from all appearances not more than fifteen or twenty years the start of you in the journey to that eternity of which you kindly warn me. And whether my tenure here shall be fifteen months or fifteen days or fifteen hours, I am equally prepared to go. There is an entire eternity behind and an entire eternity before, and the little speck in the center, however long, is but comparatively a minute. The difference between your tenure and mine is trifling, and I want therefore to tell *you* to be prepared. I am prepared. You slaveholders have a heavy responsibility, and it behooves *you* to prepare more than it does *me*."

Wise pivoted and boarded the train for Richmond. Brown and his men were hustled off to the Charles Town jail.

When the last of the preliminary hearings ended, the grand jury was ready to issue its charges. Brown and Stevens were brought to court on their cots. Stevens had complained of dizziness. Though Brown's injuries were not as serious as his cellmate's, he refused to leave his cell unless he, too, was carried into the courtroom on a cot.

Brown would continue to occupy a cot throughout his trial—rising only when he wished to participate in the questioning of witnesses or to make a statement. His insistence on lying prostrate at the feet of his accusers was partly due to his injuries and partly as a protest of what he regarded an unfair rush to judgment—though it may have been equally the result of what the late John Kagi had called a "talent for the dramatic." No matter what they felt about Brown's deeds at Harpers Ferry, how could those following his trial—either in person or in the newspapers—not find something to admire about a wounded man who defended himself from his prison bed? And though Virginians may have been in a hurry to convict him, they wanted to give the appearance of conducting a fair trial—particularly after denying his request for a delay in order that he might have sufficient time to recover from his injuries. So they felt obliged to grant Brown certain privileges, not the least of which was to allow him to be tried from a cot.

No special concessions were made, however, when it was time for the charges to be presented by the grand jury. Both Brown and Stevens were told to get up and stand before the bar alongside the three unimpaired prisoners. Bailiffs held Stevens erect. Brown used the back of a chair to support himself.

The clerk began reading:

"Conspiring with rebellious slaves to produce an insurrection . . .

"Committing treason by waging war against the Commonwealth of Virginia . . .

"Feloniously and willfully committing murder within the Commonwealth's jurisdiction . . ."

All the defendants pleaded not guilty. Brown's trial was slated to begin the following day.

———— •••• ————

And so, as he sat on his cot browsing through newspapers on the morning he was to be taken to court, Brown was convinced his God had laid out a new path for him. His war on slavery wasn't over. But the weapons of war had changed. Guns and pikes were to be replaced with words— his words—and the old man was confident he was equal to the task.

There was a rapping on the cell door's iron bars and the rattle of keys, the clicking of a falling tumbler. The door swung open and the jailer stuck his head inside.

"The guards will be here soon," Avis said. "In the meantime I have something Mrs. Avis prepared—something to warm you on this cool morning." The jailer glanced at Stevens, saw his eyes were open, and added, "For you, too." He stepped back into the corridor and reappeared with a tray that held a steaming kettle, two tin cups, and a mound of biscuits. "I know you don't favor coffee," Avis said to Brown, "so I've brought my wife's English tea." He set the tray on the table.

Brown said, "You can tell Mrs. Avis her kindnesses are always appreciated. She and this nourishment shall receive the blessing of the Lord."

The jailer retreated from the cell, returning moments later with a pair of bulky leg irons dangling from a two-foot chain. He spoke apologetically: "I think it unnecessary you should be required to wear these to your trial, Captain, but the governor fears attempts will be made to rescue you."

Brown nodded and said, "The governor seems to have taken extraordinary precautions." The old man knew that a cannon had been placed outside the courthouse and another at the entrance to the jail.

"He's not yet declared martial law," Avis said of the governor, "though a stranger in town might think so. Militiamen roam the streets, everyone is armed, and more troops are on the way from Richmond."

While the jailer knelt at Brown's feet to attach the leg irons, the old man was submissive, remarking that he was happy to be bound in the manner of those he sought to free from bondage.

After Avis departed, Stevens lifted his head. "Well, Captain," he said, "I now see what you meant when you said slavery could be frightened out of existence."

Although Brown didn't respond, Stevens's words brought to mind some things the old man hadn't shared with his cellmate. There were stories in the local newspaper of fires of unknown origin that had flared up in the surrounding countryside, and a Richmond daily reported that slaveholders in the Charles Town area had seen their barns, stables, and stockyards consumed by flames, giving the night skies a "lurid glare." It was Avis who first told Brown of the fires, that they were rumored to have been set by slaves intent on avenging the failed invasion, that some of the slaves responsible for the fires were the runaways who joined Brown at Harpers Ferry and saw the futility of continuing to fight; they had managed to escape, only to resume guerrilla activities on their own. The fires caused great fear among the residents of Charles Town and neighboring communities. But fear that grew out of revenge was abhorrent to Brown, and he worried that his efforts to rid the nation of slavery would be tainted by it, even though the fires may have been the work of men who felt they were walking in John Brown's footsteps.

The old man had spoken about none of this with Stevens. Nor had he disclosed the fact that Northern newspapers were critical of the invasion and had attempted to discredit him. Editors called him reckless, monomaniacal, someone who "met with the fate which he courted." They called the invasion the work of a madman.

The chain on his leg irons trailed noisily across the stone floor as Brown shuffled to the table. He lifted the kettle from the tray and poured the hot tea, then shuffled back to Stevens's cot. Brown helped Stevens sit up and held him while he sipped the tea—which was how the guards found them when they entered the cell.

"The judge and jury are ready for you, Mr. Brown," said the sergeant of the guard.

Brown shuffled to his cot, collected the newspapers, and put them on the table. He returned to the cot, sat down, and swung his shackled legs onto the straw-filled mattress. He nodded to the sergeant.

"Let us not keep Virginia waiting," he said, then lay down, pulling up the blanket. He shut his eyes as the cot with him on it was hoisted into the air and carried into a street crowded with onlookers. Militiamen—muskets loaded, bayonets fixed—marched alongside.

22

Minutes Later
October 27, 1859
Charles Town, Virginia

Diagonally across the street from the jail stood the Jefferson County Courthouse, a compact two-story brick building whose facade consisted of a portico and four thick columns. Were it not for a massive cupola rising from its gabled roof, the building would have been a typical example of the neoclassical style that had become a staple of Southern architecture. Immediately inside the doors was the courtroom, occupying the entire ground floor and amply lit by large windows on all four walls. Stoves provided warmth, though they were hardly needed; the body heat generated by a room packed with spectators was more than adequate. The air gave off the odor of cigar smoke and perspiration.

Brown's cot was carried down a narrow aisle and placed before Judge Parker, who sat at a table on a dais enclosed by a railing. On either side of the aisle were the tables for the defense and prosecution. To the side of the dais was the jury box.

There was a long table reserved for journalists, a number of whom were with the Associated Press, a group of correspondents employed by a half dozen New York dailies. The rest of the reporters represented individual newspapers. The journalists had chosen to segregate themselves—Northern reporters on one side of the table, their Southern counterparts on the other.

Brown lay on his cot with a blanket covering his head. He seemed oblivious to the opening remarks—until one of his court-appointed attorneys, Lawson Botts, rose from his chair and waved a piece paper at Judge Parker.

"I have here, your honor, a telegraphed message recently received that I should like to read to the court."

The judge nodded. "Go ahead, Mr. Botts."

The cracking of peanuts and chestnuts by the nonsmoking spectators ceased. The room fell silent.

Botts had only to read the first few sentences before it was evident the information contained in the message—an account of a history of insanity among Brown's close and distant relatives—was intended to show the invasion of Harpers Ferry as the work of a deranged mind. When Botts finished reading, he announced he'd shared the message with Brown earlier and that his client refused an insanity plea and sought no immunity of any kind.

Brown hadn't expected the message to be read in court. Even though Botts acknowledged that Brown rejected what the message insinuated, the specter of insanity hanging over his trial was something the old man dreaded. That Botts would even raise the issue confirmed Brown's belief that his court-appointed attorneys were incapable of providing the kind of defense he desired. He knew that the people who sent the message were well intentioned, that they were trying to save him from the gallows, but he also knew they were naive. They didn't understand that it was imperative he be perceived as a rational human being, someone who honestly believed he did what was right, even though he may have violated the laws of the nation and the Commonwealth of Virginia. To imply he might suffer bouts of insanity would ruin everything the old man was trying to accomplish; it would turn his decision to use his trial as a platform for justifying his purpose—liberating the slaves—into a meaningless endeavor.

So he pushed aside his covers, exposing his shackled legs, and—with difficulty—got to his feet. He looked at the jury, then turned to Judge Parker: "If it please the court, I should like to put an end to what I look upon as a miserable artifice and pretext of those who ought to have taken a different course in regard to me, if they took any at all, and I view the one they have taken with contempt." Brown went on to explain why he shouldn't be considered insane, putting to rest any attempt to use the claim of insanity as a strategy for his defense.

Judge Parker accepted Brown's argument and instructed the jury to do likewise.

———— •••• ————

The trial lasted five days.

Reports were transmitted by a press that had daily access to the telegraph. Newspaper editors—North and South—took the reports wired from Charles Town and transformed them into front-page copy reflecting their attitudes toward Brown and the sectional biases of their readers.

In the South, Brown was branded a fanatic and a tool of Northern abolitionists. The letters taken from his carpetbag enabled Southern editors to justify the claim that wealthy abolitionists and black Republicans were conspiring with Brown to destroy a way of life that had existed in the South for more than two centuries.

In the North, the story line wasn't so rigid. When the trial began, Brown's detractors far outnumbered his supporters. As the end neared, however, Northern papers tilted ever so slightly in his direction. This was especially apparent when the hostages spoke favorably of their treatment by Brown. When the description of his reaction to the killing of Will Thompson was printed, readers were left with a portrait of a man who was far from a cold, calculating fanatic. Brown wept when the men who shot Thompson bragged to the court about tossing him half-alive into the Potomac, watching him drown, then continuing to fire at his lifeless body.

On the fourth day of the trial, two highly regarded attorneys—hired in a last-ditch effort by Brown's Massachusetts friends to replace the defense lawyers appointed by the court—gave closing arguments. Though the arguments were forceful, they had little effect on the jurors.

It took only forty-five minutes for the jury to return with a verdict.

The spectators sat inert, the only movement coming from the table occupied by the reporters as they flipped open their notepads. Brown lay on his cot with only his bearded face visible. His eyes were closed, and his face bore a serene expression.

At the behest of Judge Parker, the clerk of the court read a brief statement recapitulating the charges, after which he turned to the jury:

"Gentlemen of the jury, what say you? Is the prisoner at the bar—John Brown—guilty or not guilty?"

Foreman of the jury: "Guilty."

Clerk: "Guilty of treason and conspiring with slaves and others to rebel and to commit murder in the first degree?"

Foreman: "Yes."

The spectators sat in stony silence. The reporters scribbled away on their notepads. The old man opened his eyes, exposed his arms in order to make a small adjustment to his blanket, pulling it closer to his chin. The expression on his face never changed.

The defense attorneys came to the bench to motion for an arrest of judgment based on certain irregularities in the original indictments and in the verdict itself. Judge Parker said he would consider the motion, then told the attorneys it had been an exhausting trial and he would announce his decision in due course.

Twenty-four hours later the judge called for the resumption of proceedings.

Brown had had a full day to think about his fate. He anticipated that the motion entered by his attorneys would be summarily denied, and it was. The only other piece of business remaining was his sentencing, and Brown had no doubts about that either.

The courtroom was once again filled to capacity as Brown lay on his cot before the bar. His attorneys stood beside him; they listened to Judge Parker overrule all objections. The clerk then came forward and asked Brown if he had anything to say before his sentence was pronounced.

All eyes were on the old man as he got up from his cot, the leg irons seeming nothing more than an inconvenience. "I have, may it please the court, a few words to say."

Two hundred fifty miles away—in his office on Printing House Square in Lower Manhattan—Horace Greeley, the forty-eight-year-old editor of the *New York Tribune*, was waiting for a copyboy to hand him the latest transcripts of telegraphed reports from Charles Town. It was the day Brown was to be sentenced, and Greeley was eager to read the transcripts. He knew the old man was to be given an opportunity to speak.

In accordance with Greeley's instructions, the reports were handed to him as quickly as his wire editor was able to transcribe them. The copyboys delivered the reports one page at a time. Greeley had paper and pencil ready. He wanted to make notes while reading.

The first transcript—an observation by the *Tribune* correspondent in Charles Town—arrived. Greeley picked it up, adjusted his spectacles, and read: "When Brown was asked by the Clerk of the Court if there was anything he would like to say, his voice remained steady and did not waver as he spoke calmly with supreme confidence. The voice with the metallic timbre silenced the murmuring spectators."

Then came the first page of Brown's speech:

"In the first place, I deny everything but what I have all along admitted, of a design on my part to free the slaves. I intended certainly to have made a clean thing of that matter, as I did last winter when I went into Missouri and there took slaves without the snapping of a gun on either side, moving them through the country and finally leaving them in Canada. I designed to have done the same thing again on a larger scale. That was all I intended. I never did intend murder or treason or the destruction of property or to excite or incite slaves to rebellion or to make insurrection."

Greeley picked up his pencil and made notes:

Words of a man convinced he fought for a just cause. Believes so strongly in his cause he bends the truth to make a point. Missouri raid not conducted "without the snapping of a gun"—a man was shot, died from wounds. Could have said the killing was justifiable under the circumstances but that would have intruded on message he wants to send.

No useful purpose served by admitting to making an "insurrection," even though his invasion fits definition of "a rising against civil or political authority."

As Greeley finished, a copyboy appeared with another page of transcript. Greeley nodded and continued reading:

"I have another objection, and that is that it is unjust that I should suffer such a penalty. Had I interfered in the manner which I admit, and which I admit has been fairly proved—for I admire the truthfulness and candor of the greater portion of the witnesses who have testified in this case—had I so interfered in behalf of the rich, the powerful, the intelligent, the so-called great, or in behalf of any of their friends, either father, mother, brother, sister, wife or children, or any of that class and suffered and sacrificed what I have in this interference, it would have been all right. Every man in this court would have deemed it an act worthy of reward rather than punishment."

Greeley made more notes:

Spoken like a true revolutionary. Came to Virginia to free the slaves. Had he done the same for a dispossessed privileged class, he would have been rewarded rather than punished.

Another page of transcript landed on Greeley's desk:

"This court acknowledges, as I suppose, the validity of the law of God. I see a book kissed here which I suppose to be the Bible, or at least the New Testament, which teaches me that all things whatsoever I would that men should do to me, I should do even so to them. It teaches me further to *remember them that are in bonds as bound with them.* I endeavored to act up to that instruction. I believe that to have interfered as I have done—in behalf of the despised poor—was not wrong, but right. Now, if it is deemed necessary that I should forfeit my life for the furtherance of the ends of justice and mingle my blood further with the blood of my children and with the blood of millions in this slave country whose rights are disregarded by wicked, cruel, and unjust enactments—I say let it be done."

By now Greeley recognized the power of Brown's words and their potential to further polarize some readers while unifying others. The editor's notes were becoming more stylized, sounding more like the radical abolitionist he was:

> The revolutionary argues the validity of his actions, and—in so doing—reveals the hypocrisy of his adversaries. And, by implication, he holds all Southerners who do nothing to expunge the evils of slavery—whether slaveholders or not—in violation of their Christian duty. Says he is ready to perform a Christ-like act and sacrifice his life for those held in bondage.

No sooner had Greeley finished making his notes when another page of Brown's transcribed remarks was laid on the desk:

"Let me say one word further. I feel entirely satisfied with the treatment I have received during my trial. Considering all the circumstances, it has been more generous than I expected. But I feel no consciousness of guilt. I have stated from the first what was my intention and what was not. I never had any design against the liberty of any person, nor any disposition to commit treason or incite slaves to rebel or make any general insurrection. I never encouraged any man to do so but always discouraged any idea of that kind."

Greeley smiled and wrote:

The revolutionary completes the Christ-like image: "Forgive them, Father, for they know not what they do."

The last page Greeley was handed seemed to the editor like an afterthought:

"Let me say, also, a word in regard to the statements made by some of those connected with me. I hear it has been stated by some of them that I have induced them to join me. But the contrary is true. I do not state this to injure them but as regretting their weakness. There is not one of them but joined me of his own accord, and the greater part of them at their own expense. A number of them I never saw and never had a word of conversation with till the day they came to me, and that was for the purpose I have stated. Now I have done."

Greeley thought for a time before writing a question:

Did he think he'd been betrayed by Cook or one of the others?

Greeley knew of the capture of John Cook and Albert Hazlett, and there were rumors that Cook—and possibly one of the men confined in a cell adjacent to Brown's—had made statements indicating they had been coerced into joining the old man. Greeley speculated that Brown was trying to address such rumors before anyone else got hold of them and that the old man wouldn't want anything to spoil the message he wished to send the nation.

The editor called for a copyboy, handed him the pages he'd been reading. "Take these to the typesetters," he said. "We'll run the story in tomorrow's edition."

When Brown finished his speech, Judge Parker waited a few seconds, cleared his throat. The old man stood motionless before the bar. The judge announced that there existed no reasonable doubt of guilt. He turned away from Brown's gaze and looked to the crowd that filled the courtroom.

"The prisoner shall be hanged by the neck until dead," he said, then paused before adding, "in a public place on the second of December next."

So saying, the judge gaveled the trial to a close.

With the exception of the journalists whose pencils could be heard scratching out words on their notepads, the courtroom remained subdued. Then—disrupting the church-like solemnity—came the sound of someone applauding. The man was immediately censured by the judge and removed by the bailiffs. Judge Parker would later apologize for the outburst, claiming the offender wasn't a resident of Jefferson County. The judge didn't want the trial to end with a breach in decorum. The nation needed to know that the citizens of Charles Town and the Commonwealth of Virginia behaved with dignity and respect when John Brown was sentenced to death.

While reporters speculated about what was going on in Brown's head, he returned to his cot. He seemed neither shocked nor depressed nor bitter about the verdict and the sentence he received. The reporters would have been surprised to know that as he lay with his eyes shut he was calculating the number of days until his execution. Since it was now November 2, he had exactly thirty days left. He would make good use of every minute that remained to him.

———— ••••• ————

It was early afternoon when Brown was returned to jail by his guards. In anticipation of his arrival, Stevens had forced himself to get up and stoke the fire; he wanted to make sure his captain would find some comfort in the warmth it provided. The flames blazed brightly by the time the guards set the cot on the floor and left the cell.

Standing with his back to the fireplace, Stevens waited for Brown to speak first.

The old man swung his shackled legs onto the floor and said matter-of-factly, "Well, my good friend, it is as I have expected all along. They will murder me on the second of December."

Though he wasn't surprised, Stevens felt compelled to say something—even though whatever he might say would be of little consequence and might even trivialize the flood of events that had carried his leader to this moment. He said, "Surely the Massachusetts men will steal you away from this prison by then, Captain."

"No," Brown responded. "I have no intention of allowing the Massachusetts men to get up a plan for my rescue. I have already given my word to Captain Avis that I shan't attempt an escape." He stroked his beard, then looked down and said,

"Besides, Aaron, I now believe I am worth infinitely more to my cause if I die on the gallows here in Virginia."

Even though Stevens had challenged some of Brown's decisions in the past, he didn't question this one. After all, it was Brown's cause that had drawn Stevens and the others to the old man. And most of them were just as willing as he to sacrifice their lives.

Brown then told Stevens that throughout the ordeal of his trial, he suffered pain from his wounds but hadn't experienced a single episode of his chronic illness—for which he was most grateful. Furthermore, his appetite was good, and he was quite looking forward to whatever Mrs. Avis had prepared for their evening meal.

Later, as the two men sat down to bowls of Mrs. Avis's stew, Brown said he was eager to get started writing letters. So little time remained to him and he had much he wanted to say. "The Lord may have taken away my Sharps carbine," he said, "but he has replaced it with the sword of the spirit. And I hope it proves *mighty to the pulling down of strongholds.*"

Stevens's head still throbbed from his wounds, but he couldn't help smiling. He'd had a feeling Brown would punctuate his thoughts with a passage from the Bible.

For the next twenty-nine days, Brown would compose a steady stream of letters, many of which found their way into print. Along with the reports of journalists who covered the trial or had come to interview him in his jail cell, the letters served to ignite the abolitionist sentiments of Northern men and women, some of whom were so moved by his words that they strove to turn him into a heroic figure, someone who would restore the nation's moral compass and whose example would lead to the ultimate eradication of slavery in the South.

23

Twenty-Nine Days Later
December 1, 1859
Charles Town, Virginia

At three thirty in the afternoon on the day before Brown was to be hanged, his wife, Mary, arrived at the Charles Town jail. It had been a long journey by carriage and rail, and along the way she'd been invited to stay in the homes of well-respected abolitionists, among them Lucretia Mott, a leader of the women's rights movement. Before crossing from the free to the slave states, Mary had to wait for Virginia's Governor Wise to give final approval to her visit and to arrange for her care and safety.

At first Brown was against the visit. He wanted to spare Mary the indignities of mobs of angry men taunting her. He also worried about the expense involved, writing her that she "would use up all the scanty means she has, or is likely to have, to make her and the children comfortable hereafter."

But Thomas Higginson—the Worcester minister and member of Brown's secret committee—was determined that Mary should go to Charles Town despite her husband's objections. Since the discovery of the letters in the old man's carpetbag, many of his supporters had been lying low for fear of being charged with conspiracy; some, including Frederick Douglass, had even fled to Canada. But Higginson had no fear of the consequences of his actions, and his loyalty to Brown never diminished. He hoped Mary might persuade him to consent to a plan of escape. So he went to North Elba, where he discovered that Mary had just received word of Brown's sentencing; she was more than willing to travel to Virginia. Higginson accompanied her to Boston and solicited the necessary funds before putting her on a train headed south.

The journey had taken Mary away from the North Elba homestead for almost a month. She was concerned about the girls, even though she knew Annie was quite capable of caring for the younger ones. She completed the last leg of the journey—a three-hour carriage ride from Harpers Ferry to Charles Town—on a bleak and chilly day. For her protection, Governor Wise provided an escort of twenty mounted riflemen. She was surprised to find Charles Town bereft of ordinary citizens. Instead, the streets were swarming with militiamen clad in a variety of uniforms, the younger men loud and swaggering, many of them no doubt absent from their homes and families for the first time. The carriage came to a stop in front of the jail.

When the jailer's wife greeted her, Mary immediately felt at ease. Brown had written of the warm relationship he'd formed with the jailer and his wife. In the parlor of their apartment, the jailer's wife introduced Mary to Captain Avis.

"I know you are anxious to see Captain Brown," Avis said. He was embarrassed at not having been made aware that Mary was much younger than her husband. She was in fact seventeen years his junior. Her hair was parted in the center and pulled back tightly behind her neck, and her high-collared dress was long and plain.

"Why, yes, Captain Avis," she said, "I am very much look-ing forward to seeing my husband."

"And you shall," he replied, then rather sheepishly added, "but first you must see Mrs. Avis. It is the governor's wish that all precautions be taken. I hope you understand."

"Of course, Captain," she replied. "Although I'm sure you realize that if I had a weapon secreted on my person, my husband would refuse to accept it. He has already written me he would do nothing to betray the kindnesses you and your wife have shown him."

It was the jailer's and not Mary's eyes that reddened and grew moist. "Governor Wise be damned," Avis sputtered. "Come, Mrs. Brown, your husband is waiting."

Avis unlocked the cell door. Brown's cellmate, Aaron Ste-vens, had been moved temporarily to an adjacent cell. Brown was standing beside the table on which lay the many news-papers he'd been allowed to acquire surreptitiously.

Avis made a quick exit; he took a seat across the corridor, out of sight and earshot. The jailer decided to ignore instruc-tions from Governor Wise that whatever activity took place inside the cell should be closely monitored.

For a few seconds Brown and Mary were locked in each other's gaze. He was wearing a black frock coat over a white cotton shirt; his trousers seemed too large, and they hung loosely from his hips. His beard had returned to its full length, as had his crown of thick, wavy hair. Mary expected to find her husband bruised and battered, but his facial wounds had healed.

Brown opened his arms and Mary came to him. Neither spoke as she rested her head on his chest. They stood for some time until Brown whispered, "I am so glad to see you, my dear wife."

"And I am so glad to see you, my dear husband."

Brown took her by the hand and led her to a pair of plain ladder-back chairs that stood near the fireplace's wide hearth.

Mary saw that her husband's gait was impeded by leg irons. He wore a pair of thick wool socks to ease the chafing to his ankles. They sat down in front of the fire.

They spoke for almost three hours, mostly of practical concerns having to do with how Brown wished his meager possessions distributed to his surviving children, the education of their daughters, and Mary's future. She in turn disclosed what little information she had of the whereabouts of Owen and the other members of Brown's company who had managed to elude capture. She was fairly certain Owen had found refuge in Ohio—either with one of his brothers or with friends. She'd heard rumors that the others had gone to Canada.

Brown, meanwhile, talked about the many visitors—other than the journalists—who were allowed to see him during his confinement. The first of these was Judge Thomas Russell and his wife, the couple that once offered their Boston home as a hideout when Brown was being pursued by federal marshals. Mrs. Russell, Brown said, mended his coat and sent it out to be cleaned. He said Judge Russell inspected the cell's large fireplace, making note of the fact that the chimney was wide enough for a man get to the roof if he ever had a desire to do so.

There also had been a visit from abolitionist Rebecca Spring and her son. Mary was acquainted with Mrs. Spring, having stayed overnight with her and her family at their home in Perth Amboy, New Jersey. In an effort to lighten the mood of what he perceived was becoming a much too somber occasion, Brown told Mary that Mrs. Spring's son had asked him how it felt to face so many life-and-death situations. "I told him I have been more afraid of being taken into an evening party of ladies and gentlemen than of meeting a company of men with guns."

Mary, however, couldn't conceal her discomfort when Brown turned to the subject of his death and the disposition of his remains. He began to detail an elaborate plan that would require her to see to the cremation of his body—along with the bodies of Watson and Oliver and the Thompson boys, Will and Dauphin. Brown wanted her to return their ashes to North Elba for burial.

Mary interrupted him. "Let us speak no more on this subject." It had been only a few short weeks since she'd grieved with her sons' young widows—Oliver's pregnant wife, Martha, and Watson's Isabella, the mother of a boy not yet a year old. She had no desire to discuss a matter that had been so painful to her. Besides, she'd already been told by Governor Wise that the Commonwealth of Virginia would handle arrangements following the execution.

"Well, do not fret about it," Brown said. "I thought the plan would save considerable expense and was for the best."

Because he didn't want Mary to go back to North Elba with the slightest doubt about how he felt about the outcome of the invasion, Brown said, "You must trust that those who were slain have not died in vain. A merciful God will not allow the sacrifices of our family to be lost." He told her that his mission was not the failure it appeared to be and that what took place at Harpers Ferry would one day be heralded as a most glorious success. "Let none of our family feel ashamed on my account," he said, "for I shall be able to recover all my lost capital in this affair by hanging only a few moments by the neck."

"Husband," she said resolutely, "it is a hard fate."

Her words weren't spoken out of self-pity but rather revealed a resilience born of devotion to her husband and his cause. The years of separation, the burden of caring for the children in his absence, the tragedies that had befallen the family, had only made her stronger. She harbored no regrets, as a weaker woman might, that she hadn't enjoyed a life bespeaking the comforts of a happy home, of a husband content to live an ordinary life, of children who would grow to adulthood free of a sense of duty thrust upon them. Instead, her husband had followed a path that required great sacrifices. Though Mary didn't feel obliged to share his certainty about God's intentions, she—like the rest of the family—knew her husband's cause was right, and that was enough.

Brown shuffled to the table and picked up one of the newspapers. "Do you remember when I said it is my duty to awaken the nation?" he asked, holding the paper aloft.

Of course she had. At every stop on her journey to Charles Town, she'd been handed newspapers reminding her of his pronouncement. When she arrived in Boston in the company of Higginson, the people were talking about a lecture by Henry David Thoreau delivered just days earlier and printed in several newspapers. Thoreau's address was the first to extol Brown's invasion as an example of civil disobedience, a courageous act designed to restore the nation to the principles on which it was founded, an act in which violence was justified. A week later, at Lucretia Mott's home in Philadelphia, Mary was handed a copy of the *Liberator*, William Lloyd Garrison's abolitionist newspaper; it contained a report of a speech made by Ralph Waldo Emerson, a man whose status as a cultural spokesman extended far beyond Massachusetts. Emerson had echoed Thoreau's sentiments and created a furor when he called Brown "a new saint, awaiting yet his martyrdom and who, if he shall suffer, will make the gallows glorious like the cross." By the middle of November, while she was still in Philadelphia waiting for confirmation of her visit to Charles Town, she picked up a copy of Greeley's *New York Tribune* and found herself absorbed in reading an exchange of letters between Virginia's Governor Wise and Lydia Maria Child, the novelist and activist from Massachusetts, who listed abolitionism as one of her several causes. The letters were published in the form of a debate on slavery and Brown's right to attack it. The debate tweaked the consciences of Northern readers and infuriated Southerners who read the reprints in their local papers.

Mary was aware of all this when she replied to the question Brown posed: "Yes, husband. I remember what you said."

"Well," Brown declared, "the journalists are sounding the trumpet." He paused before adding, "God smiles on the journalists."

Not all the newspapers stacked on the table were as kind to Brown as those handed to Mary during her journey to Charles Town. Most of them excoriated him for his failed invasion. The paper he held aloft was a copy of the *Nashville Whig*; it contained a story warning its readers that what happened at Harpers Ferry "will be but a preface to the history of a civil war in which the same scenes will be re-enacted on a larger scale and end in the dissolution of our glorious Union."

The stance taken by newspapers toward his invasion didn't bother Brown. All that mattered was that the messages sent to readers either created fear in the hearts of slaveholders, awakened the nation's citizens to the principles contained in the Declaration of Independence, or reminded those of the Christian faith of their obligation to do unto others as they would have others do unto them.

During the twenty-nine days since his conviction the old man had read enough to convince him he'd succeeded in accomplishing his purpose. The fact that he'd captured the imaginations of Thoreau, Emerson, and Mrs. Child—who, with a few others, were doing their best to transform him from a pariah into a hero—was an unexpected bonus.

The sun had set when General William Taliaferro—Governor Wise's choice to command the military forces in Jefferson County—arrived at the jail on horseback. Taliaferro and his company were to take Brown to the gallows in the morning.

24

Minutes Later
December 1, 1859
Charles Town, Virginia

Brown and Mary were sitting on a sofa in the jailor's parlor, having just finished sharing supper with Avis and his wife, when General Taliaferro was ushered in by Mrs. Avis.

Though his principal job was to convey Brown to the site of the execution, Taliaferro was also charged with ensuring Mary's safe return to Harpers Ferry, where she was to wait for the delivery of the coffin containing her husband's body.

Brown was aware that his visit with Mary was about to end, but it didn't dissuade him from standing and making an impassioned plea. "General," he said, "I ask that you allow my wife to remain with me this evening—that we may spend these few remaining hours together."

The response of the thirty-six-year-old black-bearded general—who would one day forge a reputation as an uncompromising disciplinarian—was swift and stern. "Out of the question. You already have been granted more time than allowed by the governor."

For an awkward moment there was the expectation of a rare burst of anger from Brown. But it didn't come, and he said, "Then surely the governor will allow the condemned prisoner to spend these last minutes with his wife—alone."

The general nodded to the jailer and Mrs. Avis, then turned to Mary. "The carriage will be waiting for you, Mrs. Brown." He looked to the old man. "I advise you not to keep the driver waiting. It is a dangerous time to be traveling—even with an armed escort." He turned smartly and left the apartment.

Captain Avis and his wife excused themselves, and the Browns were alone in the parlor. The old man appreciated the general's warning and didn't want to delay Mary's return to the Ferry. He rose and held out his hands, and she grasped them tightly. He told her he'd be grateful to live longer but that it was his fate to be murdered for a good cause and he was quite ready to die. Mary appeared on the verge of tears. He told her to cheer up, that his spirit soon would be with her. Then he implored her to gather the children together in North Elba. "Impress upon them," he said, "the importance of inculcating in each succeeding generation the principles that have guided our family." He pointed to a bundle of papers that sat on the floor beside the sofa. "Those are the letters I have collected since my arrest. Perhaps they can be put to some good use."

There was a knock on the door and the jailer and his wife entered the room.

"God bless you, Mary," Brown said, releasing her hands, "and God bless the children."

"And may God have mercy on you, my husband," she replied. She picked up the bundle of letters, and Mrs. Avis led her to the waiting carriage.

Brown looked to the jailer and requested the time of his execution.

"Tomorrow morning at eleven o'clock," Avis replied.

"Well," Brown said, "I must get to work. I have more let-ters to write."

"I'll not shackle you this evening," Avis said, tossing the leg irons to the floor, "although I am ordered to do so by the governor."

"I thank you, Captain Avis. You are indeed a man of good-will, and you shall have my gratitude to the end."

Back in his cell, Brown sat down at the table—now cleared of the mound of newspapers—and turned up the wick of the coal oil lamp. He began to write a letter to Mary Stearns, the wife of the most generous of his secret benefactors. The letter concluded: "I have asked to be spared from having any mock or hypocritical prayers made over me when I am pub-licly murdered and that my only attendants be poor little, dirty, ragged, bare-headed slave boys and girls led by some old grey-headed slave mother."

He finished another letter, his last to his family, and lay down on his cot fully clothed. Surprisingly, sleep came quickly.

———•••••———

Brown didn't stir until the bars of the cell's only window were projected on the wall by the first rays of sunlight. The morn-ing was cool but not exceptionally so, and the old man made no attempt to rekindle a fire. He went straight to his table and resumed writing. He wasn't aware that a tray containing a cup of hot tea and some biscuits had been slipped under the door—along with a pair of crimson slippers.

By nine o'clock he'd already met with a lawyer and made out his will. There was a gentle rapping on the door's iron bars followed by the jailer's voice. "A minister is here, Captain Brown. Do you wish to see him?"

Brown got up from the table and went to the door. He was wearing his new slippers.

In the doorway, standing next to Avis, was a man attired in the dark suit of the clergy. "I am Reverend Wilson," the man said. "I have come to offer a prayer for your salvation."

Brown asked, "Do you believe in slavery, Reverend Wilson?"

"I do," the minister said, "under the present circumstances."

"Then I thank you to retire from my sight. Your prayers would be an abomination to my God, and I shan't bend my knees in prayer with anyone whose hands are stained with the blood of slaves."

Reverend Wilson was speechless. He hadn't anticipated having to defend the merits of holding human beings in bondage. Avis took him by the arm and led him away.

Shortly after the minister's departure, the jailer returned with a half dozen armed guards. Brown was busy writing. "I'm sorry to say the time has come," Avis said, unlocking the cell door. "General Taliaferro and his soldiers are here."

Brown gathered up the several letters he'd written and gave them to Avis to be posted, then reached under his cot and pulled out a glossy black, broad-brimmed slouch hat. He placed it on his head and followed the jailer into the corridor, where the guards waited.

"May I have a last word with my men, Captain Avis?"

The jailer unlocked the cells containing the six prisoners. John Cook and Edwin Coppoc were together in one cell, Shields Green and John Copeland in another, Aaron Stevens and Albert Hazlett in a third. Brown had a brief dispute with Cook, having already expressed disappointment that Cook was the only one of the soldiers to submit a "confession" to his captors. And Brown made a point of ignoring Hazlett, who had been captured under the alias William Harrison; the old man had hopes that Hazlett might eventually be exonerated. To each of the rest Brown gave a coin, something tangible to remind them of their loyalty to him and his cause. Then he told them to meet their fate with courage and dignity.

The last soldier Brown approached was Stevens. "Good-bye, Captain," Stevens said as they embraced. "I know you are going to a better land."

"I know I am," Brown replied.

The men returned to their cells.

In the corridor stood one of the guards with a coil of rope that was to be used to secure Brown's arms.

The old man reached into his pocket, pulled out a folded note, and handed it to the guard, who took the note, slipped it into his coat, and began the task of lashing Brown's arms behind his back.

It was almost ten thirty when Brown was led by Avis and the guards onto the plank sidewalk outside the jail. The Jefferson County sheriff, James Campbell, stood beside a furniture wagon to which was harnessed a pair of white horses.

The street was bustling with foot soldiers and cavalry, among them General Taliaferro, who guided his mount toward those assembled on the sidewalk in front of the jail. He greeted them with a perfunctory salute.

Brown was amused by all the activity in the street—the mass of cavalry and foot soldiers being organized into a formation for the march to the site of the hanging. He looked up at the general and said, "I had no idea Governor Wise considered my execution so important."

Taliaferro gave a nod, turned his horse, and began shouting orders. He was intent on providing maximum security along the route, which terminated at an open field outside the town where the scaffold had been erected.

Because his arms were bound, Brown needed the assistance of Avis and Sheriff Campbell to climb onto the wagon. All three men had seated themselves on Brown's coffin as the driver, an undertaker named Sadler, gave the reins a shake. The wagon moved forward.

Taliaferro, meanwhile, deployed his foot soldiers in a double column, one on either side of the wagon. He'd split the cavalry into two units—one in front, the other to the rear.

It was an extraordinary December morning—the sun radiant, the temperature cool but not unpleasant, and not a trace of haze. The mountains to the east rose clear and sharp against a brilliant blue, cloudless sky.

There was little talk among the occupants of the wagon, though Brown offered his observations of the countryside as the procession reached the rolling farmland beyond the town. "This is a beautiful country," he said. "I never had the pleasure of seeing it before."

"Yes, it is," Avis replied.

"It is the more beautiful to behold," said Brown, "because I have so long been shut from it."

The wagon, with its retinue of foot soldiers and cavalry, neared a broad, undulating field littered with the brown stubble of harvested cornstalks. Militiamen clad in the colorful uniforms of their respective units had been formed into a large square, three ranks deep. On a mound in the center of the square stood the scaffold. There were perhaps a thousand soldiers in the formation, the bayonets of their muskets glittering in the sun.

A cannon manned by cadets from the Virginia Military Institute was situated inside the formation. By order of Governor Wise, the cannon was pointed directly at the scaffold. Wise still feared that a massive plot was underway to stage a last-minute rescue, and in anticipation of such a possibility, the cannon was loaded with grapeshot. Other cannons were placed outside the square, all under the command of Thomas J. Jackson—a VMI instructor who would one day come to be known as "Stonewall." Another notable who participated in the hanging was Edmund Ruffin, a wealthy Virginia plantation owner, slaveholder, and notorious fire-eater who had long argued for the South's secession from the Union. The sixty-five-year-old Ruffin had donned the uniform of a VMI cadet so he could witness the execution up close. Also among the troops was a handsome twenty-one-year-old wearing the uniform of the militia he'd recently joined, the Richmond Greys. The young man was just beginning to establish a reputation as an actor. His name was John Wilkes Booth.

Cavalry patrolled the field and the neighboring hills and woods, while sentries manned a perimeter outside the formation—precautions taken to ensure sufficient warning in the event of a rescue attempt. Governor Wise had declared the execution site off limits to all civilians, yet members of the press, some prominent local citizens, and visitors from out of town were gathered on the public road to see the prisoner as he approached the gallows.

General Taliaferro waved off the spectators as he led the wagon and his soldiers onto the field and marched them toward the formation. The ranks parted to allow the wagon and soldiers to pass through. As the ranks closed, Taliaferro ordered his officers to assemble his foot soldiers and cavalry and redeploy them to predetermined positions.

The wagon came to a halt. Brown was the first to drop to the ground. Though his arms were bound, it was much easier for him to exit the wagon than it had been to get on board. He moved briskly toward the scaffold.

Spectators were surprised at the old man's agility as he ascended the thirteen steps to the platform. He was followed by Captain Avis and Sheriff Campbell, the latter having taken a moment to remove a hatchet from the wagon bed.

On the platform—suspended from a crossbeam between two posts—was an iron hook. Attached to the hook was the thin hemp rope forming a noose. Under the noose was the trapdoor, held in place by a strand of rope looped over the crossbeam and tied to the base of a post.

Brown waited as Avis removed a length of cloth from his coat and tied the old man's legs together at the knees. It was imperative that the legs—like the arms—be bound in order that they not inhibit the fall through the trapdoor.

In the field in front of the scaffold, General Taliaferro's men were engaged in a series of movements integrating them into the formation. Wise had told Taliaferro that the people who witnessed the execution—especially the reporters from Northern newspapers—should have impressed upon them the pride Virginia took in the discipline and precision of her military units.

Avis, meanwhile, reached up to remove Brown's hat before producing yet another item from a pocket in his coat: a white hood.

"I have no words to thank you for your kindness," the old man said.

The jailer nodded.

Brown bowed slightly so the hood could be slipped over his head.

"You must step forward," Avis said, once the hood was in place.

"You shall have to help me," Brown said, "as I cannot see."

When the old man was positioned over the trapdoor, Avis asked if he was ready.

"Ready," Brown said calmly. "Do not keep me any longer than is necessary."

Avis guided the hooded head into the noose, made certain the rope was firm but not taut at the neck.

Though Brown was ready, Virginia wasn't. For several more minutes the old man was compelled to listen to the shouting of commands as Taliaferro's soldiers paraded in close order to prescribed locations. When they were finally in place, the shouting ceased.

Sheriff Campbell's hatchet cut the rope cleanly. The trapdoor fell and Brown plummeted through the opening.

Forty minutes later, the undertaker, Mr. Sadler, saw to it that the body was taken from the gallows and placed in the coffin in the bed of the furniture wagon. Sadler drove the wagon to the Winchester and Potomac railroad depot in Charles Town, where the coffin was loaded onto a special two-car train destined for Harpers Ferry. From there, Mary would arrange for transportation to North Elba.

———————

The militant abolitionist John Brown was dead, but his war on slavery was not yet over.

Epilogue

John Brown was laid to rest at his farm in the Adirondack Mountains of New York on Thursday, December 8, 1859. But his ghost continued to spread fear throughout the slaveholding South. Hardly a week went by that Southern newspapers weren't reporting the aftershocks of the Harpers Ferry invasion, warning of more slave insurrections, turning up the heat on the simmering cauldron of secession.

In early July 1860, a series of fires swept through Dallas and neighboring Texas communities. Editors of the *Texas State Gazette*, the *Houston Weekly Tribune*, and the *Texas Republican* blamed the deadly fires on Yankee abolitionists inspired by Brown. The papers carried stories accusing abolitionists of poisoning wells and inciting slaves to kill masters and rape their wives. In South Carolina, the *Savannah Republican* called the Texas troubles a "re-enactment of the John Brown affair." As the specter of another Nat Turner rebellion loomed, editors across the South leaped at the opportunity to tell their readers that what happened in Dallas could happen to them and that the time had come to leave the Union and create a separate Southern nation.

Even after his death, the newspapers continued to be Brown's greatest ally.

The Southern press wasn't alone in judging the effects of Brown's invasion on the nation's fragile condition. In the North, *New York Tribune* editor Horace Greeley followed with great interest the extraordinary volume of commentary appearing in Southern newspapers—most of it castigating abolitionists and Republicans. He also noted the gradual change in attitude adopted by editors in the North. To some of them, the old man was indeed a hero.

The more Greeley pondered the fiery rhetoric that filled the newspapers in the weeks following Brown's execution, the more he came to view what happened at Harpers Ferry as the latest act in a national drama whose climax would be the civil war New York senator William Seward had hinted at in a speech he'd given in 1858. Seward declared that the North and the South were engaged in an "an *irrepressible conflict* between opposing and enduring forces, and it meant the United States must and will, sooner or later, become either entirely a slaveholding nation or entirely a free-labor nation."

Fearing the *irrepressible conflict* was closer than many suspected, Greeley wrote to one of his correspondents in Indiana that Brown's "so-called insurrection" would "drive the slave power to new outrages." He concluded the letter with: "I think the end of slavery in Virginia is ten years nearer than it seemed a few weeks ago."

As it turned out, Greeley's prediction was too conservative.

———

In the predawn hours of April 12, 1861—one year, four months, and eleven days after Brown's body was carted away from a Virginia cornfield—artillery batteries from South Carolina's newly formed provisional forces began shelling federal troops garrisoned at Fort Sumter in Charleston harbor. South Carolina was the first of eleven states to secede from the Union.

And so began the war between the North and the South—the American Civil War.

Like Greeley, Brown also had made a prediction, one he wrote on the scrap of paper he handed the guard who bound his arms before he boarded the wagon that took him to the gallows. It read as follows:

> Charlestown, Va. 2nd December 1859. I, John Brown, am now quite certain that the crimes of this guilty land will never be purged away but with blood. I had, as I now think, flattered myself that without very much bloodshed it might be done.

The guard had forgotten about the note. It didn't surface until weeks later.

Brown's prediction, just as Greeley's, was too conservative. The American Civil War required an unthinkable amount of blood to be shed before slavery was expunged and the nation again was made whole. According to the most recent estimates, the number of combatants from both sides who died in battle or from related causes stands at almost three quarters of a million.

The Civil War was—and still is—the bloodiest war in America's history.

Acknowledgments

A goal of mine in writing this novel was to capture the character of John Brown by absorbing what I discovered in the many relevant sources available on bookshelves and online. I drew on works—some more scholarly than others—from the past and present, all of them permitting me to understand a complex man living in a complex era. Among my most valuable sources were Oswald Garrison Villard's classic biography *John Brown: A Biography Fifty Years After*, published in 1910, and David S. Reynolds's impeccably researched and brilliantly constructed *John Brown, Abolitionist* (2005). I am also deeply indebted to Tony Horwitz's *Midnight Rising*, Stephen B. Oates's *To Purge This Land with Blood*, Evan Carton's *Patriotic Treason*, T. Lloyd Benson's *The Caning of Senator Sumner*, Janet Kemper Beck's *Creating the John Brown Legend*, James Brewer Stewart's *Holy Warriors*, David Donald's *Charles Sumner and the Coming of the Civil War*, Richard Hinton's *John Brown and His Men*, Robert E. McGlone's *John Brown's War Against Slavery*, Robert M. De Witt's *The Life, Trial and Execution of John Brown*, W. E. B. DuBois's *John Brown*, Osborne P. Anderson's *A Voice from Harper's*

Ferry, Thomas Drew's compilation *The John Brown Invasion*, Eric H. Walther's *The Fire-Eaters*, John Stauffer's *The Black Hearts of Men* and Stauffer and Zoe Trodd's *Meteor of War* and *The Tribunal*, James Redpath's *The Public Life of Capt. John Brown*, Frederick Douglass's *The Narrative and Selected Writings*, Philip S. Foner's *The Life and Writings of Frederick Douglass* (volume 2), Edward J. Renehan Jr.'s *The Secret Six*, Robert Penn Warren's *John Brown*, Thomas Goodrich's *War to the Knife*, Clinton Cox's *Fiery Vision*, Nicole Etcheson's *Bleeding Kansas*, Merrill D. Peterson's *John Brown*, Frank Sanborn's *The Life and Letters of John Brown, Liberator of Kansas and Martyr of Virginia*, Elijah Avey's *The Capture and Execution of John Brown*, Carl Bode's *The Portable Thoreau*, Barrie Stavis's *John Brown: The Sword and the Word*, Jean Libby's *Black Voices from Harper's Ferry* and "After Harpers Ferry" in the *Californians*, Hannah N. Geffert's "John Brown and His Black Allies: An Ignored Alliance," Louis DeCaro Jr.'s *John Brown: The Cost of Freedom*, Richard O. Boyer's *The Legend of John Brown*, Fergus M. Bordewich's "Day of Reckoning," Stan Cohen's *John Brown*, Robert A. Ferguson's *The Trial in American Life*, Lacy K. Ford Jr.'s *Origins of Southern Radicalism*, C. Vann Woodward's *The Burden of Southern History*, Philip F. Gura's *American Transcendentalism*, and Ernest B. Furgurson's *Freedom Rising*.

Aside from acknowledging the foregoing, I owe a debt of gratitude to several people who provided much-needed information. They include Travis Westly from the Library of Congress, Gloria Beiter from the South Carolina Historical Society, and the most gracious staff of the Old Edgefield District Genealogical Society, Edgefield, South Carolina.

Special thanks go to the Millers—Anita and Jordan—for seeing a future for what I'd written.

To my editor, Devon Freeny, I can only express my deepest appreciation for his meticulous attention to detail in shepherding the manuscript to its conclusion.

I'm also obliged to mention those folks who provided small acts of kindness during the writing: Richard F. Dietrich and Lawrence R. Broer, scholars and writers both, and my kinfolk, Sam and Steve Nichols.

And finally there's the person without whom the book would never have been begun, much less completed. The muse of Umatilla: Robert H. Miller (no relation to Anita and Jordan). Thank you, Harv.